# BUSTED FLUSH

## The *Wild Cards* Series

A WILD CARDS MOSAIC NOVEL

# BUSTED FLUSH

### Edited by
### George R. R. Martin

### Assisted by
### Melinda M. Snodgrass

And Written by

*S. L. Farrell* | *Victor Milán*

*John Jos. Miller* | *Kevin Andrew Murphy*

*Walton Simons* | *Melinda M. Snodgrass*

*Caroline Spector* | *Ian Tregillis*

*Carrie Vaughn*

TOR®

*A TOM DOHERTY ASSOCIATES BOOK*
*New York*

This is a work of fiction. All of the characters, organizations, and events portrayed in this novel are either products of the authors' imaginations or are used fictitiously.

BUSTED FLUSH

Edited by Patrick Nielsen Hayden

A Tor Book
Published by Tom Doherty Associates, LLC
175 Fifth Avenue
New York, NY 10010

www.tor-forge.com

Tor® is a registered trademark of Tom Doherty Associates, LLC.

Library of Congress Cataloging-in-Publication Data

Busted flush / edited by George R. R. Martin ; assisted by Melinda M. Snodgrass ; and written by S. L. Farrell ... [et. al].—1st ed.
  p.   cm.
  ISBN-13: 978-0-7653-1782-7
  ISBN-10: 0-7653-1782-6
  I. Martin, George R.R.   II. Snodgrass, Melinda M., 1951–   III. Farrell, S. L.

PS648.S3  B87  2008
813'.54—dc22

2008036296

First Edition: December 2008

Printed in the United States of America

0  9  8  7  6  5  4  3  2  1

To Carl Keim,
ace architect,
good friend,
hideous mockery of a man

Keep on shufflin'.

# Double Helix

## TO THE HUNGRY SOUL, EVERY
## BITTER THING IS SWEET

### Melinda M. Snodgrass

**I FIND MYSELF AVOIDING** the passages about ashes and worms. The pages are thin, almost feathery beneath my fingers as I turn them, looking for another passage that won't fill my throat with bile. I know my father is dying. I don't have to read about it.

Here's one. It reads more like a page out of Lord Dunsany than a collection of musings by long-dead Hebrews. "Who layeth the beams of his chambers in the water: who maketh the clouds his chariot: who walketh upon the wings of the wind." I have a good voice and I know how to use it. I use it now, softening and deepening the final words. I know he should sleep. I don't want him to sleep. I want to talk to him. Hear his voice before it's silenced.

That damn lump is back. I keep swallowing, trying to make it smaller. Through the mullioned panes I can see a glint of sun on the sluggish waters of the Cam. It's August, and it feels like this endless summer will never end. The room is breathlessly warm, and the heavy air holds that sick/sweet scent of fatal illness. I can feel my shirt clinging to the skin of my back. Outside there's the sputtering growl of a lawn mower somewhere on the street, and a dog carols his annoyance. I'll probably need to mow the lawn for my parents, or find a teenager. Through the open window I can smell the green. The branches of the apple tree out back sag under the rosy burdens. *Maybe that's what happens to every living thing when they have to breed.*

My father touches the back of my wrist. His skin feels just like the onion-thin pages of the Bible that now rests in my lap. "Thank . . . you." His blue eyes are surprisingly alert in a face reduced to harsh bone and stretched skin. "There's wisdom between those covers," he adds, and transfers his hand to the Bible. "Maybe by reading to me you'll find some of it."

*Fantasies and fairy tales,* is what I think, but I keep control of my features. "So, you think I'm foolish." I grin at him. "Thanks."

"No." His expression is serious. "But I know that something is wrong. I raised you, Noel, you can't hide things from me."

He's smiling, but I still have that visceral gut clench that affects every child when their parents display that kind of preternatural omniscience. It passes quickly. After all, I'm twenty-eight, and I amuse myself for a moment wondering what he thinks I've done. No pregnant fans. I'm a hermaphrodite, so I'm sterile. I'm not in debt. Both my public job and my secret job pay me quite well. What could he imagine I had done? For a moment I toy with the idea of telling him.

*You know I'm a member of the Silver Helix, Dad, a division of MI-7. What you don't know is that I'm their designated assassin. I don't remember how many people I've killed. They say you never forget your first. His face is as blank as all the others.*

But of course I don't. Standing, I set aside the Bible and stretch. "Tea? There's lemon tarts, and some boiled tongue for sandwiches. Will you eat something?"

"I'll try."

Our kitchen is small and cluttered, and several days' worth of dishes form towers in the sink. A fat fly moves lazily between the trash can and the dirty dishes. The buzzing is almost hypnotic. *No, no, no.* A sharp head shake drives back the sleepiness. Looks like I'm going to have to hire a maid as well as a teenager.

The tongue, sullenly red and pimpled with taste buds, gleams with congealed fat under the refrigerator light. American kitchens are almost obscene with their gigantic refrigerators crammed with food. We English are starting to go the same way. Who has time to shop for each day's meal that day?

I wonder who had cooked the tongue—certainly not my mother. She never cooked. My father took care of the house and the kid, and prepared every meal, and he fit every cliché about English cooking. A spurt of anger flares in the center of my chest, but I back down from it. It isn't Mum's fault he's dying. She was the bread winner so I suppose she had the right to dodge the drudgery. But I suspect if she hadn't worked she still wouldn't have cooked and cleaned.

Her devotion to radical feminism has defined her life. Hell, she was so militant that she made damn sure I was raised as a boy. Now figure that one out. They may look funny, but I've got both sets of genitalia. I could have been raised as a girl, and even kept the same name, just changed the pronunciation.

My pager vibrates. I stand there juggling the tongue while I search through my pockets for the correct pager. I'm wearing a med-alert pager since I am so often away from England, and I have the pager my manager uses to arrange my performances, I have one from the Committee that summons Lilith, and another from Prince Siraj, the man that commands Bahir, and I have the one given to me by the Silver Helix. It's Siraj calling.

*Fuck you,* says that febrile part of my mind. But I pull out my mobile and call him. Naturally he wants to see me. Naturally it has to be now. Naturally I'll go.

The only reason it was the premier of the United Arab Emirates who received a visit from Bahir and not the president was due to an infelicitous exchange Al Maktoum had had with Prince Siraj in a Paris restaurant. The premier had mentioned how he liked to relax in a hot bath and watch the sun set through the floor-to-ceiling windows. Naked men are particularly vulnerable, and it's easy to locate bathrooms on building plans. Add to that west-facing windows, and it was a simple matter for me to use Google Earth and locate my target. The time of day was a little less felicitous. I can't use my powers at twilight or dawn, and Bahir cannot be summoned after dark. But Siraj's recollection of the conversation suggested Al Maktoum liked to read in the tub prior to sunset. And I was delivering a threat, and they rarely take long.

The rippling water in the deep glass-tiled tub makes it hard to see clearly, but it appears the premier's balls have retreated up into his belly. He stares up at me, and terror clouds his dark eyes. I risk a glance at the brace of mirrors on one wall of the marble-lined bathroom. I am a nicely terrifying figure, dressed in a black dishdasha with a pistol holstered on my hip. I had dispensed with the headdress. The trailing edges can interfere with peripheral vision, and in the desert heat my scalp sweats and itches. So my mane of red-gold hair shines under the lights. I use the tip of the scimitar to scratch at my beard. The premier never takes his eyes off that blade. I really wish that genius in operations at Whitehall who conceived of using my male avatar as a Middle Eastern ace hadn't insisted on the sword as part of Bahir's persona. It's so absurdly *Arabian Nights,* but I'm stuck with it now. Bahir's blade has decapitated a lot of people—including the last Caliph.

"Prince Siraj sends greetings to his brother, and is saddened that his brother has chosen not to honor the price of oil set by the Caliph."

"It's just a few dollars." His voice holds a quaver and a whine. As I watch, goose bumps bloom across his shoulders and upper arms.

"One hundred dollars."

"The three hundred that the prince has set is too high. The European and American economies are staggering. How does it help us if we bankrupt them? If no one can buy our oil, where is the gain?"

"You should have made these arguments to the prince. Not sought to slip behind him like a thief. His highness is not a fool. He will ease prices, but not until the westerners have paid a mighty price."

"We were not part of that war in Egypt. Why should we exact vengeance? None of our soldiers were lost." He's becoming angry, beginning to wonder if he really stands in danger of his life. I glance toward the window. The sun is perilously close to the horizon.

"You say these words without shame, which shows you are a pawn of the West."

When a blade swings quickly it really does whistle, faintly, not like in the movies, but you have that split second of sound to let you know something awful is coming. The premier flinches, and flails. Water droplets form prisms as they cascade past the window and the rays of sunlight break apart. Blood fountains and glows in the dying light. I have taken off his right hand at the wrist. He is screaming, the sound echoing and reverberating off the hard surfaces. Outside the door there is the sound of pounding feet.

The threat has been delivered. It's past time I was going.

John Bruckner, the Highwayman, is emerging from Flint's office as I arrive to report about my little mission for Siraj. Out of courtesy to our chief Bruckner had removed his stained Andy Capp hat while in the office, but he's in the process of restoring it to its customary place and customary task—covering his nearly bald pate. I retreat to the wall because the Highwayman has the build of a beer keg and about as much dexterity.

An exuberant handshake later, he's offering me one of his foul black cigars while stuffing one into his own mouth. I wave him off and pull out a cigarette. The heat from his dented Zippo fans my face as I lean into the lighter. He transfers the fire to the tip of his cigar and sucks lustily on it until the tip of the stogie glows red. The rituals having been observed, we lean against opposite walls and study each other.

"Now, how is it that I'm a bloody lorry driver and you're a bloody magician?"

"I'm prettier than you are."

"Right you are, and you dress better," he says, hitching the waistband of his baggy corduroy pants up over his paunch.

"What have you been up to?"

A jerk of the thumb at Flint's door and he says, "Old Granite Face has me running arms from Lagos to the troops out in the bush." When the Highwayman gets his rig up to speed he can move from London to Melbourne or Shanghai without passing through any of the territory in between. "Effing roads are no better than goat tracks," he continues. "They've beat the bloody hell out of my suspension. Bloody natives."

It isn't just white man's burden rearing its head. Bruckner has seen strange and disturbing things while traveling his "short cuts," and he lives in fear of getting stranded in this strange, surreal no-man's-land.

"Show a little gratitude. Nigeria is the only thing that's keeping petrol in your truck."

"Yeah, well, why can't the niggers build a bloody first world road?"

I keep control of my features. Bruckner's somewhere in his sixties. Times have changed, but not the Highwayman. He's racist and sexist, and despises foreigners with a superiority unique only to a white Englishman.

Straightening up with a grunt and another tug at his pants, he says, "I've got to push off. Join me and the lads for a pint?"

"Can't." I incline my head toward Flint's office.

"Well, next time."

He leaves, trailing smoke like the fumes from one of his lorries. I tap on the door. I can't actually hear Flint's invitation to enter, but I go on in. He's in his great stone chair, necessary because his sharp stone body would cut the upholstery of any normal chair to shreds.

I take my customary chair, stub out the butt, and take out another cigarette. The streetlights throw shadows across the bookcases. Only a small lamp on the desk is lit so Flint's eyes glow red in the gray stone face.

*"God damn it! Must you be this effective on behalf of our enemies?"*

Oh, damn, I had hoped to report about my actions in Dubai before Flint heard of it. No such luck. It seems I will not be basking in the sunshine of my chief's approval today.

"I take it the UAE has raised their prices."

*"You know bloody well they have. You cut off the man's hand! He's a friend of the prime's."*

"I must occasionally succeed, sir, or Siraj is going to wonder if his ace bodyguard/assassin is a complete cock-up."

*"Can't you exert any influence over Siraj?"*

"Bahir is viewed as a blunt instrument. I think Siraj would be just the tiniest bit suspicious if the Caliph's assassin suddenly started displaying political acumen."

Flint grunts, and gives a grudging nod. Gestures from my boss are disconcerting. It's like watching a statue come to life. He surprises me when he snaps his fingers together and produces a flame. I realize it's for the forgotten cigarette hanging between my fingers.

*My, my, this is rare condescension. I guess I'm forgiven for my unauthorized bloodletting.* Leaning forward, I light my cigarette. The harsh Turkish tobacco is like claws raking across the inside of my lungs, but the hit to the nicotine pleasure centers outweighs the discomfort and the theoretical lung cancer.

*"Where are you off to now?"*

"I've got a date." I preen and Flint makes a grinding sound like frozen gears trying to engage. "Believe me, you don't hate it as much as I. Babysitting is not my style."

I pause in the bathroom before testing my bladder control against the cold darkness of the Between. As the urine splashes against the porcelain my better nature wars with my real nature. What I really want is to call Lohengrin and cancel our date so I can go home to Dad and sleep in my old bedroom. If I go to New York I'll be eating an overly rich and heavy meal very late, and then indulging in vigorous and inept sex between sweaty sheets with the big German ace. What he lacks in finesse Lohengrin more than makes up for in stamina. I dread tomorrow. Even when I'm back in my normal body I will have an uncomfortable ache in my nether parts.

For an instant I find myself looking with loathing at my short and strangely shaped penis. Would my life have been better, easier, if Mum had let the surgeons cut it away, and make me . . .

My thoughts slam up against the reality. No amount of surgery would have made me a "real girl." I tuck myself away and zip up, and then move to the sink to wash my hands. I'm still holding the rough paper towel when I allow the transformation to twist my flesh. Breasts soon press against the front of my shirt, and my pants fit uncomfortably over female hips. Long fingernails pierce the paper towel.

The image in the mirror isn't all I could hope. The heart-shaped face looks drawn and there's the hint of a shadow beneath the silver eyes. It's rather a shock to realize that fatigue of the real body translates to the avatars. Checking my watch I calculate the time difference between London and New York. If I stop at my digs in Manhattan and repair my face and change out of pants and boots I'll be late meeting Lohengrin for dinner. But he's got a rather traditional view of women. He'll think that's typical.

I picture the flat in the Village. As my body twists into that cold, strange place I decide on the little black dress. Keep the focus on the legs. . . .

♥

# Coulda

Caroline Spector

**IT'S DARK. SUFFOCATING.** I can hear the sounds of the helicopters overhead. I've got to do something. But I can hear screams now. Oh, God, the way they scream as the flesh is seared off their bodies. I need to bubble. I need to get away from the smell of burnt skin and muscle. Screaming. I need to make the screams go away.

I try to blast my way through the darkness. For a moment, I can't bubble. It's as if there's a wall between me and my power—then a stream of bubbles flows from my hands. Dust and rubble fill my mouth and rain off my body.

There's light. The light is so clean and pure. I bubble more until I chase the darkness away and blow the weight of the debris from me.

"Stop that!"

I look around. I'm not in Egypt. There are no helicopters. No falling bodies. No fiery flesh. Just the clean, antiseptic testing room at BICC. Biological Isolation and Containment Center—who thinks these names up, anyway?

God, I hate government facilities. Why on earth would anyone build anything in an abandoned salt mine? And in the middle of Nowhere, New Mexico, to boot . . .

"The purpose of the test is to see how much force you can absorb, Miss Pond." The disembodied voice belonged to Dr. Pendergast. His voice was normally silky smooth, so it was hard to tell when he was really pissed. But there was a hint of anger and I knew I'd been bad.

But, really, how many more times could they pound the living crap out of me? I was beginning to feel like Wile E. Coyote. Drop me down into that canyon one more time, boss. Or shoot me with a death ray. Your choice.

I wasn't even certain what they were testing me for anymore. At first, it was the usual: some joker with a face that could stop a clock and biceps the size of watermelons. He gave me a left hook that I kinda felt. I tried not to laugh at the look of disappointment on his unfortunate face.

Then they started with the cannonballs, bullets, walls on springs. Honestly, who the hell has walls on springs, just, you know, lying around? I mean, did *none* of these guys watch *American Hero?* You'd've thought they'd never heard of the Amazing Bubbles.

But the superweird thing was that they didn't want me to bubble. In fact, Dr. Pendergast made it very clear that he didn't want *any* bubbling. I tried to explain to him that when I got hit with as much raw energy as they were throwing at me, I *had* to bubble. It hurt not to.

But Dr. Pendergast didn't care about that. He was only interested in how much power I could absorb. They'd already found out my max size would just about fill an eight-by-eight room. But I was no Bloat. They told me that when I stopped growing in size I started getting denser. Heavier, but no larger. I kinda got the feeling this was very interesting to them.

The problem was, after they got me as fat as I could get, and they kept throwing more and more force at me, I was finding it more difficult to bubble it off after the tests. The denser I got, the more powerful I became, but the harder it was to access my power. Hell, I could barely lift one of my pudgy fingers.

And it didn't help that every time I got hit, it brought back memories. Memories that I didn't want to face. So I did what I usually do—I thought about something else. Thought about anything that would distract me from what was rattling around my head like a bad Rob Zombie movie.

Thinking about Ink naked usually did the trick.

"Okay, Miss Pond, we'll go again."

"Yeah? I don't think so," I replied. I flung my hands out and released an enormous stream of bubbles, and I could feel my clothes getting looser. I grabbed a handful of waistband with my left hand to keep my pants from falling off.

The bubbles bounced around the room, but I kept bubbling with my right hand. As I filled the room, the bubbles just sort of vibrated against one another. I'd made them soft and rubbery so they wouldn't hurt anyone. But it would take a while for them to dissipate. The room would be useless for any more games of Kick the Bubbles. At least for a while.

"Miss Pond, you agreed to be tested."

"I know, and now I'm done with testing. I don't recall this being anything other than voluntary on my part."

"You're acting like a child. We have only just begun to discover the true range of your power."

I glared at the one-way mirror. I couldn't see Dr. Pendergast, but I could imagine the patronizing look on his face. That and how he would stroke his Vandyke when he was trying to "reason" with you.

"Yeah, well . . ." Crap, I always sucked at pithy-line moments. "You're not the boss of me." I marched out with my pants hitched up, trying not to smack myself on the forehead.

There was a knock on my door. They were lodging me in one of the officers' quarters. I suspected the hoi polloi got far less kind treatment.

I pulled the door open. One of the homeliest women I'd ever seen was standing there. Her hair was cropped short like she'd cut it with safety scissors. And her cheeks and forehead were acne-scarred, with an angry red breakout in full bloom. "Miss Pond?"

"That's me," I said.

"I'm Niobe." She paused.

"Niobe!" I pulled her to me in a bear hug. We'd been corresponding via e-mail since *American Hero*. She had really touched me, as many of her e-mails had been heartbreaking. Her parents had been less than supportive when her card turned, which was like saying Joker Plague had some unattractive members. But there had been something else in her e-mails, something unspoken.

"What are you doing here?" I asked. "Not everyone gets an all-expense-paid vacation at the lovely BICC."

"Well, my parents weren't too pleased that their only daughter wasn't going to have the perfect coming-out party. It's hard being a debutante with this." Her thick tail swished on the floor. I hadn't noticed it before. It was an ugly gray, thick and mottled, and there were stiff bristles sticking out of it.

I turned and started putting the rest of my things into my suitcase. She looked so forlorn it made me uncomfortable.

"They're studying me," she said, "just like they were studying you."

"God, I hope not," I replied, looking over my shoulder. "They've been pounding the crap outta me."

She gave me a wan smile. "No," she said. "I don't have a power like yours. You know, you're prettier in person."

I laughed. "Whoa, Non Sequitur Girl, er, Woman."

"I mean, I guess you're different than you looked on TV."

"You mean I'm not as fat now." I shoved the last of my clothes into my bag. "Yeah, I just bubbled the hell outta the test room. I'm leaving, and I don't want to be as recognizable when I head back to New York."

She shoved her hands into her pockets and looked unhappy. "I guess this means you're not going to spend any time with the other patients."

"I didn't know anyone wanted to see me," I said. "They've pretty much kept me in the dark about everything except for the whole, 'Let's see what we can throw at Bubbles this time.' "

Niobe looked even more morose at this. "Yeah," she said. "They treat us like rats in a cage."

"Look," I said. "I've got plenty of time before my flight—if they even have enough fuel to get off the runway today. Why don't I come and meet whomever you want me to meet?"

"You'd do that?" My God, her eyes were so sad.

"Sure, let me grab my things."

"Is it cool being a part of the Committee?" Niobe asked as we sped along the silent corridor in a BICC golf cart.

"I guess," I said. "I mean, it's great being a part of something that's supposed to be doing good, but sometimes . . . sometimes it's hard."

There was a faint whiff of burning flesh. I glanced around, but there was nothing but smooth, unblemished wall flashing by.

"But you get to do a lot of other cool things, too."

"True. I got to go to the Academy Awards and the VMAs, and they had a parade for us at Disneyland after that mess in Egypt. So that was okay. But doing press junkets, not so great."

The cart slowed as Niobe lifted her foot from the pedal and looked at me. "But isn't it fun having them ask you questions and then they actually pay attention to you?"

"Yeah . . . not so much," I replied. "When we got back from Egypt they sent us out on a goodwill tour. It was pretty hellish. Not because of the people who wanted to meet us—they were almost always cool." *Except for the woman who threw pig's blood on me and called me a murderer,* I thought. "But that press stuff is less than thrilling. Trust me, no fun at all."

We sped up. "Oh," Niobe said. "I just thought that after *American Hero* and being on the Committee that your life would be, you know, perfect."

"I don't think life's ever perfect."

"It was pretty perfect when Tiffani got knocked off *AH*." She gave me a sly smile.

I smiled back. "Yeah, that was kinda perfect."

"Have you seen any of the promos for the new season of *AH*?" Niobe asked. She sounded excited.

"Yeah," I said. "They wanted me to do some teasers, but I was out of the country when they were shooting."

"What do you think of the new aces?"

"I think they have no idea what they're getting themselves into."

Being an ace, sometimes you forget that other people who get the virus aren't so fortunate. Everyone knows that the virus kills, but people forget that it also maims.

Niobe led me through a pair of swinging doors into the children's ward. There were bright mobiles, stuffed animals, and posters on the walls. Some of the girls had wrapped their IV stands in beads and Mylar stickers. At least I think they were girls. This was the place where they put the sickest kids—the ones the wild card virus had not transformed, but had crippled.

"We have a special guest today," Niobe said. "She was a contestant on

*American Hero* and she's now a member of the Committee: the Amazing Bubbles!"

There wasn't thunderous applause, but I hadn't expected any. I'd done my share of hospital appearances in the last year. From Walter Reed to Beth Israel they were mostly the same—sick people who just wanted anything normal in their lives again. Even seeing an ace in person seemed normal. After all, I'd been on the TV in their living rooms.

Niobe led me to bed after bed. In one, a boy lay wrapped in a plaid robe. He was indigo. He looked like Violet Beauregarde after that unfortunate gum incident. We passed another bed where a child floated above the covers like a balloon. Balloon Girl gave a little wave as we went by. It was obvious that Niobe liked all these children and they liked her. But at one bed, she stopped and began laughing before she could introduce me.

Sitting in the middle of the bed was a tiny boy. He was perfectly proportioned with a shock of black hair. As I watched, his features began to change. It was like watching a live-action version of computer morphing.

His hair grew longer until it came to his waist. His features changed, became more feminine. Then I realized: he looked like Cher.

"Okay," I said. "That's just wrong."

Niobe giggled. "Watch this."

The boy's body began to bulge, arms and legs expanding as if there were balloons in them.

"You've got to be kidding me," I said. "The Michelin Man?"

Niobe and the boy started laughing together and I realized that this was one of Niobe's children. I knew she was psychically linked to them, but that was about all I knew about her power. She'd been pretty close-mouthed about it. When she stopped giggling and could speak again, she said, "This is Xerxes."

I reached out so we could shake, and he slipped his tiny hand into mine. "It's very nice to meet you," he said. He sounded like Marvin the Martian.

"You should take that act on the road," I said.

Niobe stopped laughing. I was baffled. I mean, I'm not the greatest joke teller in the world, but I didn't think my comment had sucked all *that* bad: besides, as deuce powers went, Xerxes's wasn't a bad one.

"Uhm, I guess we should move along," I said. "It was nice to meet you, too, Xerxes."

Niobe led me to another bed. I wasn't certain of this patient's gender, so I decided to follow Niobe's lead.

"This is Jenny," she said. "Jenny's card turned about a month ago. She isn't sick, but she keeps expelling her internal organs when she gets too excited."

"Hey, Jenny," I said. "You're not going to spew on me, are you?"

Niobe gave a little gasp, but Jenny laughed. Or kinda gurgled. "Usually people are too freaked out to say anything to me," she said. "You know, I was rooting for Drummer Boy on *American Hero.*"

"I can see why," I said. "He's a musician and chicks dig musicians." That was my polite response when people said anything about Drummer Boy. I still thought he was a massive douche even after Egypt.

"Would you sign my book?" One of her flippers shoved an autograph book across the bed.

I flipped through it. She had an astonishing number of famous people. She must have started it before her card turned. I found a blank page toward the back and scrawled my name and a dedication across it.

"There you go. I can give Drummer Boy a call and see if he can send you a signed picture. I mean, if you'd like that."

"That would be so great!" Jenny said. "Oh, dear, I think you better stand back."

Niobe and I moved back and, sure enough, Jenny hurled her innards. It was not only disgusting to look at, but the smell was awful.

"Okay, well, I think Bubbles has a flight to catch," Niobe said.

The flight to New York had been about what I expected: long, boring, and way too crowded. (The less said about the flight from Carlsbad to El Paso the better. Terror in the skies.)

I was ready to get back home to Stuyvesant Town. It wasn't in the hippest part of the city, but it felt like a real home to me. It was at Fourteenth Street and Avenue A. Lower East Side, but not quite trendy—yet.

The neighborhood was only just beginning to be gentrified. It still had lots of cheap clothing shops, good ethnic food (also cheap), and some great bookstores within walking distance. And the Stuyvesant Town complex remained what it had been designed for—middle-class housing.

Of course, I was living there illegally, subletting from a couple who had moved to Columbus after their baby was born. They'd wanted to be closer to the relatives, but hadn't wanted to give up the idea of being New Yorkers. So we'd agreed that when they wanted to come back, I would vacate. That had been two years ago, so I felt pretty secure where I was—for now.

But I couldn't get home from the airport without transportation, and today there were only a handful of cabs and a wicked-long line to get one.

I eventually found myself in the back of a makeshift cart being pulled by a joker. He was at least eleven feet tall, almost all of his height in his legs. It was weird as hell being dragged through NYC by daddy longlegs. I wondered where he got his pants tailored. At the Big and Tall Men's Shop?

Traffic was almost nonexistent. But we still had to navigate around cars that had been abandoned by their owners. Bikes shot around us, the riders whooping at us as they went by. The buses were running, as there had been an executive order to keep them operating.

Things had been bad when I'd left, but they seemed worse now. There were boarded-up shops on almost every street. And the places that were open, mostly bodegas, had signs out with shocking prices on them.

The joker pulled over to the curb in front of my building and I paid in cash. Between the Committee stipend and the endorsement work I'd had over the last year, I was doing okay. Who knew letting a Volvo hit you could be so lucrative? And with commercials, I didn't have to wonder if the rest of the people involved were going to be alive the next day.

I walked up to the fourth floor. *Good for the muscles,* I thought.

When I absorbed energy, I didn't just get fat. My muscles got bigger, too. That much I'd figured out by myself. So I'd started training to give myself as much muscle as I could pack onto my frame. I was certainly more buff now, but my body type didn't bulk up. I wanted to be more agile when I was fat. The muscles helped with that, too.

The air was stale in my apartment. I cranked open all the windows and turned on the ceiling fans. My mail was piled up on the table. Only in Stuyvesant Town would I have trusted a neighbor with the key to my apartment.

I pawed through the mail, pulling out the bills and fan mail, trashing the junk. Then I booted up my computer. There was a ridiculous amount of useless e-mail and one or two from Ink:

To: prettybiggirl@ggd.com

From: tatsforless@ggd.com

I know we talked this morning, but I miss you already. When you finally get done at BICC, we need to have a long, long conversation about your mouth and my clit. Or vice versa.

Honestly, a girl can only masturbate so much. . . .

Come home soon!

Your ever-changing girl toy,

Juliet

There were more e-mails from her, but you get the idea. And there was also one from Niobe.

To: TheAmazingBubbles@committeepost.net

From: Genetrix@BICC.gov

Dear Michelle,

It was wonderful to finally meet you in person. I wish we'd had more time together, but I was so happy for the time you spared.

And I wanted to especially thank you for meeting the children. It meant the world to them. Xerxes thought you were funny and Jenny thought you were "very cool about the whole unswallowing thing." (Her words, not mine.)

I hope we will stay in touch. Your friendship means a lot to me.

Yours,

Niobe

At least Niobe's e-mail made me feel better. I missed Ink, but not as much as I thought I should. And it made me feel like a lousy girlfriend. But I was feeling disconnected from a lot of things these days.

My cell phone began to buzz. I picked it up and saw a text message from John Fortune asking me to come to his office at the UN. Crap. I really didn't want to go down there. I left the rest of my e-mails and turned off the computer.

"Look, you know I hate to ask this," I said.

Fortune sighed and put his head in his hands. *Oh, great,* I thought. *The guilt trip. Passengers boarding now for the nonstop . . . stop that!* "I just need a rest," I said. "It's been over a year and I've done too many missions."

"But that's why we need you," he said, lifting his head from his hands. "You've done mission lead. You were in Egypt. You were at Behatu Camp. How many people can say they stopped genocide in the Balkans?"

I closed my eyes and took a deep breath. When I opened them again, Fortune was staring off into space. I knew that Sekhmet was talking to him. And, boy, did that give me the willies. I mean, who would want a massive scarab living under the flesh of your forehead, attached to your skull, and communicating with you via God-only-knows-what? Ew. I didn't know how he did it—living with someone else constantly in his body, always listening in on every conversation. Not to mention the giant scarab forehead zit—*not* a look I'd recommend.

"I know you need a break, but the way things are going, I just don't know if I can spare you." He gave me his "I'm a sensitive guy" smile. I was pretty sure that last bit was Sekhmet's doing. "Here's the thing," he continued. "Jayewardene wants a team to investigate charges of genocide in the Niger River Delta. The People's Paradise of Africa is making the accusations, and it's turning into a massive political shitstorm."

"Another genocide?" I said. My stomach clenched and I thought I might be sick.."I don't think I can do another genocide."

And then he gave me that "do it for the world" look. Honestly, I liked him better when he was just a PA on *American Hero.*

*That* John Fortune had been a nice guy. *This* John Fortune was so absorbed with whatever it was that was driving him so hard that he didn't care about much else. Except maybe Curveball.

"I've done plenty for the Committee, so don't try to act as if I haven't,"

I said. "I need a break. You could send Gardener or Brave Hawk. They've only been around for a few months. They'll be fresher."

"But you would be the best choice if we have to do an African mission," he replied. "If it really is genocide, a woman as lead would be better PR. You could do that whole teary-eyed/angry thing you do."

"Gardener is a woman," I said. I glared at him, but I didn't say anything else. He frowned and then stared off into space again. Sekhmet was talking some sense into him—I hoped.

"I'll think about it," he said at last.

"I'm going to see Ink in D.C.," I told him.

"Fine," he replied, "take your cell phone." But I could tell he wasn't paying attention to me anymore. He was planning his next big thing.

When I got to Washington the next day, I had to walk from my train stop to Ink's apartment. There weren't even any joker cabs here, and the subway looked crammed.

I had a key and let myself in. There were clothes strewn everywhere and newspapers and magazines piled up on every available surface. I dropped my duffel and started tidying up. It would annoy her to no end. She said she could only find things where she left them.

I'd been at it for a while when my cell started buzzing. I looked at the screen. It was Ink.

"Hey, baby," I said, answering.

"You made good time," she said. "You're not cleaning up the apartment, are you?"

I looked around. The newspapers and magazines were in neat piles and the clothes had been put in the laundry or folded and put away. The bed was made with clean sheets, and I'd put the dishes away.

"No—of course not—I know how you feel about that."

"Liar. You are such a liar."

"It's true. I am a filthy liar," I replied. "Unlike you, who's just incredibly messy."

"I've got to work late," Ink said. "How about you meet me here and we can get some dinner?"

I rolled my eyes. More walking.

"Sure, honey. Whatever you say."

◆

The SCARE offices reminded me of BICC. Cold, impersonal, and indifferent to human needs.

They held me at the front desk until Ink came down to escort me upstairs. It was annoying. Just because I worked for Jayewardene and the UN and not for the U.S. government, I was being treated like I might be a security threat. Honestly, if I had wanted to I could have blasted the front desk area to smithereens.

The elevator opened and Ink stepped out. It was still a surprise to see her now. The short, spiky hair was gone; in its place was a sleek bob. She didn't have her tats on all the time, either. And instead of her ubiquitous Converse high-tops, she was wearing pumps. Her business suit was tasteful and modest in a sober gray. It made me want to weep.

We were in the elevator when Ink got up on her tiptoes and kissed me.

"What was that for?" I asked.

"I missed you," she said. "Good grief, I can't even kiss you without you thinking something weird is going on. You haven't been having those nightmares again, have you?"

I didn't answer.

"You have," she said. "And you've been having those flashbacks, too."

"John asked me to lead a group to Nigeria," I said, hoping to change the topic.

"I hope you turned him down. You don't need any more stress."

Annoyance ripped through me. My mother had once said that it wasn't the big stuff that screwed up relationships. It was the little things—the everyday stuff that went on and on, annoying the hell out of you. I hated that Ink's concern and attention were so grating. And I *really* hated the fact that she was right. "Yeah, I turned him down, but I told him I was available if he needed me for anything else."

Luckily, the elevator doors opened and she didn't have a chance to reply. As we walked through Cubicle City, I noticed that a lot of the employees were giving Ink sympathetic looks. She nodded to a couple of them.

"What's going on?" I whispered.

"In a minute."

We stopped in front of a large door. Ink slipped a key on her wrist coil into the lock. When the door opened, we were in a beautiful waiting room. There was a desk at one end next to a second door. Ink went to the desk and sat down behind it. "Grab a chair," she said.

I got a chair and dragged it next to her desk, then plopped down in it. The phone rang and she answered it.

"Yes, this is the office of the director," Ink said. "No . . . I'm sorry . . . He's out for the rest of the day."

There was a pause.

"Of course, I would be happy to answer any questions."

She stuck out her arm and I could see words scrolling across it: *There's nothing more I would rather do this afternoon than talk to you. And your inane questions will ensure that I'll never get this half hour of my life back.*

"Yes, the new director is wonderful to work for."

*As long as you don't mind a self-absorbed, narcissistic jackass with penis-size issues.*

"Of course, we'll all miss Nephi Callendar. As Straight Arrow he was a force for good and as head of SCARE he looked out for the best interests of the American people."

She put her leg up on the desk so her skirt fell back a little, and I could see in Gothic lettering:

*Who was a decent human being, unlike this new guy, who has the IQ of warm milk. Of course, Nephi would have had a conniption fit if he had known that you and I were more than "best" girlfriends.*

"But the new director has some exciting plans for the department."

She lifted her shirt so just her stomach was bared. Written on it was: *When he isn't working out or obsessively cleaning his office every hour. What a freak! And not in a good way.*

"Well, his plans are secret at the moment. It would be inappropriate for me to reveal them at such an early date. I'm certain that when he's ready, he'll be making an announcement to the press. Yes, of course. I was happy to help."

"I didn't know that Callendar quit," I said.

"He didn't quit. He retired. It happened while you were at BICC. He really did take a chance on me. After all, I'd only done PA work on *American Hero*. But he said that he needed all the aces he could get working for him and what I'd done on *AH* was just as hard as anything I'd do here. Crap, I am so depressed."

I stood up and went around her desk to hug her. "Don't worry about it.

If this doesn't work out, I'm sure I can get you hooked up with the Committee."

"Let's just get some dinner and go home," she said, coming over and kissing me. Then she said, "I'm pretty sure I can think of a fun way to pass the evening."

♥

I was walking through Behatu Camp. It must have been early morning because the heat hadn't really hit yet. My footsteps made puffs of dust along the unpaved street. The mountains ringing the village were so close I thought I could smell snow. How many centuries had people been fighting over those indifferent Balkan peaks? All this dying—for what?

Lying a few feet in front of me was a girl. She was only ten or so. It was hard to tell because she was so thin. I didn't want to get any closer, but it was part of my job. I squatted down next to her and pushed the hair back from her face. There was a deep gash along her neck. Blood was pooled underneath.

"I found another one," I said loudly.

"We'll get there in a minute." Was that Curveball? Or maybe Earth Witch?

I touched the girl's face. There were bruises and small cuts. Her lips were swollen. I didn't need to see the rest of her body to know she'd been raped. That's what happened here. Women, girls, grandmothers were all systematically raped and tortured. That's why we were here. We were supposed to stop it.

But we were too late for her.

Her eyes snapped open. White, unseeing eyes. I jumped back and fell on my ass.

"Murderer," she said. "Killer."

Blood spurted from her mouth, covering me.

*"Wake up!"*

My eyes opened, but for a moment, I didn't know where I was. Ink gave me a hard shake. "C'mon, Michelle. Wake up."

"I'm awake," I said. But my mouth was dry and it came out as a croak.

"Jesus, you scared the crap out of me."

"I'm sorry," I said woodenly. I could smell fear sweat on myself.

"You should just quit the Committee," Ink said as she grabbed her robe and slid from the bed. I heard her go into the kitchen and turn on the faucet. Then she came back and handed me a glass of water.

"I can't quit," I said. The water was cold and tasted so good it hurt.

"Why not? You don't need the money."

The sheets were damp with sweat, so I went to Ink's closet, pulled out a fresh set, and then started stripping the bed.

"I can't quit because I still have work to do for them."

"Have you even told them what's been going on with you? You've got post-traumatic shock, for crying out loud."

I jerked one of the pillows out of its case. "I don't recall when you got your psychiatric license."

"Fuck you!" she snapped, yanking the sheets off the bed. "I *hate* this macho bullshit you're doing. You don't have to impress me. I know you. I know your heart. I know you'd give anything to help someone else. But you can't rescue the entire world."

A hard lump was stuck in the back of my throat. I was not going to cry. I hated women who cried. "Please, can we just leave it alone?" I turned away. If I looked at her I would start bawling.

"Fine," she said. I could hear her tucking and snapping the sheets. I turned back around to help her.

We finished making the bed, then got back in. But she stayed on her side and I stayed on mine, as if there were a chasm between us. I guess there was, but I didn't know what to do about it.

♠

# Double Helix

## THE SWORD SHALL NEVER DEPART
## FROM THY HOUSE

### Melinda M. Snodgrass

STANDING AT THE WINDOW in Flint's office looking out at the traffic. Unlike New York, horns still blare and engines cough and rev, but even with our North Sea platforms and the Nigerian oil, gas is very expensive and the number of cars on the roads is substantially reduced.

"*There have been a number of incidents in the oil fields. The People's Paradise is casting it as oppressed locals reacting against the central government in Lagos, but it's happened very suddenly and it seems very well targeted. I think the President-for-Life Dr. Kitengi Nshombo has a strong interest in securing those oil fields for himself.*"

"We can't lose that oil. Bruckner would be *very* upset if he couldn't run his truck." It's part of my persona that I keep everything light and rather sarcastic, but in truth I feel a surge of very real fear that cuts through the fog of exhaustion that seems to enfold me. What if there wasn't gas to run the ambulances? What if I wasn't around and Mum couldn't get Dad to the hospital?

"*And now the damn UN and the Committee are getting involved.*" Flint actually rises from his chair. Even with the reinforced floor I feel the wood flexing and trembling as he walks to join me at the window. "*You must reduce their effectiveness. Separate them from Jayewardene. The UN with an army of aces is a distressing development and the secretary-general seems very eager to use them.*"

"Look, it would be rather bad form for me to remove Jayewardene, but

Nshombo . . ." I allow my voice to trail away suggestively. "I could pay a little visit to Kongoville."

*"His sister would only take his place. He's a true believer in his Socialist Paradise and murderous in pursuit of his beliefs, but she is a sadist and would be much worse. Also, the real power there is this ace, Tom Weathers. He has an alarming array of powers. Any one of them would be potent. Taken together . . ."* He pauses. *"I think he may well be the most powerful ace in the world."*

Reaching into my pocket, I pull out my case, remove a cigarette, and tap it on the lid. The silver gives back a distorted image of my face. "That may be, but I'm betting a bullet in the back would still kill him."

*"It may come to that, but not just yet. If the ruling class in Kongoville starts dying while they're locked in a dispute with us . . ."*

"Right you are. Clean hands, plausible deniability, and all that."

*"Is there any way for you to break up this Committee?"*

"I'm trying, but I only have nights. And not every night because Noel Matthews also has a life as a stage magician."

*"I thought Lilith does her best work at night."* It's bizarre hearing ponderous sexual innuendo from those stone lips.

"Yes, well, but I can only fuck so many men a night, and my choices are a little limited. But if Lohengrin and DB were to go after each other . . ." The image is irresistible—Lohengrin's sword against DB's sonic attack. It would be an interesting match-up. "It wouldn't be hard. Men are so predictable."

Flint cocks his head in query. *"Only because you are playing the slut. Why do you do that? Is that how you view women? And you're not very charitable toward men, either."*

"Yes, but I hate people. They are universally such shits."

*"Hmmm."* And then Flint is back to Africa. *"Try to get posted to Africa. That way we can control the information coming back."*

All this talk of controlling information and stopping an investigation finally registers in my sleep-deprived mind. "We're sure nothing is going on in the Niger Delta . . ."

*"Perfectly sure. And we will not allow the PPA to invade on a pretext."*

"And if they do?"

*"They'll be dealt with."*

♣

The room has a sour, musty smell. I want to open the window, but it's a raw day with wind and rain squalls. Dad's breath seems to rattle in his chest, and his skin looks gray. I need to keep him warm.

I shouldn't be here. I should be in New York with Lohengrin. But I had to come home. Even though I canceled dinner I can still teleport into Lohengrin's bed. He'd probably prefer that. To be fair the big German ace doesn't begrudge the money he spends on me. God knows, he's got enough with all his product endorsements.

Thinking about food has my gut clenching with hunger. I can't remember the last real meal I ate. A cup of tea is at my elbow, and a plate of macaroons I picked up at the bakery sits on the bedside table. But Dad wants me to read to him. Once he falls asleep I'll eat. He hands over the Bible with a shaking hand. It's open to the Psalms. I just start reading. They're all the same to me.

" 'I love the Lord, because he hath heard my voice and my supplications. Because he hath inclined his ear unto me, therefore will I call upon him as long as I live. The sorrows of death compassed me . . . ' " My voice cracks, and an aching vise closes my throat. "Excuse me." It comes out as a rasp.

I plunge into the bathroom until I compose myself. It takes a long time.

Wearing loose-fitting clothes that will accommodate Bahir's bulk I decide to stop at the Highwayman's favorite watering hole for a pint. I need to wile away another hour until the sun has set. I check my watch. That will put me in New York at 2:00 A.M.

I don't particularly enjoy the sweat, diesel, and overcooked boiled vegetable smell that fills the working-class pub, but I like to keep on good terms with my fellow members in the Silver Helix, and I want to hear from Bruckner about his runs to Nigeria. Not that I don't trust Flint . . . it's just that I don't trust anyone. And it was Flint who taught me that.

From the alley I can see the big lorry parked illegally in front of the pub. There's the twist and pull as my flesh resumes its normal shape. I tighten the belt a couple of notches and cross the street to the pub. It's called the Saracen's Head, and a picture of a turbaned, bearded head with blood flowing from the severed neck adorns the sign. I'm glad the Highwayman doesn't know that in my other life I'm Bahir.

Bruckner has seated himself where he can look out a window every few minutes and check on his ride. A bell over the door rings as I enter. Bruckner's foul cigar has trumped the cigarette smoke. I don't even think my Turkish fags could compete.

The bartender, who is bald with a sagging heavy belly and an array of tattoos on his wobbling upper arms, pulls me a pint of stout. Everyone in the pub is white. Not the easiest thing to find in London today. The big men hunched at small tables eye me as I cross the room, but relax into acceptance when I sit down with Bruckner. John is obviously the arbiter of social acceptance here. A modern-day and male version of the patronesses of Almack's.

"What the fuck are you grinning at?"

"Nothing." I reluctantly release the image of Bruckner in a poke bonnet and Empire dress. Still, I had better get control of my errant thoughts. I take a pull on my stout and savor the dark, peaty taste. I like a beer you can practically chew. "John, have you run any armaments down to Port Harcourt or in the Urhobo region?"

"Yeah, that's where we're having a spot of trouble."

"And what is encompassed in the word . . . 'trouble'?"

"The bloody jigs in the Oil Rivers region have started mucking about with the pipelines."

"Why?"

"Usual bloody whine." He pitches his voice into a high squeaky plaint. "Oh, we're being oppressed. We're so poor. Those big mean corporations. The evil government is making us get off our lazy black asses and work." He grunts, coughs, and takes an enormous swallow of lager.

"Anybody dying?" I ask.

"Good Christ, when aren't they dying on that miserable continent?"

"I'm just trying to find out if the Lagos government is doing something naughty. We don't want our ambassador at the UN to plead innocence, and then find himself with his knickers down."

"As far as I know the bloody niggers in Lagos are no worse than the rest of the bloody wogs in any other crown colony. And why does it have to be Britain's problem when they are shits?"

I drain my mug. "White man's burden?" I suggest sweetly and leave.

♥

The mattress sinks under my weight as I arrive in Lohengrin's bed. The steady rhythm of the thunderous snores doesn't alter. For some reason it infuriates me. I think about the long thin knives I carry stashed about my person, and contemplate letting the boy wake up to find a blade at his throat. I always get cranky when I'm tired, and right now I'm positively homicidal.

I plaster on a smile, and lay a hand on his bare chest. He snorts, jerks, and comes up from beneath the sheets like a broaching whale.

"*Was? Was ist?*" He finally focuses on me. "Ah, *Liebling,*" and I'm crushed in a massive embrace. "When you called I thought I would be alone and lonely all night, but now here you are." His lips find mine. I can taste the beer and sauerkraut in his sleep-clogged mouth, not pleasant, but I close my eyes and think of England while we fence with tongues. Eventually he comes up for air.

"What did you do today?" I've settled back in the crook of his arm while he jams pillows behind his back.

"Ah, we heard a report from China. Tinker is doing very fine work there building pumps for wells. We do *such* good things, my Lili." Just listening to him maunder on about all the *wunderbar,* fabulous, brilliant things the Committee has done in the past twenty-two hours gives me *mal de tête.*

Even though he's blond he's got a pretty good mat of chest hair. I twine my fingers through it. "Tinker is quite a charmer, isn't he?"

"*Ja,* nice fellow."

"It seems that DB has abandoned us to be a rock and roll star." I inject regret. "I understand why he did it, but it makes us so vulnerable."

Lohengrin's arms tighten around me. "Are you afraid? Don't worry. I'll keep you safe."

"I know you'll try, but we're not always paired together and it just seems that the problems never stop and never get easier."

"We destroyed a much more formidable foe in Egypt." He pokes me playfully in the side. "And you didn't think we could do it."

"Well, DB did it. He really is the most powerful ace we have."

There's a shadow in the wide blue eyes. Satisfied, I pull his head down and start kissing him in earnest. Oh, I'm going to be sore tomorrow, but I've got him already wincing.

♠

# Just Cause: Part I

Carrie Vaughn

ECUADOR

**THE HILLSIDE HAD MELTED,** engulfing the street. Mud was moving, swallowing structures. The rain poured, and the slough of mud had turned into a soupy flood, drawn down by its own weight. There had been a town here: the edges of tin roofs emerged from mounds of gray earth, mangled fences stuck up at angles, cars tipped on their sides were mostly buried. And the rain still fell.

Before the jeep even stopped, Ana jumped out and ran into the thick of it.

"Ana!" Kate called.

"Curveball, we got other problems," Tinker said. He gestured to a crowd shoving its way along the road. Some of the people saw Ana and called out to her, *"¡La Bruja! ¡La Bruja de la Tierra!"* Earth Witch. They recognized her, and knew she'd come to help. The refugees needed to get to higher ground, up the next hill, to escape the flood. Ana could handle the mud. Kate and Tinker needed to get those people to safety.

Not every rescue depended on ace powers, she'd learned over the last year. Sometimes you just needed to offer a hand. Provide a working vehicle for people who couldn't make the hike.

Kate's jacket wasn't doing anything to keep her dry, but she wore it for warmth. This was supposed to be the tropics, but they were in the mountains, and it was cold. Didn't seem fair. Water dripped in streams off the brim of her baseball cap, a blue one with the UN logo John had given her.

The poor thing was starting to look ragged, like it had been through a war zone or three. Which it had.

She helped Tinker with the evacuation, but she always kept an eye on Ana.

Now Ana knelt on the muddy slough covering one of the houses. She looked feral, kneeling in mud that had splashed her legs, shorts, and T-shirt. Her black hair was coming loose from its braid and sticking to her round face. Hands on the mud, she glared at it with a knotted expression, setting her will. She called to someone in Spanish, and someone shouted back. People were digging, scooping, and flinging away buckets of dirt in the search for survivors.

A sound rumbled, like distant ocean waves. A couple of the guys on the roof cried out and jumped to the road. The dirt under them started moving, particles slipping, falling in waves, dirt pouring out of windows, slumping away from the house. In moments, Ana knelt on a sheet of mud-streaked corrugated tin.

Bodies broke free.

A woman and a child rode the swell of earth that came out the windows. They were limp, their limbs pushed to odd angles by the dirt's movement, their clothing tangled around their bodies. Another child remained hung up on the windowsill. Shouting erupted, and people surged toward the victims.

Kate fought her way to the woman. She was still warm, still had color. Still had a pulse. Her hair and skin were caked with mud. Kate cleaned the mud out of her mouth. *Please, let us have gotten here in time.*

The woman choked, sputtering back to life. Other rescuers revived the children. People wearing Red Cross jackets appeared. The convoy must have caught up with them. Kate, Ana, and Tinker had pushed ahead in the hopes that Ana's power could save lives.

Ana didn't stop after freeing the house. She scrambled off the roof and set her hands on the road, which cleared before her. Buildings emerged, and still the wall retreated, groaning, reluctant. Ana crept forward, always keeping one hand on the ground, and pushed the earth back. Rescuers searched the other houses and found more victims who'd been swallowed up, and now spit back out. Not all of them lived, but many did.

When Ana reached the end of the street, a wall rose at the edge of the town, a barren mound of churned-up mud, a tumor against the backdrop of the green jungle. The wall of mud served as a dike, diverting the flood of water around the village, buying them time.

. Kate approached her, hesitating, not wanting to break her concentration. Ana, head bowed, was breathing hard, her back heaving.

"Ana?" Kate touched her shoulder.

Ana said something in Spanish. Then her eyes focused, and she smiled. "Wasn't that something?"

"Will it hold?"

She shook her head. "Not with this rain. They're still going to have to evacuate."

"What about you? You holding up?"

"Same as always." She took a deep breath and briefly touched the quarter-sized medallion she wore. Kate offered her a hand up and was startled at how heavily Ana leaned on her. She held her side, at the place where a bullet had struck her a year before. The wound still hurt her sometimes. "I'm going to go help clear the rest of those houses."

Kate knew better than to try to argue, however hurt or tired Ana seemed. She went back to Tinker and the jeep.

The Red Cross had set up a tent and was distributing blankets and coffee. Hypothermia was an issue in the rain and cold. Tinker—Hal Anderson, a burly Australian ace with a beach-bum tan and weight-lifter muscles—had let the jeep stall out, which meant he was now burrowed under the open hood, doing who-knew-what to the engine. He'd rigged the thing to run on tap water—great publicity, not using any of the local fuel supplies during a global oil crisis. If he could mass-produce his modification, he'd be rich. But the device needed adjusting every time the engine shut off.

They'd been at this for three days, driving from village to village, staving off mudslides and evacuating towns. They needed a chance to catch their breaths. That was all she wanted.

Someone screamed and cried out a panicked stream of Spanish.

A river was pouring off the mountain. Water lapped the top of the wall Ana had made to hold back the flood. The edges crumbled. Suddenly the whole thing disintegrated. It was just gone, turned to soup by the rain, and the flood roared through the village. Ana was in the middle of it. Holding a little girl's hand, she knelt in the street, hand on the ground, looking up at the wave pouring toward her. This wasn't the slow, creeping wall that Ana had pushed back earlier. This was a mass of water so powerful it had picked up tons of debris—rocks, trees, a mountain's worth of topsoil—and carried it barreling down.

Too fast for Earth Witch to hold it back. More water than mud, she couldn't control it.

"Ana!" Horrified, helpless, Kate watched.

Ana reacted instinctively. She held the child close to her body and hunkered over, protecting her. Then, both of them disappeared in the torrent.

Kate started to run to her, but Tinker held her back, hugging her to him.

"I can break them out, I can blow through the mud!"

"No, you can't!"

She struggled anyway, trying to break free, but he held her trapped.

Then someone yelled, *"¡Mira!"* Look.

The river of mud flowed in a steady stream, but something in the middle of it moved, turning like a whirlpool. Then, a shape broke the surface. A platform of stone rose, carrying two figures clear of the flow, which frothed around the interruption. The tower of bedrock stopped some six feet above the surface. It was only a few feet in diameter, but it was enough. Ana crouched there, the child safe in her arms. Both were drenched in dripping mud. Even from where she stood, Kate could see Ana gasping for breath.

"Christ," Tinker breathed.

Kate cheered, laughing with relief.

The little girl shifted in Ana's arms and clung to the woman. Ana cleared the mud from both their faces. She looked up, raised her hand. Kate waved enthusiastically.

Ana touched the ground, and a faint rumble sounded, even over the sound of the flood. More ground broke free, a line forming a narrow bridge from the platform to the hillside. Soon, Ana was able to walk to safety, carrying the girl.

One of the refugees, a young woman, broke from the crowd and cried out. The girl in Ana's arms struggled. "Mama!"

Ana let her go, and she ran to the woman, who swept her up, sobbing. Holding her child, she went to Ana, touching her reverently, crying, *"Gracias."* The ace bore it with a smile.

Kate ran to meet her and pulled her into a hug, mud and all. Like she would notice a little more mud after this week. "Are you okay? Come on, you have to get warmed up, get something hot to drink."

Smiling vaguely, Ana hugged her back. "I'm okay. It's nice to be saving people for a change."

And it was.

The next morning, back in their hotel room at Quito, Ana was asleep. She'd been asleep for ten hours. She didn't even look relaxed, curled up in a ball, hugging the blankets tightly over her shoulders, like she was trying to protect herself from something.

They all needed a break. They'd been running all over the world for a year now. Ana, Michelle, Lilith, and a couple of others had been asked to use their powers almost nonstop. What did that do to a person?

Kate pulled a chair close to the window, took out her cell phone, dialed. John answered on the first ring.

"Hey, Kate. You okay?"

"Hi, John," she said, smiling. That was always his first question: you're okay, you're not hurt, you're coming home. "I'm fine. We're all fine. We saved a lot of people."

"I know, the networks have been carrying the story. What a mess."

"Yeah, half an hour in the shower and I still haven't gotten all the mud off."

"Maybe I can help you with that when you get back." She could hear the suggestive grin in his voice and blushed gleefully. "Speaking of which, aren't you supposed to be on a plane back?"

She sighed. "I made an executive decision to stay an extra day and give Ana a chance to sleep. She's really wiped out, John. I've never seen her this bad, not since Egypt." Egypt, when she was shot in the gut, after she'd cracked open the earth wide enough to swallow an army.

"Is she going to be okay?"

"I think so, eventually. But she could use a break. We need her too much to let her burn herself out."

"I know. She's not the only one." He sounded as tired as she felt.

"Promise me you'll give her a break after this. She hasn't seen her family in months. I think a trip home would do her good. You've brought in half a dozen new aces, more people from *American Hero*—surely you won't need her for a few weeks."

"Okay. Yeah. That should work." Then he sighed, reminding Kate that Ana wasn't the only one who was wiped out. "I'll figure this out."

There he went, taking it all on himself again. I, not we. This was the Committee, not a dictatorship. But Secretary-General Jayewardene had named him the chairman, and John took that position seriously.

She was too tired to argue about it right now.

Then John said, "How about I send Lilith to come get you—"

Ah yes, Lilith, who could wave her magic cloak and whisk them around the world in a heartbeat. But only at night, which was somehow appropriate, considering what seemed to be Lilith's other favorite activity. She'd turned the Committee into a soap opera all by herself.

"It's daylight here, John."

"Oh. Right. Maybe later, then."

Or not. "We'll be home tomorrow anyway."

"Fine, okay. But there's something else I wanted to talk about."

"Oh?"

"I was watching news footage. You weren't wearing your vest."

She wrinkled her face, confused for a moment, then remembered: the Kevlar vest that had spent the trip stuffed in her duffel bag.

"That's because no one was shooting at us," she answered. "There weren't even any soldiers. It was the Red Cross and us."

"They don't have to be soldiers to have guns, and you never know when someone might take a shot at you."

"It wasn't a Kevlar situation," she said.

"Is it really that big a deal to wear the vest?"

"It is when you're in a humid tropical country and need to move fast. The thing makes it harder to throw."

"And you couldn't throw at all if anything happened to you."

"And a Kevlar vest is not going to save me from drowning in mud. Or from getting hit by some lunatic jeep driver."

"Now you're making shit up just to argue with me."

Funny how he got all worked up over her not wearing Kevlar, but didn't seem to notice that Ana had been in shorts and a T-shirt. This wasn't supposed to be about *her*, it was supposed to be about the team.

She opened her mouth, ready to snap back at him, her pleasant flush at hearing his voice turning to frustration. These were stupid arguments, which didn't stop them from happening.

Sitting back, she made herself relax and said, "This is when I'd kiss you to break your concentration."

Saying so had about the same effect. She could imagine the nonplussed look on his face. Then he laughed, and the knot in her gut faded.

"I worry about you. I don't know what I'd do if something happened to you."

This, too, was an old conversation. She should have been pleased at how much he wanted to protect her, and she was. But it also felt like being put in a box.

"I'm sorry you were worried," she said. "But the only way you can really keep me safe is to not send me out here at all. And that would just piss me off."

"I know, and you can get killed crossing the street at home. Doesn't mean I'm going to stop worrying."

She smiled. "I love you, too, John. I miss you."

"I miss you, too. Get some sleep, okay?"

"Yes, sir."

NEW YORK CITY

Kate and Ana shared an apartment on the Lower East Side. They went home from the airport, and Ana crawled into bed for another round of sleep. Kate checked in on her, then went to see John.

While she and Ana had gone for austere college chic in a close-quarters studio, John lived in his mother's penthouse overlooking Central Park. Peregrine was in Los Angeles for the second season of *American Hero* and had given her son the run of the place.

Kate felt the disconnect every time she went there. She'd grown up with Peregrine on TV and all over the covers of magazines. She was an icon, probably the most visible and famous wild carder ever, with her stunning presence and spectacular wings. And here was Kate, dating her son.

The penthouse was beyond posh. It wasn't opulent or over the top—that was just it. Everything was tasteful and perfect, from the clean lines of the gray leather sofa set and glass coffee table, to the giant arrangement of hyacinths on the twelve-seater dining-room table. Real flowers, not silk, changed every week by the housekeeper. Last week had been orchids.

John grew up with this. He walked in here, and it was home. Kate still felt like she'd landed in a photo spread in *Vogue*. She was getting used to it—it was definitely easy to get used to. But sometimes she wondered if she'd fallen down a rabbit hole.

She set her bag by the wall of the living room and took a deep breath, happy to be anywhere that didn't smell like a third world country.

"Hello?" she called. Her voice echoed.

"Hey!" John appeared from the kitchen, a bottle of wine in one hand and a corkscrew in the other. She was on him in a heartbeat, arms over his shoulders, pulling herself into a kiss. Awkwardly, hands full, he hugged her back. Their kiss was warm and long.

"Hi," she said when they managed to separate.

"Hey," he said, his smile bright. "Let me put this down so we can do this right."

John set the bottle on the coffee table, where two glasses were waiting. Kate pulled him down to the sofa next to her.

The light from the other room glinted off the lump in his forehead. Sekhmet. A scarab-like joker living in John's head. She gave him his power—he wasn't an ace on his own, not anymore. But Kate didn't like to think about it, that she and John were never really alone. Right now, moments like these, John was all hers.

"Are you sure you're okay?" John said. "You still look beat."

"I'm just starting to wake up."

She pulled her leg across his lap, half straddling him, and kissed him again. She rested her hand on his cheek, ran it across his curly hair. His lips moved with hers while his hands crept under her shirt, pressing against her back. She drew on his warmth, and the tension faded. They sighed together.

"Welcome home," he said.

"Thanks. It's really, really good to be here." She could curl up in his arms and never leave.

"Yeah. I worry less when you're with me." He ducked his gaze, hiding a smile. "If it weren't for you, I don't think I'd have lasted this long."

So serious. Of course he was, this wasn't a game. The pundits sometimes joked: what, you kids think you can save the world? But they could. They did. Little parts of it at a time.

Not wanting the anxiety to creep back, she joked, "And if it weren't for you, I'd have a million dollars and be the designated ace guardian of San Jose."

He laughed, and she laughed with him, their heads bowed together. He said, "You really want to be the designated ace guardian of San Jose? Showing up for your guest appearance on *Dancing with the Stars?*"

"Oh, my God, no. Poor Stuntman. No wonder he went to work for the government."

John's eyes held uncertainty again. Still worrying.

"John, I wouldn't change anything. I don't want to be anywhere but right here."

Their next kiss was slow, studious almost, like neither one of them wanted to miss a single sensation. He worked her shirt off, and she helped, raising her arms, leaning into his touch as his hands slid up her back. He dropped her shirt on the floor, then tipped her back onto the sofa, and it was some time before they actually made it to bed.

Kate heard a voice. She thought she was dreaming, some kind of weird, lucid dream, because her eyes were closed, but she felt awake. Familiarity intruded. John's voice, muttering.

But it wasn't John. He wasn't speaking English. She opened her eyes.

He was looking at her, but it wasn't him. Part of him belonged to Sekhmet, and sometimes she took over. The look in his eyes became older, harder, more experienced. That other gaze was looking at her now, with an expression that was both sad and annoyed. The situation was complicated: Isra the joker had been waiting for a great ace with whom she could join her powers and become Sekhmet, the handmaiden of Ra. But John didn't become Ra. He'd been cured of the wild card virus. Isra might call herself Sekhmet, but she never got the power she'd longed for. There was no Ra, now. Her frustration with John, and with those around him, was plain, whenever she came to the fore.

The voice whispered in Egyptian. Kate wished she knew what she was saying. She was afraid the joker was saying, "This won't last."

Self-consciously, Kate pulled up the sheet to cover her chest. "I wish you'd leave us alone," she whispered.

Isra heard her. "You're children. Just children. You don't understand."

Kate frowned. "That's not fair. After what we've been through, after what you've put John through—"

"It wasn't supposed to be like this. He's such a boy."

"No. You ask too much of him." But how could she argue with something that was so much a part of him?

"*You* are just a child."

Angry, Kate started to sit up, ready to yell another retort. But John closed his eyes, sighed, and seemed to sleep again.

She touched John's arm. "John? John, wake up." She kissed his bare shoulder, then again, until he stirred.

"Hm? What's wrong? Is it the phone?" He thought Jayewardene was calling with a new disaster. He started to sit up, but she held him back. It was John this time, looking out of his own eyes.

"Nothing's wrong. I'm sorry, I shouldn't have woken you up."

Only half awake, he stroked her cheek absently. "You okay?"

She thought about telling him he'd been talking in his sleep—or that Sekhmet had been talking in his sleep. She'd told him on other nights when it had happened. This time, she didn't. "I had a nightmare or something. It's nothing."

Then John's phone *did* ring. They both lurched at the noise. Reflexively, he grabbed it and listened. His frown deepened. Jayewardene. Had to be.

"Got it. Okay. We'll send someone down," he said, then hung up.

"What is it?" she asked.

"There's been an explosion in West Texas. Feds are saying a grain elevator went up, but that's not what the people on the ground are saying."

"What are they saying?"

"Terrorists. Sabotaging the oil."

"Oh, my God. And we're going?" She pushed the covers back. But John shook his head.

"Lilith and Bugsy can go. They can check things out and report back before we've even gotten to the airport."

"But I want to go—they'll need people, there's got to be some kind of rescue operation—"

"We don't know the story yet, so you're not going."

"John, I want to go. If you're trying to keep me safe—"

He smirked at her. "Are you ever going to stop arguing with me?"

"You ought to be used to it by now." She tried on a smile. Hoped he knew she was teasing.

He ignored the phone for the moment, wrapped his arms around her, and kissed her. Which was just what she needed. She leaned into him and kissed back.

And for a moment, everything was just fine.

# Double Helix

## AN ABOMINATION OF DESOLATION

### Melinda M. Snodgrass

"**I THOUGHT WE WERE** going to Texas," Bugsy says, seconds after we arrive in the bar on the twenty-eighth floor of the Beekman Tower Hotel. We're still in our party clothes. The blogger surprised me by actually knowing how to dress. Unfortunately the piping on his tuxedo shirt draws attention to his burgeoning paunch.

Through the wide window I can see tendrils of fog swirling around the Brooklyn Bridge. The long gray streamers are like fingers plucking at the guy wires, and for an instant I consider what that music would sound like.

"We are. And while John might prefer for us to gallop off like white knights, I prefer that we go smart. We need information about this explosion."

"It was big, and we sure as shit know it wasn't a grain elevator." He rubs at his scalp, and gives me his signature sneer.

"Yes. And I don't think you'd look good bald, toothless, and bleeding from your eyes, ass, and nose."

He blanches and takes his hand out of his brown hair. "Nuclear?"

"I'm going to find out."

"How? If the government is trying to cover it up—"

"They're idiots to try. There are seismic monitors all over the world. We work for the UN. One of our affiliated organizations is the International Atomic Energy Agency."

"Will they tell us?"

I lie. "I have a boyfriend who works for them."

There's a central area in the room delineated by art deco–style metal columns. It holds the bar, some comfortable sofas, and a baby grand piano. I take Bugsy's hand, lead him over, and push him down onto a couch. "And while I talk to him you're going to have a drink and relax. Try the green apple martini. It's really good."

I retreat into the observation area on the left, and sink down at one of the small tables. I use the Silver Helix phone. The signal is heavily scrambled and it will put me directly through to Flint. I also keep a close watch, and sure enough a small green wasp lands on a small serving table.

"Yes."

"*Gruss Gott, Liebling.*" I give it a throaty purr.

"*Ja,*" comes Flint's reply. I love that I work for someone smart. It helps me continue to suffer the Committee.

"I need to know about the explosion in Pyote, Texas," I continue in German. If a bug could look disappointed this one would. The wasp gives a sharp buzz and flies back into the main bar.

Over the phone I can hear papers rustling, and I reflect on generational differences. I only carry a pen because they can make quite a decent weapon. My notes are on my Palm, my BlackBerry, my phone, and most often in my head.

"*They're still crunching the data from the monitoring stations. I can't give you the exact magnitude yet.*"

"Just tell me if it could have been conventional explosives."

"*No.*" Flint anticipates my need. "*Do you need a suit?*"

"I'll need two."

"*How will you explain that?*"

"You're my boyfriend in the IAEA."

"*Right. One more thing. Could it be Siraj?*"

"If we . . . they have a nuke and Bahir doesn't know about it, then Bahir's usefulness is definitely at an end. *Ciao.*"

The natural flora of Texas burns well. Our boots are soon streaked with black soot. In the distance a single tree stands naked and twisted, ghostly in the light of a nearly full moon. In places there are black hummocks of varying sizes. Closer examination reveals dead jackrabbits, coyotes, cattle, and a few horses. Lilith's long hair is plastered to my sweat-damp cheeks. Because of the helmet I can't pull it loose. I purse my lips and try to direct a puff of air, but I can't get the right angle.

It's not just the heat of a Texas night or the bulky lead-lined suit that creates my discomfort. I feel like my skin is crawling, prickling, burning. Even though I know the various radioactive particles aren't actually penetrating my suit, I decide we're not going to stay long.

We can't get close to the former town of Pyote. We know it's crawling with federal agents and scientists from the NRC because at my suggestion Bugsy had unlimbered a few hundred wasps before donning the suit. They have been scouting for us. What they've seen is a large crater, a handful of blackened buildings, and dozens of burning oil wells. Ironically, the grain elevator is still standing. Occasionally a National Guard helicopter goes thrumming by overhead, the wash from the rotors stirring the ash, searchlights sweeping across the devastation. So far none of them have spotted us, but it's only a matter of time.

I become aware of a new sound over my helmet's radio. It's Bugsy's teeth chattering. "Shit, this is what it looked like. In Hiroshima and Nagasaki." A handful of his wasps crawl across the back of his gloved hand. They don't look well.

"Exactly like it." I pause for an instant, then add, "Only there were a lot more people and buildings in Japan."

He turns so he's facing me and we can see each other through the faceplates. He looks hurt and angry and very young. "You know what I mean. This is awful. People need to know about this. They need to see what one of these bombs can do. It's been sixty years. Everybody's forgotten."

"You go, tiger." But it's all bravado. There's a quivering in my gut like I've never experienced before. Such is the power of The Bomb.

Bugsy turns away. Shame is like a taste on the back of my tongue. This is his country, and someone has attacked it in a particularly horrible way. I lay a hand on his shoulder. "I'm sorry. I'm scared, too."

In this direction we can see a plume of fire. The hot wind racing across the West Texas plains bends and dips the flames, revealing the black shadow of a pump jack. I wonder how long the steel can withstand the heat from the burning oil.

Bugsy points at the burning oil well. "Do you suppose that's why they did it?"

"These fields are almost played out." I shake my head. "There wasn't enough oil here to make any appreciable difference."

"Then why do it?"

"As a warning? Next time it will be Alaska or the refineries in the Gulf." I put an arm around his shoulders. "We need to get out of here."

I-20 runs right by Pyote. A portion of the interstate is now inside the federal cordon, so the vast emptiness of West Texas seems even emptier given the dearth of traffic. It's also 1:20 A.M. as Bugsy and I stand in the coin car wash in Pecos hosing off each other's suits. We're on the outskirts of the town, which seems to consist entirely of fast-food joints, auto body shops, and junkyards conveniently located for the cars that can't be fixed. Every small American town seems to possess this leprosy as if it were a protective asteroid belt shielding the core planet. Not that the center represents any kind of nirvana.

Once the suits have been sluiced off we climb out. The pungent reek of male sweat fills the still air. I'm hoping Bugsy's stink is so strong that he won't notice my particular musk. I can change the form, but my body chemistry remains the same, and men's and women's sweat smells different. I know from my training that we need to rinse off any errant particles that might have penetrated the suit so we turn the hoses on each other.

The water pours out of the hose at high pressure. I actually find the pounding soothing on the sore muscles in my back. My T-shirt and jeans cling to my skin. Behind my lids it feels like I've used eye drops made from sand. It doesn't occur to me until I turn around that getting a soaking as Lilith will provoke quite such a reaction from my companion. Bugsy's eyes are unfocused, and he's sporting a gigantic hard-on that presses against the fabric of his wet trousers. I can understand why—when you're faced with this much death the urge to life is strong. It's also Bugsy. He doesn't see much action. A man who changes into bugs at stressful or exciting moments would not be the ideal lover.

"You want to . . . ?" His voice is husky. "It would only take a few minutes," he says.

"An excellent reason for me to say—*no.*"

A car glides past and I realize a fraction of a second too late that it's a police cruiser. My gut clenches and I reach for Bugsy, but the cop has spotted us and we're pinned in the glare of his spotlight. The lights start flashing, and he noses up into the car wash bay.

The cop is a large, shadowy form standing prudently behind his open car door. "What are you two up to?" The drawl is hard and suspicious.

I'm acutely aware of the Hazmat suits, and I can't seem to think. Bugsy steps in. He is quick. I'll give him that. "Uh . . . wet T-shirt competition. We're practicing." There's a faint interrogatory rise to the words. I hope the cop misses it.

I also hope he's a redneck and not a Baptist. He shines his flashlight on my chest. The leer dispels any doubt as to which camp he belongs. "Well, you two better get on out of here. There's a bunch of Feds just down the road, and they're detaining everybody who ain't local—and some who are."

"Thanks, sir," Bugsy says. The cop steps back into his car and drives away.

"Good save," I offer the compliment because I want to get Hive out of Texas, and I'm afraid it won't be easy.

"You didn't say anything," Bugsy says.

"I was the prop." I'm looking for the right approach when Bugsy makes it unnecessary.

"Can you get me home? I gotta write my blog."

"And tell the world what?"

"That a nuke went off here."

"Is that wise?"

"It's the truth."

I study him. He really doesn't get it that sometimes—often—the truth is overrated. But I take him home to Washington, D.C.

I can't believe I'm actually checking into the Best Western Swiss Clock Inn in Pecos, Texas. The walls are painted white with a green roof and an absurd clock tower rising from the center of the building. The nearest town to Pyote is Wick, but it lacks any kind of accommodation, and it is now behind the law enforcement cordon.

At first the woman at the reception desk tells me there are no rooms available, but I milk the British accent for all it is worth, with a hapless Bertie Wooster sort of demeanor. She loves it, and soon she loves me. I get a room. As I'm walking to the elevators I pass the ubiquitous wooden stand filled with flyers detailing all the wonderful things to do in Pecos. The Pecos Cantaloupe Festival seems to be most prominently displayed. Pity I'm here too late for that excitement. Another flyer shows a Schwarzenegger looka-like dressed as Conan the Barbarian. BARBARIAN DAYS! it announces, JUST 259 MILES AWAY IN SCENIC CROSS PLAINS, TEXAS. Yes, 259 miles, just a Sunday drive for a Texan. If there was gasoline.

I dump the garment bag in the room, and crank the air-conditioning to high. It's one of those low, under-the-window affairs, and it sets up a frightful clattering. It does pour cold air into the stuffy room. I'm tired, but I've got to hit the town. My guess is that evacuees from Wick and any survivors from Pyote will be in Pecos. I need to find them, buy rounds, and loosen their tongues. But God I'm tired.

I'd dropped Bugsy in D.C., and had to wait for dawn so I could make the daylight-to-daylight jump as Bahir. Once the Hazmat suits were back in London I stopped at my flat and packed a bag so I wouldn't arrive back in Texas without luggage. I checked on Dad, and prepared him a cup of tea and a slice of toast smeared with Nutella. He ate three bites. I finished it, and now it lies in the pit of my stomach like a piece of lead shot. It's early afternoon in Pecos. Someone will be at the local watering holes.

While I walk I use my phone to link to the Internet. Bugsy has been a busy boy. His post is already up.

> It was a Nuke, boys and girls! The coyotes are glowing at night—at least the ones that aren't dead. I know, I know, it's so twentieth century to be talk-ing about The Bomb, but it's clear that MAD has stopped working, and now it's time for everybody to get Mad.

I pass one of those white metal boxes that pass for a newsstand in the U.S. The local Pecos paper is still yammering about grain elevators.

I regret not wearing a hat, and my usual black attire amplifies the heat. The sky is painfully bright, and the sun doesn't so much shine as glare. My skin prickles. I'm acutely aware of radiation right now. I pause and survey the dining choices—a Pizza Hut, a Dairy Queen, a Subway. I spot a Mexi-can restaurant. What I don't see is a bar. Equally unfortunate is that the most cars are in the parking lot of the Pizza Hut. Well, they might have a beer and wine license. And then I spot the fire truck parked near the back. Yes, this might be the right place.

Inside, the harsh smell of undercooked tomato sauce is an assault on the sinuses. Conversation fills the room with a droning sound, as if a hive of bees were moving in. People don't even fall silent when I enter. They really are upset.

The waitress is cute and small and round and Hispanic. She has an expression that is both alarmed and delighted. People on the edges of a catastrophe always have that particular look.

"I'll take a small meat pizza and your salad bar. And what kinds of wines do you have?"

"Red and white."

I mentally sigh. *Of course.* "I'll take red." I give her my best stage smile. She smiles back. "I say, dear, I'm a producer with—" I time it so her exclamation of excitement makes it unnecessary to say with whom.

"Movie?"

"Well . . ." I look about conspiratorially. "I don't want to say too much. So often these things come to nothing, but I think you all have quite a story here, and if that's true, well . . . things might happen," I hastily add, "And of course anyone with information would be compensated and probably be in the film."

She scuttles away. Satisfied, I drift over to the salad bar. In a surprisingly short time a number of people have joined me around the giant bowl of iceberg lettuce. I can smell the MSG as I drop it onto my plate.

"You're a movie guy?" says one man whose cheap suit suggests insurance salesman or local banker. I move my head in a particularly noncommittal way. "But you're not a journalist?" He has that dried leather skin so common in Americans who live in the West, and the wrinkles deepen with suspicion.

"I can assure you I am not a journalist."

"You're English," says a large woman in spandex pants. The worried frowns ease. That seems to make me somehow more trustworthy.

"Well, I can tell you right now it wasn't no grain elevator. We don't grow wheat in these parts," says an elderly geezer whose bald scalp is not so much tan as covered with age spots.

"There's an elevator in Pyote," another local objects.

"Yeah, but it's a little teeny thing, just for the local feedlot," says the geezer.

"There was no warning. The sky just lit up," says another man with skin like jerky, and a big sweat-stained cowboy hat pushed far back on his head. "I was shifting cattle to new grazing, and the dark caught up with us. I was just going to wait out the night—then boom. Damnedest noise you ever heard."

"Has anyone from Pyote spoken about it?" I ask.

"We haven't seen anybody from Pyote. Wick, yes, but not Pyote." The cheap suit drops his voice. "I think they're all dead."

"Not all," says a burly man whose head seems attached to his shoulders without benefit of a neck. I watch the muscles in his upper arms flex and move. I think I've found one person who belongs with the fire truck. "I saw a medevac helicopter going in. Somebody survived."

"Whoever it was, I don't think they were hurt," says the fat woman whose plate is so full that lettuce is starting to cascade off the sides. "I heard they're under guard. Locked up." The door of the Pizza Hut opens and my old nemesis from the car wash enters. "I bet it's the guy who caused the explosion. My niece is married to a policeman over in Wick." I wish she would keep her voice down because the cop has stopped walking and is staring at us—hard. I'm a stranger in town, which is a red flag to a cop.

"Nobody could have lived through that. I was real close by and I'm damn lucky to be alive."

"They could if they was an alien," argues the old man.

"Or a joker."

I can't really tell who said that, and I find it interesting that the mind would go to joker rather than ace. It's far more likely one of the meta-powered would survive, but there is still an enduring discomfort and disgust with jokers.

"It's probably them damn rag heads," says the man in the cheap suit. "Going after our oil. Making sure we have to pay through the nose. We should nuke them."

It's a typically jingoistic American reaction, and I reflect that if Siraj could hear that he might reconsider his stand. The door closes and I realize the cop has left. I try to tell myself that he decided he wanted a burger rather than a pie—

—but it was a vain hope. They are waiting in my hotel room. One is your typical FBI agent, white, big, broad, with an ill-fitting brown suit and a crew cut. The other is a SCARE agent and an ace. The Midnight Angel is clad in black leather. Every curve of her lush body is revealed by the skintight jumpsuit.

"Please come with us, sir," says the Fucking Big Idiot.

It's a very quick helicopter ride to scenic Wick, Texas. SCARE has set up headquarters in city hall, and the fact that SCARE rather than the FBI is in charge tells me that the Americans suspect some kind of wild card involvement. The mayor's office has that small-town-politician-trying-too-hard-to-seem-important feel. The walls are lined with pictures of the potbellied little mayor posing with various national politicians and movie stars, with commendations from the Elks and the Moose and various other odd American organizations including, in fact, the Odd Fellows.

A woman sits behind the desk, and if the mayor were still here she would dwarf him. Joann Jefferson, aka Lady Black, is the Special Agent in Charge. As she stands she pulls her reflective cloak more tightly about her statuesque body. A tendril of silver hair has slipped from beneath the hood of her black bodysuit, and it seems to shine on her ebony cheekbone. She sketches a greeting with a black gloved hand, and then waves me into the chair across the desk from her. I don't offer my hand. I know the suit and cloak are supposed to protect me from her energy-sucking power, but I'd rather not test the limits of the technology.

"Noel, what the fuck are you doing here?"

I lean back in the chair and pull out my cigarette case. "Ah, I see we're dispensing with the pleasantries." I take my time lighting up, and judge when she's just about to lose it, then I say, "Someone set off a nuclear device. Normally I'd argue that in this godforsaken part of the world no one would notice and it would make little difference to the general ambience, but I gather some people died."

She rubs a hand across her face. Despite great cheekbones her features look like they're sagging. I sympathize. I'd really wanted to catch a nap back at the Swiss Clock. "I know we can't hide this from other governments, but we don't want a panic. If people knew a nuke went off . . ." Her voice trails away as if she's just too weary to keep talking.

"Look, let us help. You might recall that we are allies. That special relationship and all that rot that our prime minister and your president mutter lovingly to one another."

She's considering. I decide to help her along. "Sorry about the directorship. We frankly couldn't believe the news when we heard who replaced Nephi." Her brows draw together in a sharp frown, but I can sense it's not meant for me, and she's a good little soldier and doesn't take the opportunity to complain. "Well, just know that Flint is on your side, as am I," I add.

For a brief moment the hard-charging law enforcement agent is replaced by a woman who looks pathetically grateful and vulnerable. It's gone in the flick of an eyelash, and Jefferson says in a terse, clipped tone, "It's got to be the Arabs. I guess they're not content with destroying our economy, now they have to smuggle in a suitcase nuke and bomb us, too."

"But Pyote, Texas? I mean, really. Not much of a splash with that. No, they would pick a far more visible target."

"There are oil fields here," she counters.

"And the Midland/Odessa fields are just about played out, and believe me, the oil ministers in Riyadh and Baghdad and Amman know that."

She fingers that errant strand of hair and stares at me for a long time. "You people do know the Middle East better than we do."

"You're quite right. We've been oppressing them and manipulating them for *far* longer." I stand. "I'll see what I can find out. I have a few contacts over there."

Even through the thick walls of one of Saddam's former palaces I hear Baghdad humming. Everyone in the Caliphate—and any Muslim nation whether they are part of the Caliphate or not—gets subsidized petrol. It used to be said that every crane in Europe was in Berlin. Now every crane in Europe and a few more to boot are in the Middle East. Siraj is trying to jump fifty years in one. He may just succeed, unless those of us in the Western nations kill him first.

Siraj is neither a religious ascetic like the Nur nor a hedonist like Abdul. Instead, he's a Cambridge-educated economist, so we are meeting in his state-of-the-art office in the midst of marble splendor. Every few seconds the computer dings, indicating a new e-mail. In the outer office a highly competent secretary answers the constantly ringing phone, and the fax machine whines and buzzes and shakes as it extrudes pages.

I'm in my Bahir form: red-gold hair and beard, traditional garb, shimmering golden cloak, and that damn scimitar. The teleporting ace who beheaded the enemies of the Caliphate had appealed to the Nur, but no assassin likes to get within arm's length of a target. Give me a McMillan TAC-50 any day, and a location a mile from the objective.

Siraj is chain-smoking Turkish cigarettes. He's the one who taught me to like the strong tobacco back when we were housemates at Cambridge. I would love a fag, but can't—Bahir is a very good Muslim, even down to having a wife. For a moment I think about the girl I married seven months ago under pressure by the Caliph. The old man felt that the Caliphate's remaining ace needed to set an example. But I need to put her aside. It's dangerous for someone in my line of work to allow anyone too close to them for any length of time. Fortunately I have the perfect excuse—she's barren. That accusation will probably keep her from marrying again. There's an uncomfortable tightness in my chest. The truth is that it's my fault, I'm the one who's sterile.

I realize I've missed whole sentences of Siraj's diatribe, and it shocks me. I've got to stop woolgathering. I'm going to get myself killed.

". . . Texas? *Texas!* Why in the bloody hell would I bomb Texas? As if I have a nuclear bomb. Would that I did. Then they wouldn't threaten me." He snatches up a sheaf of papers off the desk as he roars past, and shakes them in my face. The rattling is like hail on a tin roof, and the gold ribbon that marks this as an official diplomatic communication waves before my eyes, causing me to flinch and pull back.

"The secretary of state is holding me *personally* responsible for this explosion. They are the ones with nuclear bombs buried everywhere. They should take a count."

"I am sorry, Most High—"

"I told you not to call me that." His tone is snappish and peevish. "I'm not Abdul, and I don't want us acting like it's 1584."

"Yes, sir, I am sorry. I just thought you should know what they are saying."

"And you know this how?"

"I have a contact who works in Whitehall. The Americans are enlisting the aid of the Silver Helix to investigate whether we're involved."

Siraj pauses, and a humorless smile puts grooves in his gaunt cheeks. A year ago he was a portly man with a smooth, unlined face. Now he's thin, and worry and responsibility have gouged grooves into his forehead and etched lines around the soft brown eyes. "Maybe they'll send Noel. He is their reputed Middle Eastern expert. I'd like to know how he evaded my hospitality last time, and extend it again."

I incline my head. "Would you like me to kill him, sir?" It's totally surreal. Usually I'm amused by these situations, but this time it gives me an odd crawling sensation.

"No, I'm tired of the world viewing us as ignorant barbarians. I'm teaching them to respect us."

"But hate us all the more." I pause, then add, "And they have the armies."

"I'll moderate prices before we reach that point."

"And how will you know you've reached that point without crossing it?"

He looks at me oddly. I've taken a misstep, but to say anything more will only make it worse. I bow and teleport away.

# Political Science 101

Ian Tregillis & Walton Simons

**THIS WAS NO PLACE** for a thirteen-year-old kid.

He didn't remember how he got to the hospital, or even why he was there in the first place. His room smelled funny and the walls were painted a color so bland it didn't even register in Drake's mind. He was sick of being stuck with needles and hooked up to machines all the time. The gown they'd given him to wear did a lousy job of covering his chubby body.

The nurse had that fake friendly look on her face. She was middle-aged and skinny and she wasn't going to tell him anything. Drake was going to ask anyway, though. So far, all he'd found out since his blackout was that he was at Brooke Army Medical Center in San Antonio. Which was hell and gone from his dad's ranch outside Pyote.

"I want my mom and dad. Where are they? Where are my brother Bob and my sister Sareena? Why can't I go home?" He crossed his arms across his hefty stomach like a pouty, underaged sumo wrestler.

"By now you should know better than to ask, young man. You know what's going to happen if you keep this up."

Drake knew exactly what would happen. "I don't want to sleep anymore. I have nightmares. I've told you that."

"A new doctor is coming here later on today, to ask you some questions. Are you going to be a good, cooperative little boy, or not?"

Drake shook his head and gave the nurse his coldest stare.

She sighed. "I'm asking you nicely, son. Please try to help us."

Drake wasn't interested in cooperating. Maybe if he caused enough trouble they'd kick him out. "Go away. Leave me alone." He pulled the pillow from behind his head and threw it at her.

She caught it with one hand and used the other to open the door. "Orderly. I need assistance in here."

He put up a decent fight, but the orderly was a big guy who didn't play games. Eventually they got the needle into him. Seconds later, he felt like his body was an empty shell; his skin made of brittle clay that shattered and collapsed in onto itself. Darkness came, but it wouldn't last.

He was naked and curled up in a ball on the ground. Something was wrong with the ground, though. It was hot and his feet hurt. Drake saw small fires here and there. There was a big fire, too, behind him and to his right. He could feel the heat on his back and legs. He stood up and started walking away from it.

He started shuffling forward, feeling with his toes for anything he might be able to cover himself with or use as a weapon. Unfortunately, if there was anything on the hot ground, Drake didn't find it. His legs began to hurt and he collapsed to the ground, crying.

After sobbing until his tears were gone he stood back up and wiped his runny nose.

He continued shuffling slowly forward. The fire he was heading away from still seemed close, or maybe it was the other fires. There was no way to tell. Drake felt the ground rising slowly beneath him. It was a small hill, but by the time he made it to the top, his sides were burning and he was gasping for breath.

In spite of the fact that Drake was scared and uncomfortably naked, he lay down and closed his eyes.

Waking up from the drug was like swimming up from the bottom of a very deep pool. His hospital room came slowly into focus. Drake rubbed his eyes. The good nurse was there. Gerald, that was his name, was friendly and would talk to Drake about video games.

"Hungry, buddy?"

Drake's senses were coming back online. His stomach was empty enough it hurt. "Is it breakfast or dinner time?"

"Foodwise, it's whatever time you want it to be," Gerald said with a smile. "But timewise we're talking late lunch. I can get you a sandwich or a burger with fries. Maybe some ice cream."

"Oh, snap. A burger and fries would be killer." Drake's mind was now firmly focused on food and wasn't turning loose until he was comfortably full.

Gerald gave him a high-five. "I'm on it. You may have a visitor before I get back, or so they tell me."

"Another doctor?" Drake asked.

Gerald laughed. "I expect so. There's not much of anyone else around here." He ducked out the door with a wave.

Drake was annoyed when the new doctor showed up before Gerald got back with his burger. Drake had been expecting a mad scientist type, mostly because this all seemed like a bad movie. Instead, the man was younger than Drake's dad, maybe in his mid-thirties, had all his hair, and didn't wear glasses. He did have a white coat and a clipboard, but that was standard issue for this place.

"Hello, Drake. I'm Dr. Fitzhugh." He extended a hand. Drake shook it warily. "I understand you've been having bad dreams."

"Yes. It's because they give me this stuff to make me sleep." He looked straight at the doctor. "Can you make them stop giving it to me?" Although Drake's first idea was to find his parents and go home, he was also sick of being put to sleep.

The doctor nodded and scribbled on his clipboard. "I see. That medication is a nonopiate, but it can turn loose the subconscious in an uncomfortable way. I'll make a note of it."

Drake smiled. "Okay. Can I go home soon?"

"I'm also recommending that you be transferred to another facility." He put a hand on Drake's shoulder. "I'm sorry, son, but we have to figure out exactly what happened to you, and we don't seem able to do that here."

"Will my folks be at this place?"

"Just remember everyone is trying to help you. Have a good trip." The doctor stood and left the room with a rustle of his white coat and no further explanation.

♥

*Mom? I don't feel real good.*

Niobe Winslow felt her oldest child dying, felt him melting away like so much ice cream dropped on a summer sidewalk. Soon there would be nothing left of Xerxes but memories. And another hole in her heart.

Through their bond she felt the warming lamps perched over his incubator; needles squirting filtered blood and synthetic proteins into his forearm; plush swaddling.

*Hang in there, kiddo. Momma's coming.*

Month-old Xerxes was the longest-lived of Niobe's seventy-six children. Xue-Ming had lived nineteen days, thirteen hours. Xander, eleven days and change. Xerxes's breakthrough longevity had slipped through her defenses, bolstered her with vain and foolish hopes.

He'd been so strong. So healthy.

Her chair clattered to the floor as she jumped to her feet. The joker to whom she'd been reading rocked back and forth on his bed. His head, a featureless extrusion of flesh and bone, knocked against a white-spackled patch on the wall. The orderlies had given up on repainting it.

She righted the chair with her tail as she yanked the door open. "Sorry, Mick. Gotta go. Back tomorrow."

Knock. Knock. Knock. Little flakes of plaster rained down on Mick's sheets. The door slammed behind her.

A bell chimed the hour. She ignored it.

*I feel funny. My tummy hurts.*

*Almost there, kiddo. Just hang in there, 'kay?*

She ran through the corridors of the Biological Isolation and Containment Center, a facility carved into the caverns of an old salt mine deep under southeastern New Mexico. The corridors glowed with light from fiber-optic skylights connected to an array of heliostats on the surface. The skylights shone brightly; one could forget that the desert was half a kilometer overhead.

As both a voluntary committal and a trusty, Niobe had the run of the place. It was the nation's foremost biological research center, where an army of doctors and scientists struggled to cure hundreds of patients of their afflictions. The facility resembled a wagon wheel tipped on its side: a central hub, with radial spokes connecting it to an outer ring. In places, the outer ring connected to the original warren of mine tunnels, some large enough to swallow a freight train. The pie sections of the wheel were color-coded, like a Trivial Pursuit piece.

Niobe ran around the rim of the wheel. This wing (minimum security, voluntary committals) was decorated in shades of green, complete with oil paintings of forests and verdant hillsides. The corridors turned orange and red as she approached one of the medical wings.

Her tail caught an orderly's medicine cart as she skidded around the corner toward the infirmary. The cart flipped. Hundreds of pills skittered along the floor.

Over her shoulder, she yelled, "Sorry!"

"Damn it, Genetrix . . ."

Half the staff thought that was her real name. Genetrix. The Brood Mother.

The connection to Xerxes strengthened when she entered the infirmary. But still their telepathic link felt staticky, like a radio tuned slightly off-station.

Niobe weaved through a maze of EEGs, EKGs, respirators, dialysis machines, and still other devices constructed specifically for her children. Doctors and nurses surrounded the oversized infant incubator where Xerxes lay, working frantically to keep him alive.

A tangle of tubes and wires snaked from Xerxes's body to the machines. His skin, smooth and rosy-pink just this morning, hung waxy and sallow from sunken cheeks. Rheumy cataracts leaked sour-milk tears down his face. Even the thick black head of hair he'd styled into a little Elvis pompadour to make her laugh was coming out in clumps.

She had promised to take him to Las Vegas.

*Mom? I'm scared.*

"I'm here now," she said. "Don't be scared, okay?"

"Mom . . ."

"Hush, kiddo."

A single thought, through a blizzard of psychic static: *I love you, Mom.*

And then Xerxes was gone. The blanket sagged, empty but for a slurry of organic molecules. The ammonia-and-hay odor of dead homunculus wafted out of the incubator. Niobe sobbed. One nurse hugged her tightly, patting her on the back and murmuring encouragements, while another collected the dead child's remains in a sample jar.

The chimes sounded again, louder this time. A low voice on the PA system. "Genetrix to therapy two. Genetrix to therapy two, please."

She didn't want to go. But Xerxes's death had slipped a knife into her gut, and every secret, selfish thought gave it a vicious twist. Regularity was crucial. Generations yet unborn—but cherished no less—would drop like mayflies, if not for BICC's rigid methodologies. And so she went, for the sake of her future family.

Therapy room two mimicked the layout of Niobe's own quarters, except for the larger bed (a California king-size mattress) and the curtains along one wall.

Christian was seated on the edge of the bed. He looked up when she walked in. "Where were you? They're going nuts in there." He gestured at the curtains with the long, knobby fingers that always felt warm and strong on her hips.

"With Xerxes." She wiped her eyes. "He passed. Just now."

He grunted, pulling the shirt of his BICC uniform over his head. The soft blond hair on his body didn't catch the lights, so his chest looked slick and bare.

"He was scared," she said, walking behind a bamboo privacy screen in the corner. Niobe had insisted on the screen. As she draped her sweatshirt over the top of the screen, she added, "He would have liked it if you visited."

"Who?"

"Xerxes."

"Oh."

The bristly hairs at the base of her tail snagged the waistband on her sweatpants. As she worked them free, she added, "You could come, next time." Christian said nothing.

She scooted under the covers while Christian had his back turned. The linens made scratchy noises as she pulled the sheets around her. She wished she had shaved her legs, wished the wild card hadn't given her pig hair.

The nightstand clunked as Christian dropped a prescription bottle into the drawer. He popped a pill in his mouth. She pretended not to see any of it. The pills made her feel ugly. Uglier.

She lifted the covers for him, but he paused to draw the curtains, revealing a long mirror along the far wall.

"Maybe we can leave the curtains closed, just once."

The mattress bobbed as he climbed in next to her. "They go ape-shit when we do that." As he plumped a pillow under his head, he added, "Besides, it's all for the kids."

A cotton tent raised itself farther down the bed, below Christian's

waist, as he laced his fingers behind his head. The pill had worked, whatever it was.

She leaned over to kiss him, but he pulled away.

"C'mon, Niobe. They're waiting."

No warmth between her legs, no tingling desire. Not that it mattered.

Niobe sighed. She took care not to glimpse the mirror as she straddled
Christian, not to see her shapeless, doughy body; her tail; her acne.

Christian laid his hands on her waist, strong fingers wrapping around
her hips. He never touched her stomach, or her back, or her breasts. She
wanted his arms around her, but resigned herself to holding his shoulders.
His fingertips dimpled her flesh as they found a rhythm.

Her tail convulsed. Niobe groaned. The ovipositor widened for peristal-
sis with a tearing pain that robbed her of breath. The first egg in a clutch
was always the worst.

Christian finished with a little convulsion of his own, but not before
she was already climbing down. She wanted to hide behind the privacy
screen, but Pendergast and the others were adamant about recording every
detail of the birth process. At least the sheets made a passable toga; Niobe
had a lot of practice.

Christian rolled off the bed. He pulled his boxers on.

The first egg formed at the base of her tail. Through clenched teeth, she
said, "Won't you . . . unhhh . . . stay?"

He pulled his shirt back over his head. "What?"

"Don't you want to"—another burst of pain as the first egg passed midway along her tail and the second formed—"meet the little ones?"

"Can't. Docs gotta examine me." Christian combed his hair in the
mirror. "I've explained this before."

She wondered why they couldn't examine him *before* each session, but
couldn't catch her breath enough to ask. The tip of her tail tore open to
pass a sticky, pineapple-sized egg. She deposited it in the square marked on
the floor, where the cameras on the other side of the wall and in the ceiling could film the hatching from multiple angles.

Christian opened the door.

"Maybe you could come by and see them later?"

"Maybe," he said. And then he was gone.

Niobe dressed while the trio of eggs wobbled, shuddered, and expanded.
The first disintegrated with a little *pop,* overlaying a talcum-powder smell

on the odors of antiseptic and sex. In its place stood a three-foot-tall homunculus: stocky, bald, but with a bushy, fiery red beard.

He rubbed his scalp and looked around the room with wide, coal-colored eyes. "Mommy?"

Niobe smiled. She opened her arms. "C'mere, Yves."

They hugged, her son strong and healthy in her arms. She tried not to dwell on that. He felt the twinge through their bond, though, and said, "Look what I can do!"

He ran up the wall on two feet. She watched him dance upside down on the ceiling while the second egg hatched.

Yvette was tall and lithe—or would have been, were she of normal size—with waist-length auburn hair, sharp cheekbones, and almond-shaped eyes. Stunning.

*Thanks, Momma.* The girl kissed Niobe on the cheek, then settled in her lap. She smelled like summer rain.

"Mom!" Yves kept dancing overhead. He moved on to an Irish jig, complaining, "Mom, you're not LOOK-ing!"

"That's fantastic, kiddo! We should sign you up for Riverdance." Better yet, Niobe imagined, a trip to Ireland.

The third hatchling, Yectli, had pale, nearly translucent skin, a shock of white hair, and eyes like the wide, bright New Mexico sky. Albinism as a mild form of jokerism? The kid got off lucky.

"Better than that, even," he said, reading her thoughts. He swelled his chest and cocked a thumb at himself. "Watch what *I* can do."

Yectli turned toward the mirror and held his arms out. Ten little lightning bolts crackled from his fingertips to the mirror. Through the wall Niobe heard a crash, then somebody yelling for a fire extinguisher.

"I did it for you, Mom," said Yectli. "I zapped that camera good!"

The room smelled like ozone.

Drake was securely belted into a helicopter seat with a soldier on either side of him. This was so nuts it almost made him laugh, but he was too miserable for that. He wondered why he needed to go someplace else in the first place. The doctors and soldiers scared him, but he wasn't going to show it. And he wasn't going to let them make him cry.

The helicopter was flying over desert scrub and they were headed more or less toward the setting sun, so Drake figured they were headed west. They might be flying over Pyote. Hell, it could be New Mexico or Arizona for all Drake knew. Desert didn't look like much from the air. The soldiers spoke to each other every now and then in some kind of military talk that didn't make much sense to him, but most of the time they were quiet.

Drake was already tired when they took off, and by this point he could barely keep his eyes open. The seat hurt his butt, but the discomfort didn't keep him from sliding off into sleep. He couldn't tell when the dream started.

He was naked in the middle of a landscape covered with fires. His feet burned. His ass hurt. Even his nose and eyes hurt. The *whoop-whoop-whoop* of helicopter blades caught his attention and he began waving his arms. The chopper door opened and something silvery fell heavily to the scorched earth.

"Pick up the garment and put it on," boomed a voice. The helicopter settled to the ground, sending a cloud of dust into Drake's nose and eyes.

Coughing, Drake unfolded the silvery suit. It was like nothing he'd ever seen before, one-piece, but zippered everywhere, and he struggled to get his arms and legs inside. He was relieved to have something to cover himself with, but this was bulky and he'd sweat like a pig in it. There was a hood with dark plastic where his eyes would go, but Drake didn't pull it over his head.

A person dressed in a suit like the one Drake had just put on beckoned to him from an open door. Drake squinted and ducked down as he moved toward the helicopter.

"Hey, kid. You okay?" The soldier on his right side was nudging Drake in the ribs.

Drake sat up straight, straining his belly against the confines of the safety belt. He was still having the dreams, even without the medication. Maybe there was still some left in his system. That must be it. "Yeah, I'm fine."

The helicopter slowed and descended rapidly. Drake craned his neck and peered through the window plate. The chopper was kicking up a bunch of sand around the small, asphalt landing area that was ringed with a few blinking lights. There were more soldiers, or guards of some kind, waiting when he stepped outside.

One of the soldiers from the helicopter held Drake aside while the other one talked to a uniformed man who'd been waiting for them. The man was young, Hispanic, and built like an athlete. His uniform was sharp and pressed, but it wasn't the same as the soldiers' outfits. Drake squinted and made out the letters "BICC" on a badge he was wearing. The soldiers got back into the helicopter and the BICC man walked over to him. Drake felt a powerful hand on his shoulder.

"Hello, Drake," he said. "Welcome to your new home." He headed down a concrete ramp with Drake in tow.

"I don't need a new home," Drake puffed. "I want to go back to Pyote, where my family is."

They reached a large, metal double door with guards on either side. One of them waved Drake and the BICC man through. The door opened into an elevator. The man guided Drake in and waited for the doors to close, then inserted a key and turned it. They began to descend. It took a long time. In fact, it was probably the longest elevator ride of Drake's life.

"Who are you?" Drake tried unsuccessfully to push the hand off his shoulder.

"You can call me Antonio," the man said. "Or you can call me Justice. It's up to you, but use a respectful tone in either case. That goes for how you speak to everyone here."

"Yes, sir." Drake almost choked on the words. The doors opened into a reception area with more guards and a couple of people sitting behind their desks, typing or maybe just trying to look busy. They all stopped what they were doing when they saw Drake.

Justice guided Drake over to the nearest desk. There was a woman sitting behind it. Her pinched face and ugly-ass hair made Drake think she hadn't had any fun in her entire life. "Show Drake Thomas as arrived."

"Affirmative, sir." She pushed a button on her desk and another door opened with a faint hiss.

Drake followed Justice into a huge, brightly lit area. The illumination came through a glassed-in ceiling at least twenty feet above the floor and looked like natural sunlight. Drake didn't see how that could be the case given how far down they'd come. Corridors radiated out from the center in several directions, like the spokes of a bicycle. There was a kiosk in the very center with a couple more guards. Drake could see they were carrying automatic weapons and heavy batons. Again, no one was smiling. This was feeling more and more like a prison to him.

"Follow me," Justice said. Drake did as he was told. His footsteps echoed noisily off the metallic flooring. Justice paused about fifteen feet down the hallway at a doorway. He inserted his BICC badge. The mechanism beeped, and he pushed open the heavy door. "This wing of the facility is the taupe area. All the sections are color-coded based on the type of guest who's staying there."

"What kind of guest am I?" he asked.

"The kind who isn't going to be any trouble, I'm sure," Justice replied. His tone wasn't mean or taunting, just instructive.

*I just want to go home. Someone get me home,* Drake thought.

The walls were painted a soft tan. The hallway itself branched in several different directions from the main corridor, reminding Drake of an ant farm. This place was bigger, much bigger, than he'd imagined. Halfway down the hall, Justice opened a door, this one leading to a small room. There was a single bed, a half-open door leading to a bathroom, and a television bolted to the wall. Drake brightened at the sight of the TV. He hadn't had access to one since things went all to hell.

"At least you gave me a TV. That's something." Drake looked around for a remote.

"Right. All you can watch right now are the DVDs. There's only a few but we'll try to get you some more," Justice said. "I'll give you a tour of some of the facility later on, but for now you'll be required to stay in your room. We also need you to take that." He pointed to a pill in a plastic cup, sitting next to a glass of water on the end table.

"I'm sick of pills and stuff."

"I'll make it worth your while."

Drake shrugged and took the pill. They'd only force him if he didn't, and he was curious about the payoff.

Justice walked over to a paper bag on the floor and fished out a T-shirt, which he tossed over to Drake. "Just so you know we're not the bad guys." He gave Drake an unconvincing smile and left, locking the door behind him.

Drake unfolded the shirt, which had the familiar Joker Plague logo on it. He tossed his other shirt and pulled it on, stretching it tightly over his belly. *Score one for me,* he thought, wondering how long it would be before he could get full access to the TV. He'd worry about that later. Right now he was getting sleepy.

Dr. Pendergast leaned forward in his easy chair, scratching the salt-and-pepper Vandyke on his chin. "It's healthy to grieve," he said.

Niobe wiped away a tear. She looked around the room, looking for words. Diplomas on the walls documented Pendergast's extensive medical pedigree. The photo on his desk showed Pendergast in a tuxedo, smiling, with his arm around the shoulders of a centaur. Niobe gathered that the horse guy was some famous doctor. Pendergast often spoke fondly of his time at the Jokertown Clinic.

"They're scared," she said. "But if I'm strong, if they feel that, it gives them hope, you know?"

"It isn't healthy to ignore your feelings."

"I'm not. But I need time." She glared at the doctor, twisting the tissue paper in her hands. "You called me for another session even before Xerxes had died. I can't do it that often. It was too soon."

Pendergast nodded. "Unfortunate timing. I am sorry about that. But consistency is crucial to our work."

She exhaled through pursed lips, crossed her arms over her chest, and looked away.

"You've grown much self-awareness since you came here. You should take comfort in that, Genetrix." She'd lost the name battle long ago. The new identity was his idea. "You've come a long way. Do you remember how you first came to BICC from your parents' estate?"

Of course she did. She remembered lots of yelling, lots of blood, an empty bottle of scotch, a straight razor. If one of the maids hadn't found her in time, she might have bled out right there on the floor of the master bath.

Her tail still had the scars. Little ridges of skin where the ugly pig hair wouldn't grow.

Quietly, so he wouldn't press the issue: "Yeah. I remember."

"You're a different person now. I'm proud of you."

Niobe lowered her eyes, nodded. She sniffed again. "It helps having people who care about the kids. Like you. And Christian."

"And we're making progress. Two years ago, a full month would have been unthinkable. We'll beat this thing. The important thing, Genetrix, is not giving up."

Niobe didn't say anything. More tears came. The room went out of focus.

Pendergast stood. He paced over to his desk and picked up the candy jar. In a lighter, more jovial tone, he said, "Quite a trio in this clutch!"

He offered her a chocolate. Niobe declined. Sweets made her break out even worse than normal.

"Yectli certainly was a shock."

One corner of her mouth curled up in a half-smile at the pun. She snorted. Then she looked up, worried.

"Was anybody hurt? He didn't mean to. He just wanted to impress me. Kids are like that."

Pendergast waved away her concerns. "No worries. He frightened the technicians, and fried an expensive camera, but otherwise no harm done. I found it funny, myself."

"Do you think he's a joker? The albinism, I mean?"

He shrugged. "Who can say? Your hatchlings vary so greatly from one to the next . . ." He trailed off. "Do *you* think he's a joker?" He narrowed his eyes and scratched his beard again. "Were you thinking about jokerism when you were with Christian?"

"No. Why?"

"I want to show you something." Pendergast opened a wooden cabinet to reveal a flat-screen television and a DVD player. He pressed a button and the static blinked into a view of therapy room two from behind the mirror.

She watched herself saying, "Maybe we can leave the curtains closed, just once."

Then Pendergast fast-forwarded until Yectli hatched. Yves's head kept bobbing into the frame as he danced on the ceiling. "Watch what *I* can do," boasted Yectli.

*Zap!* The image returned to static.

"Quite a coincidence," said the doctor. "You expressed unhappiness with the camera, and then poof! A manikin with the power to address your unease."

"You think I did that on purpose somehow?"

"Perhaps your mental state during copulation determined Yectli's power."

"Jesus, Doc! If I had any control over their abilities, don't you think *not dying* would come first?" Niobe threw up her arms. "God!"

He raised his hands, palm out. "Fair enough." As he closed the cabinet, he said, almost as an aside, "Has Yvette demonstrated her power to you yet? We're still unclear on whether she's an ace or a deuce."

"Nope. She's a quiet one." *Aren't you, sweetheart?*

*Better to be thought a fool, Mom.*

After a happy but bittersweet lunch with Yectli, Yvette, and Yves, Niobe loaded up one of the kitchen carts with books, magazines, and a cooler of ice cream. She promised to rejoin the children for a movie night as soon as she finished her rounds.

Mick absorbed ice cream through his fingertips while Niobe read another chapter of *The Catcher in the Rye* to him. She always let him have a little extra. His body contained the cure for cystic fibrosis; the wild card had cured him even as it rendered him a joker at age eight. By studying Mick, BICC researchers would one day save thousands of kids.

When she tugged the empty bowl from his fingers, he grabbed Niobe's wrist. He tapped the book with his free hand while bobbing his head at her. Tap, tap. Nod, nod.

"Mick, I don't understand. What? What's wrong?"

*He's saying you're like that catcher in the field of rye,* said Yvette.

*Because I remind him of Holden Caulfield?*

*No. Because you care so much.*

*Oh.*

Niobe smiled. "Thank you, Mick. I like you, too."

He let go. Plaster dust rained down on his sheets once again as he went back to knocking his head against the wall, just as he'd been doing when Niobe arrived.

"See ya tomorrow, Mick."

In addition to voluntary residents like Niobe and Mick, the low-security wing housed a library, cafeteria, gym, and television lounge. The lounge also contained a computer with Internet access. Niobe swung through during her rounds to check her e-mail. She watched a few minutes of a football game, socializing with the patients and off-duty orderlies, while waiting for a turn at the computer.

Nothing from her parents, of course, but she did find a new e-mail from Bubbles, who was in New York. Another city on Niobe's list of places to visit someday. Niobe decided to respond with a note about Xerxes's death—Bubbles had met him and would want to know.

Moans went up around the lounge. The game had disappeared, to be replaced with the words "Special Report." Niobe kept one ear on the TV while she typed. Several people threw things at the screen when President Kennedy announced a new gasoline rationing program. Niobe finished up the e-mail to Bubbles and resumed her rounds.

The earth-toned medium-security wing (brown, taupe) housed patients moderately dangerous to themselves and others. Some were here voluntarily; others at the behest of family, or the courts. Niobe's first room had been in this wing. There were no voluntary committals in the yellow high-security wing.

Powder blue Q Sector, BICC's maximum security wing, housed the worst of the worst. It was also the reason Niobe never let her children accompany her on the rounds.

The wing had been built into one of the spurs off the outer ring. Each cell required special construction tailored to the particular occupant, and the old salt caverns offered the space to do so. If you wanted to lock somebody up and lose the key, this was the place to do it.

Niobe hurried past the cell housing the joker woman covered in dozens of baby mouths. The active soundproofing never completely nullified their combined wailing. She also passed a lead-lined cell that housed a glowing, mummylike figure, and a watertight cell filled floor to ceiling with glycerin to prevent its occupant's skin from igniting.

One denizen of Q Sector she didn't skip, though she might have liked to, was known as the Racist. She tapped on the Plexiglas window of his cell. She never met his eyes when he looked at her; their darkness, their intensity, unsettled her. Prison gang tattoos covered most of his skin not covered by his jumpsuit.

"Bookmobile."

"You still here, kike?" At some point in the past, he'd decided she was Jewish.

She slid his requested book—a dog-eared copy of *The Turner Diaries*—through the lazy Susan. It was originally his own copy, found on him when he was captured.

"How many times are you going to read this crap?" she asked. "Why don't you read something educational instead?"

"How long until Uncle Shylock takes you back to Jew York City so I don't have to see your ugly face no more?"

"I've told you," she said, wheeling the cart away, "I'm not from New York." She left the Racist to his solitude.

"Nibble they toes, nibble they fingers . . ."

Her last stop was outside the cell of Terrence Wayne Cottle, aka Sharky, in reference to his gray skin and the serrated, triangular teeth that filled a mouth extending halfway around his head. Cottle embraced the identity enthusiastically. He'd eaten his victims to death.

". . . chew they skin, chew they guts . . ." Featureless black eyes popped open when Niobe pushed her squeaking cart to a halt outside his cell.

". . . chomp they tail and all them kiddies!"

"Something to read, Terrence?"

"Not bored. Hungry." Thin lips pulled back from his teeth as he said this. "So hungry." He licked his lips.

A single scoop of butter brickle sat at the bottom of her cooler, but of course she couldn't give it to him. Pendergast and the security techs were adamant that Cottle could never receive any utensil. Even a plastic spork.

"Can't help you there, Terrence." Niobe held up a few magazines. "How 'bout a *National Geographic*?" Even staple-bound magazines were off-limits.

"What I'd really like, *Genetrix,* is a copy of *Modern Gourmet*."

"Sorry, *Sharky,* no such luck."

Cottle shook his head. "Shame. Been looking for a good recipe for roast joker tail." He laughed. "Something that'll tell me how to debone that thing."

His shouts followed her back up the hallway. ". . . or a marinade for fat little kiddies?"

Yves, Yvette, and Yectli were extra quiet. But she knew how to cheer them up.

*Hey, you kids ever been to Disneyland?*

Yectli clapped. *Of course not!* said Yves.

*Well, let's fix that,* thought Niobe. And this time, no putting the trip off until it was too late.

All they needed was a few days. She'd let Pendergast know they'd be gone, and then find some tickets online. The oil crisis guaranteed that she'd have to pay a king's ransom to get all four of them to California and back, but she hadn't touched her trust fund in a long time. It might have taken a hit, thanks to market craziness brought on by the crisis, but odds were that her parents' goodbye-and-go-away-forever gift was still pretty hefty.

*You guys are gonna love Space Mountain.*

Returning through the medium-security wing, Niobe found one of the cells open. The cot had been stripped, and a pile of new linens rested at the foot of the mattress.

"Get a move on, Genetrix."

She turned to find Tom, one of the BICC orderlies, standing next to her.

"Oh, hiya, Tom. What's going on? New guest?"

"I'm not kidding. Beat it."

"What? I'm just asking."

Tom shrugged. "I got my orders." He pointed down the corridor. "Scram." He glared until she turned the corner.

She waited a moment before peeking back.

Justice—the head of BICC security—escorted a boy down the corridor and into the cell. Young, based on his height, and a little pudgy.

The boy turned just as Justice slammed the cell door behind him.

He looked terrified.

The interrogation room was cramped and dim. Drake was sitting on one side of a metal table; facing him from the other side were a doctor, or so he guessed from the man's white coat, and another BICC guy. Justice was behind Drake, but he was letting the others ask the questions.

"Mr. Thomas, you're aware of your medical condition, are you not?" The doctor leaned forward and adjusted his glasses.

Drake shook his head. "No, no one's told me anything."

The BICC man, wearing a badge that said "Smitty," opened a folder. "Well, it's time you learned why you're here. Let's start with exactly what you remember?"

"Nothing," Drake said defensively. This was going to be just like the army hospital, nothing but questions. "Why don't you tell *me* something for a change. Like where my family is or why I can't see them, for instance."

"Well, there is a bit of information I can provide you with about your medical condition." The doctor had a really nasty look on his face, reminding Drake of his fourth-grade math teacher. His badge read "Dr. Pendergast," which sounded like something made-up. "You've been infected with xenovirus Takis-A, the wild card. As for your family, they're all presumed dead."

"Doctor," Justice said, a serious look on his face, "are you sure . . ."

"Yes," Pendergast interrupted. "This young man needs to come to grips with the situation he's in. It might help overcome his memory suppression."

Drake went numb. "You're lying about my folks." He had a feeling, deep down, that it was true. "Tell me you're lying." He'd been afraid they were dead, but until someone said it Drake wasn't going to believe it. Now, someone had said it.

"What did you think happened to them, Drake?" Smitty asked. "Did you think they survived a nuclear explosion?"

"I didn't even know there *was* an explosion." Drake was holding back the tears with everything he had. "How did it happen?"

"That's what your government wants to know, Drake." Smitty gave Drake a cold stare that momentarily replaced his grief with fear. "It's possible that your parents were part of a terrorist plot, and something went wrong."

"My mom and dad terrorists?" Drake shook his head in disbelief. How could these people be such morons? "That's stupid. They sat outside almost every night watching the sky for aliens as part of the 'Watch the Skies' volunteers. They would never hurt anyone." Drake was telling them the truth. His folks had joined the volunteer program after the Swarm invasion, which happened before he was even born.

"Try to see things from our point of view, Drake." Smitty looked like he was trying to force his face into something like a sympathetic look. It was ugly. "There's a small nuclear detonation in a largely unpopulated area. The size of the explosion is consistent with a suitcase nuke, something a terrorist might use. The location suggests it was an accident, except for the fact that there was a little boy in the middle of it. An ace who survived the blast and is immune to radiation. Does that seem like a coincidence to you?"

It was too much for Drake to take in all at once, but these asshats wanted answers, and they expected them from him. "I can't tell you what

I don't know," Drake said. Skeptical stares greeted his response. "Maybe the explosion did something to my memory. I'll try."

"It would be worth your while to do so," Smitty said. He nodded to Justice. "Take him back to his room. Keep him on the medication."

Drake felt his chair sliding backward and he quickly stood. "I'm doing the best I can."

During the short walk back to his prison, Drake's fear gave way to despair. His family was dead. Even the few people who cared about him, like his aunt Tammy in Austin, must think he was dead, too.

Once alone in his room, Drake fell on the bed and pulled the pillow over his face. He could hear Justice's footfalls echoing away down the hall. Only then did the tears come, and he couldn't stop them for a long time.

He wasn't sure what time it was when Justice showed up again, knocking at his locked door. "What do you say we take a walk and get some exercise?" Justice stepped out into the hall and gave Drake a look that made him understand this was not a suggestion.

"Whatever you say." Drake popped up from the bed. He'd never been very big on exercise, but stretching his legs beat the hell out of rotting in his crappy little room.

"Excellent." Justice led him down the corridor and into the central area. The vast room was still mostly deserted except for the guards at the kiosk, who were talking and laughing about something. "We're cleared for green section today," Justice told the men.

Along the way Drake paid attention to where the surveillance cameras were. He'd counted at least five. Once inside, though, Drake almost felt relieved. He hadn't had any idea what to expect from "green section," but the first room they came to was a big one with couches and a couple of TVs, one of which was turned on. It wasn't like a real living room, but was still lots nicer than anything Drake had seen here so far. His eyes tracked like radar to the TV set. A couple of people were watching *American Hero*, and it was the end of the show where the contestants had the cards in front of them and someone got voted off.

Justice quickly guided him away from the TV and into another hallway.

Only then did Drake notice the walls were like classroom green, only brighter and friendlier.

"Maybe we'll stop back here on the way back," Justice said, grabbing Drake more gingerly than usual by the shoulder and ushering him out. "Right now, I've got something else in mind."

They continued down a long hallway. Most of the doors here were closed, although one that was open led to a room with Ping-Pong tables and an old quarter-gobbling arcade game, as well as candy and drink machines. Two young women were going at each other in Ping-Pong.

"Keep moving, Drake," Justice said. "We're almost there."

The next door opened into a cafeteria, which was even bigger than the one at his school. It was mostly empty, although a few tables had two or three people sitting at them.

"This is where your meals come from, just in case you wondered."

Drake's enthusiasm level dipped a bit. He wasn't wild about the bland food he'd gotten, but maybe they had something good he hadn't seen yet.

Justice pointed to a woman standing behind a glassed-in corner counter. "Interest you in some ice cream, son?"

Drake hustled over as fast as his heavy, out-of-shape legs would carry him. There were over a dozen flavors, some of which were dangerously low in their containers. He walked around behind the counter and looked up at the middle-aged woman. "Can I get a free taste or two?"

She shook her head, then smiled. If she was surprised to see a kid in the cafeteria, she didn't show it. "Sure, son. Just show me what you want to try."

Drake quickly pointed out a couple of chocolates, French vanilla, and some rainbow sherbet. "Let's start with those." When the woman bent over, he noticed the badge attached to her pocket. Justice was directly on the other side, but wasn't looking his way. Before he could do anything she turned around with a spoonful of ice cream.

"Here you go."

Drake took the sherbet into his mouth but couldn't focus on how it tasted. "Mmmm," he said. "Vanilla next, please."

The vanilla was in the front row of the ice cream display and the woman had to bend over for it. The chain holding the badge must have broken at some point and was now held on with tape. Drake leaned into the woman, as if trying to get a better look at the ice cream, and tugged the badge free. He held his breath and tucked it into the front of his pants.

"Our French vanilla is a big favorite." She offered him a heaping spoonful.

Drake exhaled heavily and downed the ice cream. It was actually great, for vanilla. More important, neither the woman nor Justice had noticed him sneak the badge. "Oh, yeah, that's what I want."

The woman handed Drake a couple of small paper napkins and sent him on his way. He felt the cool plastic of the card against his belly and hoped it didn't show under his clothing. Drake sat down across the table from Justice and gobbled his ice cream down so fast he got the cold thing in his forehead.

"Ate it too fast, didn't you?" Justice didn't say it in a smug way. "I'm sorry you found out about your family the way you did. The doctor is just trying to help you get your memory back. This place can be comfortable for you, Drake, if you just settle in and help us to help you."

"I'm trying," Drake said defensively. "How would you feel if your entire family was dead and somehow you were the only one left alive? And people stuck you in a place and asked you questions you didn't know the answers to?"

Justice nodded silently and sat for a moment in thought. To Drake it almost seemed like Justice felt sorry for him. "I think I'd be pretty unhappy, but I also think I'd try to adapt to my new circumstances." He held out an open hand. "Give me the card, Drake."

The ice cream went sour in his mouth. Drake pulled the card out and dropped it into Justice's large palm. "It was just a game."

"Right. But we don't want to get Alice"—he nodded toward the ice cream woman—"in trouble, do we?" He tucked the card into his pocket. "And this wouldn't get you out anyway."

"Like I said, it was just a game."

"We'll have to find you some different games, then. Make the best of your time here, Drake. Nobody wants you to be miserable." Justice stood, straight and tall and solid as a brick wall. "Let's get you back to your room."

Drake got up and began trudging from the cafeteria, dragging his feet as he went. So they'd caught him. So what? No way was he giving up. Sooner or later they had to make a mistake, and that was when he'd make a break for it.

♠

Pendergast's office had no waiting room. Niobe stood next to a watercolor landscape of grama and piñon, shifting her feet often. Her tail made it impossible to rest her back against the wall, so she had to lean one shoulder against the hard concrete. It put an ache in her hips.

Muffled voices leaked into the corridor. She knew the doctor's voice, and Justice's, but the third was unfamiliar.

*I was thinking. Maybe your dad would like to come to California with us.* Perhaps Christian would be more eager to spend time with her children—their children—if he had the chance to vacation away from BICC for a while.

*Yeah!* thought Yectli. Yves liked the idea, too. But Yvette thought, *Don't trust him, Mom.*

*Why? He's your dad and he loves you.*

*But he's not—ouch.*

*Yvette, what's wrong, honey?* Niobe knew the answer but she asked anyway, hoping to be wrong.

*Owey! Momma, it hurts.*

Niobe found herself silently pleading with the virus. *No. No, no, no. Just a few more days. Please. I promised them Disneyland. All three.*

The door opened. Justice exited Pendergast's office, pulling the new arrival—the boy—after him. The kid's head hung low, and his face was flushed. Niobe wanted to give him a wink and a smile as they passed, but Justice pulled the kid in the opposite direction when he saw Niobe. The kid didn't even look up.

She entered the office. Pendergast himself sat behind his desk, scribbling notes into a file.

The doctor looked up, saw her, and reared back in surprise. "Genetrix." He shut the file folder, with his pen still inside. "This is a surprise."

Niobe jerked a thumb over her shoulder. "New kid?"

"Hmmm? Oh. Yes."

"Looks pretty unhappy."

Pendergast fished his pen out of the file, saying distractedly, "He's still adjusting to his new environment." He looked pensive for a moment, then added nonchalantly, "Have your children said anything about him?"

Niobe had deflected several days of leading questions about Yvette.

Clearly Pendergast suspected the girl was some kind of mentalist. But if her daughter wanted privacy, she'd have it. As much as could be had at BICC, anyway.

"No. Just wondering about him."

He recapped the pen and opened a filing cabinet. "I have another appointment. Do you need something?"

"Nope. Just letting you know I'll be on vacation for a few days." She grinned. "Taking the kids to Disneyland."

"Ah. I see," he said quietly. He slid the file into a drawer filled with many others. "You'll be leaving soon, I take it?" Niobe heard the cabinet lock click when he pushed the drawer shut.

"The sooner the better. Want to take them before . . ." She didn't want to say it aloud; bad enough they already knew she was thinking it.

"Of course." Pendergast nodded. He looked pensive again. "Tell you what. If you'll do something for me first, I'll personally see that your leave paperwork is expedited."

"Great. Name it."

"Drake. The new arrival. Introduce yourself; try to make him feel welcome. Let him know he has friends here."

"Sure. I can do that. Why *is* he here, anyway?"

"The important thing," said Pendergast, "is that he feels comfortable and relaxed."

*Don't trust him,* Yvette repeated.

The evasion wasn't lost on Niobe. But poor Drake did look like he needed a pal. And if cheering him up would get the kids to Disneyland that much sooner, that was win-win.

There was a knock on the door. "Come in," Drake said, trying to get his brain working.

After being unbolted, the door opened a bit and a young woman poked her head in. "Can I come inside for a minute?" Something about her tone of voice was different than what he was used to around here. Then it clicked that she was being polite.

"Sure." Drake swung his legs over the bedside and onto the floor, then stood up.

"Hi, my name is Niobe."

"Holy crap." Drake couldn't keep himself from staring once all of her was inside. For the most part she was a normal woman, pretty young still, but there was something attached to her. It was like a big tube coming out from her lower back, almost like a third leg, but with no bones. Her clothes were the kind fat girls wore, all floppy and worn. "Sorry," he said. "I've never met anybody like you before."

"You mean a joker?" If she was bothered by her appendage or Drake's reaction to it, Niobe didn't let on. "It's okay. You must be pretty special yourself for them to ship you here."

"Not really, just another little fat boy from West Texas." Drake was suspicious, but decided to give her the benefit of the doubt. "Well, maybe a little bit special. You want to sit down?"

The corner of her mouth turned up in a smirk, and the thing stuck to her back wiggled over her shoulder, like it was waving at him. "Easier for me to stand. Have they turned on your TV yet?" She nodded to the set on the wall.

"Only the DVD player, and most of the movies are pretty lame." They'd given him *The Rescuers, SpongeBob SquarePants,* and *Dumbo.* He hadn't made it all the way through *Dumbo,* it was just too depressing. Drake slumped a little.

"That figures." She pulled something from a large paper bag she was carrying. Drake had been so distracted by her tail, or whatever it was, that he hadn't even noticed it. "Don't tell anyone I gave you this. And keep it hidden."

Drake immediately recognized the Game Boy and grabbed it from her with a grin. "Geez, thanks."

"I thought you might like that. I've only got one cartridge, arcade classics, but I'll try to get you a couple more and some extra batteries." Niobe handed over the rest to Drake. "Like I said, though, keep it hidden or they'll take it away and we'll both be in trouble."

Drake began to really relax. "You're not one of them. I mean, you don't work here."

She shook her head. "Not exactly. They're conducting, sort of, tests on me. You know how that goes."

There was no reason to believe she was lying, although Drake thought she was holding something back. That was okay, so was he. "Yeah. I really appreciate this, Niobe. Trust me, I won't get caught."

"Good. Because if you do, they probably won't let me visit again. One more thing. I heard you liked the ice cream, so . . ." She fished a moist carton out of the bag, and a plastic spoon. "Mint chocolate chip. Tastes incredible, believe me."

"Oh, snap." Drake's appetite, which had been next to nothing, came back to life and he had the carton open in a flash. The ice cream was as good as she said. Maybe better. "Why are you being so nice to me?"

Niobe shrugged. "I have a soft spot for kids." Her expression went distant for a second, like she was listening to something only she could hear. Then she continued. "Er, handsome young men like yourself. Anyway, I know this isn't the friendliest place in the world. You're probably not happy with how they're treating you, and I'll bet you miss your family and friends, too. Am I wrong?"

He didn't want to think about his family and friends right now. "No. It's just that you're the only nice one so far." Drake took another extra-large mouthful of ice cream. His mouth was happier than any part of him had been in a long time. "I'm not complaining, though."

Niobe smiled. It was a grown-up kind of smile, like she knew so much more than he did, but Drake didn't care right now. "I've got to get back to my rounds," she said. "Have fun with your Game Boy."

"Oh, I will," Drake said. Niobe opened the door and pulled her tail-thing through to the outside of the room. "My name's Drake."

Niobe nodded. "Hang in there, Drake. See you soon." Then the door closed and she was gone.

Drake polished off the remainder of the ice cream and tossed the carton on the floor. He popped the Gameboy cartridge into the slot and powered the machine on. Moments later a menu of several games, most of them older than he was, showed up on the screen. Drake almost went for Missile Command, but decided Defender was more his speed. He paused a moment before starting the game. Niobe might be the person, the friend he needed, to get out of here. He didn't want to get his hopes up, but he had to hope for something or give up entirely. He'd think about it later. Right now there were aliens to kill.

Early-morning sunlight poured down through the skylights. Far above, Niobe knew, the sky would be a brilliant azure. *Just wait 'til you see it with your own eyes, kiddos. There's nothing like it.*

Niobe found Pendergast coming out of the cafeteria. He held a cup of coffee in one hand and a foil-wrapped bundle in the other. She could smell the green chile and chorizo from his breakfast burrito, and the chicory in his coffee.

"All done," she said.

He breezed past her. "What's done?"

"I introduced myself to Drake, like you asked." She walked backward, keeping abreast of him. "I think he was glad for the company. Seems like a nice kid. I'd be happy to visit him again."

"Good." Pendergast said nothing more.

"Meanwhile," Niobe said, hoping to jar his memory, "the kids and I will be taking our leave this morning."

Pendergast shook his head. "No. I'm afraid not."

"What do you mean, 'No'?"

"No, you're not taking your children anywhere."

She stepped in front of him, arm raised, blocking his path. Coffee sloshed over the brim of his cup. "I'm not asking your permission. I'm telling you as a courtesy."

He sighed. "Niobe. Taking your children out of this facility—the only place where they can receive the specialized medical attention they need—is a reckless and irresponsible act. And so I've decided, for the sake of your children, to revoke your leave privileges."

Anger made Niobe's tail quiver against her back. "You forget. I have a key card for the elevator."

"Which you'll find quite useless. It hasn't worked for many weeks, in point of fact."

Her knees felt weak. Watery. "But . . . I promised them Disneyland . . ." She slumped against the wall. "Please don't do this."

"It's for the good of your children," Pendergast said. He stepped around her and was gone.

*Don't trust him,* said Yvette. *Either of them.*

♥

# Double Helix

## BETTER TO DWELL IN THE WILDERNESS THAN WITH A CONTENTIOUS WOMAN

### Melinda M. Snodgrass

**THE CONCRETE WALLS OF** the locker room at Invesco Field at Mile High seem to exhale the scent of old sweat, gym socks, and cheap aftershave. *This,* I think as I lift the champagne bottle out of the ice and survey the label, *is the downside of being so famous and popular that you have to play in stadiums rather than theaters.* Thank God my performances are played in more intimate venues. I would so hate to make a 747 disappear.

Even here, far beneath the stadium, I can faintly hear the beat of the bass and the roar of the crowd as Joker Plague performs their final number. I find myself thinking about a Roman holiday when I was in high school and how we had toured the cells beneath the Colosseum. Places for enslaved gladiators and wild beasts brought across oceans solely for sport and blood. *Not so very different from modern football.*

An unexpected yawn cracks the hinges of my jaw. My shoulders feel like they're slumping beneath invisible weights. I toss back my head and press my shoulder blades together. Lilith's breasts thrust aggressively against the silk of my halter top, and I bite back a hiss. My nipples are sore from Lohengrin's teeth.

There is the thunder of footfalls approaching the locker room. The door bursts open and Joker Plague has arrived. Michael, aka Drummer Boy, leads them into the room. Sweat is running down his chest and four of his six hands are still tapping at the tympanic plates on his torso. Trailing after him are the other four members of Joker Plague. The Voice's presence can only be guessed at by a towel floating in the air. Occasionally it moves as if wiping a face. Bottom and Shivers are just standard jokers—one with the head of an ass, and the other looking like a Disney vision of a demon complete with blood red skin. The worst for me is S'Live, a floating balloon of a face, and a multitude of tongues like flicking snakes thrusting from between the lips of the unnaturally wide mouth.

Flanking the boys is their manager, who reminds me a lot of my manager. BlackBerry in hand, headphone in his ear, a too-sharp suit and a too-sharp face, and a phalanx of security guards. Female arms thrust through the closing door, and hysterical soprano voices call out to the various band members. A broad, tall guard gets the door closed and turns with a look like a contented bull. There's not enough Plague for every groupie. Some of them will doubtless fuck the guards in hope of getting closer to a band member next time.

I work the cork out of the champagne just as they enter, and the explosive *pop* stops them all. Most of the men gawk. Black leather pants, silver halter top, and spiked heels will work every time. One rent-a-cop reaches for his hip as if expecting to find a pistol.

"Hello, Michael." I pour champagne into a glass. "Thirsty?" He's incredibly tall, so I have to throw my head back to see his face. He ignores the glass, takes the bottle in one of his six hands, and drains it. I rescue the glass and take a sip. It's not bad.

"Committee business?" he asks and the unseen Voice makes himself heard with an audible snort followed by—

"Oh, shit, not now. We're in the middle of the tour."

"Fuck off," he says to the room at large. "You knew this was the deal when you booked the tour."

There is grumbling between Shivers and S'Live, but they move away to gather up their street clothes. The manager continues to hover.

"The girls are gonna want to see you," he whines.

"Tell them he's got a girl," I say. An odd range of emotions cross Drummer Boy's face. For an instant there is naked lust (good), followed by grim resolve and a subtle physical retreat (not good).

The peanut gallery gives us some space. I take another sip of champagne. "Why are you here?" The tone is challenging, not encouraging.

I move in on him again. "I've always wanted to see Denver. Rocky Mountain high and all that. And . . ." I drop my lashes to veil my eyes, and allow my hair to fall over my shoulder and brush across one of his hands. "I wanted to see you and tell you . . ."

"Tell me what?"

I inch closer. This time he doesn't retreat. "That you did a good job in India." His breath increases in tempo and flutters across the top of my head. I drift away and pick up another of the twenty champagne bottles. "Why don't we take this to a nicer venue?"

"Are you trying to pick me up?"

I decide to match directness with bluntness. "No, I'm trying to fuck you."

"You're sleeping with Lohengrin."

"Does that mean I belong to him? How very antiquated of you. And you a rock and roll star. I thought you'd be more broad-minded."

He looks over toward the row of sinks and the mirrors set above them. He is frowning at his image. "That kind of thing can tear a group apart." Three of his hands are drumming nervously at the tympanic plates that cover his immensely long torso. It's like a strange syncopated heartbeat echoing off the concrete walls.

"And you care. How sweet." I move up next to him and lean against his side.

"I think the Committee is important. We do good work."

"*You* do good work. In fact, you seem to do more than anyone else. Except for me, of course. Taxi Girl."

One side of his mouth twists up in a reluctant smile. I run a hand up his shoulder, noting the elaborate colors and designs of the tattoos, and cup the nape of his neck. A gentle tug and his head drops. I match it by going on tiptoes and press my lips on his. I can't risk tongue, but I keep my lips soft and parted, inviting him in. For an instant I can taste and feel the mounting passion, then he pulls back, coughs, and asks in a too-casual tone. "What about our Fearless Leader?"

"Oh, Fortune's very good at photo ops and press conferences." DB gives a bark of laughter. "So, do you want to sleep together or not?"

He cocks his head to one side. The light glints off his multiple piercings. "You always use the crudest, most distancing phrases—fuck, sleep together. You never say 'make love.' Why do you do that?"

It's strange, but the question takes me aback, and leaves me feeling naked. I fall back on flippancy. "I don't believe in love?"

"I do."

I point toward the door. "You have an army of groupies waiting out there."

"Yeah, but they're different from an ace."

The champagne bottle hits the ice with a crash as I drop it back into the bucket. "Curveball is sleeping with John Fortune. Why reject what I'm offering?"

"I love her."

"My God, you're a hopeless romantic. What? You think you're going to win her by limiting your fucking to nats?" His expression darkens and I realize I've allowed my disdain to show. How to recover? My mind flits over the past year and the things DB has done, and I see it. Dad was right, there's something to the Bible. "Though I doubt you'll live long enough."

One of his hands closes around my upper arm and turns me around to face him. I'll have bruises tomorrow. "What do you mean by that?"

"You seem to draw all the most dangerous assignments. You never just hand out food aid or deliver medical supplies."

"Yeah? So? I've got a lot of power. As I showed in Egypt."

"Do you read the Bible, Michael?"

"What? What the fuck?"

"Of course it's mostly fairy tales, but those old prophets were pretty perceptive about human nature. It hasn't changed much in three thousand years. Take the story of David and Bathsheba. Such a romantic story. What people forget is that she had a husband. 'Set Uriah in the forefront of the hottest battle, that he may be smitten, and die.' "

Our eyes lock, and we hold the stare for a long, long time. "He wouldn't," DB finally forces past lips gone stiff with anger.

"If you say so. I'm sure he's your very good friend."

DB turns away, his broad, powerful shoulders hunch as if he's trying to protect himself. "I wish you hadn't come here."

"Me, too. It's going to be a lonely night." And I prepare, visualize home, and teleport away. As I travel the Between I think it's been a good night's work.

♠

# Just Cause: Part II

Carrie Vaughn

**KATE AND ANA RUSHED** to catch the subway. Dinner at Stellar, the posh restaurant at the top of the Empire State Building, was one thing, but a cab ride during a fuel shortage was too much of an extravagance. They rode standing, holding on to one of the bars, talking in hushed voices about this and that, phone calls home, how Ana's brother was applying to the University of New Mexico and how Kate's parents were still upset that she'd dropped out of college. They got stares. They always got stares, and a few whispers, "Is that really them? It couldn't be . . . They look so much like . . ."

Street level was quiet. Perpetually gridlocked traffic had vanished. A few government vehicles, a few cabs, and very few private cars were active. Fifth Avenue might have been a street in any small town. The air actually smelled decent.

As soon as they turned the corner, shouted questions began from the group of reporters waiting outside the Empire State Building. Kate and Ana stood shoulder to shoulder and prepared to run the gauntlet.

"Curveball! Earth Witch! Who's your pick on the new season of *American Hero?*"

Be nice, Kate reminded herself. Keep the press on your side. Those were the rules from *American Hero,* and they still worked. She shrugged and smiled her sweetheart smile. Cameras flashed. "I don't know, I'm not really watching."

"We've been a little busy," Ana added.

More questions. Kate couldn't make them all out.

"Earth Witch! Reports say you collapsed from exhaustion in Ecuador. Is it true? How's your health?"

Ana's face was a mask, the smile frozen in place. "I'm fine," she said.

Someone pushed her way to the front and stuck a digital recorder out. "Is the Committee going to intervene to stop the genocide in Nigeria?"

Amid the way-too-personal questions about romances, diets, and clothes, the political ones struck like bolts of lightning.

Kate's sweetheart smile turned apologetic. "No comment. I'm sorry."

With the doorman helping to clear the way, they slipped inside, leaving the reporters crowded on the sidewalk.

Ana let out a sigh.

"You okay?" Kate asked.

"I'm sick of people asking me that," Ana said.

"We're just worried—"

"I'm fine," Ana said, her smile tight. It was what they all said. They were all so tough.

They took the express elevator to the restaurant. They were nearly the last to arrive.

John turned to the elevator when it opened; his face brightened. "Kate! Wow, you look great!" She beamed back at him. She'd been hoping for that reaction. She wore a silky, floral halter dress with heels, and her hair was up. That alone made her look about five years older and a ton more sophisticated.

"You don't look too shabby yourself." He wore a suit with a band collar shirt, giving him sophisticated polish. Definitely his mother's son. She reached for him, and they joined hands to pull each other into a kiss.

"You two are, as ever, awfully cute," Bugsy said. "But I'd like to point out that Ana looks *fabulous*."

Ana wore a black wraparound dress with a low-cut neck and flowing, knee-length skirt that clung and flattered in all the right places. Add her long black hair, dangly gold earrings, and ever-present St. Barbara medallion, and she looked exotic. And now, she was blushing. But smiling, too.

"We went shopping today," Kate said.

"It called to me from the store window," Ana said. The two of them giggled.

Bugsy said, "What a surprise, we all clean up pretty good."

"Maybe someday *People* will stop picking on how I dress," Kate said.

"They named you best dressed at that UNICEF fundraiser last month," Ana argued.

"Only because John's mother picked out the dress."

John got a dreamy look in his eyes. "That was a great dress."

It had been a great dress, with enough architecture to give even Kate cleavage. A picture of the two of them from that night ended up on the cover of *Aces!* They were arm in arm, looking at something off to the side, smiling. They'd looked like royalty.

The Committee: Rusty, wearing a big grin, waved from the far corner, where he was talking with Bubbles and Holy Roller; Gardener was pointing out something on a potted fern to Toad Man and Brave Hawk; the Lama (from Nepal, who was able to turn insubstantial) and the Llama (from Bolivia, who was almost a joker, with a foot-long neck and fuzzy gray hair, and who could spit a gooey venom incredible distances) were glaring at each other across the foyer. Both had refused to change their ace name to avoid confusion. And Lilith, the British teleporter, standing with Lohengrin and surveying the room critically, like this was all beneath her. She wore an amazing gown, V-neck coming to a point between her breasts, slit in the skirt climbing to her waist, the diaphanous black material deceptively translucent. All the guys were stealing glances—and Lilith knew it.

Being America's ace sweetheart didn't count for a whole lot sometimes, thought Kate, in her cute and completely boring dress.

The absent member was obvious: at seven feet, DB dominated any room he was in.

"Where's Michael?" she asked.

John frowned. "In Chicago wrapping up his concert tour, I think. Let's make the introductions," he said, turning their attention to the two women Kate didn't know. Even more new members. "From Canada, this is Simone Duplaix, aka Snowblind, and Barbara Baden, the Translator, from Israel."

Simone had dyed magenta hair that screamed *look at me.* She wore a black miniskirt, crop top, and a nose stud, and glared like she expected someone to challenge her on the dress code. Also in her twenties, Barbara was a little more upscale, with a clingy, midnight blue cocktail dress. She kept her hands folded in front of her and was a picture of calm.

"Simone, Barbara, this is Kate Brandt and Ana Cortez." Handshakes all around.

"There's hardly a need for introductions," Barbara said. "Everyone knows who you are."

"Introductions are more polite," Kate said.

Tinker came in from the next room, holding one of his gadgets, a gunmetal gray box that looked like a cross between a TV remote and an eggbeater.

"What's that?" Ana asked.

"Bug detector," he said cheerfully in his thick Aussie accent. "John wanted the place swept. Can't have spies now, right?"

"How do you know it even works?" Kate said.

He pointed it at Bugsy, and the device let out a high-pitched squeal that left them all wincing.

"Well," Bugsy said, glaring at the thing. "My confidence is truly won over."

Tinker huffed. "I built it to track down covert listening devices. I think you got a few of those on you, eh, mate?"

For the punch line, a small green wasp crawled out of the pocket of Tinker's suit jacket.

"Hey!" Tinker swatted the bug, and it crunched. Bugsy winced. "Don't you ever get tired of that trick?"

"I have another one, but you wouldn't like it any better."

The center of the next room had been cleared to make way for a long table draped in white linen. The arrangement lent a somber weight to the evening. This felt like a state dinner. And here, in this luxurious setting, on the eighty-sixth floor, Kate really felt on top of the world.

In keeping with its location, Stellar had a neo/retro art deco motif, with muted colors like pale grays, soft blues, streamlined chrome fixtures with inset lighting, ferns pouring from silver planters. The chairs and tables were mahogany and modernist. Movie stars of the 1930s in tuxedos and ball gowns might have come sweeping past at any moment. It was romantic, especially the balcony overlooking the Manhattan skyline.

"This place is amazing," Kate said, taking a chair between John and Ana near the head of the table.

John gazed around, smiling. "This used to be a different restaurant. Aces High. All the big aces used to hang out here, and the owner did this aces-only dinner every year on Wild Card Day. Mom met my father there.

My real father, I mean. She says it's the only reason she comes here, since Hiram retired. I guess I thought it'd be cool to come back. Start some new traditions now that aces are heroes again."

He wore a wistful look, like he gazed through a window into that by-gone time when everything was bigger, flashier, better. The woman he knew as his mother had been a different person then. And his father was dead.

Dinner first, meeting after. The staff brought out course after course of gourmet dishes: perfect breads, exotic pâtés, oysters with caviar, salmon, quail, and more. Maybe not more food than Kate had ever seen in one place, but certainly more different kinds of food. No holds barred. John ordered champagne, and they drank a toast to friends old and new, to jobs well done. And, as had become tradition, a toast to the friends who were missing. They'd lost people. They wanted to remember.

They relaxed into conversation and gossip.

"Guess who called me yesterday," Kate said.

People threw out names, movie stars and pop singers, and she shook her head for each one. "Apparently, Michael Berman is looking for some-one for the rogue ace challenge on *American Hero*."

Groans greeted the name of the network executive who rode herd on the show.

Rusty said, "You actually talked to him?"

"God, no. He left like five messages. But I'm warning you—you all may be next."

Ana said, "Depends on how desperate he gets."

Kate wanted to argue, but she was probably right. Berman wouldn't be calling her. Ana wasn't considered as photogenic as the more convention-ally sexy women who'd been on the show. Didn't matter, because she could still kick all their asses with her power.

Kate rolled her eyes. "The guy's an ass. I mean, have you seen who they picked for this season? Space Cadette? What's up with that?"

"I thought you weren't watching," John said. Kate huffed.

They were finishing the main course when the restaurant doors slammed open. Drummer Boy appeared, lining all six hands on his hips.

"Hey," he called in a booming voice. "Am I too late? No? Good."

He had to duck to enter the room. He was bald, shirtless, showing off not only his impressive canvas of tattoos, but the tympanic membranes on his torso—his namesake.

John frowned, and Kate tensed. "Aren't you supposed to be in Chicago?" John said.

"Not tonight. Had a little extra time so I thought I'd drop by. This meeting is for the whole Committee, right?"

Bugsy tried to divert the tension, opening a space by the table near him. "DB, pull up a chair. Meet the newbies. Simone, Barbara, DB."

DB didn't cooperate. "Ladies," he said, nodding a minimum polite greeting, then grabbing a spare chair from another table and pulling it next to Kate. He couldn't squeeze himself between her and Ana, so he remained behind them. Turning the chair backward to sit on it, he leaned one set of arms on the backs of Kate and Ana's chairs, crossed another set, and Kate lost track of the third. Now, Kate had John on her left, DB on her right, and the two of them were glaring at each other over her head.

Ana, thank God, distracted him. "How's the tour going?"

"It's been fucking amazing. We're playing stadiums. Hell, we're not a stadium band! We started out punk in two-bit bars. Now here we are." That third set of arms spread in a gesture of offering.

"I still haven't seen the show," Ana said.

"You should. When the next tour starts. I'll get you the VIP treatment, front row seats, the works."

"Cool," Ana said.

"Bring earplugs," Bugsy said. "I *have* seen the show."

Lilith, sitting on the other side of the table, licked a bit of sauce off her fork. "Michael, dear, you look so uncomfortable hunched in over there. Why don't you come sit here with me? There's plenty of room at this end."

In fact, there wasn't, except for a sliver of space at the corner. And Lohengrin, already sitting by Lilith, straightened and puffed up his chest, as if he could fill the space by himself.

Kate half hoped DB would move. Except that would involve making Lilith happy.

DB smirked. "That's okay. I wouldn't want to upset Prince Valiant there."

"Oh, Klaus here? He won't be upset. He's a big puppy." She gazed up at the German ace through slitted, silver eyes.

*What an amazing bitch,* Kate marveled.

A clink of metal on glass rang out. A goblet tipped and splashed water over part of the tablecloth, plates, and people.

"Aw, cripes, would you look at that?" Rusty was half on his feet, reaching uselessly after the mess. "Sorry. I'm pretty clumsy, don't you know." His iron jaw creased into a bashful smile.

The tension broke. At least for the next half a second or so.

John made a production of digging in an attaché case for a set of manila folders, which he distributed. Moving on, then.

"Time for business, I'm afraid," John said, standing at the head of the table. "A lot's landed on us all at once, but I think we have the resources to handle it. At least, I'd like to prove that we do." He flashed a smile, almost shy. "We're still keeping an eye on the situation in Texas. We know there was an explosion. Lilith and Bugsy concluded that it was nuclear. We still don't know what caused it, but the Feds think it was terrorists. For the moment, there isn't much we can do until we hear further developments. But here's what we *can* do."

Secretary-General Jayewardene had given the Committee three separate missions, all of them deemed urgent.

First: a brutal hurricane season appeared to be developing in the Gulf, and Jayewardene had a hunch. The secretary-general had a track record of accurate hunches. If he wanted a team there to help, the Committee would go.

Second: the UN had received reports of genocide in Africa, in the oil region of Nigeria near its border with the People's Paradise of Africa, a newish, self-declared nation that was either the latest in a long line of corrupt, despotic regimes or the beginning of a new, empowered Africa free of colonial influences. It depended on who you talked to. A Committee team would investigate the genocide claims and make recommendations.

And third: the current oil shortage was artificially induced. Prince Siraj of the Caliphate had manipulated production and forced prices to their current, stratospheric level of three hundred dollars a barrel. In the opinion of the secretary-general, this was nothing short of economic terrorism that was impacting the entire world and causing widespread hardship and depression. A team would go to the Middle East to open oil production again, and UN troops were assembling in anticipation of direct intervention.

"I don't think I have to tell you that this last objective is top secret," John said. "We don't want any leaks to the press clowns downstairs. No blogging." He pointed at Bugsy, who held up his hands in a show of innocence.

This was a new development, and Kate was surprised that the

secretary-general had decided on such direct action. They'd almost be causing an international crisis rather than fixing one.

John read from his notes.

"Earth Witch, Gardener, Bubbles, and Holy Roller. You'll head to New Orleans tomorrow. See what you can do about reinforcing the levee system and aiding in the evacuation, if that becomes necessary. DB, you'll be leading the team going to the PPA. You'll have Brave Hawk, Snowblind, Toad Man, and the Lama—Han, not Juan—with you. Curveball, Lohengrin, the Translator, Rustbelt, Tinker, and I will be going to Arabia. Bugsy, you and Juan will hold down the fort here, and Lilith will keep us all in communication, and provide emergency transport if needed—"

DB was shaking his head, chuckling quietly.

John regarded him a moment. "Do you have something to add?"

"I see what you're doing," DB said. "Pretty slick, actually." He tapped a couple of beats on the edge of the table.

"And what is that?" John said tiredly.

DB seemed happy to explain. "Here it is. You're taking all the hotshots to Arabia to be the saviors of the Western world. And you're sending me and the second stringers to some shithole in Africa—to do what? Observe? Investigate? To do *jack shit* is what."

"Hey, who are you calling second string?" said Buford, glaring at DB with bulging eyes.

Bugsy smirked. "Turning into a giant toad is not exactly A-list."

"Got me further on *American Hero* than you."

*Ouch.* A year later, people were still throwing that at each other.

"DB," John said, "I'm just trying to put people where their powers will be most useful. I don't know what you think—"

The joker's sarcastic smile fell. "I'll tell you what I think. I think you're a glory hound, I think you're—"

John dropped a folder on the table with a slap. "Who's the glory hound between us, Mr. Rock Star? Really?"

DB didn't slow down. "You're setting me up to fail, maybe even get me killed . . ."

Kate closed her eyes. Counted to ten. So help her, if either one of them brought her up as an excuse . . .

". . . and I think you'll do anything you can to keep me away from Kate!"

That was it.

John actually laughed. "Geez, would you let it go? This isn't about Kate!"

Kate stood. Picked up a steak knife. Hefted it in her hand, testing its weight. Felt a warmth flow like flames through her arm. Eventually, everyone was staring at the knife in her hand. Things got real quiet.

She looked at John on one side of her, DB on the other. They stared back, stricken.

"Finished?" she asked. "Can we all sit down and play nice?"

DB muttered, "Tell Captain Cruller to stop rigging the missions in his favor."

"You're being paranoid," she said. He had to realize how monumentally bad this looked. Halfway down the table, Snowblind and the Translator stared in fascination.

"Kate, maybe you should put that down." Ana nodded at the knife in her hand. Kate was gripping it, white-knuckled. In her mind's eye she could almost see the glow, the buildup of power. In a temper, she'd let it fly and not even realize it. Ka-boom and fireworks. Wouldn't that impress the newbies? But Ana recognized the mood. And Ana was about the only person who could say anything and not piss Kate off.

Carefully, she set the knife on the table and shook the tingle out of her arm.

John shuffled the folders in front of him, a mindless gesture. "Fine. We'll switch. DB, you're on the Arabia team. I'll go to Africa. It's not a big deal." He pulled his chair back and sank into it. Catching her gaze, he was trying to tell her something. Maybe: *See? I can play nice.* But his solution left her feeling a little sick. She hated to think that a squabble like this might damage a mission, any mission.

Mostly, she hated that they were fighting over her. As if her own choice hadn't had anything to do with which of them she'd ended up.

Seemingly mollified, DB sat, flexing his arms and running a quick riff on his torso.

John was talking again. "You have your assignments. The New Orleans team will leave first thing—"

A commotion sounded from the restaurant's foyer: heavy footsteps, voices arguing. Just what they needed—more excitement. So much for a nice dinner.

A waiter spoke. "I'm sorry, we're—"

"We have a warrant."

Bugsy stared at the entrance and said, "I have a bad feeling—"

Three men and a woman, all wearing suits and an air of government-backed smugness, came through the door. The guy in front, above average in height and notably fit, filled his expensive pale suit well. He had a buzz cut and a face that was hard to describe. Not ugly exactly, but definitely not right. Crooked nose, uneven eyes—broken bones that had knitted a little off, and laugh lines that had developed oddly because of that.

That disconcerting face twisted in a smile that suggested he was enjoying the situation.

"If you'll all remain seated and quiet we'll get this over with as quickly and painlessly as possible," he said in a decisive, cop-in-charge voice.

John didn't stay seated and quiet. "Billy, what—"

"That's *Director* Ray to you, Mr. Fortune. Now please sit down." That was possibly the shit-eatingest grin Kate had ever seen. John sat.

Director Billy Ray drew a folded pack of papers from the inside pocket of his jacket.

"Mr. Jonathan Tipton-Clarke?" He scanned the group like he was looking for someone, but Ray knew exactly where Bugsy was. His gaze fell on him in a second. "I have here a warrant for your arrest."

"What?" John demanded. "What for?"

"For disseminating classified information in a public venue and potentially damaging national security," Ray said.

Bugsy smirked. "I blogged about Texas."

"Geez, don't admit anything," John said. "He's an affiliate of the United Nations, there are proper channels for this."

It was a valiant effort, but Ray wasn't interested in proper channels, obviously. He was probably *very* interested in parading a handcuffed member of the Committee past the paparazzi downstairs. "Mr. Tipton-Clarke, if you'd stand, please."

Bugsy did. Ray gestured, and one of the agents produced handcuffs.

"You can't do this, mate," Tinker said. Murmurs around the table agreed with him.

"An American citizen engaging in activities damaging to the safety of the American government and people? I certainly can."

Kate glanced around the table. Eighteen aces and jokers, all—most—with formidable powers. All of whom were tense, glaring at Ray and his goons with unhappy expressions. In one of New York City's poshest restaurants. This could end badly.

Obligingly, Bugsy turned his back to the agent and put his hands behind him, letting them cuff him without complaint. That meant Kate saw him smile and wink, right before he disintegrated.

Thousands of green wasps buzzed as clothing and handcuffs fell. Ray lunged with what had to be ace-fueled reflexes. All he managed to do was snatch the shirt before it reached the floor.

"Shit!" Ray said, ripping the shirt and tossing it aside. "I *hate* when that happens!"

The agent who'd been trying to cuff Bugsy yelped and jumped back, reaching inside his jacket for a gun. The other agents did the same.

All around the table, aces and jokers braced for battle.

Kate had hoped her teammates weren't stupid enough to start something against Ray and his goons. So much for that.

John shouted, "Stand down! Back off!"

The bugs swarmed the four federal agents, clouds of them fogging around their heads. The agents slapped and swatted, hissing as they were stung. Ray swore, snarling as he slapped at himself, crushing wasps when he found them, and scratching at new welts.

With a whoosh and crash, a giant toad bounded onto the table, knocking aside water glasses and tea lights. His mouth was already open, the hideous tongue lolling, before Kate could stop him. A few drops of mucus hit her as the tongue whipped out and grabbed a gun out of the nearest agent's hand. Stunned, the guy regarded his slime-covered hands with a look of horror.

The Llama—the Bolivian one—was the second to jump on the table. His long neck stretched forward, his fists clenched at his side, and he puckered his lips.

"Michael, grab him!" Kate yelled at DB, who was closer.

The big joker reached behind the Llama and took hold of various parts—arms, shoulders, back, legs—with all six arms and yanked him backward, off the table and onto the floor, but not before he got off a shot of spit.

Fortunately, the spit bomb went wide. Only part of it landed on the sleeve of Billy Ray's suit jacket.

The federal ace regarded the spot for a moment. Then, with a sigh, he drew a handkerchief out of his pocket and wiped off the glob. He seemed resigned as he tossed the handkerchief aside.

Buzzing, the bugs formed a loose cloud, circling the room and occasionally dropping to take another sting at one of the agents.

"Stand *down!*" Kate shouted. Facing her team, Kate planted herself between them and the agents. Buford had opened his mouth for another go with his tongue, the Llama was unsuccessfully wrestling with DB, the other Lama had his eyes closed and seemed to be meditating, Brave Hawk had sprouted his wings and gripped a steak knife but hadn't actually done anything yet. Lohengrin had donned his armor and looked like he wanted to march forward—but John planted a hand on his chest. The others seemed caught between decisions to stay put and take action. Lilith stood at the end of the table, arms crossed, regarding the scene with an aggravating lift to her brow.

A sudden breeze ruffled Kate's bangs—the door to the balcony had opened.

Bugsy's swarm banked around the room, stretching into a streamlined shape, shot out the balcony door like an arrow, and disappeared into the New York sky.

Scratching at a swollen spot on his nose, Billy Ray glared at the balcony, and at the Amazing Bubbles, who knelt by the open door with her hand on the latch.

"I thought we needed a little air," Michelle said, shrugging with an air of innocence that wasn't entirely genuine.

The room was quiet, finally. Lohengrin's armor faded. Buford, human now, climbed off the table.

Billy Ray stood at Kate's shoulder. Literally breathing down her neck.

"I am this close to dragging all of your asses to jail," he said to her, holding his thumb and forefinger so they barely touched. "But because you're cute, and I like blondes, I'll give you a break. Today."

Kate rolled her eyes.

Ray wasn't finished with them. As he regarded them, his gaze sweeping from one end of the table to the other, his frown deepened. For a moment, the ace almost looked tired. He muttered, "You kids are going to get yourselves killed. And I'm probably going to be the one who has to scrape your guts off the pavement."

He stalked out, gesturing at his underlings, who fell into step with him. They were all scratching at angry, swollen bug bites. Kate ran a hand through her hair and sighed. When was her life going to stop feeling like reality TV?

A woman giggled. Snowblind, stifling the laugh with a hand over her mouth. The hand was trembling, just a little. "I knew joining the Committee would be exciting, but I had no idea."

Nervous chatter dispelled some of the tension as people straightened chairs and returned to their seats. Some of the wait staff crept out of hiding.

Kate pulled out a chair and sat. John brought over another chair and sat with her.

"So. Bugsy's wanted by the Feds," he said. "I guess that's another line on the to-do list."

"What are we going to do about it?"

"Normally I would call the director of SCARE to clear this up. But Billy Ray *is* the director of SCARE." He winced. "And how the hell did that happen?"

It never ended. Always another mission. Three more missions, in this case. Kate leaned close to John and spoke softly. "You promised Ana would get a break. But you're sending her out again tomorrow?"

John had the grace to look chagrined. "I know. But we need her. No one else can do what she does. This isn't going to get fixed by . . . by a giant toad."

She couldn't argue, because he was right. Ana herself wouldn't want to be left out of this. Even now, the ace was helping the staff pick up scattered glassware and table settings, like she could never sit back and let someone else do the work.

"I'll make it up to her," he said, earnest. "I promise."

"Hey, John," Tinker called. "What do you want to do with these?" He held up Bugsy's discarded clothing.

Someone said, "Whoa. I never would have pegged Bugsy as a boxers guy."

John just shook his head in long-suffering bemusement. Smiling, Kate wrapped her arm around his and rested her head on his shoulder. "You sure know how to show a girl a good time."

♣

# Double Helix

## HIS ENEMIES SHALL LICK THE DUST

### Melinda M. Snodgrass

Dear Sir,
And now for *As the UN Turns.*

I SET ASIDE THE laptop feeling the residual heat on my thighs and take a sip of scotch and a drag on my cigarette. Once in a great while I worry that I'm taking too light a tone with my superior officer, but Flint seems to like it. I think I actually manage to amuse the joker/ace.

My manager has me in a suite at the Marriott so I'm comfortably ensconced in the sitting room with my feet up on a hassock, and Sonique playing on the radio. In two hours I'm going to be onstage performing my magic act. I need to get this report typed and into a diplomatic pouch within the hour so I can spend an hour working my hands, and checking over my equipment at the theater. Through the hotel windows I watch the sun setting behind the Golden Gate Bridge. The sky burns in shades of red, orange, melon, and lavender, and the waters of the bay seem to be dancing quicksilver.

I return to the task.

Jonathan Hive's blog post regarding the explosion in Pyote, Texas, roused the ire of the Powers That Be in Washington, and SCARE sent agents to arrest him for violating national security—Bugsy must be viewed as a fearsome threat to national security because Billy Ray himself showed up. But as tough as Ray might be he can't capture a cloud of buzzing insects. After bestowing several dozen stings to Ray, Bugsy . . . er, bugged out. It was a wonderful sight watching a swarm of green wasps heading down 33rd St. to the consternation of the dinnertime crowd.

Net result—Hive is holed up inside the UN. The Department of Justice is blustering, Jayewardene is being saintly and noncommittal, and I'm sure I'll be tasked with getting Hive out of the country at some point. It does raise interesting legal questions regarding the status of an American citizen seeking sanctuary with an international body located on American soil. I'm sure in four or five years the Supreme Court will give us a definitive ruling.

I know this won't make Whitehall happy, but these really are third-rate aces who have accompanied Fortune to Africa, and Fortune has been very clear that none of the Committee members are to take part in the fighting. We should be able to brush through this without any overt interference in Nigerian affairs, and I really can't refuse without damaging my status within the Committee.

Oh, and one more thing. I want a raise.

Sir.

◆

# The Tears of Nepthys

## THE FIRST TEAR: ISIS

### Kevin Andrew Murphy

SUNLIGHT GLINTED ACROSS THE waves, postcard perfect for a Nantucket summer. Ellen's mother had loved mornings like this, watercolor mornings she'd called them, time to take the paints and easel and a flap of Bristol board and a daughter by the hand, and drag them off to Brandt Point by the lighthouse, sketching the sailboats like the one Ellen lived on now.

An easterly wind was already wisping away fingers of fog as Ellen let go of the ladder. She settled herself into the dinghy, then paused, one hand on the mooring line. She raised her free hand to the cameo at her throat, her mother's brooch, resting a fingertip on the velvet band.

She decided against it. Today was her day, Ellen alone. She let go of the line, unknotted the rope, and slipped the oars into the water. She rowed in silence, passing the sailboats of the purists, and on past the cabin cruisers tied to mooring posts. The latter waited like wallflowers at a dance, all but three bearing FOR SALE signs faded to gray and Nantucket red.

Ellen sculled the water until the smooth lee gave way to the rough rippling of open harbor. A gust sprang up and the salt wind stung her eyes, threatening to start tears. Even the most beautiful morning was nothing if you had no one to share it with. The gulls cried mournfully, gabbled and shrieked, some skimming near her, hoping she were a fisherman with lost bait or a tourist with spare bread, but all Ellen had was a rueful smile. Nothing to a gull.

She found a space at the end of the pier, pausing to check her outfit before she stepped into view: a pair of ivory clam-diggers, nicely cut but unremarkable; a blue-and-white-striped nautical pullover, equally classic and unmemorable; and finally Top-Siders, standard footwear among the yachting set. As for herself, a willowy blonde on the inner cusp of forty might still turn a head or two, but one virtue of classic features was their anonymity, a face glimpsed in a gallery of old masters and fin de siècle poster art, and forgoing makeup was its own disguise. Sun and salt had bleached her wavy hair a shade lighter than the honey blond most would remember, and scrunching it back into a ponytail was not what most would expect of her, either.

About the only thing anyone looking for Ellen Allworth would expect was the cameo, the one whose profile she usually consciously styled her hair to mirror. But despite being anonymous in its beauty, black and white carved portrait jewels were no longer a popular fashion item, and the only woman known to wear one as a constant was her, Cameo.

She could always take it off, of course, but then again, Ellen could always cut off her left arm. Instead, she reached into her satchel and withdrew a long red Isadora Duncan–style scarf, looping it once around her neck, concealing the heirloom and source of her ace name. The scarf trailed like a pennant as she came on the dock, an anonymous fashion plate from a yacht magazine.

There was a peculiar smell in the air. *Incense,* Ellen realized as she got her land legs and looked for the source. Nearby, uncomfortably close to the gas pumps and their extremely hopeful OUT OF GAS—CHECK BACK NEXT WEEK sign, was a bowl filled with sand, a dozen sticks planted in it, embers glowing like jacinths in the morning light.

Beyond that, a dark-haired woman knelt on a prayer rug. In her right hand she held a musical instrument that looked like a tuning fork, gilt brass crossed with jangling metal bars—a sistrum, Ellen remembered dimly from the memory of one of her ancestresses; they'd been all the rage back in the twenties, part of the Egyptian Revival when they'd cracked King Tut's tomb. The woman holding the sistrum looked like she'd have fit right in back then, garbed as she was in a long linen gown with an elaborate scapular beaded with faience and gold. Given the current tensions with the Caliphate, wearing that outfit took either guts or religion.

Ellen took a deep breath and reached into her satchel as casually as she could. She and her ace had been in hiding ever since Cardinal Contarini and his mad monks had called a hit on her, and given the cardinal's fondness for ace assassins and their fondness for odd getups . . .

Her fingers closed around soft felt, and in a practiced motion, she donned Nick's fedora.

"What . . . ?" Nick began, looking around.

*Quiet,* Ellen said in the back of his head, her head. *That woman. I think she's an ace.*

Nick looked, noting the sistrum and prayer rug. "Elle," Nick said in a soft undertone, "if that woman's Catholic, then the Pope's a Unitarian." He sighed. "If the Alumbrados ever do send anyone, it'll probably be a guy in an I AM THAT MAN FROM NANTUCKET T-shirt."

*Nickie, I'm not being paranoid. . . .*

He grimaced, all the response she needed. "Elle, please, just live a little. For both of us. It's not like being up the sleeve ever did me any good. No one but you even knows who Will-o'-Wisp was, or even remembers half of what I did. And in the end, I still got killed. . . ."

Before she was born, Ellen knew, but before she could respond, Nick took the hat off and she was alone inside her skull. Again.

Ellen clutched the worn fedora for a long moment, then slipped it back inside her satchel, shouldering it as bravely as she could, and soldiered on, wind stinging her eyes. Nick was right. Live a little. She smiled and nodded to the woman on the prayer rug and walked on past.

The woman stopped shaking her sistrum and stared at Ellen's throat. *"Kamea."*

Ellen paused, her free hand coming up to where the wind had whipped the scarf aside, almost touching the exposed brooch. "Excuse me?" she asked, stepping back a pace.

*"Kamea,"* the woman repeated, a word in what sounded like Arabic or Hebrew, then gestured to Ellen's cameo with her free hand. "You bear the charm, the face of Nepthys, the white goddess in the black night. You are her avatar and my prayers have been answered."

"Nepthys?" Ellen echoed, trying to place it as she fumbled for Nick's hat.

"The wife of Set," the woman supplied, "the mother of Anubis and the sister of Isis. And, oh, my dear sister, I am Isis. Isis of the Living Gods. My brother-husband, Osiris, he-who-rose-from-the-dead, had a vision that the avatar of Nepthys would arise at dawn on this morn from the waves at the whale road's end." She gestured with her sistrum, bars chiming softly, indicating Nantucket. "Nepthys would rise, surrounded by the dead that walk and the wind that wails."

The morning wind was brisk but not yet wailing, and as for walking dead, at this hour, there weren't even any hungover tourists. Ellen raised an eyebrow. "See any of those?" she asked, her hand inside her satchel, a death grip on the dead man's fedora.

"No," Isis admitted. "My brother-husband's visions are sometimes confused. I'm afraid he was a little drunk when he had this one. He gets free drinks at the Luxor. I believe his exact words were 'zombies and hurricanes.'" She covered her eyes. "I'm sorry, my daughter has died and I have been clinging to Hope's slimmest thread. . . ." Isis fell to her knees, her sistrum vibrating in a white-knuckled shake. "O Nepthys, send me a sign!"

Ellen bent down, hugging the woman hard before she started ululating. "Hush," Ellen hissed, then whispered in her ear, "I'm the ace you're looking for, but please, I'm up the sleeve."

"O Nepthys be praised," she breathed. "Thank you, O sister."

"I can't promise anything. Just get your stuff and follow me." Ellen rubbed at the bit of Isis's makeup that had smeared on her own cheek and led her back to the dinghy, placing her satchel with Nick's precious hat by her feet. "We can speak when we get to my boat."

The wind was stronger rowing out than rowing in. By the time they were at the boat it was seriously whipping Ellen's ponytail. Isis's circlet was at least keeping some out of her face. "Will-o'-Wisp . . ." Isis read the name on the sailboat's stern. "That is . . . a drowned soul?"

"Yes." Ellen tied up, clambering up the ladder, then helped Isis ascend with her bag. "Let's go below deck." Ellen ushered Isis into the main cabin and shut the door securely behind them. Sound carried, and when dealing with mad monks, one never could be too paranoid.

Isis stood in the middle of the cabin, taking in the Philippine mahogany, the easel, the sketches, the assorted bits and bolts of cloth, and the vintage sewing machine with a half-finished dress strewn inside-out across the galley table. "I wasn't expecting visitors." Ellen shoved aside the unfinished dress, making a place for Isis. "I don't cook, but do you take tea?"

"Yes, please," said Isis. Ellen nodded. A kettle would have been nicer, but a microwave was a small luxury for a single woman. She didn't bother to ask what type Isis preferred—Taylor's of Harrowgate was good enough for anyone—and in a minute and a half, it was done.

By the time she turned around, the Living Goddess had conjured a bowl of sugared dates, either from her bag or thin air. Ellen didn't much care which. She set the mug in front of Isis, considering, then sat down opposite. "So," Ellen said, "what did your, uh, brother, tell you?"

"That only Nepthys, of all gods, can raise the dead. We were bewailing the loss of our beloved Aliyah and . . ." Isis raised her mug, inhaling the steam like an oracle with her bowl, then put it plainly: "Can you help us?"

It had been a long while since Ellen had sat with a client. "Perhaps, but I have to tell you that it's going to be less than what you want. I have to be up-front about that. The last time . . ." How was she supposed to put it? "My last client was expecting the Second Coming and just got a Broadway Revival. I'm a psychometric trance channeler. Most objects"—she hefted her mug as demonstration—"I can feel the psychic impressions on, like smudged fingerprints or whispers on the other side of a wall . . . but if an object is very important to someone, I can tell that, and if that person has died . . ."

Isis finished her thought: "You can channel the soul of the departed?"

Ellen took a sip of tea, letting it linger on her tongue as she thought of the best way to phrase it. "I think they're souls, but the dead . . . well, when I call them back from the darkness, they don't recall an afterlife. They only remember up to the last point they touched an object."

Isis's dark eyes were limned with kohl. "My daughter left the world as she came into it, naked and screaming. But at least . . ." Her voice caught. ". . . at least, your gift is kind." She reached into her bag. "You will spare my darling Aliyah the torment of her end."

Ellen moved the mugs and the untouched dates aside, making room for Isis to unroll a tightly furled bundle of denim. It was like unwinding a burial shroud, revealing at last a pair of low-rise jeans and a black baby-doll T-shirt with the *American Hero* logo, the legend EVERYONE WANTS TO BE-LONG TO THE CLUBS!, and the image of a pretty brown-haired girl wearing nothing more than a whirlwind of glitter, the name SIMOON stenciled below. Isis then added a pair of earrings, small bits of silver and Swarovski crystal in the shape of the Egyptian Eye of Horus, the same as you could get in any Cambridge or Greenwich Village Goth shop. "My daughter wore these her last day on *American Hero*."

Ellen blinked. "Your daughter was an ace?"

"We called her Simoon, the child of the whirlwind. Though the name on her birth certificate is 'Aliyah Malik,' 'Malik' for 'daughter of the King.' "

"Oh . . ." What Ellen did not usually tell her clients was that when the person she channeled was an ace, she channeled their power as well. The contestants from *American Hero* included some pretty potent aces. If occasionally wonky ones. Ellen pursed her lips. "Before we go any further, there's one other thing we do have to discuss: payment."

"I am not rich," Isis said, "but you will have the eternal gratitude of the Living Gods, this I promise you. And you may join us at any of our temples as our Nepthys."

"No offense, but I've got Catholic nutjobs after me. Rather not have Muslim ones, too."

"Osiris foresaw this. As payment, he offers prophecy. *The night hawk has killed the red bird,* he told me. Does this omen bring ease to the heart of Nepthys?"

Ellen sat back. A red bird? A cardinal? Contarini was *dead?* That would be welcome news—mostly—but she'd like better assurances than a vision from a Las Vegas lounge act. She made a counteroffer: "Just let me keep your daughter's things."

"They are mere mementos. If you can make my Aliyah live again . . ."

Ellen composed herself, picking up the jeans. They were . . . unimportant. "You can keep these." She touched the T-shirt, feeling a touch of excitement, a thrill of passion, and a great deal of disappointment, quickening as she touched one, then the other of the earrings.

"Aliyah very much wanted to have her ears pierced," Isis explained, Ellen hearing her words as if from the end of a long tunnel. "I would not let her until she was sixteen."

Ellen unwound her scarf and pulled off her pullover, shedding them along with her identity as she slipped on the T-shirt, adding the earrings, and then . . .

Aliyah yawned, coming awake muzzy-headed as if from a dream. In the back of her head, Ellen stayed silent, watching and observing as Aliyah shook her head and focused on Isis. "Mama?" She blinked. "When did you get here?"

"Aliyah," Isis breathed. "Oh, you are back. You are back. Nepthys be praised."

"Uh, when did I leave?" Aliyah looked around the messy cabin, taking in the oddments and fabric notions, then looking back to her mother. "Mama, where the hell are we?"

"We are in the bark of Nepthys. She has brought you back from the dead."

"The dead?" said Aliyah, standing up, then looked at Ellen's hands, her hands, in incredulity. Then she touched them to her small breasts. "Where the hell are my tits?"

"You are in the body of Nepthys. She has lent you her form."

Aliyah grabbed her chest and squeezed, feeling herself up. "I haven't worn an A cup since I was twelve." She scanned the room. "You expect me to believe I'm suddenly some flat-chested old lady so I can freak for the cameras? What sort of fucked-up illusion is this?"

*Actually,* Ellen thought, *it's not an illusion. You're in my body. And I'm not flat-chested. Or old. Hell, I'm not even forty.*

"Aliyah," Isis cried, tears forming in her eyes, "it is no illusion. You died in Egypt."

"Egypt?" Aliyah echoed incredulously. "I've never even *been* to Egypt!"

"Yes, you have. You were killed by a villain named the Djinn. But your uncle Osiris foresaw a way for you to return, and so I quested until I found Nepthys . . ."

"Then why don't I remember anything about it?"

*Because,* Ellen thought, *when I channel someone, I can only channel them up to the point where they last touched or wore something. I'm channeling you from your shirt and earrings.*

"Oh, this is utter crap," said Aliyah, "and I'm not buying it. Watch." She grabbed the front of her shirt and pulled, ripping it straight off over her head and tossing it into the corner.

The connection faded a fraction, becoming appreciably weaker, and Aliyah staggered.

Isis caught her. "Aliyah, my dear one. It is true. But Nepthys has brought you back."

Aliyah hugged her mother. "Egypt . . . why would I go to Egypt?"

"The Djinn was killing the Living Gods. You went with John Fortune to save them."

"The PA?" Aliyah had a flash of memory. It was as if a dam broke, belief and realization crashing through, coming out as tears and great gasping sobs. "Oh, Mama . . . Mama . . ."

Ellen stayed silent. It was best at these moments.

"Hush, Aliyah. Hush, my dear one. Mama is here." Isis rocked her in her arms, stroking Aliyah's hair, Ellen's hair, one and the same. "Mama is here. It is all right."

"I didn't tell you how much I loved you . . ."

"Nor I, Daughter," Isis said, tears at last beginning to fall, "nor I."

They held each other for a long while, rocking in time with the boat, Isis crooning some wordless Egyptian lullaby.

♥

# Volunteers of America

Victor Milán

**TWO TALL MEN IN** Nigerian Army uniforms stretched the young boy's arms out to the sides. A third stepped forward, raising a machete.

Screaming, the boy's mother bolted from the flock of Ijaw villagers kneeling under the patrol's guns. Sergeant McAskill, mercenary "advisor," bellowed a command. Beneath his boonie hat his face was redder than usual, clashing with his ginger mustache. A buttstroke took the mother down, blood and teeth flying. Her husband sobbed in his mush-mouthed wog English that they were innocent.

Watching from well back among the cluster of shacks that rose on stilts from pale green swamp weeds and white sand, patrol leader Captain Chauncey grinned in his beard. *Sod that for a game of soldiers,* he thought. LAND, the Liberation Army of the Niger Delta, had blown an oil pipeline two kilometers away last night. The lump of black smoke still hung in the sky to the northeast.

These people knew the game. Prices must be paid. And as for innocence— "It's bloody Africa," he said aloud, shaking his head. He inhaled deeply from his cigar.

The blade fell once, twice. It chopped the boy's arms off just below the shoulder. If the boy made any noise it was lost amid the villagers' screams. His blood spurted bright red in the morning sun.

From the corner of his eye Chauncey saw something in the sky. He looked around right quick. A man was flying low over the village. It was the blond-haired pretty-boy ace from down south in the People's Paradise.

Quickly Captain Chauncey stepped back out of view under the overhang of a roof meticulously hammered out of scavenged soup cans. Once when the sergeant didn't think his CO was listening, McAskill had dared to call him a "podgy, pasty-faced git."

The captain smiled again. Now he'd learn what happened to those who said shite like that about Butcher Dagon.

The flying man stretched out his hand. A line of bright fire leapt from his palm. It hit McAskill in the back.

With a scream that was mostly superheated air expelled from already-dead lungs McAskill flung his arms out straight as flame enveloped him. His FN-LAR rifle went flying.

Gunfire began to flash and thunder from the surrounding weeds, raking the Nigerians. The Butcher flicked his butt to the ground.

"Sod you, McAskill," he said, and took himself off.

Crouched among weeds the twenty-one-year-old woman felt fear spread like sickness from her belly. Though it was probably no hotter nor more humid here near the Bight of Bonny than in her home city on the Congo River, now part of the People's Paradise capital of Kongoville, the sweat streamed down her face and from her armpits inside the camouflage blouse she wore.

Her desire to rush forward and save the child from the blade had burned like fire. But the hard men around her in their Ray-Ban sunglasses and distinctive spotted camouflage, elite Leopard Men commandos, would shoot her if she gave away the trap about to be sprung. As surely as their comrades, fanning out to surround the village on three sides, were about to cut down the Nigerians and their SAS advisors.

Her breath caught in her throat as the golden-haired hero of the PPA, of whom her people said his skin was white but his soul a black man's, touched lightly down by the man he had incinerated and swatted away the soldiers who had mutilated the boy. As the Leopard Men opened fire she unfolded long slim legs and stumbled forward.

Her escort let her go. They were intent on shooting at the now-fleeing remnants of the Nigerian patrol. Stealth was no longer a concern.

As if drawn by an invisible tether she approached the boy flopping and bleeding his young life away into the white sand. The risk of accidental shooting meant nothing. Her whole being had narrowed to needle focus on her duty: to succor the hurt. As only she could.

She walked as though she sank to her knees in the soft sand at every step. Because she walked also into her own private world of pain.

"This is gold!" Sun Hei-lian's cameraman exclaimed. "Holy shit, this is great."

Annoyance stabbed Hei-lian as behind her a new crew member turned to lose his lunch in the weeds among the palm trees a hundred meters from the village. She had spent much of the last two decades working third world crises, seen a hundred people's share of horrors. Yet her own pulse ran almost stumbling fast and her skin prickled with adrenaline from what she'd just witnessed.

It was so horrible she had actually felt an urge to intervene. But their Leopard Society guards had made abundantly clear that while her CCTV news team represented the People's Republic of China, whose fraternal assistance to the PPA they greatly appreciated, if they got out of line, they'd be killed without hesitation.

*If I can take it,* she thought, *the newbie can, too.*

Her longtime sidekick and cameraman, Chen, a chunky crew-cut gargoyle kneeling at her side, seemed focused as tightly as his camera. Hei-lian had to agree that what they'd just captured, the boy's mutilation followed by the ace formerly known as the Radical leading a surprise assault on his tormentors, was electric. A victory for her team as complete as the one the commandos were even now mopping up.

A young native woman, willowy-tall and fresh-faced as a child, emerged from tall grass to Hei-lian's left. Hei-lian's instincts started barking like excited guard dogs. "Chen," she said urgently. "Track left."

A brief scowl creased his big round face behind his viewfinder. She actually thought that in their years of working together as a team he'd learned to overlook the fact that she was a mere woman—as well as the indignity of having to take orders from her. He swung the camera left.

"What's with this chick?" he asked. They spoke English in the field, for practice. "She's moving like a zombie from *Dawn of the Dead.*"

"Get that sat dish set up now," Hei-lian shouted. The use of Mandarin instead of English made the young tech wiping puke from his mouth with the back of his hand jump like a jolt from a cattle prod. He and his assistant didn't fumble as they unfolded the small metal flower of the portable uplink. They didn't dare. "Get us a signal."

"Why bother?" Chen said. "The healer ace. Oh, boy. What? She's going to conjure bandages out of thin air? *Bo*-ring."

"Just keep shooting," Hei-lian said.

"All right, I know. Human interest. Yada-yada-yada."

But Hei-lian knew something more was happening. She wasn't really a telejournalist. Or rather, she was that among other things. And she was getting the intuition in stereo.

The African girl's smooth face showed keen suffering now, as if she felt not just sympathy but the brutalized child's actual pain. *An empath-ace?* wondered that specialized part of Hei-lian's mind. The Ministry of State Security, the Guojia Anquan Bu, Guoanbu for short, had no information on the girl: she was new. Their would-be allies, the PPA, were holding out on them. Again.

"*Hong,*" she said.

"Got it!" the tender-tummied tech sang out. "You're live, Sun."

She straightened and shifted so that Chen could frame her briefly with the young woman in the background. "This is Sun Hei-lian, CCTV, reporting live from an Ijaw village in the disputed oil lands of the Niger River Delta, where Leopard Men commandos from the People's Paradise of Africa, led by the ace they call *Mokèlé-mbèmbé* after the legendary hippopotamus-slaying river dragon, have just stopped a Nigerian platoon advised by British SAS troopers from carrying out a massacre. Now PPA ace Dolores Michel is about to heal a youthful atrocity victim."

Hei-lian moved to clear the frame. Obediently Chen focused on Dolores. She had slowed even further, as if the air had congealed around her. Tears streamed down her cheeks. Tendons stood out on her throat. Hei-lian could see her shaking from here.

Ten feet from the boy she stopped. Her body spasmed violently. She threw back her head and screamed.

In great gushes of blood her arms blew off her body at exactly the same points at which the boy's had been severed.

◆

Sun Hei-lian and crew emerged first from the Gulfstream that had brought them from a strip in the recently incorporated PPA province of Cameroon, into the hot green twilight of Kongoville's Patrice Lumumba International Airport. They set up on the apron next to the mobile ramp to shoot.

Medical technicians carried Dolores Michel down on her gurney, moaning in agony unallayed by painkillers. Briefed by a propaganda officer during the return from the Delta, Hei-lian now knew they interfered with her ace.

Tom Weathers stepped into the sunset light slanting across the Congo River. The crowd held back by Simba Brigade soldiers roared adoration.

A striking woman, tall and slim with blond hair flying, ran from the knot of waiting dignitaries through heat that rose from the pavement like shock waves. She caught Weathers in a passionate embrace. For all her self-control Hei-lian couldn't prevent a mouth-twist of distaste.

The woman detached herself from Weathers. To Hei-lian's keen discomfort she ran up and hugged her. She was taller than the Chinese woman, who was middling tall even by Western standards.

"Hei-lian," she said.

She had the voice of an adult woman, the inflection of a child. Sprout was not Weathers's lover, but his daughter—protected fiercely throughout his mercurial career as the last international revolutionary. She had the mind and emotional development of a seven-year-old.

*Disgusting, that he indulges the creature so,* Hei-lian thought as Sprout released her. She fought the urge to dab at herself, as if to wipe away some unseen contagion.

There was mystery, too, that caught at Hei-lian's mind like a cat claw snagged in the skin of her arm: though her face was unlined and lovely, Sprout, close-up, looked to be on the cusp of middle age. Perhaps not much younger than Hei-lian's forty-one years. She actually looked older than her father did.

Yet, Guoanbu knew, the Radical had aged normally since bursting on the world like a car bomb over a decade before.

Chen had panned around to catch President-for-Life Dr. Kitengi Nshombo and his sister Alicia, flanked by Leopard Society men in dark suits, leopard-skin fezzes, and their inevitable aviator shades, advancing to welcome the homecoming heroes. The president was a head shorter than his sister, handsome in an austere way. In his heavy-framed glasses he looked a little bit like Malcolm X, but scaled down, *concentrated,* with skin almost as dark and hard-looking as obsidian.

Dr. Nshombo gave a short speech in French, the official language of the People's Paradise. Though she understood it perfectly Hei-lian tuned it out: boilerplate.

Alicia enfolded Tom to her vast bosom. "*Mokèlé-mbèmbé,* you have struck a mighty blow for revolutionary justice everywhere!"

Chen caught Hei-lian's eyes and rolled his.

"There is good news, Tom, my friend," the president said as they walked toward limousines waiting to carry them to the palace. He said "my friend" as if barely familiar with the words. They were probably almost true. No one quite knew how the Africa-for-Africans ideologue with the charisma of a plank of wood and the white-skinned global guerrilla idol had formed their partnership. But there was no question it had proven highly profitable for both.

*And soon it will profit China,* Hei-lian thought. She felt . . . as close to happy as she ever did.

"What's that?" Tom asked. He spoke French with an outlandish American accent that Hei-lian suspected was part of his act. He walked hand in hand with his daughter, who took all the fuss surrounding her daddy in stride. She was used to it.

*At least she's a well-behaved thing,* Hei-lian thought.

"A delegation of UN aces are on their way from New York, Tom, *cher,*" said Alicia, beaming from behind her glasses as if announcing the advent of Santa Claus. She acted as her brother's right hand. She was also head of the Leopard Society, which among other things constituted the secret police. "They're going to investigate whether to intervene—to help us free the oppressed people of the Delta from Nigerian and British imperialism."

"The Committee dudes?" Tom flashed that grin of his.

"Indeed," the president said. "Your video from the Delta has stirred outrage worldwide. The UN at last heeds the calls for action."

He flicked a look at Hei-lian. As usual his face was expressionless. A warm flush ran from her stomach to her cheeks. *Our video,* she thought. That in itself was a victory for the PRC.

The president's Mercedes limousine waited with top defiantly open, in contrast to the bulletproof carapaces beneath which most world leaders cowered to "meet" their subjects. "Wait one," said Weathers.

If the delay annoyed Nshombo he gave no sign. He seldom did. If you managed to annoy him, you found out about it from Alicia.

A medical crew was about to load Dolores Michel into a nearby ambulance. Weathers walked up to her in that long-legged swagger of his. Hei-lian gestured her crew along and followed.

The girl was conscious. Even Hei-lian winced at that. Her face was ashen green and streamed with sweat. But her eyes were clear.

*The Angel of Mercy.* That was what the Information Ministry man told the CCTV team to call Dolores.

Bloodless lips moved. She seemed to be praying repetitively. Hei-lian recognized it. Her father had been a priest, albeit of a different confession.

"You really gonna heal up, there, girl?" Weathers asked. Dolores's eyes met his. She actually tried to smile. She managed a nod.

"You did a great thing back there in the Delta," he said. Bending down he kissed her forehead. "When you get up you'll be a heroine to the whole friggin' world."

"Tell me a little about yourself, Dolores," the Chinese woman said.

Dolores sat in a wheelchair in the vast rose garden on the presidential palace grounds. It was the day after their return from Nigeria. Because of the need for strong light to shoot by they couldn't be in shade. The high hedges were gloriously colored, but they also cut off any breezes that might have relieved the oven heat. And the concentrated fragrance made her woozy.

Despite all that, Dolores felt much better. She only wished she weren't so afraid of the reporter. Though totally old, maybe even over forty, she was quite lovely in an alien, austere way. Certainly she moved with the grace of a jungle cat.

The gaggle of Chinese men filming and recording her didn't help put her at ease. But she had been ordered to do this for the People's Paradise.

"I was born here," she said. "In 1988. The city was Kinshasa then. My father was a clerk with the Ministry of Transportation. My mother was a schoolteacher. We were good Catholics. Our life was good despite political upheavals and outbreaks of violence; they were worse in the countryside."

She smiled. "We welcomed it when Dr. Nshombo and his . . . war leader took power, united the Democratic Republic with our neighbors the Republic of the Congo, and combined Kinshasa with Brazzaville into Kongoville. It brought peace and stability at last."

The journalist smiled and nodded. Dolores was a child of a mass-media generation; her family had satellite TV. She understood the smile was purely professional. Yet she couldn't help responding to it.

"You did something remarkable yesterday, taking that poor child's injuries on yourself. They tell me both you and he will heal with astonishing rapidity—that you'll actually regenerate the severed limbs. Is that true?"

"Yes. Already my arms grow back. They—they itch terribly. I wish I could scratch."

She laughed. She did not mention how badly she still hurt. Laughter gave blessed if temporary relief.

"You're an ace."

"Yes."

"When did you turn your ace?"

"I was a student nurse at Liberation University. I was given . . . a test."

Dolores bit her lip. The Ministry of Information woman had coached her carefully. She hoped she'd get her lines right. Mistakes cost. It was part of the price of order.

"So it revealed your ace."

"Yes."

*No.* But the true nature of the facility she had been taken to, far out in the bush, was a state secret. And if she mentioned the experimental injection she and the others received there . . . even her sudden heroine status wouldn't save her.

"Once they found out I had an active wild card I was taken to a special school for wild cards. They gave me more tests."

*And I failed them.* The memory still brought on a cold sweat. Those who manifested no useful ace powers met the same fate as jokers and deuces. And the black queens, for that matter. They were taken away. What happened then no one knew.

If they guessed, no one dared whisper. Those who spoke too candidly also disappeared.

"There was an accident on the training ground," she said. "A young man, Pierre, was terribly burned by a new ace who didn't know how to control his power. They brought him in as I was being taken out."

*To meet my own fate.* The State had lost patience with her. She knew the survival of the People's Paradise in the face of imperialist hate and envy required harsh measures. But she feared death.

Almost as much as she feared pain.

"As he was rushed past on a gurney, I—I felt as if I had caught fire. I fell down screaming. My flesh blistered. Actually charred."

"How terrible."

"The pain was—unbelievable." She blinked away tears of remembrance. It was never easy; but that was still the worst. "My injuries exactly mirrored Pierre's. And we both healed totally within a few days."

The reporter shook her head. "So you actually experience it all? The wounds, the pain?"

"Oh, yes."

"You are an exceptional young woman."

"I'm just a normal girl. I don't mean to be a heroine."

"But to walk up to that poor Ijaw boy, knowing what would happen to you—where did you find the courage?"

"It's my gift." *My cross.* "Because I *can* do this, I feel I—can't *not.*"

The reporter nodded. Clearly she had what she needed.

"Thank you, Dolores," she said. "I can well see why they call you the Angel of Mercy."

Dolores made herself smile and nod. That, too, was duty. But the Ministry had hung that name on her.

What people *really* called her was Our Lady of Pain.

"I'm John Fortune," said the kid with the lump in his forehead, shaking Tom Weathers's hand.

*No shit,* Tom thought, glancing once at the bump and then forgetting it. What meant something to him was the presence of a *class enemy.* Even if he hadn't known Fortune was a celebrity brat he'd take him for a rich kid. He squeaked with privilege.

Worse, he was Establishment all the way. Head of the Committee. In tight with UN boss Jayewardene. *The Man,* junior fucking varsity.

President Dr. Nshombo stood there, grave and graven in the cool dark room in his palace depths with all the monitors in it, to ensure this first meeting between the UN aces and his field marshal went smoothly. Tom would keep his personal feelings in check. Basic revolutionary discipline.

"Yeah," he said.

The guy flashed his eyes at him. For a moment Tom thought he might take a swing at him. But no such luck.

An image of a different John Fortune flashed through his mind: a little boy, clutching the hand of his slim, beautiful mother with her wings folded at her back. He hadn't had the lump in his forehead then. . . .

Tom shut his eyes and shook his head once, quickly. *Not my memory,* he thought. *That dude's dead.*

"So you are the famous Radical," said the slim Goth chick beside Fortune. She had chin-length hair, brass red, streaked electric chartreuse. Her English had a French accent. "I'm totally excited to meet you."

"This is Simone Duplaix," Fortune said. "Also known as Snowblind. She's from Quebec. That's in Canada."

Ignoring the gibe, Tom grinned as he shook her hand. "Pleasure's mine. But these days I just go by Tom."

Her grip lingered on his. "I had your poster on my closet door in college," she said. "To me you are a hero."

"Long live the Revolution," he said. He let her hand go and turned to the next visiting fireman. Sure, Snowblind was ready to get it on. But not really that cute. He was doing better. And if he was going to get some on the side, that ace chick who'd gone with them on the Oil Rivers raid was pretty foxy. Before her arms blew off and all.

Briskly, Nshombo introduced Buford Calhoun, a big blond redneck who wore a dark business suit and tie, but looked as if he ought to be wearing greasy coveralls with his name on the chest. "Pleased to meet a famous ace such as yourself, Mr. Weathers," he said. Southerners always sounded dumb to Tom. He right away suspected that *dumb* ran a little bit deeper with ol' Buford.

"And this is Mr. Tom Diedrich," Nshombo said. "He also goes by Brave Hawk."

Nshombo spoke English not with a French but with a touch of stuck-up-sounding English accent. Tom usually talked French with him anyway to keep his hand in. He'd learned the language during an earlier go-round in Africa. He picked it up pretty easily. He did most things pretty easily. Except keep a gig.

Until now. Nshombo might be a stiff. But the man had *vision*. And he wasn't afraid to leave Tom free to do his thing. To let him be . . . Radical.

Even before he heard the ace name, Weathers had this other Tom pegged as Native American. He stood six or seven inches less than Weathers's six-two, copper-skinned, hair black as a crow's ass. He wore cowboy duds: pointy boots, faded denim jeans, blue denim shirt. A coral-bead necklace with a smooth-polished stone hawk fetish encircled his neck.

To Tom's amused delight he actually tried the hand-crushing game. Diedrich had pretty strong hands. For a nat.

Tom Weathers's grip could powder brick. Literally.

He was above that kind of macho posturing. He squeezed back just hard enough to make the Indian's eyes water and bandy knees buckle. Then he let him go.

*Gotta admit the little fucker's pretty hard-core,* he thought. *He'd let me squash his hand before he cried uncle.*

Diedrich gave him a flat look and a tiny nod. "Hear you fight for the rights of indigenous peoples," he said huskily. "Don't see a lot of white-eyes actually step up and do that. Mostly they're just talk."

Looking as if Brave Hawk's implied slam had put his aristocratic nose a bit off true, John Fortune said, "And this is the Lama, from Nepal."

He'd saved the weirdest for last. The Lama was a skinny little brown guy in a yellow robe who sat in the lotus position.

Two feet off the hardwood floor.

He didn't offer a hand. Tom didn't push it. "The Llama?" he said. "Isn't he some South American guy, spits, like, sticky tear-gas slime, kicks real hard?"

"That is properly pronounced *yama*," the floating man snapped. "I must mention he is merely a poser with a cape and a pencil-thin mustache. Whereas *I* am being a seeker after spiritual truth."

"Whoa! Hang on, Mr. Holy Floating Dude," Tom said, holding up his hands. "Don't get your dharmic diapers in a wad."

The Lama looked pissy. Before he could say anything Tom heard a pop and felt air puff against his face. A woman appeared in the briefing room.

Tom blinked. An *amazing* woman. Gleaming black hair flowed down over her shoulders to blend in with a black cloak worn over a white jumpsuit.

Her eyes were silver in her exquisite heart-shaped face. Zippers slashed this way and that across the jumpsuit. Tom noticed they offered ready access to ripe breasts and pussy. His heartbeat picked up.

"Fashionably late again, Lilith?" Fortune asked acidly.

"Right on time, I'd say, Johnny dear," she said. Her voice was a kind of purr that tickled right up Tom's nut sac. Complete with one of those velvety Brit accents. "I've just missed the boring parts, it seems."

John Fortune clenched his hands. His lips moved. So did the lump in his forehead. Tom stared at it with horrified fascination. *Christ, is that a fucking bug?* He almost imagined he could see little legs twitching under the coffee-with-cream skin. He'd first thought it was just some physical thing that came along with Fortune's ace, a minor joker manifestation. . . .

"She brought us here yesterday," John Fortune said with what seemed unnatural control. "She's been away on business of her own. As is often the case."

"She only comes out at night," Simone said. "Like a vampire." Tom wasn't sure if she was being—what was the word?—snarky, or if she spoke with a certain admiration. Outside he knew the sun had just dropped below the horizon with equatorial abruptness. In here it was never day or night, warm or cold. It just *was*, like Limbo.

"And you must be the famous Radical," Lilith said, ignoring the editorial commentary. She smiled at Tom. He forgot all about John Fortune.

It took a strong man to withstand the sheer sensuality of the look and not get knocked flat on his ass. They didn't come stronger than Tom. *Rest easy, sweetheart,* he thought at her. *I'm Alpha Male of the whole fucking continent of Africa.*

Except the little dapper guy at his side. But Nshombo never showed any interest in sex. What got him off was *power*.

Tom Weathers had charisma in buckets. He knew that. He used it—for the Revolution, of course. But if he'd had any of what the petit bourgeois wimps called "people skills" these days, he wouldn't have had to tuck Sprout under his arm and run away from the collapse of a score of revolutionary movements in a dozen years, brought about by the sudden onset of pissed-off government troops or mutiny by capitalist running-dog lackey traitors in his own band. Or both. Still, he couldn't help noticing that if either Hei-lian or little Goth-punk Simone had drawn a *death glare* ace, the newcomer would be a smoking heap.

"Now that we are all present," the president said through silence thick as the sex in the air, which hung heavier than the humidity of the Kongoville night outside, "has your delegation had sufficient time to peruse the evidence we provided you, documenting Nigerian crimes against the native peoples of the Niger River Delta, whose land they plunder of oil?"

That was the problem with the man. He really talked like that.

"Not really, Your Excellency," Fortune said. "You loaded us down pretty well."

"My eyes are turning around in my skull from all this stuff," Brave Hawk said.

Buford gave him his lights-on/nobody's-home smile. "I don't bother my head with none of that," he said. "I just go where they point me and do what they tell me, and leave the thinking to them as're good at it."

Nshombo nodded his big head precisely. He was very good at it. "We wished to leave no doubt in your minds as to the justness of the cause we share with the oppressed people of the Delta. Now, please give your attention to our guests from Chinese Central Television. As you may know, Ms. Sun and Mr. Hong accompanied yesterday's attack which interrupted the Nigerian atrocity."

He nodded to Hei-lian and one of her pet geeks, who had hung back playing furniture during the introductions. Hei-lian smiled that gorgeous smile of hers. It lost a little bit of its luster with Lilith in the room. But not all.

Tom slid his tongue over his underlip. He was starting to get *ideas*.

"Thank you, Mr. President," Hei-lian said. "Gentlemen, Ms. Duplaix, Ms.—Lilith. If you'll just look at the monitor here—"

"I am *so* not watching that horrible arm-chopping video again!" the Goth girl exclaimed.

"I quite understand your feelings," Hei-lian said. "Fortunately, we need not. My crew has blown up and enhanced certain frames from footage taken moments before the counterattack began."

Hong diddled dials. To Snowblind's visible relief—*and what's somebody called* Snowblind *doing here just south of the equator?* Tom wondered—what appeared on one of the big flat-screen monitors was huddled Ijaw huts, distance-grainy. Among them stood a figure. It looked up and to its right, then backed into a doorway out of sight.

"Wait," Fortune said. "Run that back."

Hong did. The man stepped back out into sunlight. He was short, plump, white, and bearded, and wore the same style bush hat, khaki shorts, and short-sleeved shirt as the red-haired guy Tom had torched. He carried a long old-style Brit assault rifle.

"Freeze it," Hei-lian said.

"Son of a—" Fortune cut himself off just before he said something a well-behaved little fascist type didn't say in front of presidential guys. "That's Butcher Dagon!"

"He is familiar to you, Mr. Fortune?" Nshombo asked.

"*Le bête!*" Snowblind hissed.

Fortune controlled himself with visible effort. "Yes, Mr. President," he said. "Yes, he is. The Committee knows him way too well. His real name's Percival Chauncey. I'm not sure if he's number one on the list, but he's definitely one of the most-wanted ace criminals in the world today."

"So my intelligence analysts tell me," Nshombo said. "He currently styles himself a captain, although his actual military record is spotty. The Nigerians, it would seem, have added a rogue ace to the SAS advisors who lead their death squads."

"If that Limey prick's involved," Diedrich said, "something bad's definitely going down."

He and Tom gave each other hard grins. Tom may've been like *that* with Nshombo. It didn't mean he had to go sucking up to him like Fortune did. He appreciated Brave Hawk's disrespect for authority. Even if he'd be smart not to push it here in the PPA.

Nshombo ignored the crudity. He gazed intently at the delegation's young leader. Despite modern A/C Fortune's forehead shone with sweat. It made the strange bulge gleam in the fluorescent light.

Fortune's eyes flared. He clenched a fist and raised it. "*We'll—*"

He cut off. He unwound his hand, dropped it behind his back, as if it suddenly embarrassed him. In a less clotted voice he said, "We'll have to study the situation carefully before committing to a course of action. A lot's at stake here. And Nigeria's not the first country to hire a dodgy mercenary ace."

Tom smiled a slow smile and glanced at Nshombo. The president's face showed no more emotion than the polished teak idol it resembled. But if he'd been a betting man, he would've just lost to Tom Weathers.

Tom stooped and opened a red and white cooler that sat discreetly against a wall. A wisp of dry-ice fog puffed out. He took out a white plastic garbage bag. It was full of lumpy, pokey objects.

"*Here's* what's at stake here, man," Tom said, handing it to Fortune. "See for yourself what we're up against."

Its weight caught the slick Committee ace off guard. He'd forgotten how strong Tom was. Fortune fumbled the bag and it fell open, spilling its contents down his pants and across the floor.

"Fuck!" he yelled.

Snowblind screamed.

It was a bag of severed hands, their dark skin gone ashen.

"Daddy! Oh, I want my daddy!"

Sun Hei-lian prided herself on her ability to keep cool under the most demanding circumstances. Being interrupted while concentrating so intently snapped her equally well-honed survival reflexes into play against her. Startled, she jumped up from elbows and knees.

Tom slid out of her. She bounced on her bare buttocks on his disordered bed.

"It's all right, honey," said Tom from his knees behind Hei-lian. "I'm here."

Sprout's hair was disarrayed, her eyes puffy with tears. She wore an oversized Hello Kitty T-shirt that came down almost to her knees and clutched a well-worn teddy bear to her breasts.

Lying supine to receive Hei-lian's ministrations, Lilith raised her head from her pillow with one brow raised. "And what might this be?"

"My daughter," Tom said. "She's—special. You know."

"I see. Does she often burst in under such . . . circumstances?"

"Hey. Sex is a natural thing."

But Hei-lian noted he swept up the sheet to cover his rampant erection and turned away as he folded the woman weeping into his arms, so as not to give her an inappropriate prod in the flank. He also left both women completely uncovered.

"I had a bad dream," Sprout sobbed. "I want my daddy."

"Hey, sweetheart," Tom said. "You got the world's greatest ace right here. I'll always be here for you."

Sprout buried her face in his shoulder. Tom embraced her, stroking her long blond hair with genuine tenderness.

To muster such modesty as was available to her with minimum commotion Hei-lian lay down on her belly. Now that the passion-spasm had been broken she felt glad enough for a break.

Her mind whirled with thoughts. There was the odd phrasing Sprout had used—twice saying she *wanted her daddy,* when he was right here in front of her. But that struck her as a likely product of the creature's retardation. One could read nothing into it.

What stuck in her mind, though, was the stricken look in Lilith's silver eyes as she watched Tom Weathers comforting his daughter like any loving father.

◆

"So," Lilith said, "however did a Western man of mystery wind up warlord of a Central African revolutionary movement?"

The lovemaking was done. Hei-lian was glad. Although the pleasure had been seismic she was both exhausted and sore. And now that the passion had subsided she felt a certain shame at what she had done.

*You've done worse for the People's Republic,* she reminded herself.

She raised herself to prop elbow on bed and cheek on palm and gazed with half-lidded eyes across the golden length of Tom Weathers in the light of the bedside lamp. He lay on his back with hands linked behind his glorious halo of hair. Sweat didn't seem to dampen its spirits. Hei-lian wondered if that was another facet of his ace. He certainly displayed a remarkable array of powers.

On his other side Lilith lay in similar pose, all silver skin and gleaming midnight hair. She had asked her question lightly, almost teasingly.

Hei-lian kept her expression neutral. She was skilled at that. She felt a visceral dislike for the other woman. Even though she still had the smell of her on her upper lip.

*It's not jealousy,* she told herself. *That's personal sentiment. This is national security.*

Tom's eyes flicked from Lilith to Hei-lian and back. He smiled lazily. If he made an effort to hide his smugness, Hei-lian thought, he failed.

"If I tell you, I won't be mysterious," he said.

Silver eyes narrowed. Hei-lian watched the British ace raptor-close. Lilith seemed as skilled and imaginative at pleasing a female lover as a male one; the more so when the object of their exercise was to excite a man who scarcely needed erotic encouragement. Until the fourth or fifth time, any-way . . .

And Tom—before sleeping with him the first time, weeks ago, Hei-lian expected his lovemaking to be brisk and perfunctory, perhaps even brutal. And indeed when his passion mounted he was forceful as a stallion. But before that he was both remarkably sensitive and skilled.

As he had been tonight, despite devoting greater efforts to the inter-loper. *I suppose I can assuage my ego with the fact Tom can actually enjoy my aging face and body at the same time as this perfect black and silver succubus.*

"You've fought many brilliant guerrilla campaigns, Tom," said Lilith, running a black-painted fingernail down his chest. His pectoral muscles were defined but no more: without his remarkable ace gifts he would have been strong, but wiry-strong, not a steroid-pumped freak. "Each time be-trayal brought you down."

"Damn straight," Tom said. "It was the only thing that could."

"Yet your partnership with President-for-Life Nshombo endures. A few years ago, he was just another minor faction leader in the endless, bloody Congo wars. The next thing the world knows you're at his side; he's van-quished his rivals, conquered the Democratic Republic of the Congo, then the Republic of the Congo, and is well on his way toward carving a new resource-rich superpower from the heart of Africa. What transformed both your fortunes so?"

Tom shrugged. "Nothing succeeds like success, like the capitalists say. Dr. Nshombo's objectively Marxist. We're after the same ends. We agree on the means. Especially that to make an omelet you've got to break a few eggs."

Hei-lian *wasn't* objectively Marxist. Far less Maoist. Never had been. She had learned all the right words, and parroted them with appropriate conviction. She had her Party pin, which always delighted Tom when she wore it. But to her it was no more than a necessary token, a kind of union card. Had she actually *believed* the rhetoric, the Ministry would have purged her years before as an idiot or a dangerous loon.

A brow-furrow marred the smooth perfection of Lilith's face. Hei-lian repressed a smirk. She almost wished her opposite number—for Guoanbu agreed with the world intelligence community's consensus that Lilith was a spy for the Crown, although her background was if anything a darker secret than Tom's—luck in learning anything. Hei-lian had gotten little more from Weathers than anyone could get from a quick Google. And Hei-lian was good.

"And then there's your daughter, Sprout," Lilith said. "She's quite lovely, make no mistake. Yet one almost gets the impression she's older than you. How is that possible, really?"

Hei-lian felt Tom tense. "It's an ace thing."

"But when first you burst upon the scene, twelve years ago, you looked to be a man of twenty. In the interim you'd appeared to have aged quite normally."

"Yeah. Shit happens."

Lilith drew back slightly. Hei-lian allowed herself the ghost of a smile. Lilith clearly wasn't used to men talking to her like that.

"Speaking of your daughter," Hei-lian said. Not to let her rival off the hook. She had her own agenda. Or, she amended quickly, her country's. "I'm concerned by her, Tom." *Appalled* would be a better word, but she'd never dare say that. It was absurd to indulge a real child as he did Sprout. To so indulge an adult—and for an adult to act so utterly like a child—made Hei-lian's flesh crawl.

"She's happy here," Tom said.

Lilith seemed not to resent Hei-lian speaking. If anything she seemed mildly hopeful Hei-lian, as a lover of some standing, could winkle out of Tom some scrap that a mere one-night stand, however spectacular, could not. Neither did Lilith show jealousy of her. *She wouldn't,* Hei-lian thought, *any more than Tom would feel jealous of the world's strongest nat.*

Any more than she herself would feel jealous of an ant. Although she envied them, sometimes, the mindless simplicity of their drudge work.

"But wouldn't Sprout be better off in a proper institution?" Hei-lian said. *Locked away where real humans wouldn't have to endure her?* she didn't say. As Sprout surely would be in the People's Republic. "Wouldn't she be safer?"

"Hey, she followed me from camp to camp for eight years," he said. His tone stayed light. It didn't deceive Hei-lian. "We had some narrow escapes, sure. But I kept her with me. I kept her safe. People asked lots of times why I exposed her to that. The answer was: I'd never turn her over to the Man. *Never.*"

Intelligence agencies had long speculated that their relationship was not decently that of father and daughter. Weathers was a notorious womanizer, a male chauvinist as unapologetic as the 1960s revolutionaries he aped.

But no one had turned up a whiff of incest. Even before Sprout's interruption of their ménage à trois, Hei-lian had known the relationship was not incestuous. Tom was fanatically protective of Sprout. He was capable of many things—some, Hei-lian knew, quite dreadful. Harming his daughter in any way was simply not among them.

That vulnerability appealed to the *yin* in Hei-lian, her feminine side. But the *yang* knew it was a vulnerability.

"Living is obviously easier in a palace than in the bush," she said. "But doesn't it make her a more visible target?"

His smile was ugly. "Anybody makes a move on her gets to find out how they like orbit. Without a spacesuit."

"But you can't be always around. Especially with the war to liberate the Oil Rivers heating up."

"She stays," he said, like a door shutting.

Hei-lian felt the pressure of Lilith's eyes. *Don't you dare pity me!* she thought.

She made herself smile. "Whatever you say, lover."

She lay back beside him. Tom stayed tense, staring at the ceiling.

Lilith leaned in to kiss his lips. She swept her hair back to give Hei-lian a clear view. Was it gloating? An invitation? Beneath a pang of resentment Hei-lian felt arousal stir. She almost resented that more than Lilith's casually proprietary way with Hei-lian's lover—and asset.

"I'm sure your life story is fascinating," Lilith breathed. "I'd love for you to share it with me. I'd find that . . . exciting."

Tom responded. Not the way either woman expected. He got up abruptly off the bed.

"I wanna show you something," he said.

He went to a chest of drawers and opened the bottom one. The two women knelt naked at the edge of the bed to watch. The drawer was full of clean socks and underwear, neatly folded and placed by the palace staff. Great egalitarian Tom Weathers saw nothing incongruous in being waited on hand and foot by people of color like a colonialist of old, it seemed. Then again, neither did the president, nor his sister, nor for that matter any "revolutionary" leader Hei-lian knew of. And she knew them all.

Tom brought out what looked like nothing more than a roll of athletic socks. When he unrolled it a big peace medallion fell into his palm.

"Here." He handed it to Lilith.

Her eyes went wide. By its obvious weight in the other woman's palm

Hei-lian guessed it was solid gold. At today's prices Weathers had a young fortune stashed in his sock drawer.

"Your old medallion!" Lilith said. "I've read about it. You used it a lot in your early career. People theorized it served as a sort of focus for your powers. I've wondered what became of it."

Tom shrugged. "I guess I just stopped needing it."

"Didn't it used to glow?" she asked, handing the golden peace sign back.

His face shut down briefly. "Used to," he said. He rerolled the medallion in the sock.

"It just got dimmer and dimmer," he said, putting it back. "Then it went out."

He shut the drawer with a bang.

Wearing only an outsized Grateful Dead T-shirt of Tom's, Sun Hei-lian padded into the suite's darkened living room. He had wakened her, moaning in his sleep. Another of his nightmares. They seemed to be coming more often.

Nshombo and his retinue temporarily occupied a palace built by Mobutu Sese Seko, the longest-lasting Congolese dictator, who had named the country Zaire. A colossal new People's Palace was being built in the heart of the former Kinshasa. Dr. Nshombo had no known vices. A vegan, he ate sparingly. He neither smoked nor drank. His personal quarters were ascetic in the extreme: a pallet, a lamp, a well-stocked bookshelf.

Yet while Alicia Nshombo enjoyed power's perquisites quite visibly, even her extravagant tastes couldn't account for the new palace's sheer *scale*.

Hei-lian understood. The colonialists, like their feudal ancestors, had built their residences and administrative buildings in order to cow their subjects. Kitengi Nshombo built to cow the colonialists *back*.

Sitting on a sofa with legs tucked beneath her she switched on satellite TV. The first thing she saw was . . . herself, reporting from the Niger Delta swamp with the pale grass blowing about her legs and the pipeline on its scaffolding gleaming like bone in the background. Her face pleased her: quite well preserved. She could even see beauty of an austere kind. She might stay before the cameras for years yet, if her masters so decreed.

Again she wondered at her appeal to Tom, her junior by at least a decade, if appearance didn't lie. Wondered if it could last.

He'd been interested enough after the odd interlude with the amulet, when Lilith, laughing, had led them through one last intricate three-way erotic ballet. Then, the jumpsuit rolled beneath one arm, Lilith had swirled her black cloak around her nakedness and vanished.

Hei-lian lit a cigarette and laughed at her own foolishness. Her life's trade was that of a moth testing how close it could fly to flame. Everything was ephemeral. Humans most of all.

Tom's unease concerned her, though. *Only because he's vital to our plans,* she hastened to think. Things were about to come to resolution, to triumph or calamity. And he was acting strangely.

She recalled an incident at dinner that night. The Lama excused himself to go to the lavatory. Brave Hawk made some contemptuous comment about him.

"Yeah, he seems pretty useless," the American with the curious lump in his head, John Fortune, had said. Hei-lian marveled at the UN's idiocy, sending a mere youth in charge of such an important mission. "When I was a kid, my mom, Peregrine, used to take me to Aces High. Sometimes there'd be like this weird guy, this old hippie who wore a purple and green Uncle Sam suit. Called himself Cap'n Trips. Nobody seemed to know what he did, or what he was doing there. Maybe he was just buds with Tachyon. Anyway, this Lama dude kind of reminds me of him, for some reason."

And Tom paled and went still. As if he had seen a ghost.

Hei-lian shook her head, as colorful electric shadows washed unseen over her face. Who knew the mind of a *gweilo?* Tom Weathers's mind was disordered and undisciplined even for an American.

*Is that why he appeals to you?* a voice in her head asked. She shook it off.

If she had learned one thing, it was that worry never helped. The People's Republic had won. *She* had won. For now. The future would bring what it would bring. She would adjust. Or fail and die.

She stubbed her cigarette and lay down. Smiling, replete almost despite herself, Hei-lian fell into the deepest sleep she had known for years.

On the television the images of horror her own team had captured endlessly replayed themselves.

Tom Weathers slept, too. Not well: but this sleep, it seemed, was a pit he couldn't escape no matter how he tried.

*He* was coming. Tom could sense it. His nemesis. The one being on all the earth—as a good Marxist he disbelieved in heaven, and as a rebel laughed at hell—whom Tom feared.

He sauntered, long-legged, loose, scarecrow gaunt. With his shoulder-length hair, silvered blond, and his beard and mustache, he looked like the WASPiest Midwest Baptist Jesus portrait ever. His shirt was a tie-dyed tee; his pants were elephant bells.

Just an old hippie. To anybody else he'd be a figure of fun. Almost a clown.

Some people dreaded clowns. That was irrational phobia. This was anything but.

"I know what you really did," the newcomer said, smiling sadly. "I know what you really are."

His words filled Tom with terror. "You don't know anything!" he screamed. "You don't know shit!"

"I created you." He shook his head. "To think I tried to bring you out again for so long. I wanted to be you. And for the last dozen years I've *been* you. Watching helplessly while you trashed everything I stood for: peace, love, justice."

"Don't talk to me about justice!" Tom shouted. "You're just another bourgeois poser, man!"

"Maybe," he said. "But I'm still a man."

"You're nothing! You don't even fucking *exist*."

The man looked at him. The eyes were the same eyes that looked at Tom in the mirror every day: light hazel. Even though the other's were magnified by Coke-bottle lenses. Round and rimless, of course.

"I'm sorry I ever created you," Mark Meadows said. "But I feel even sorrier for you. You're losing it, Radical. You can feel it slipping away. And when you lose it—well, I'm waiting, man. Right here. I never go away."

He flashed a peace sign and faded into mist.

Tom Weathers woke screaming.

♣

# Double Helix

## FOR NATION SHALL RISE
## AGAINST NATION

### Melinda M. Snodgrass

SIRAJ AND THE CALIPH stand at the window of his office gazing into the sky. The Caliph was short to begin with and age has bent his shoulders. I can easily see over his head. The plane is a small spot of darkness against the intense blue of the sky. It's rapidly gaining altitude.

"*Kill him!*" says the Caliph. "Send the sword. They will see we are not to be treated as children to take their discipline!" Even through the old man's quaver I can hear the snap of command, the charismatic presence that could send a hundred thousand of the faithful into the streets in reaction to a slight, real or imagined, against Islam.

I keep very still, wishing for invisibility, but Siraj looks back over his shoulder at me. I can see the slow burning anger in his eyes, and I wish that Jayewardene had taken a different tack. What the secretary-general had perceived as sweet reason Siraj had read as condescension.

"Could you teleport to it?" Siraj asks, nodding toward the plane. He is formally attired in a snowy white *thobe* with a gold-trimmed *bisht* thrown over top. A gold signet ring glitters on his little finger as he holds the cloak closed.

"No." I keep it a short lie. You always get into trouble when you try to explain things. And a lie is necessary. All I need is to be ordered to kill the secretary-general of the United Nations.

Now the Caliph is frowning at me. "Why not?"

"I can't calculate the speed and adjust for distance. And if I miscalculate . . ." I shrug. "I cannot fly, sir."

"You are afraid?" It's more of an accusation than a question. The Caliph is staring at me. His eyes are like dark coals held in a cobweb of lines that gouge the skin that's not covered by his luxurious beard. "You will not act for the faith? For your people?"

I nod at Siraj. "The president has not commanded me to act."

"You could just teleport somewhere else . . ." A sudden smile softens the lines in Siraj's face. "While you're plummeting toward the ground."

"And that might be a problem, sir." I offer him a quick smile.

"Why will you not take action?" the Caliph demands of Siraj.

"Because my predecessor made that mistake, and it's one of the factors that brought down disaster upon us in Egypt."

The old man throws his hands in the air and stalks toward the office door. Siraj watches closely until it closes behind him.

He sighs and moves to a table of elaborately inlaid wood and mother-of-pearl. A chess set is off to one side. A couple of decks of playing cards and a score pad rest on one corner. Siraj is an obsessive bridge player. We had spent many hours with Kenneth and Chris playing rubber after rubber in our house in Cambridge. I find myself wondering what became of Chris. Kenneth is a bond trader—

I pull back my wandering thoughts when Siraj says, "I think Jayewardene would like to have found a solution."

"So, why didn't you agree, sir?"

"Because I'll lower prices on my timetable, not theirs." Siraj's expression has hardened again. He picks up a deck of cards, and begins to shuffle it absently.

It's a risk, but I have to speak up. Partly for the oil, but partly for these people I've lived among. "The UN, NATO, and the Americans are massing troops in Israel, Lebanon, Turkey, Upper Egypt, on aircraft carriers. Our army is shattered. We left its bones along the Nile. And they have aces. Loh . . ." I turn it into a cough and, I hope, cover the mistake. "The Crusader is with them, and the Iron Man."

"They will not invade." Siraj hands me the deck and I automatically take it. "The West has covertly stolen our oil for decades. They will be too squeamish to openly steal it."

"But, sir, your speciality is bridge. This is poker. Are you sure they are only bluffing?" And I'm betrayed by my nervous hands and tired mind.

I, too, riffle the cards, but it turns into a bridge of cards flowing like bird wings between my palms. I quickly stiffen the muscles in my fingers, sending cards spurting in all directions.

I drop down and feel my *thobe* tug at the back of my neck as I kneel on the soft black material. I'm scrabbling for the cards, not daring a single glance at Siraj. Fear and tension form an aching knot in my belly. I can't keep doing this. I've got to get a night's sleep. Spend a day in Cambridge.

Flint, Weathers, Fortune, Siraj, Jayewardene. Oh, yes, I've got quite a little list.

*And none of them would be missed.*

◆

# Dirge in a
# Major Key: Part I

S. L. Farrell

"DB, WHEN ARE YOU getting back? It's been damn near a goddamn month now. S'Live wrote a new song he wants us to get on the album. Yeah, it's last minute but KA says he can get it done. We're using this crappy sequenced track right now, but it ain't making it. We need you to really lay it down. And the engineer thinks we need to retake a couple tracks while we still have the studio reserved, and there are all your dubs we've been waiting on for fucking forever. . . ."

Michael was lying on his bed, in the room he and Rusty shared on the aircraft carrier USS *Tomlin,* currently sailing with its escort cruisers in the middle of the Persian Gulf. Michael thought he could feel the slow roll of the ship in the swells, but that was almost certainly an illusion. They'd been on the ship for almost three weeks now. The initial adrenaline rush at the thought of going into action had long ago vanished, to be replaced by simple boredom.

Here, it was two in the morning and the lights were off except for sleeping lamps. Michael stared up at the shadowed gunmetal gray ceiling with its lacework of piping. He'd snagged a pizza from the mess as a late-night snack an hour ago; it felt like a brick sitting in his stomach. Rusty snored on the bunk below him—both of their beds specially widened and reinforced to accommodate them—as Michael listened to The Voice talking half a world away. In the background, he could hear Bottom and Shivers discussing music: *"Y'know, I wonder how would it sound if you played a low G under that Cm chord rather than the tonic . . . ?"*

Once, hearing that, he would have wanted nothing more than to be back there in the studio with them. Once, it would have been *him* driving the band to get the tracks down, to get the final mix in the can, to get a tour together since that's where the money was in the music business now, to get all the reviews and interviews they could. Now, it all just felt . . . distant.

He felt disconnected from everything. From everyone.

"Soon," he told The Voice. "I gotta do this thing."

"For the fucking Committee."

"Yeah."

"So where the fuck are you?"

"I can't tell you. All that secrecy and security shit, y'know."

The Voice gave a huff of exasperation. "Ain't it enough they've damn near killed you a couple times over? Ain't it enough that you've been doing publicity crap for them and campaigning for Kennedy and getting sent to every damn third world dustup more than you're gigging with us?" The Voice's scorn was flint on steel, sparking anger. "DB," The Voice continued, "KA and the rest of the suits are fucking screaming. They expected us to get this CD wrapped up a month ago. And our fans are screaming, too—all those dates we canceled in the last year because of your 'work' with the Committee. That's great for you, but we gotta make a living, too."

"I know. I know. Look, I gotta do this, then I'll be back, man. As soon as this is over. As soon as I possibly can. Things are gonna break now. They are. I'll be back soon. I promise."

He heard the sigh and an under-the-breath curse. "Yeah. You promise. I have the great DB's word and everything. There's something we can take to the goddamn bank." He heard the click a moment later.

The brick of undigested pizza slammed hard against his rib cage.

"Ya think soon, huh?" he heard Rusty say sleepily.

"I don't know. It was what he wanted to hear." That was only the truth. Michael didn't know; Rusty didn't know; Lohengrin or Tinker or Kate or even Babs didn't know. No one in this damned flotilla circling the Gulf for too many tedious, hot, and numbing weeks knew. Only Jayewardene and Fortune had the answer.

Michael understood the arguments, or thought he did: industries were shutting their doors throughout the industrialized countries; rapid inflation threatened the world economy; in the U.S. and other countries, cars were being abandoned in the streets; hundred of thousands couldn't get to their jobs and thousands more were being laid off or fired every day; the entire transportation system was under immense stress; there was talk of a burgeoning worldwide depression. UN forces were being staged all around the Caliphate as a threat, because without oil's economic lubrication, people were going to die. He'd heard the arguments.

He wanted to believe them.

"Who the hell can tell," Michael said into the dimness of the room. His fingertips pattered on his torso and drumbeats answered. "I mean, Jayewardene's talks with Baghdad didn't go anywhere, and Babs is back here on the *Tomlin*. Everything's all 'we're not bluffing; this is fucking serious' but nothing's happening." Michael shrugged even though he knew Rusty couldn't see the gesture. "I've lost count of the number of fucking card games I've played, the bad movies I've seen, and those new episodes of *American Hero* they keep sending us are about as exciting as watching grass grow."

"Kate's here."

Two words, uttered in that flat, quiet voice; they stopped Michael's tirade. He chuckled into the semidarkness. "You're not as dumb as people think. You know that, Rusty?"

"Cripes, get some sleep," came the response.

*Can't stay the same, can't stand still*
*Go on, try it, it might work*
*And if not what have we lost*
*Only something that was never ours*

*Around, around, around we go*
*Where we start, nobody knows*
*Inward, outward, up we go*
*Or is it down and out to close?*

The words were from "Staying Still," one of the cuts on Joker Plague's second release. The guy singing—a shaven-headed ensign named Bob—didn't have The Voice's range or power, but he was doing a decent job. None of the four guys with Michael on the makeshift stage—all of them

Navy personnel—were a match for S'Live or Bottom or Shivers, but it was good just to be playing, to banish some of the pent-up energy and tension with a barrage of furious, driving rhythms. While he was playing, while he was onstage, the rest of the world went away. That's the way it always was, always had been. Onstage, there was only the moment and the energy and the applause. The drug of music was terribly addictive, and he'd long been in its thrall.

Three-quarters of the crew were gathered around the stage placed against the flight deck island: standing in the warm Arabian evening, listening and bobbing their heads, some of them dancing up front. Michael could see the aces there, too, standing in a group off to the side: Rusty, his arms folded and his head nodding in half-time to the beat; Lohengrin—in jeans, a blue USS *Tomlin* T-shirt and ball cap—looking more like a pudgy graduate student than a formidable ace; Barbara Baden, the Translator, back on the *Tomlin* since the collapse of the talks in Baghdad; Tinker, one of the new "recruits" in the Committee, whom Kate claimed could make useful tools out of anything.

And Kate. Curveball. Michael nodded to her, standing off to the side next to Lohengrin and Tinker. He moved to that side of the stage, his six arms flailing hard at his body, the drumbeats fast and loud and insistent. He opened one of his throat vents wider, letting the low *thrump* of the bass drum pound directly at her. He knew she'd feel the concussion, slamming against her body. She grinned at him, waving as he swayed to the beat in the improvised spotlights placed on the catwalks overhead.

The song finished to loud applause and whistles from the crowd. "Thanks for listening!" DB called into his throat mikes, waving. He tossed his signature graphite sticks into the crowd. "You've been a great audience! Thank you!" He high-fived the other musicians in the pickup group as the captain's voice came over the intercom, telling everyone to clear the flight deck and return to duty stations. "You guys were great. Great. That was lots of fun. . . ."

The spotlights went out. From the stage, the *Tomlin* seemed to be a brilliant platform floating in blackness pricked by the running lights of the cruisers flanking her, the wakes streaming out phosphorescent and white from their bows. There were no other lights but the stars in this universe, and the horizon in all directions was the unbroken, dark line of the Gulf.

He hopped off the stage as the crowd began to disperse and sailors swarmed over the improvised stage to disassemble it. Michael walked over to Kate, who applauded as he approached. Babs and Lohengrin were already walking away, talking earnestly to Colonel Saurrat, commander of the UN troops. Rusty loomed behind Kate and Tinker. "Cripes, you guys were loud," he said. Tinker wore the too-wide, open-mouthed smile of an awed fan getting to meet his idol.

Michael ignored Tinker, smiled at Rusty, and cocked his head toward Kate. "Well?"

"That was fun," Kate told him. "Just what everyone needed, I think." Her hand—her right hand, the deadly one—touched one of his arms momentarily, then dropped back to her side.

"You should hear the real thing sometime. If you liked this, you'd be blown away. I'll get you guys tickets to our next show." *Whenever that might be. . . .* The thought came unbidden, and he shook his head to banish it.

"That'd be *fantastic!*" Tinker said, his Australian accent broader than usual. "Sure. That'd be great. Just great. If you want, DB, I could whip you up something better than those mikes you use around your neck, though. I'd be happy to do it for you, mate. Y'know, I heard you blokes a couple times now; in New York on your first tour right after Egypt, and, let's see, I think it was . . ."

"Hey, fella," Rusty interrupted. "What's say you and me get some chow, huh?" Rusty clapped Tinker on the shoulders, staggering the man, and half dragged him away. Kate chuckled.

"You have a fan," she said.

"Fans are good. Sometimes. Hey, I'm thirsty and it's getting chilly out here. Take a walk with me?"

Kate shrugged. "Sure."

He walked with her toward what the crew called "Vulture's Row," the collection of catwalks climbing the island of the flattop. They went down a few levels, below the flight deck to the crew level. One of the crew lounge doors was open, and they went in, Michael snagging a couple bottles of water for them before they sat on a couch in the room. There was a TV set at the far end set to local broadcasts, a half dozen male sailors gathered around watching the screen, the sound tinny and distant. The channel was showing "spontaneous citizen protests" in Baghdad as Arabic lettering scrolled across below; there were bands of protesters filling the streets and firing weapons into the air. UN DEVILS! proclaimed one of the signs, with a caricature of a scarab-browed face on it. MURDERER! said another, and on that one, a six-armed man beat his chest like a multiple-armed King Kong while smashing a minaret-adorned mosque.

"I talked to John," Kate said. Michael grimaced around the mouth of his water bottle. "He couldn't really say much over the phone, but he said that things can't stay at stalemate for very much longer."

"Fine by me. I'm tired of cooling my heels here. Let's either go in for the oil or go home. One or the other." Michael was watching the cartoon of himself jump up and down as the man holding the sign screamed invectives in Arabic.

"Home would be good."

"But you don't think that's what's going to happen? Or Fortune doesn't."

A shrug.

"Yeah, I get it," Michael told her. "It's all kinda weird. Hell, we've both seen what the oil crisis is doing, but maybe we can fix that. Maybe. I've talked to Kennedy and I know how important he thinks this is, and I'm with him, even if . . ." He lifted one set of shoulders. "Even if I'm not entirely sure that oil is what we should be going after right now. But I don't mind being here." *Because you're here, Kate. That means more than the rest.* He didn't say that. He didn't have to. She knew his thoughts—he could see it in the way her gaze drifted away from him, as if she wanted to say something but had decided against it. "You think this is important, too, right, Kate?"

"I'm here," she answered. "So yeah. I do." Her voice was unconvincing.

"Yeah." Michael leaned back and put his top right arm around the back of the couch. Kate didn't move away; he found himself inordinately pleased by that. "Though I ain't looking forward to another fight in the desert, I gotta admit."

She frowned. "Maybe you should have taken John's advice and gone to Africa, Michael. Or maybe just stayed back home this time, given where we're going and what happened last time. They don't like you here—you especially, out of all of us." She nodded toward the television.

One of the sailors picked up the remote. The video of the Baghdad protests faded into a series of flickering channels. Michael was tapping on his chest softly, quick arpeggios of percussive notes, his throat openings flexing quickly to shape the sound. Kate's hand touched one of his arms and he stopped the drumming. He put his middle left hand on top of hers so that she wouldn't pull away. "So they don't like me. Big deal. I'm glad that we're together on this one, Kate."

He saw her glance away with that, biting at her lip. "Michael—"

"Yeah, I know. Sorry." He let go of her hand, but she left it where it was. It seemed a small victory.

"Michael," she began again. "I want to stay friends, but I'm with John and you're not going to change that. Please—quit pushing. It's just pissing me off."

"What pisses me off is that you don't seem to notice the fucking she-bug in his head," Michael spat out. Kate pressed her lips together, and her grip loosened on his arm and pulled away. "Sorry," he told her as her eyes flashed angrily. "That was reflex—and a lot of pent-up crap that doesn't have anything to do with you, or even with John. I guess . . . I guess that if you like John, then there's gotta be something good about him. I'm just tired of all this fucking waiting around, Kate, and worried about what's going to happen next. Sorry. Really. I won't do it again."

He could see that she didn't believe him. She started to get up from the couch. He forced himself to remain seated and not rise with her to try and keep her there, when that was what he wanted to do most of all. "Kate, don't give up on me. Not now. I'm here. I'm here and you're here and at the very least we have to work together to get this done."

Halfway up, she paused and sat again. "Michael," Kate said, her voice quick, quiet, and earnest. "I need you to cooperate with everyone. Every-one: with John, with Barbara, with Lohengrin, everyone. None of us feels good about this, but I've made my arguments. And, well, I'm here. The lousy politics keep getting in the way of the Committee, and the publicity garbage that goes along with all this—yeah, that's all getting to me, too. More every day. But . . . I trust John, and I believe that he's try-ing to do the right things. It's hard enough for him and the Committee to accomplish anything without us fighting among ourselves. So let's stop."

"Okay," he said. "Sure. You got it."

She looked away from him toward the television screen, picking up her water and taking a sip. The sailors had settled on a channel: this season's *American Hero* was playing, one of the interminable "introductions" with Buffalo Gal's lumpy and hairy face staring laconically at the screen, a cud bulging her left cheek as she chewed contentedly against the western mountains in the background. The sailors watching the episode cheered as the video cut quickly to Auntie Gravity, whose ace was the ability to render objects temporarily weightless. Especially with the low sound, it was difficult to focus on anything about Auntie Gravity beyond her breasts, which appeared to have been cut-and-pasted from a bad pornographic cartoon: a massive chest far too large for her frame and defying the pull of gravity, straining at the cloth of her custom-made T-shirt. One of Michael's multiple throats closed, a finger tapped his chest, and a mocking cymbal crash rang out in the lounge. The sailors turned, gave Michael a thumbs-up, laughing.

Kate grimaced. She set down the bottle of water and pushed herself up from the couch. Michael thought she was going to say something, but she just looked at him, her head shaking slightly.

"Sorry," Michael said. "But, hey, *they* thought it was funny."

"Yeah, they did." She sighed and touched Michael's top shoulder. "Hey, I gotta go. See you later, okay?"

"Sure," Michael told her. "Later. I'll be looking forward to it."

"Want another?" Rusty handed Michael a can of Old Milwaukee beaded with sweat. Michael took it in his middle left hand and opened it with the top left. Rusty shook his massive head as foam hissed at the opening. "That just looks weird, fella," he said.

Michael grinned and tilted the can over his open mouth, draining half the beer in one swallow. He could feel it running cool down his wide throat on its way to join the other four he'd already had. He wiped at his mouth with the back of a hand.

The fierce Persian sun had set over an hour ago, and Michael and Rusty were sitting in the area called the Junk Yard, aft of the island, sheltered a bit from the wind by one of the Tilly cranes. They were sitting near Elevator Three, which was down. They could look over the edge to the well-lit and cavernous hangar below the flight deck, where sailors were working on one of the fighters. A female mechanic walked into sight in the floodlights, and Michael's gaze followed her. "Man, look at the ass on her," he said. "Even in those overalls, she looks fine."

Rusty set down his own beer and belched loudly. "Kate," he said. "Remember?"

"Don't mean I can't look." Michael finished the rest of the can and tossed it toward the paper bag that held the twelve-pack. He wasn't entirely sure it went in, but he shrugged. "Hey, I learned my lesson after *American Hero*." He leaned his head back against the Tilly. His eyes closed, and he started awake. Rusty was still looking at him, so he figured it had only been a moment. "After that, I realized there's no way . . . Hey, got another one of those?" Rusty reached into the bag and handed him a can, popping another one open for himself. Michael opened his and took a long swallow. "No *way*," he said, the "way" coming out loudly enough that the young woman in coveralls glanced up at them, "that I can get involved with any aces or anyone famous 'cuz Kate would hear 'bout it. Some bastard like Hive would go an' tell her, an' then she'd just get fucking *pissed* all over again and go runnin' off to goddamn Beetle Boy. So I made me a rule: don't fuck aces, don't fuck *anyone* famous, so Kate don't think I'm just some asshole chasing after pieces of ass. 'Cuz I do love Kate. I do. Man, if I were with her . . ." He was gesturing with all six hands. He heard the can clatter against the deck, and managed to rescue it before all the beer spilled.

"That's a *good* rule?" Rusty asked. One steely eyebrow climbed the oxidized metal of his forehead.

"Fuck yeah it is. It takes care of the whole problem." Michael leaned closer to Rusty, his voice dropping to a conspiratorial bellow. "Now, if something happens after a concert, well, what happens in the dressing room or my hotel room stays there, right?" He nudged Rusty with an elbow and grimaced at the too-solid contact. "Right? As long as she's not famous or some ace."

"I hear you saying that, yeah."

"Y'know, I could see settlin' down with Kate one day. Though 'cuz of the virus, we couldn't have kids—I already got myself taken care of, y'know." He made a snipping motion with two fingers. "I'd love to have kids, too—did'ja know that? I would. Fucking *love* it. You 'member those joker kids back in Egypt—always around me, trying to play drums on my chest?" Michael laughed and pounded on his torso, sending a wild, unrhythmic cascade of drumbeats echoing from the island. Below, the mechanics glanced up again. "Hell, that was a blast. Kids would be great; maybe we could adopt some. . . ." He paused, blinking. His eyelids felt impossibly heavy. "But hey, what about you, Rusty?" Michael asked. The beer can was on its side again. He looked at the foamy puddle mournfully. "How is it with you and the women? I bet you get your share, right, big guy like you?" Michael touched his chest, and a cymbal crash rang. Rusty said nothing. "Right?" Michael asked again.

"I never—" Rusty began, then grated to a halt like a broken locomotive. He was staring out at the dark Gulf.

"Never what?" Michael asked, then the import of the words hit him and he sucked in salt air in a great gulp. "Shit, you mean . . . ?" He could see the answer on Rusty's face. "Wow," he said. "I really don't know what to say, man. Never?"

Rusty shrugged. "I was seventeen when I turned my card. Before that, I dunno, I was a kinda shy fella, that's all. And after . . . Now . . ." Another shrug. Even through the haze of alcohol, Michael realized it was the most words he'd ever heard Rusty say about himself at one time.

"Never," Michael repeated, and belched. "We're a hell of a pair, ain't we?" he said. He put all three right arms around Rusty. They sat there a moment, just staring. Then Rusty reached into the bag and pulled out two more beers.

"'Nother?" he said.

Michael took his and popped the top. He reached over to clank his can against Rusty's. "To us," he said.

They drained the cans as one.

Barbara Baden had called the meeting of the Committee members aboard the ship. Michael knew what it meant; they all knew. He could see it in their faces as they entered the meeting room belowdecks of the *Tomlin*.

"Hey, Kate," he said. He took the seat next to her at the table. Rusty sat on his other side. Across the table, Lohengrin nodded to him, and Tinker smiled. Barbara was at the whiteboard near the head of the table. There were notebooks in front of each of them, with the UN logo prominent on the cover. "We're the last, I guess. Sorry, Babs."

Baden smiled. "Not a problem, DB. I just finished talking with the secretary-general and John Fortune. So here's the situation: unless something changes in the next day, we'll be going in before dawn two days from now; the *Tomlin* is already heading to a new position just off Kuwait City."

"Going in where?" Lohengrin grunted. *Goinguh in vhere?* "To the oil fields?"

Baden shook her head. "We need a better staging area for that—there will be several UN battalions involved, not to mention the ground and engineering support we'll need when we take control of the actual oil facilities. We plan to take Kuwait International Airport first."

Michael couldn't contain his laugh. Six arms waved like a spastic tarantula. "You're kidding, right? We're going to take Kuwait International, in one of the Caliphate's biggest cities, and the Caliph and Prince Siraj are going to just let that happen? Hell, they'll have every inch of the ground covered with troops."

"We're hoping that won't be the case," Baden said stiffly through the smile that appeared to be chiseled on her face. "Even though negotiations have broken off, Secretary-General Jayewardene has kept the lines of communication open with Prince Siraj. He has reminded the prince and the Caliph what happened the last time they attempted to interfere with the Committee aces. We hope that they understand that 'permitting' a small incursion into the Caliphate would be better for them politically than resisting one and losing."

Rusty grumbled something unintelligible, Kate said nothing. Tinker was staring at his hands. Michael looked at Lohengrin. "You buying this?" he asked.

"Well . . ." *Vell* . . . A shrug. "I trust that John won't give us anything we can't handle."

"Must be nice to have that kind of trust in him." Michael felt Kate's gaze snap toward him with that.

Barbara continued to smile at him. "I'd also remind you, DB, that you're here because you specifically requested this mission. John told me to tell you that if you've changed your mind, he'll arrange to fly in another Committee ace to take your place. Should I tell him to make that call?"

Michael had no good answer for that. They were all staring at him. His fingers tapped his chest involuntarily and the sound of sticks on a hi-hat reverberated in the room. "No," he told Barbara, not daring to look at Kate. "I haven't."

"Good, then," she said. Smiling. "Then we're in agreement. Now, if you'll open your notebooks, we'll look over the initial attack plan. . . ."

*I know you hate me,*
*I know seeing me gives you pain*
*I don't care, but*
*You better not try to stop me again*

Michael tugged on the cord to pull the earbuds from his ears. The current studio mix of "Stop Me Again" and The Voice's acid voice went to shrill, insectlike piping, to be replaced by the *thrup-thrup-thrup* of the CH-47 Chinooks' rotors and the shriller whine of fighter jets and attack helicopters farther overhead. Each of the aces had been placed on a separate chopper—Michael declined to consider the obvious logic behind that. He glanced down through the smeared windows and saw the buildings of Kuwait City's southern outskirts below them. His stomach churned; at any moment, he expected to see the bloom of antiaircraft fire, or fighter jets with the insignia of the Caliphate on their wings diving on them, or the fiery stem of an RPG arcing up toward their Chinook from the houses below to bloom in death and fire. He leaned toward Lieutenant Bedeau, with thick earphones over his blue helmet. "Anything?" he half shouted.

Lieutenant Bedeau—in command of the troops in Michael's chopper—shook his head and gave a thumbs-up. It did nothing to reassure him.

Taking Kuwait International couldn't be easy. At any second, it was all going to go to hell. Michael knew it. He could feel it. Any second now, he was going to hear the chatter of machine guns and the sinister *thrump* of mortars. Helicopters would be pinwheeling down to crash to the tarmac. There were going to be explosions and smoke choking the air, and blood. Too much blood.

They dipped and turned sharply, and Michael's eyes widened. Below, he could see the concrete lines of the airport, coming up fast toward them. A couple of the flotilla of choppers had already landed alongside the main terminal, and he felt their own craft touch down. No chatter of guns. No explosions. The rear door of the Chinook slammed open, letting in a wash of harsh light and swirling sand. "Go! Go! Go!" Lieutenant Bedeau shouted in French-accented English, waving his arms. The cord of the headphones jiggled heavily. "Move!"

*It's gonna happen now. Now.*

The troopers from his Chinook piled out from the rear ramp in a quick, nervous double line, fingers caressing the triggers of FAMAS G2 automatic weapons. There was no answering gunfire. There was no resistance at all: no Caliphate soldiers eager to defend the airport, no tanks clanking toward them, no fighter jets dropping bombs, no RPGs streaking red death. No Islamic aces. Nothing.

*Yet,* DB reminded himself. He was lugging two M-16 rifles himself, one in each set of his four lowest arms. A custom-made armored vest was pulled tight around his heavily muscled, tattooed body, and he wore one of the blue helmets over his shaved head. He was the last one out, hitting the ground under the wash of chopper blades and blinking at the gritty sand that still managed to get past the plastic goggles.

The landscape was dun dotted with green, pinned under a vicious, relentless sun. *Back in the desert. Fucking lovely.*

Around the tarmac, the rest of the Chinooks had also landed, UN troops spilling out like blue-capped coffee beans from broken bags, the aces of the Committee team—one to each chopper—following them: Lohengrin and Rusty, who like Michael might also be having flashbacks to Egypt; Barbara Baden; Tinker.

And Kate. Michael waved to her—a hundred yards away. She waved back perfunctorily. The dry air felt cloying, as if somehow, impossibly, a thunderstorm was about to break. He hoped not too many people were going to die when that happened.

"DB!" Lieutenant Bedeau was gesturing at him. "Let's move!" He pointed toward the terminal.

Michael grunted assent and took a single step. That was as far as he got.

Something whined past his ear—like one of Hive's wasps in some great hurry—then a duller *k-chunk* came from the fuselage of the Chinook behind him. He half turned his head to see a ragged, circular hole torn in the metal. The sharp report of a rifle came in that same breath. "Sniper!" he yelled.

That was when an invisible semi slammed into his chest and knocked him to the ground. He went down hard, barely able to breathe from the force of the impact. The world went dim around him momentarily and he nearly blacked out. He heard the M-16s he was carrying scratch along the concrete of the runway, dropped from stunned hands; he heard other people shouting and the familiar, bowel-churning rattle of automatic weapons fire. Hands pulled on his multiple arms, dragging him away. He shook his head and pulled away from them. "I can do it," he growled, but the effort of moving and talking hurt like a son of a bitch. He half crawled, half limped to the other side of the Chinook where the blue helmets were crouched, scanning the rooftops and windows of the terminal. He fell more than crouched. The fingers of his middle right hand probed his chest: there was a hole torn in the Kevlar-and-steel vest, right above his heart.

With the realization, the world spun around him once.

Another bullet ricocheted from the ramp, leaving a bright scratch close to Michael's head. "There!" one of the soldiers shouted, pointing to a puff of smoke from the terminal. M-16s and FAMAS chattered and stone chips flew from the building's facade. A Tigre Eurocopter attack helicopter, looking like a monstrous wasp, lifted fifty feet in the air. Weapons fire spat from the front guns of the Tigre, then stopped. A soldier waved from the chopper's open window, then drew a finger over his throat. The Tigre banked and moved away.

"Drummer Boy!" Lieutenant Bedeau was crouched next to him, his thin Gaelic face concerned. "You are okay?"

"Yeah. Okay. At least I think so." Michael used his lower hands to push himself up to a sitting position. He grimaced. "Fuck, that hurt."

"There was only one man, and he wasn't a very good sniper, luckily for you. A trained sniper would have gone for the head shot." Bedeau tapped his own forehead and grinned suddenly. He slapped DB's shoulder. "Now he's a very dead amateur."

"Good," Michael told him.

"The people of the Caliphate, they don't like you very much because of what you did to the Righteous Djinn." Bedeau said it with a faint smile. DB was damned if he knew what was so amusing about any of it.

"Yeah," Michael answered, rubbing his chest through the vest. "So I gather."

♣

# Double Helix

## THE WORDS OF A TALEBEARER ARE AS WOUNDS

### Melinda M. Snodgrass

**I'VE LEFT THE MOISTURE-LEACHING** heat of Baghdad for the steaming heat of Kongoville. The tropical heat makes me wish I could strip off not only clothes but skin as well. What is it about the British that we seek out such dreadful climes in our pursuit of empire?

Exhaustion has left my mind feeling like a gray blank. I wasn't sure I could effectively picture one of the rooms of the palace so I gave myself more room by picking the garden. The night air is filled with the sounds of insects and frogs. I wonder if one of those deep *ribbets* is Buford out grazing on bugs. I giggle.

It dies when I hear the distinctive sound of a gun being cocked. Whirling I see one of the Leopards, his eyes glittering in his dark face. The gun is coming up. He recognizes me before his finger tightens on the trigger. The barrel drops, and I can feel my knees trembling with released stress. The wash of adrenaline is ebbing, taking with it the last of my energy. I grope in my pocket, pull out a Black Beauty, and toss it into my mouth. It seems monstrous passing down my throat. I have to cough before I can ask, *"Où est John Fortune?"*

He takes me.

Fortune is slumped in a large armchair, dressed only in boxers, staring blindly at the insects circling the table lamp. Sweat gleams on his bare chest, and forms drops in his sideburns. Sekhmet humps beneath the skin of his forehead like some grotesque tumor. I wonder how Curveball feels with this voyeur present at every tender fuck.

"Lilith," he says as if remembering who I am.

There's an overstuffed ottoman near his feet I sink down onto, and feel the leather stick to the moist skin of my calf.

"We're getting some blowback from the Caliphate," I say.

"What does that mean?"

"That annoyed locals are shooting at us."

That makes him straighten. Suddenly another soul is looking through his dark eyes. It's old and cold and I recognize a kindred spirit.

"They have brought it upon themselves."

"Yes, well, that may be the case, but however naughty they are or pure we are, bullets are still lead and they still kill. As DB nearly found out."

"What?" The decibel range goes high and the young man is back.

"Bullet to the chest. Fortunately his vest sucked most of it. But it was a near thing." I pause for just the right amount of time. Cast down my eyes, then look back up at him. "Kate seemed very concerned. She was still with him when I left to report to you." I pause again. "Oh, she said to give you her love."

There is again that strange snapping shift in the eyes, and Fortune's voice rasps as he says, "You are an evil thing. Dark and—"

My lips skin back in a smile. "John, dear, do exert a little control over your senile mummy."

Fortune seems like an inexpertly controlled marionette as Isra tries to propel him out of his chair, and he struggles to stay seated and composed. There's something so wrong and disturbing about this symbiosis that I find myself taking a step back. Fortune was supposed to have the power of Ra, the power of the sun itself, but it was taken from him when his father cured him of the wild card. Sekhmet was to be the handmaiden of Ra. Two powers wedded to form a whole. But Fortune is just a nat, which makes them only half of what they were meant to be.

Thank God. Fortune's self-righteousness melded to Isra's vindictiveness would be a truly terrifying prospect.

◆

# Political Science 201

Ian Tregillis & Walton Simons

**YVETTE:** Fourteen days, nine hours.
**YVES:** Fifteen days, eighteen hours.
**YECTLI:** Sixteen days, two hours.

**CHRISTIAN WAS OUT THE** door on the way to his regular postcoital physical before the first egg appeared.

*Don't trust him,* Yvette had said.

Zoë, a petite girl with a pageboy bob of strawberry-blond hair, asked, "Why not?" *Not-not-not-not . . .* The echoes came from every corner of the room. They made concentration difficult. A strange deuce.

Her brother Zane flashed his chromatophores into ripples of firetruck red by way of response. He snuffled at Niobe's palm with his tentacles.

Zoë frowned. "What does that mean?" *Mean-mean-mean . . .*

"It means shut the hell up," said Zenobia, the frail and birdlike baby of the clutch.

"Mom! Zen swore at me!" *Me!-me! . . .* Zane recoiled, covering his earbuds. He retaliated, using a camouflage ability that extended to projecting invisibility. Zoë bumped, loudly, into an invisible nightstand.

"Ouch!" *ch!-ch!-ch!-ch!-ch!*

Niobe said, "Hey. Be nice, you two."

*But why would she say that about trusting people?*

*I'll find out, Mom.* Zenobia walked to the door, dispersed into a cloud of mist, and was gone. Niobe considered calling her back. But in the end she wanted to know what Yvette had meant, too.

Zenobia drifted through the entire medical wing and found no sign of Christian. He was nowhere to be found. It appeared he'd left the facility, until Zenobia heard laughter and muffled voices coming from a storage room.

Behind the industrial-sized cans of tomato paste and five-gallon tubs of elbow macaroni, four folding chairs were arranged around a card table. One chair sat empty, but Christian was there, chatting with two men.

*Mom, I found him!*

*Good work, sweetie. I see him.*

*I don't think he had a physical.*

*I know.*

A fourth man hurried in. He sat across from Christian.

"What's the good word, Pham?"

"Girl, boy, girl. Deuce, joker, ace." The man named Pham summarized Zoë, Zane, and Zenobia for the others.

"Good work, Pham," said Christian.

"Why can't you just stick around to see what pops out of those eggs, Chris?"

"Would *you* stay any longer than you had to?"

Twin pangs of hurt and betrayal passed each other on the way up and down the bond between mother and daughter.

Smitty slapped Christian on the back. "He does the hard work. Who can blame him, wantin' to get out of there?"

"Yeah, speakin' of hard, how the hell can you do her, anyway? She's disgusting."

"Gentlemen, I just sit back and think about my bank account." Christian grinned. "Every litter of freaks is another hefty little bonus."

"Yeah, so's you can afford all the child support!"

"You get paid extra to screw her?"

"Of course, retard. Would *you* do it for free?"

Far on the other side of the complex, Niobe cried.

"I would if she looked like Curveball. Shit, I'd pay to screw *her*. Yeah, I would wreck that girl. I'll bet half the guys on the Committee are bangin' her."

"The way I hear it, Tom, you got no choice but to pay for it." More laughter all around the table at this.

"This season's better. Green chick? Talk about hot."

"I like that acrobat, Minx. Now *she's* bangable." Tom leered. "And I'll bet she's freaky in the sack, too."

Smitty laughed again. "Could you imagine Genetrix on *American Hero?* Fucking before each challenge? Her teammates would have to draw straws." Pham pounded the table with his fist, laughing.

Christian took a deck of cards from the table. "Okay, so we got a deuce girl"—Christian removed the deuces of hearts and diamonds and set them in the center of the table, faceup—"a joker boy"—he added a joker to the deuces—"and an ace girl"—the aces of hearts and diamonds went into the mix. "Someone do the honors."

*Mom? What are they doing?*

Niobe didn't say anything. Even Zoë had fallen silent. Zane's mantle faded to gray.

Pham flipped a coin. Christian added the deuce of hearts back to his deck. They repeated the process, and the ace of diamonds went back.

After shuffling and letting Tom cut, Christian dealt four cards to each player.

"Okay, gents. Ante up."

Niobe gasped. *They're gambling, Zenobia. They're gambling on you and Zane and Zoë.*

A little salad of green bills accumulated in the center of the table. It grew as bets and raises and calls swirled around the table.

"Fifty bucks says the octopus croaks first."

A pang of terror and anguish through the bond. Niobe stroked Zane's head. His mantle turned ink black. "Shhh, shhh. Don't listen to them. They don't know what they're talking about."

Back at the game, Pham said, "I'll take that action." He dropped a few bills on the table. "Bet the octopus outlasts the chubby kid Justice brought in a few weeks ago."

*Drake . . . ?* A cold, sickly feeling took root in Niobe's gut. Why would they say that?

*Zen, that's enough. C'mon back now.*

*I'll get him! I'll drift right into his body and—*

*No. Leave him alone. That goes for all three of you.*

Zane ruffled his tentacles. His sisters nodded.

*I need to think for a while.*

He was asleep the next time they came for him, although the dreams kept him from sleeping very well. Drake didn't really know if it was day or night. There was no clock in his room and he'd watched all the DVDs, some more than once.

Drake could barely feel his feet on the floor as they shuffled him down the hall in the direction of the interrogation room; Justice seemed to be lifting him more than guiding him. Once there, it was going to be more of the same stupid questions and he really couldn't tell them anything.

Smitty and Dr. Pendergast were waiting for them inside the interrogation room. There was someone else, a woman who was about the same age as his teachers back at school. Her dark hair was pulled back and her eyes darted around the room like a fish in an aquarium. Drake flopped heavily into the empty chair and put his head onto the desktop. "Please let me leave. I can't help you." He closed his eyes, hoping it would all just go away.

"We're going to try something different this time, Drake," Smitty said, in his flat but somehow scary voice. "Something to help you remember. Your file from BAMC indicates a reaction to a particular type of sedative. Dr. Carlisle will be sitting next to you while you're under. She has the ability to see into your mind somewhat and will share that with us."

Dr. Carlisle pulled up a chair next to him. Pendergast moved around the table and stood by Drake's other side, a hypodermic in one hand. He grabbed Drake firmly by the shoulder, and before the boy could struggle had the needle into him.

"You may feel a little uncomfortable for a moment," the doctor said, "but . . ."

The rest of the sentence was a hopeless garble to Drake, like someone was speaking a foreign language to him from inside a well. The room tipped and rolled beneath him. The light over the table dimmed and went out, and it seemed he was falling slowly into a dark hole filled with cotton candy, but the hole didn't have a bottom. He closed his eyes.

This wasn't like the dreams. It felt like someone pushing open his mind and chipping bits of it loose.

He was sitting at the computer playing WoW . . . His brother Bob was behind him, yelling, saying it was his turn . . . Drake hitting the floor, coming up punching wildly . . . one flailing fist catching Bob in the balls . . . Bob choking him and demanding that he give . . . Drake trying to get air any way he could, no air . . . Bob saying "What's wrong with your eyes?" . . . Drake feeling like he was growing . . . A flash of light, blinding, blotting out Bob, and Sareena downstairs, and his mom and dad out by the stock pond . . . A feeling of collapsing, darkness . . .

*Where was he?*

Drake opened his eyes again, back in the interrogation room. His head was over a trash can and he was throwing up. Drake couldn't believe how much was coming out of him. He hadn't been eating much lately.

"That's all right, Drake," Pendergast said. "That's what it's there for."

Smitty glanced up from the notebook he was writing in. Dr. Carlisle was whispering in his ear. She looked scared. "Get him out of here," Smitty said. "We're done for now."

Drake tried to get to his feet, but his thick legs were wobbly beneath him. "What did you do to me? Does this go away?"

Dr. Pendergast handed him a glass of water. "You'll feel better if you get some of this down." Drake took this glass in an unsteady hand and balanced it against his lip, gulping down as much as he could. At least it took a little of the vomit taste from his mouth.

When he was finished, Justice tugged at him. "Time to get back to your room, Drake."

Drake tried to take a step but lost his footing and collapsed face-first to the floor. His forehead bounced heavily off the cold linoleum. Smitty laughed. Drake clamped his jaw shut. He wasn't going to let them get him to go emo if he could help it. At least whatever they'd drugged him with dulled the pain as well as making him a spaz.

Justice lifted Drake up by his armpits. "Shut up, Smitty." He glared at his fellow BICC agent.

"Thanks," Drake said. "I'm okay now." It was a lie, but he was going to do his best to pull it off. He could tell that Justice wasn't taking up for him because he liked Drake. It was because he thought Smitty was a jerk-off. It was one of the few things they agreed on.

On the way back to his room Drake tried to get Justice to tell him what they'd injected him with, not to mention what it had done to him.

As expected, Justice told Drake exactly nothing except that it was an advanced interrogation technique. Justice gave Drake a stick of gum when they got back, "to take the taste out of his mouth." Then he left Drake alone again.

Drake lay on his bed, chewing the gum slowly to keep the taste for as long as possible. As near as he could tell, they were going to keep him here forever. All he knew was that he had to get out of here soon, and he was going to need help. Major help.

Niobe, Zoë, and Zane pretended to watch *American Hero* in the lounge while Zenobia snuck into Pendergast's office. Zane chuckled (in the form of cyan and burgundy cross-hatching) when the Laureate, the weakest of the competing aces, managed to get Tesseract, the most powerful, voted off the show. Team Clubs was screwed.

Niobe turned inward, focused on Zenobia. The filing cabinet was locked. Zenobia reached inside with a phantom finger and tripped the latch. It took a bit of searching to find Drake's file.

*Got it, Mom.* Zenobia pulled out a thin hanging folder. The tab said "Thomas, Drake."

*Good job, kiddo. Don't keep me in suspense.*

Zenobia started reading. "No. Freaking. Way."

Drake was, apparently, the only survivor of the accident in Texas that had been on the news. An Air Force reconnaissance patrol had found him, naked but otherwise apparently healthy, near the center of the devastation. SCARE suspected that Drake had played a role in the event. Whatever it had been, it *wasn't* a grain silo explosion.

A page slipped out of the folder and fluttered to Zenobia's feet. It was the end of an e-mail. Pendergast believed in paper trails, apparently, and kept hard copies of everything.

In a report to his superiors in Washington, Pendergast had concluded: ". . . constant danger to this facility, its staff, and the other patients. As the trump virus has failed, I see no choice but to euthanize the subject."

*My God.* Reading those words revived the sickly feeling in Niobe's gut.

The newest entry in Drake's file, dated that morning, recommended that he be moved to the deepest part of Q Sector for "containment" in case of an accident. Pendergast stressed the importance of keeping Drake calm—which Niobe found at odds with tossing him in BICC's worst neighborhood—until he could be subtly euthanized. Pendergast suggested piping carbon monoxide into Drake's new cell.

The television blared. Zane jumped. Pham, a player in Christian's secret mistigris game, had picked up the television remote and was cranking the volume.

"Hey, not so loud!" *Loud!-loud!-loud!-loud!* . . .

He ignored Zoë's echoing protest, plopped down in a recliner, and tore open a bag of corn chips. Niobe hoped his lewd fantasies of superpowered starlets would distract him from wondering where her third child had gone.

Pham shifted around in the chair, trying to get comfortable. After a moment he grunted, unhooked the jangly key ring from his belt, and tossed it on a side table.

"Mom." *Om-om-om-om.* Zoë whispered, "It's too loud for Zane." *Ane-ane-ane-ane-ane* . . .

"Hush, kiddo. Don't make me lose my train of thought."

*Zen, can you put Drake's file back and pull mine?*

The file marked "Winslow, Niobe" was twice as thick as any other. It began with a capsule biography summarizing her life, the long journey from a Connecticut mansion to a subterranean government laboratory.

Next, the file detailed every child she hatched at BICC: photographs, medical examinations, descriptions of their abilities. But they weren't catalogued by name. The paperwork reduced each child to a serial number, starting with 1-A-1 for her darling and dearly missed little strongman Aaron, all the way to 1-Z-3 for Zenobia.

Like Drake's, Niobe's file contained Pendergast's handwritten observations. Not long after her admission to the facility, Pendergast had enthused to his superiors: "The subject's unprecedented ability to circumvent the natural statistics of the wild card virus, most notably the routine suppression of the Black Queen among her hatchlings, presents tremendous possibilities. Isolating the mechanism should be our highest priority."

Back in the lounge, Niobe hugged Zane and Zoë to her. Zenobia kept reading.

Unraveling the peculiarities of Niobe's children had proven difficult.

Slow progress dampened Pendergast's tone. Six months in, he'd become paranoid that Niobe might decide to leave the facility before BICC could achieve its research goals. He'd had her elevator card deactivated, and as a further precaution he'd filed papers with SCARE.

She'd been a prisoner for over a year and hadn't known.

Six months after that, he'd written: "We have met with moderate success extending the mean hatchling life span. If more resources are devoted to this work, future clutches may be turned into deployable assets. In this vein, the subject should be utilized as a biological reactor until reliable suppression of the Black Queen has been achieved."

Niobe hugged her children until they gasped. *Reactor? That's all I am? An egg factory? You want to turn my children into weapons?*

Zoë huddled closer to her mother. *Mom, what are they going to do to us?* It was hard to believe she could sound so quiet, so mousy, so frightened.

Niobe didn't know what to say.

Zenobia read further. Pendergast had been reading all of Niobe's incoming and outgoing e-mails. Her correspondence with Bubbles prompted lengthy and graphic speculations on Niobe's sexuality.

The final entry, dated two days earlier, was terse: "Fulfilling our research objectives will require several hundred clutches. Recommend accelerated schedule, with multiple partners." A chart accompanied this note. Pendergast intended to pair her not only with nats, but also with aces, deuces, and jokers. Including some from Q Sector. "Staff should develop techniques for forced insemination should subject prove uncooperative."

Niobe shivered. The entire family fell silent. Niobe wiped at her face, flicking away tears before Pham or another orderly noticed.

Zane rode on her shoulder as they walked back to her quarters. The picture frames on her shelves rattled when the door slammed shut behind her. Her children—row upon row of them—smiled, grinned, mugged, gave the thumbs-up from dozens of photographs. The picture frame on her desk housed an autographed photo of Michelle Pond. Two photos cropped side by side, in fact, contrasting thin Bubbles and large Bubbles.

Niobe clicked the remote for her stereo. The little Bose player was plugged into her iPod. Haunting vocals and mournful guitars echoed from the cinder-block walls and wrapped around Niobe like an acoustic blanket. Espers's "Children of Stone" had become her anthem the moment she first heard it. Stone children never age, never die.

She flopped down on her bed and cried. Christian's betrayal had been painful enough. Two years. *Two years,* she had let them poke her, prod her, humiliate her, all in the stupid belief that they wanted to cure her children. But they didn't give a shit about any of that.

She felt stupid. Ashamed.

They were going to chain her to a table and use her like a machine. But not before they murdered Drake.

Zoë and Zane climbed into her lap. Zane, a mournful cobalt blue with spots of jade, nuzzled her hand. Zoë's tears, hot with sorrow, trickled down Niobe's neck. They sat that way until Zenobia said, *Uh, Mom?*

She had unlocked the lower compartment of Pendergast's TV cabinet. The shelves were crammed with DVDs. Many had austere white labels on the spine: "Genetrix Insemination Session, 1-H," and so forth. But others had garish sleeves plastered with titles such as "All Joker Action," "Tentacle Tramps," and "Herne Takes Jokertown, volume 3."

*Mom, there's magazines here, too, with—*

*Oh, my God. Oh, my God.*

She'd thought nothing could be worse than how he viewed Niobe and her children as tools, means to an end. She was wrong. He spent half his time jacking off to her sessions and the other half trying to turn her children into weapons.

She felt *filthy.*

"Mom," Zoë whispered, "we can't stay here."

Niobe blew her nose. "If we leave, you'll get sick." She didn't add "soon." "If we stay, you have a chance."

"No." Zenobia shook her head. "No we don't. A few extra weeks at best."

Her siblings agreed. "Besides." *Ides-ides-ides-ides.* "Drake needs our help." *Elp-elp-elp-elp-elp-elp.*

His arm still hurt from the shot they'd given him. Whatever it was supposed to do, it hadn't worked, and the doctors weren't happy about it. Justice had him in tow again. The hallway they'd entered was blue and the doorway to it had two heavy bolts on the outside.

"Is that you again, spic?" a voice came from deep inside one of the rooms. Drake couldn't see inside because the heavily barred window was too high. Justice didn't reply and kept walking.

A horrible face appeared at another one of the windows. It was gray and the mouth had huge teeth. "Love to eat them fat boys. Fat boys what I love to eat. Bite they fat-boy heads off. Nibble on they fat-boy feet." The voice put a cold knot in Drake's stomach.

"Why are you putting me in here with them?" he asked.

"It won't be for long, Drake. That much I promise you." Justice unbolted the door to an empty room and herded Drake inside. There was a bed, a toilet, and not much more. Justice closed and bolted the door in place. His footfalls receded evenly down the hallway.

"Love to eat them fat boys." There was a laugh that sounded like gravel being poured down a garbage disposal.

Drake sat down on the hard, lumpy bed and closed his eyes. There had to be a way to make all this go away.

Zane waited in the television lounge, mimicking the color and wood-grain pattern on one of the tables. The same table where Pham tossed his key ring when he watched TV. He didn't notice when his keys disappeared.

*Good work, Zane! I'm proud of you,* said Niobe. *Okay, you two, it's your turn.*

They had until the end of Pham's break, a little under half an hour. Niobe headed for Q Sector. She stifled the urge to run. Hurrying would arouse suspicion.

Meanwhile, Zoë and Zenobia crept toward the central guard station. Zoë hid around the corner while her wraith-sister drifted down the corridor to take a position under the console. She studied the controls until she found the switch that unlocked Drake's cell.

*Ready, Mom?*

*Ready, kiddo.*

Zenobia flipped the switch. *K-chunk.* A four-inch steel bolt slammed into the solenoid situated on the outside of Drake's door.

Niobe tiptoed inside. "Psst, Drake," she whispered. "It's me, Niobe." She nudged his shoulder. "Wake up."

"Go 'way. Sleeping."

"It's Niobe. Please, get up. It's important."

A heavy sigh. "Fine."

Drake sat up, a sad and pudgy figure in his underwear. His hair was pressed flat on one side and sticking straight up on the other.

She licked her thumb and wiped little crumbs of sleep from his eyes. He pulled away. "What?"

"Get dressed, kiddo. We're leaving."

His eyes opened a little wider. "What?"

Niobe opened the bag she carried and yanked out shirts, pants, socks, and underwear. "Do you like it here?"

"No."

"Well, you're gonna like it here even less when you find out what they have in store for you." She handed him the bundle of clothes, then looked away while he changed. "They're gonna hurt you, Drake."

"Done."

"Here," she said, pulling a handful of cotton balls from her pocket. "Shove these in your ears."

Drake looked at her. "Are you nuts?"

"Trust me." She winked.

"Why should I?"

"Please? Just take them."

She held her hand out to him. Slowly, reluctantly, he took the cotton, but he didn't put it in his ears.

"What now?"

"Now we wait."

Now it was up to Zane. Pham's key ring would unlock the elevator, but Zane had to get there first. There was a limit to how quickly he could shift his coloring. He could make other things invisible, but not himself.

Niobe watched through his eyes as he snuck through the complex. Twice he had to stop in plain sight while orderlies and security techs made their rounds.

Ten minutes until the end of Pham's break. Five.

The elevator doors came into sight at the end of a long corridor. Close enough for government work.

"Get ready, Drake."

*Zen, now.*

Zenobia, still hunched under the central guard station, reached through the console with ghost fingers to flip a row of bright red toggle switches.

*Click, click, click-click-click-click.*

Cell doors started to open throughout the medium- and high-security wings of the facility.

"What the—" The security tech immediately slammed the switches back. Zenobia reflipped them from her vantage inside the console, and then trashed the wiring.

"Shit, shit, shit." The tech punched the alarm panel, drew his fléchette pistol, then bolted down the corridor.

Warbling sirens sounded throughout the facility at ear-shattering volume. Drake fumbled the cotton into his ears. "Happy now?" he shouted.

Niobe filled her own ears as best she could. It helped, but not much. But the cotton wasn't intended for cutting down on the alarm noise.

As soon as the security tech left, Zoë joined her sister at the console. Niobe watched the monitors through her daughters' eyes. Just as Zoë had predicted, the guards stationed outside the exit up top hurried down to help contain the escapees. Meaning they helpfully brought the elevator down for Drake and Niobe.

The corridors throughout the complex echoed with screams and gunfire. The corridors between Drake's cell in Q Sector and the elevator, however, were empty.

Niobe squeezed Drake's hand. It trembled. "Time to go, kiddo. Ready?"

"I guess so." He nodded, though he looked scared.

"Stay close. Follow me."

They slipped out of Drake's cell. As they scooted down the corridor, a voice echoed from the far end of the wing.

"Chomp they tail, chomp they kiddies . . ."

*Oh, no,* said Zenobia. *Mom, I think I opened some of the other cells by accident.*

Flames erupted out of another cell. The heat was so intense that liquid salt dripped from the ceiling.

"Run!" Niobe took off at a dead run, but Drake couldn't keep up. Soon he fell behind, hunched over and panting. Niobe grabbed his hand and dragged him away from the burning salt caverns. The floor was slick with gallons of spilled glycerin.

"Outta my way, kike!" The Racist blurred past. The wind bowled them over, fanning the flames higher. Niobe shoved Drake toward the exit from Q Sector. Shouting and gunfire echoed through the facility.

*Zoë! You know what to do, honey.*

Zoë reset the alarm panel. The sirens stopped. She pressed the "general call" button on the PA system. "I'd like to dedicate this first number to my mother."

Zoë, it turned out, had a lovely singing voice. It echoed throughout the complex both by virtue of electronic amplification and her own deuce. Security techs and inmates forgot what they were doing. After a few verses they started wandering aimlessly.

The cotton didn't help much. Staying focused was a chore. Niobe chanted a mantra—*elevator, elevator, elevator*—as she half dragged Drake past scenes that could have been culled from some of the major riots of the 1960s. Her eyes watered, her nose ran freely, and her throat burned; somewhere, the techs had resorted to using tear gas. The HVAC system was circulating it through the complex faster than the filters could cleanse the air.

They hurried past one corridor where a pair of security techs grappled listlessly with an inmate. They had pepper spray and a Taser, but as long as Zoë sang, they couldn't concentrate long enough to use them.

They rounded another corner. Niobe tripped over a body sprawled on the foor. Smitty lay faceup, eyes open, staring at the ceiling. Unblinking. Blood trickled from his eyes and nose.

"Don't look, Drake." Niobe covered his eyes as she pulled him along.

They were halfway across the cafeteria when Christian appeared in the doorway. His lips moved soundlessly, as though he was struggling to form a coherent thought—Zoë's deuce at work again. He gave up, holding out his hand palm out. *Stop*, it said.

"Christian . . ."

Screams echoed from farther up the corridor. Christian frowned, turned, then frantically scrabbled at his holster for his fléchette pistol. Niobe and Drake scrambled backward, away from a surge of heat. Torrents of fire swept down the corridor. They swirled around Christian, and then he was gone.

*Dad . . .*

Niobe concentrated on finding a detour, on getting Drake to the elevator. *Later. I'll think about it later.*

Drake jumped when a section of the cinder blocks next to the gleaming steel elevator doors pulled away from the wall. Niobe tickled her son under the chin.

"I'm so proud of you, Zane."

He nuzzled her hand with his tentacles, using one to push a key into the slot next to the elevator doors. They slid open without a sound.

"Going up." Niobe ushered Drake into the elevator.

*C'mon, kiddos.* She beckoned to Zane, and mentally waved a finger at Zoë and Zenobia. *All aboard.*

Zane climbed her shoulder; Zenobia drifted through the walls toward the elevator; Zoë didn't move.

*I have to stay behind, Mom,* she thought. *Zane and Zen can help you on the road. But the longer I sing, the better your chances of getting away.*

*But—*

Zenobia thought, *You know we're right, Mom.*

Niobe cried. "No . . ."

A tiny frown touched the corners of Drake's mouth as he watched Niobe.

*No! That's not what we agreed on.*

Zane laughed, ripples of marigold orange limned with hints of sorrowful cobalt.

"*We* agreed to this. I love you, Mom." *Mom-mom-mom . . .*

Zenobia rematerialized halfway down the corridor from the elevator. "Almost there, Mom!"

". . . Chomp, chomp, chomp . . ." Sharky turned the corner. ". . . Chew, chew, ch—" He paused when he saw little Zenobia running toward Niobe and Drake in the elevator. "Love to eat them kiddies." His grin was a flash of serrated enamel as he set off at a loping run. "Yes, yes, yes. Fat boys what I love to eat."

"Zen! Run!" Niobe punched the button to close the door, but didn't send the elevator up yet. The doors moved with agonizing slowness. She shielded Drake with her tail. "Drake, get behind me." Sharky reached for Zenobia, but his fingers passed ineffectually through her mist. He swiped at her, hissing and spitting, as she wafted through the doors.

The doors stopped with just an inch between them. Sharky had wedged three claws into the gap. He slid the rest of his long, pallid digits into the space and pried the doors apart. "Bite they fat-boy heads off . . ."

Niobe used her tail to push Drake as far away from Sharky as the tight space allowed. "Stay away from him!"

Sharky stepped inside. The doors closed. The elevator started moving up. He took another step, shoved Niobe aside, and grabbed Drake—whose eyes had begun to glow—by the collar. "Nibble, nibble, nibble on his fat-boy face."

Zane flashed the truest black Niobe had ever seen. Drake disappeared.

"What—" Sharky faltered.

Niobe reached for Drake, managed to get a handful of shirt, and yanked him out of the cannibal's grasp.

Sharky lunged toward the corner where he'd thrown Niobe. But Zenobia leapt onto his back, and the pair dissolved into clouds of mist. The clouds passed harmlessly through Niobe.

Drake reappeared. Niobe shoved him to the opposite corner of the elevator. Zenobia released Sharky. One of his forearms was stuck inside the wall, up to the elbow. He flailed, tugging viciously at his encased limb. It didn't budge.

"Let me go! Let me go, you bitch!" Niobe pulled Drake near the door, out of Sharky's reach.

*Zane, Zoë, Zenobia, I love you more than I can say. You're good kids. And I'm proud to be your mom.*

*We love you, too, Mom.* Somewhere down below, Zoë sang an old Vera Lynn song.

Niobe put an arm around Drake. "I'm gonna look out for you, Drake. I promise." Tears made it sound unconvincing.

The elevator sped up, up, up, until it spat them into a cold, dark desert, big as the world but somehow smaller than her promise.

♥

# Mortality's
# Strong Hand

John Jos. Miller

**RAY REACHED OUT TO** grab the kid, saying, "You're under arrest,"
and Bugsy dissolved like smoke in his hands, green, razor-laced smoke
that stung him a hundred times. He grimaced at the pain and the shrill
whine of the telephone ringing by his bed stand.

*Telephone.* Shit. He'd been dreaming again, this time about that asshole
Hive. How can you arrest a swarm of wasps? Ray opened his eyes and
reached out in the darkness and grabbed the phone. "Yeah."

"Mr. Ray." He hated being called mister, but as Attorney General Rodham
had explained to him numerous times, his status required it. He'd been director of SCARE—the Special Committee for Ace Resources and Endeavors—
for a bewildering half year now. He still wasn't sure it had been a good idea
to take the job, but he hadn't been able to resist President Kennedy's request.

"Yeah."

"Trouble." Finally free of the cobwebs of nightmare, he recognized
Dolan's voice. Dolan was agent in charge of the night shift. Ray knew it
had to be pretty serious to wake him—he squinted at the clock by his
bedside—at 3:00 A.M.

"What."

"There's been an incident at BICC."

Ray hated bureaucrateese, something which didn't endear him to the
agency lifers. "Incident?"

He could hear Dolan swallow. "Yes, sir. A riot. Actually, a riot and
breakout. We're still assembling data—"

"Christ. I'll be right there. Call in everyone. This is going to be a bitch and a half." Ray hung up the phone and sat up in bed. Why did shit like this always happen at 3:00 A.M.? He'd had just three hours of sleep, but it was the first time in two days he'd managed any at all. He was having trouble sleeping and when he did, he dreamed, and the dreams were worse than the sleeplessness. An arm snaked out from the other side of the bed and went around his flat, corded stomach.

"What is it, sugar—hey!"

He flicked on the overhead light and glanced at the girl. She was lean, blond, and naked with one well-tanned arm thrown up over her eyes, blocking the light. Jenny, from the secretarial pool. He'd been sleeping with blondes lately. Especially lean ones, with long legs and small breasts. The one time he'd taken a busty brunette to his bed had been a disaster. He rubbed his face with his hands. *Can't dwell on this shit,* he thought. *Don't have time for it now.*

"Sorry, Jen. Emergency. Got to get down to the office."

She sat up in bed, short blond hair tousled, looking like a sleepy pixie. Ray didn't notice.

"Oh."

"Going to take a quick shower. Call you soon."

"Oh."

Ray went into the bathroom, jumped under the shower for perhaps twenty seconds, and gingerly patted himself dry. His hide was still peppered with angry red marks. They were slow to heal. Maybe he was allergic to that goddamn slacker Hive. He momentarily pictured his hands wrapped around Hive's throat, but that was minor solace to his physical and mental pain. He had more worries now. There seemed an endless supply of them in this job. He dressed quickly in the walk-in closet off the bathroom. Jenny was gone by the time he returned. He took a moment to make the bed, then went out into the Washington night. In a way, he was thankful for the phone call. It saved him from that unpleasant morning awkwardness of shuffling off his latest one-night stand. He didn't need that crap. Lately there was a lot of crap that he didn't need. And some that wasn't, he thought, that maybe he did.

The CIA had Langley, the FBI Quantico. SCARE had a suite of rooms in a Justice Department building on a floor that was partly outsourced to Fish and Game. *Damned lousy budget,* Ray thought.

Lights were already shining in the office windows as he alighted from the taxi. The place was hopping. He signed in at the security desk in the lobby and rode up to the seventh floor, turned right down the corridor (Fish and Game was to the left), and came to a reception area where half a dozen clerks and agents were hustling around pretending they knew what they were doing. Ray suspected they were just trying to get noticed.

At least Juliet Summers, his secretary, was on the ball. She had a pot of coffee ready as Ray strode through reception to Summers's tiny private domain, and his office beyond. Summers, adopted out of Korea as an infant, had parlayed a job as a production assistant on *American Hero* into a SCARE position. A holdover from Callendar's regime, she was efficient, hardworking, and quite reliable. Cute, in a waifish way, only five feet tall and petite all over, with short bobbed hair and dark, intent eyes. She wore expensive business suits and always looked immaculate, even at four in the morning. If she'd been a man Ray would have asked her the name of her tailor. The tattoos flashing over her skin sometimes repelled, sometimes intrigued him. He often wondered what she looked like naked, but that was not an uncommon thought for Ray to have about an attractive woman. He was pretty sure she was hot for him, but he wasn't about to mess around with that. Good secretaries were harder to find than one-night stands. She followed him into his office and closed the door on the chaos behind. Inside, it was quiet and neat, just like Ray liked.

"Talk to me, Ink," he said. She handed him a steaming mug of coffee as he perched on the edge of his desk. Its spotless surface was marred only by a basket with a neatly stacked pile of memoranda that Ray was supposed to have read.

"We're still trying to sort out exactly what happened. The reports from BICC have been confusing. We know there was a riot. Casualties. We know some of the detainees escaped."

"Shit. Names?"

"Sharky. The Racist. Genetrix—"

"She was a trusty," Ray said, outraged.

"Now she's an escapee." Ink paused. Ray sensed more bad news coming. "Drake Thomas."

"Son of a bitch." As SCARE director he'd been privy to the memo on the kid they'd dubbed Little Fat Boy, and he *had* read it. Drake's escape was about the worst news imaginable. Chumps like Sharky and the Racist were small change in the wild card world. Sure, they were murderous thugs, but murderous thugs were a penny a dozen. Kids who caused nuclear explosions were rather more unique. In fact, there was already a signed termination order in case the kid ever did slip his leash. Ray didn't like the thought of taking down kids, but Drake had already accounted for Pyote, Texas. What if he'd let loose in El Paso or, say, a city that someone would actually miss? They had to find him, fast.

Ray rubbed his face, thinking. "Do they know up the chain yet?"

"AG Rodham's waiting for your report."

"Son of a bitch," Ray said again. Knowing his boss, she'd blame him for the fuckup even though he'd been thousands of miles away and it was probably all that asshole Justice's fault. Rodham was a treacherous bitch, and ambitious as hell. To her, AG was just a springboard to a higher position. She hadn't been in favor of Ray's appointment as SCARE director, and Ray knew why. She was jealous of his press, which, of course, was ironic. He'd never in his life sought out the media. It just found him. He couldn't help it if he was colorful. Rodham, on the other hand, lived for publicity. Lusted for it. Probably why she'd never married. She couldn't stand to share the spotlight with anyone, and she'd be very happy to get rid of Ray and replace him with another bland asshole like Callendar.

*Yeah,* he thought, *and what's your excuse?* For a second he didn't know what he was thinking about, and then it hit him. She'd never been far from his mind since she'd left, but thoughts of the Angel intruding on business time were unproductive. Even dangerous. It didn't help that he had no real answer for that son of a bitch in his head asking these stupid questions. *She's gone, asshole,* he told him. *Deal with it. I've got Rodham to deal with.* She'd use this sorry mess as another excuse to chew on his ass. She was already on him to fly to Hollywood to recruit promising contestants from the second season of *American Hero.* Promising. Yeah. He'd seen their dossiers. Buffalo Gal. Eight feet tall, horny, hairy, and humped. Fucking great. Or maybe Professor Polka and his frigging accordion. One bullet in the bellows and the dancing would stop, wouldn't it? Christ. Well, he wasn't inclined to put up with errands like that. Important shit had to be done, and he needed to do it. Trips to Hollywood, endless meetings talking budgets, hiring quotas, mission statements for the twenty-first century, blah, blah, blah. Only one solution to this problem.

Road trip.

Ray looked at Ink, his gaze narrowed. "Whistle me up a Lear. I'm headed for BICC. When Hillary calls tell her I'll report on conditions as I observe them personally."

Ink cleared her throat. "Are you sure that's wise, sir?"

The "sir" irritated him. He didn't like hearing it, especially since most of the time it was insincere blather covering up the speaker's real feelings. He wished he had someone he trusted to discuss problems with. Someone who would tell him the truth. Someone to make up for what he realized was sometimes his own hardheadedness and, let's face it, recklessness. He saw where this train of thought was heading and consciously derailed it. He almost sighed, but stopped. It was all over when you started sighing to yourself.

"Hell, no," Ray said. "But that's what I'm doing. Who's on the EDR?"

That was another thing about this fucking job. He'd been talking in acronyms ever since taking it. Ray watched a Chinese-style dragon fly through a bank of puffy clouds and glide across Ink's left cheek as she leafed through the memoranda in the in-tray, eventually finding the Emergency Duty Roster. "It's a light night," she reported. "Just Crypto and Stuntman."

Ray nodded. Crypto was a longtime SCARE man. He was good at figuring out codes and shit, but not much in a fight. Stuntman was another hire out of that *American Hero* crap. In fact, he'd won the damn thing, but apparently his hoped-for movie career had never developed, so he'd gone into government service. Ray had never worked with him, but had read his file. He was supposed to be pretty much indestructible. That was something, at least.

"All right," he said. "Crypto can stay home and work his crossword puzzles. Tell Stuntman to meet me at the airport." Ray's face was looking fairly normal, though his smile was still crooked. It was almost endearing. "What can I bring you back from New Mexico?" he asked. "How about a piñata?"

Ray had known Jamal Norwood, aka Stuntman, for only an hour, and hated him already. He was a young, good-looking African-American with fairly light skin and more Euro than Afro features. Ray approved of his clothing sense, though his suit was a little too flashy and expensive for so young an agent. It was his attitude Ray couldn't stand.

"I'm Billy Ray," he'd said, strapping down next to him as the Lear was prepped for takeoff.

"Yeah," Norwood replied, unimpressed. "Heard all about you. They call me Stuntman, but I've given up that shit. No future in it. Doubling for Denzel and Will Smith and low-life ghetto rap stars making the real money while my ass—"

"I thought you were a millionaire. Didn't you get that much for winning that crappy show?"

"Un-uh, Carny. After taxes and agent's fees there was barely five hundred thousand left."

"Carny?" Ray asked.

"What?" Norwood looked at him. "That's what they call you."

"My code name is Carnifex."

Norwood shrugged. "Not what I heard. Everyone calls you Carnivore."

Ray looked at him blankly, finally understanding a little of what Nephi Callendar had gone through all those years. Norwood fiddled with his iPod, and fell asleep a minute after takeoff. And he snored. Loudly.

Ray stared stonily ahead as the Lear flashed west, wanting to sleep but unable. It seemed like forever, but took only a couple of hours. Norwood woke up after they'd touched down at the private landing strip outside the Biological Isolation and Containment Center, located in the middle of nowhere in the southeast corner of New Mexico, within stone-throwing distance of the Texas border, if you could throw stones pretty far. A jeep was waiting for them with a security tech wearing BICC insignia and the Haliburton company patch. *Justice doesn't even have the guts to show up himself,* an unhappy Ray thought, getting unhappier.

Stuntman wasn't happy, either, as he surveyed the mostly flat, mostly empty desert. He was already perspiring in the morning heat. "Any place to get breakfast around here?"

"Just the BICC cafeteria, sir," the tech said.

"Swell," Norwood grumbled. "Nothing like government-contract food."

Ray was hungry, too, but he wasn't going to bellyache about it even if Stuntman was right. They climbed into the jeep and the driver sped off down an obviously recent asphalt road that led from the airstrip to the containment center. BICC consisted of a very large, very ugly, very angular concrete building set in the middle of nowhere, surrounded by a gaggle of outbuildings that looked like a motor pool, storage facilities, and barracks. These buildings were enclosed by a razor-wire fence with a central guard station manned by more Haliburton cannon fodder. As they were waved through Ray looked down the fence line to where the chain link and razor wire had been smashed outward as if by an invisible avalanche.

Norwood noticed it as well, and looked at Ray with raised eyebrows. "You're not dealing with fake bank robbers now," Ray said pointedly.

"Bring 'em on," Stuntman said. His grin was almost convincing.

The Haliburton stooge accompanied them into the main building. At least it was cool inside, compared to the killing desert heat. They took an elevator down a half-dozen levels, Stuntman staring at the bloodstains that still discolored the elevator's walls and floor. For once the newcomer kept silent, and Ray didn't feel the need to prod him.

The guide escorted them down a hallway with industrial-quality carpet that probably cost the taxpayer a C-note a square yard. He knocked once on the door at the end of the corridor, saluted sloppily, and slouched off.

"You know," Ray said to Stuntman, "he probably makes six or seven times more a year than you do."

"Yeah," Norwood said, "but that uniform he has to wear just sucks."

*Good one,* Ray thought, and then a voice called, "Enter."

The corridor leading to the director's office had been furnished in mid-twentieth century industrial, but inside was a different story. Ray pursed his lips. The decor here was a lot more luxurious than in his own office. He made a mental note to ream out whoever had let the decorator run amuck.

"Ah." Pendergast, the BICC director, was sitting in an expensive ergonomic chair that matched his teakwood desk. On the other side of the desk Justice occupied an equally comfortable-looking chair flanked by two straight-backed wooden ones. "Mr. Ray. Good of you to come—"

"Yeah, good of me to do my job," Ray said without inflection. He looked at the young, slim, handsome Hispanic agent sitting in the comfortable chair. The last young, slim, handsome, Hispanic agent he'd had to deal with had turned out to be a fucking traitor and Ray had gutted him with a glass shard. Ray hated to generalize, but he also hated to be reminded of bad experiences. If it hadn't been for the Angel, he would've cashed in a couple of times during that particular dance. She . . .

He gritted his teeth. "Hello, Justice. Hell of a mess you've got here."

"Yes, sir," the SCARE agent said sulkily. His handsome features were marred by a lumpy purple and yellow bruise on the right side of his jaw. Probably why he was so pissy. "It—"

He stopped, realizing that Ray was frowning at him, and rose quickly to his feet, flushing. He stepped aside clumsily and Ray took his seat. Ray nodded at Stuntman, who took the chair to his left, while Justice sank down into the chair on his right.

"Right," Ray said. "Agent Norwood"—he nodded at Stuntman—"Dr. Pendergast, BICC director. Agent Echeverria, head of BICC security. Now that we're all comfy and we all know each other, suppose you tell me what the hell happened here."

Pendergast and Justice looked at each other, and Justice started to explain the sequence of events as they'd been reconstructed. It took a few minutes to tell the whole story.

"So," Ray said when he'd finished, "let me get this straight. You're head of security with a hundred agents under you. Granted, most are contractors, but still—you couldn't stop a little fat kid and an ace whose power is getting pregnant from engineering a breakout out of a multibillion-dollar facility with a high-tech security system? Is that about right?"

Stuntman broke the silence with a snicker.

Justice reddened again. "Their breakout was well planned—and they had help."

Ray looked thoughtful. "Oh, that's right. Genetrix had her three kids. How old were they? Three days? Four?"

Stuntman's snicker threatened to turn into a guffaw.

"Let me see her cell," Ray said.

"Why—," Pendergast began.

"Because I want to," he said, interrupting.

Pendergast sighed, then stood. "All right. This way."

"She had more help than her current brood, sir," Justice said as they walked down the depressingly appointed corridor to an even more depressingly appointed room block that still showed signs of the recent ferocious struggle. "There were twenty-seven escapees, including nine from the high-security wing. We recaptured most before they got half a mile away—"

"Casualties?" Ray asked.

"Four dead. Two security techs. One orderly. One patient."

"Who's still on the loose?" Ray looked at Pendergast.

"Well," the director said, "as you said, Drake and Genetrix. And also Sharky, Deadhead, the Racist, Covert, the Whisperer, and the Atomic Mummy."

Ray nodded, looking grimmer at each name mentioned.

"Here we are."

They stopped before one room in a row of rooms. Ray looked inside. Cheery. The only personal touch was the dozens of portraits of kids set on wall shelves. Some looked normal. Some looked like nightmares. Most were somewhere in between. Frowning, Ray stepped inside the tiny room and picked up a framed autographed photo. Actually, it was two photos, side by side in a frame. In one the subject was model slim and beautiful. In the other she'd ballooned to elephant size. Ray got out his cell and hit the speed dial.

"Ink," he said. "Oh, fine. Just great. Listen, get ahold of that fat chick from *American Hero*. The one that's on the Committee. Tell her that her number-one fan has just escaped from a federal detention center and is traveling with an extremely dangerous killer ace. If Bubbles hears from her, we need to know about it, at once. Right. See you." He turned off his phone, and looked thoughtful. "Whatever happened to Genetrix's last generation of kids?"

Pendergast hesitated a moment. "Deceased," he finally said. "Old age—"

"Old age, hell," Justice broke in. "Two escaped with her. I told you the one we captured wouldn't stand up to the grilling you put her through—"

"We *had* to find Drake quickly—," Pendergast interrupted.

"And did you?" Ray asked.

"No," Pendergast said quietly.

"Interesting," Ray said. "Not only are you incompetent fuckwits. You're also sadistic incompetent fuckwits." He turned to Justice. "I want your report on these interrogations ASAP."

"Yes, sir," Justice said stonily.

Life flared on Pendergast's face with a furious blush. "No one talks to me like that!"

"I'm not no one," Ray said conversationally. "I'm Billy Ray. I was spilling my blood in service before you tortured your first rat in Psych 101. I've encountered plenty of assholes like you over the years, Doc. Let me clue you in. Chumps like you are tolerated as long as you deliver the goods. When you fuck up, the politicians higher up the food chain will throw you to the wolves to cover their asses and find another white coat to run the rats through their mazes. Count on it. I don't know what kind of snake pit you're running here, but this breakout was engineered by desperate people. How'd Genetrix get so desperate, Doc?"

Pendergast's face had taken on the hue of someone who'd bitten into bad sushi. He was about to reply, but was interrupted when his cell phone tootled. He grabbed it, held it up to his ear. "Yes," he said, and as he listened his face became even queasier. He hung up.

"What?" Ray asked.

"Four dead state troopers have been found on Interstate 70 outside Alamogordo. They were pretty badly mangled. One seemed partially eaten."

"Sharky," Justice said quietly as Norwood grimaced in disgust.

Ray nodded. "Sounds like a clue to me. Where, exactly?"

"I've got the map reference," Pendergast said, noting some figures down on a notepad, which he handed to Ray. Ray accepted the pad with one hand while hitting his cell phone's speed dial with the other. He knew that they needed to run this down fast and he knew who to contact for help. Lady Black was in charge of the team securing the blast site down in Texas, and she had a bunch of aces with her.

"Ray," he said.

"Yes, Mr. Ray."

"Since when have I been 'Mr. Ray' to you, Joann?" he asked.

"Since you got to be the Man, Mr. Ray."

"Let's have this pissing contest later," Ray said. "I'm at BICC right now, but we're headed for Alamogordo. We're going to need Moon. Can you spare her, and someone to bring her?"

"Are you asking or ordering? Sir?"

Restraining himself, Ray answered, "Asking."

There was a short silence. "I suppose."

"Fine," he said. "Thanks."

"You're welcome. Sir."

Ray broke contact, suppressing a sigh. More shit to clean up. He never thought that he'd piss off an old comrade like Lady Black. They'd both been in SCARE a long time, and she'd wanted the directorate herself. Truth was, Ray knew she'd be a better director than him, but he wasn't in human resources. It wasn't his job to make everyone happy. Suddenly, he looked at Pendergast and smiled.

"Pack your knapsack and slip into your Birkenstocks, Doc. We're going to Alamogordo." He turned to Justice. "Get in touch with local and state law enforcement. Give them descriptions of all escapees, but tell them they're not to approach if they're spotted. We don't need any more half-eaten state troopers. Just relay any info about sightings to us." Ray looked back at Pendergast as the director made a sputtering kind of noise. "Something wrong, Doc?"

"Why do I have to accompany you?" Pendergast asked indignantly. "I'm not a field agent."

"No," Ray said with faux patience, "but you are the foremost authority on the escapees."

"Yes," Pendergast admitted reluctantly.

"I'm going to need that expertise, Doc." He stood quickly and stretched. Action was right down the road. He could smell it. "You got fifteen minutes to get ready."

Pendergast stared at him.

"You've just wasted five seconds."

Pendergast turned, muttering.

"I sure hope there's someplace in Alamogordo where we can get breakfast," Stuntman said.

Alamogordo, a town of thirty-five thousand about fifty miles from the Texas border, was noted for two things. The first, its proximity to White Sands Missile Range, had led to its Museum of Space History. The second, its proximity to Holloman Air Force Base, had led to a string of water bed motels on its main drag, as well as the town's ubiquitous wild card theme.

"I don't get it," Stuntman said through a mouthful of honey-fruit-and-nut pancakes. It was afternoon and they'd stopped at the first roadside diner they'd seen outside Alamogordo, the Interplanetary House of Pancakes. It had a billboard flying saucer on its roof being smothered by a deluge of maple syrup from a large upended bottle. Inside, it was unrelentingly cheerful with a shiny chrome ambience and a decor that a modern, cutting-edge bistro would kill for. And it smelled like pancakes and waffles. Unsurprisingly, the three of them had ordered breakfast. "What's with all this space stuff in the middle of cowboy country?"

Ray shrugged. "You can't blame the locals. Much. They're stuck here in the middle of Nowhere, New Mexico, hemmed in by desert on one side and missile range on the other. They can't *all* work for the government. They have to make a buck somehow, so they latched on to Tachyon's landing here back in nineteen forty-five."

"Nineteen forty-six," Pendergast said around a mouthful of omelet.

"Right." Ray stared him into silence. "Forty-six. Even if they have to dress up as Tachyon imitators and perform quickie marriages, there's worse ways to make a living."

"I guess," Stuntman said. "So that explains the tacky gift shops, the T-shirt emporiums, the Famous Alamogordo Joker Dime Museum, Dr. Tacky's No-Tell Motel and Wedding Chapel, not to mention the tours to two competing Tachyon landing sites—"

"Which," Pendergast pointed out pedantically, "are both nothing more than obvious tourist traps, since Tachyon landed on the base . . ." He ran down to silence as Ray and Norwood both stared at him. "Excuse me," he added, after a moment, "I have to go to the boys' room."

He got up and slid out of the booth. Stuntman polished off his sausages and held up his coffee mug as the waitress went by with the pot.

"Here you go, hon," she said, filling up his cup. Ray waved her off. His kidneys were already floating, and he didn't know how much longer they'd have to wait until Moon showed up with her handler, as Ray had texted them to meet at the diner. The waitress turned, paused, stared. "Oh, hon—you can't bring your dog in here."

"She's not a dog," the Midnight Angel said. "She's a government agent."

Ray looked over the back of the booth and their eyes met and something passed between them. Ray didn't know what it was, but he guessed that it wasn't good. For a moment he swore quietly to himself. Lady Black knew that he and the Angel were on the outs. She could have sent someone else to shepherd Moon. But part of him was glad that she hadn't.

The Midnight Angel was taller than Ray's near six feet, and roundly, richly curved. She wore a black leather jumpsuit that was tight as the skin on the now-forgotten sausages on Ray's plate. Her long, dark, thick hair was bound in a braid that fell nearly to her waist and, as usual, a number of escaped strands gave her a tousled look, as if she'd just gotten out of bed.

The waitress looked uncertain. "Couldn't you at least put it on a leash?"

Moon, who currently looked like a German shepherd, growled at her as the Angel said, "We're both with the government, ma'am."

"Well, I guess that's all right, then," the waitress said.

Stuntman turned in the booth to look over his shoulder, and dropped his fork. "Holy mother," he said in a voice that almost didn't carry to the approaching SCARE agents. "Is that the Midnight Angel I been hearing about?"

Ray nodded.

"And you broke up with her? Are you crazy, Carny?"

Ray nodded twice more. Stuntman wasn't exactly right—*he* hadn't broken up with *her*—but Ray wasn't going to open that can of worms again. Not now. He stood, slid out of the booth. "Agent Norwood," he said, on his best behavior, "agents Angel and Moon."

Moon wagged her tail as Stuntman murmured hello, essentially ignoring the caniform.

"Care to join us?" Ray smiled winningly. "I know you have a hearty appetite."

The Angel smiled back. Stuntman snorted coffee. Ray felt his pulse accelerate as if Butcher Dagon had just turned into his fighting form right in front of him.

"Thanks, Billy." Her voice had a Southern accent that felt like honey on Ray's ears. She looked around. "Your booth's too small for all of us. Moon, why don't you join Billy. I'll sit here," she said, indicating the two-seater across the aisle.

"I like the way she moves," Stuntman said in a low voice as she slipped into the booth.

*You don't know the half of it,* Ray thought. He looked at Moon, who jumped up on the bench next to him. The waitress, still dubious, nevertheless took their orders. The Angel got the He-Man Breakfast with a side of biscuits and gravy, and she ordered a steak, rare, for Moon.

They sat in silence for a long moment that Ray felt was unusually tense. It surprised him to feel this way. He wasn't usually sensitive to nuance, but everything, it seemed, had changed since the Angel had come into his life. He groped for something to say.

"So, how's things at Pyote?"

"Still devastated," the Angel said.

Ray nodded. He was becoming familiar with the feeling. He glanced at

Norwood, who had a wincing, almost sympathetic expression. Stuntman started to say something, saw the look on Ray's face, and thought better about it. Moon wagged her tail tentatively, while the Angel sipped delicately at the large glass of iced tea that the waitress had already brought.

Fortunately Ray's cell phone buzzed. He reached for it in obvious relief. "Yeah."

"Director Ray."

He knew that voice. "AG Rodham."

"What are you doing in New Mexico, Director Ray?"

*Sitting on my ass in a diner outside Alamogordo watching my eggs and sausage go cold and Stuntman drool over my girl,* he thought. He got as far as "sitting on my—" before he thought better of it. "Uh, that is, sitting in conference with my agents while mapping out a strategy to contain the danger posed by the escapees who are in imminent threat of recapture. Ma'am."

There was a longish silence, then the voice said, "Imminent?"

"Yes, ma'am."

"They had better be."

"Yes, ma'am." He gritted his teeth.

"Since you're two-thirds of the way there, I'd like you to take that trip to Hollywood we've discussed and interview some of the new *American Hero* contestants."

Ray gritted his teeth harder. "Yeah. I've heard great things about the Kozmic Kowboy and the Jackalope."

His phone went dead. He felt Angel's eyes on him, and looked at her.

"Good news?" she asked.

Ray was saved the embarrassment of answering as the food arrived. The waitress put several platters before the Angel, and then slid a barely singed steak in front of Moon. Her tail thumped more certainly.

"Oh, Billy?" the Angel asked.

"Yeah?"

"Can you cut Moon's steak up for her? She can't manage a knife and fork with her paws."

"Sure." Ray savagely slashed at the steak for the smiling dog. He felt . . . he felt . . . he didn't know how he felt. Except that he wanted to hit something. Really hard. That reminded him. Where the hell was Pendergast?

"Where the hell," he asked Stuntman, "is Pendergast?"

The agent shrugged. "I don't know. Maybe his zipper got stuck." He sighed, looking put upon. "Want me to go check on him?"

Ray glanced over at the Angel, who was unconcernedly tucking into her food. She could eat, he thought, like no one else he knew. She needed the food to fuel the metabolism of her fierce and hungry body. He used to love to watch her eat, especially in bed after a long bout of lovemaking. There was something satisfying in watching her quell her appetites. Something vital and vibrant, like watching a cheetah run.

But now, seeing her, it made him feel, what? Lonely? *Christ.* "No," he said. "I'll do it."

Muttering, he got to his feet. He thought he saw the Angel glance at him as he went down the aisle between booths, but he wasn't sure. *What am I,* he thought, *back in middle school? No, because I wasn't this bad, even then.*

He went out the diner's front door and circled back through the parking lot, which was the only way to reach the restrooms at the rear of the building.

*So I didn't want to get married,* he thought, still able to work up anger at the nature of the Angel's grievance. *Was that so bad? Why ruin a good thing? Hell, it was a great thing.* He stopped at the door to the "Spaceman's Room." There was a thumping sound inside. "Pendergast," he called out, "you still in there?" *Why take a chance at messing it up? Who cares what a priest or judge says?* "Pendergast? You all right?"

Muttering to himself, Ray pushed open the restroom door. Even he was stunned by the sight of blood everywhere, splattered on the floor, geysered onto the ceiling, still running down the metal divider that had once separated the stall from the rest of the room and was now torn from its wall brackets and crumpled as if it had been struck by a giant fist.

Pendergast himself was crammed into the urinal, sitting in it as if it were an uncomfortably small throne. At least what was left of him was. He was covered with blood and missing chunks of his neck, chest, abdomen, and his entire right arm. Sharky, standing in a pool of blood that had drained from Pendergast's body, was gnawing on it. Pendergast's eyes were glazed and only mildly annoyed. In a flash of horrified insight Ray realized that the BICC director never knew what had hit him.

"Yum, yum," Sharky crooned as he ripped meat off Pendergast's flabby arm and wolfed it down. "Nice and fat, yum, nice and fat. Sweet meat."

They stared at each other for a long, long moment. Sharky's predator eyes gleamed with sudden glee. "Yum," he said, "more meat," and he dropped Pendergast's arm and leapt at Ray.

Ray slammed the door in the creature's face, but Sharky came right through it, smashing it and tearing it off its hinges. Ray automatically ducked the flying fragments, but he couldn't avoid Sharky's grasp. *He's missing his right hand,* Ray had time to think. It looked like it had been removed by a dull knife or determined teeth. And then Sharky engulfed him.

He hit Ray like a sumo wrestler and bore him down. Ray twisted. He almost pulled free from Sharky's one-handed grasp, then the cannibal fastened on with his immense jaws. Ray screamed with pain. Sharky gnawed where Ray's neck met his shoulder. He might have had him for good if he hadn't torn off a chunk of flesh and bolted it down, quickly making a face and saying, "Ugh, stringy!"

Ray screamed again, in anger this time. "You fucking son of a bitch freak!"

He felt muscles rip and blood spatter. He hoped Sharky hadn't hit the jugular, or he was a dead man. He swung a fist, but only skinned his knuckles on Sharky's tough, pebbly hide. Without wasting a moment he jammed his knee up between Sharky's legs, and Sharky's eyes crossed at the sudden impact and he blew a fetid stream of breath on Ray's face, splattering him with a mist of his own blood and spatters of his own flesh.

Sharky rolled off, grabbing his crotch and panting too hard to moan. Ray staggered to his feet, clamping his right hand to his neck. It was instantaneously drenched with blood. "Good thing he has gonads," Ray muttered, moving in on the groaning Sharky.

Ray heard the sound of feet on gravel, approaching fast. Very fast. He turned to see a blur descend upon him, then something bit deep into the back of his right leg at the knee. Tendons severed, and he fell. The blur braked to a stop in a flurry of dust and pebbles. Looking at him and smiling was a lean, tallish man wearing a dirty, sweat-soaked BICC jumpsuit. The torn-off sleeves exposed lithely muscled, crudely tattooed arms. He had cold, hard eyes, and close-cropped hair, and was carrying an open clasp knife with a bloody eight-inch blade.

"Racist," Ray muttered to himself. He tried to get up, but his leg wouldn't work.

"Best stay down, boy," the Racist said, "I cut you good. Hamstrung you like a deer."

Sharky lurched to his feet. "Gonna eat your head, little man. Gonna snap it off your neck and suck the meat off your skull."

He opened his maw. It looked big enough to do the job. Ray lurched upright, his weight on his left leg, ready to do something, anything, so he wouldn't die on his back in the parking lot of the Interplanetary House of Pancakes outside of goddamn Alamogordo, New Mexico.

From between the parked cars Moon flew by, growling. She hurled herself at Sharky, taking him low in the legs, cutting them out from under him. He went down in the dust again, Moon snapping at his hand and head like a wild beast. He windmilled his arms furiously and one caught Moon like a club across her ribs, hurling her to lie panting at Ray's feet. She was up instantaneously in a guard position before him.

"Well, what we got here?" the Racist drawled as Sharky shook his head and mumblingly dragged himself to his feet again. "A cunt and a nigger. You government boys sure are getting pussified, hiding behind women and mud-men."

Ray was afraid to turn his neck to look. He could still feel the blood pumping from it, and more running down his leg.

"Oh, Billy," a familiar voice said. "Get down before you bleed out."

He *was* feeling a little woozy. He sat down on the gravel parking lot, barely able to focus on her. *At least,* he thought, *she looks concerned.*

"Hey," he protested, "stop ripping up my suit."

"Quiet." The fabric tore like paper towels in the Angel's strong fingers. She pressed a wad of cloth into the hole in Ray's neck and shoulder.

"That was Italian," Ray mumbled.

"Now it's rags," she said. "Moon. Hold this in place."

Moon shimmered and shrunk in size. Now a fox, she pressed her warm little body against Ray's neck, holding the rough bandage against his wound. It soaked through instantly. The Angel stood up. Ray didn't like the look on her face. Actually, he realized, he did.

"Norwood," she said in a hard, steady voice, "you take the Racist. Watch him. He's fast. I got the cannibal."

The Racist smiled. "You get the pussy meat, Sharky. I get the dark meat. Let's take 'em." He started to run. *Away* from them.

"What the hell?" Stuntman said.

Ray wanted to warn him, but he was having difficulty speaking. He was dazed. A little confused. A little cold. The only warm thing was the fox curled up against his neck, licking his face and yipping softly at him. He should be on his feet, but he couldn't seem to rise.

Sharky lumbered toward the Angel. She just stood there. He wanted to warn her, too. He wanted to call her name. To tell her that he loved her. He wanted to beg her to come back to him. But his tongue and mouth couldn't work.

Sharky reached her, slobbering, "Nice meat, soft, rich, *nice* meat," and Ray wanted to say, "Get your frigging sword," but he could only think it. She stood her ground, and pivoted away from the joker's embrace, her hands low and clenched together, and she bought them up and around and slammed them in the middle of Sharky's stomach and lifted him up off his feet and tossed him a good dozen yards away onto the surface of the parking lot.

"That *hurt*," Sharky said like an outraged child, and the Angel said, "Save my soul from evil, Lord, and heal this warrior's heart," and her flaming sword appeared in her ready hands.

Ray managed to croak, "Look out," and the Racist descended on Stuntman like a tornado, full speed, total impact. They bounced apart. The Racist skittered backward, but somehow maintained his balance. Norwood slammed into a parked car, crushing in the door panel and setting off the alarm. He bounced back and fell face-first on the gravel, then scrabbled to his knees. The Racist looked at the knife in his hand. The blade had snapped off. There was no blood on the metal stump protruding from the hilt.

"Goddamn. You made out of rubber, boy?" he asked Norwood.

The Midnight Angel stalked toward Sharky, who had gotten up and was shaking his head, smiling, his rows of teeth gleaming in the sunshine. Flaming wings sprouted from the back of her shoulders. *That's new,* Ray thought groggily.

"Eat your titties like candy," Sharky said, and the Angel cut him. His left arm came off. Blood showered like a fountain. Ray, watching, grinned.

"Ow," Sharky said, and she cut him again. This time, his head came off. Sharky took a lumbering step toward her, and then he fell, blood pumping with each beat of his slowing heart.

"Shit," the Racist said, as the Angel turned to him.

A car screeched toward them from the back of the lot, the driver shouting, "Get in, get in."

He braked, showering the Racist with pebbles and dust, and the ace flung the passenger side door open. He started to climb in, turned, and looked at Norwood, who was coming at him with a hard look on his face. "We got business to finish, boy," he said, and slammed the door just as Norwood reached for him, and the car fishtailed out of the lot.

The Angel moved her hands apart and her sword and wings disappeared. She went to Ray and knelt down by him. "Hang on. We'll get you to the hospital—"

Ray reached out and grabbed the front of her jumpsuit and pulled her face close to his.

"Tell the doctor," he said, making a supreme effort, "to stitch the tendons. Staple the goddamn things together if he has to—"

"Billy—"

"*Tell him!*"

"All right. Yes."

He lay back a little, grinning woozily. "Anybody get the license plate of that car?"

Moon, still pressing against his neck, made a little yip of affirmation.

"Good job," Ray said, and closed his eyes.

His cell phone rang.

He opened his eyes. "Somebody get that," he said, and closed them again.

Ray felt a strong hand clutching him with the relentless strength of a giant, and he knew that no matter how hard he fought, he would never break free. *If I'm going down,* he thought, *I might as well go down with my eyes open.* With a supreme effort of will he pried his eyelids apart and blinked, though the light was dim and the air was cool. He realized that the Angel was bending over him in her dusty leathers. He was lying in bed in a small, antiseptic room, with tubes in his left arm and various electronic monitors stuck up on shelves all around him. He realized that he was in a hospital. He should have. He'd been in plenty during the course of his career.

"Hi," he said, surprised at the croaking sound that was his voice.

"Hi yourself."

Ray blinked. "What the hell happened?" The words came out in a husky whisper. He felt kind of hollow. Drained.

The Angel shrugged. "After you passed out I got you into the rental and drove to the hospital at Holloman as quickly as I could."

Ray was glad that he'd been unconscious during that drive. "And Moon and Stuntman?"

"On the trail of the Racist and his accomplice who was driving the hot-wired car. Another one of the escapees named Deadhead."

Ray nodded, satisfied. "Good. And did you give my message to the doctors?" He lifted his head and looked down his body. His neck hurt like a son of a bitch and his numb left leg felt like dead weight and was swathed in bandages, like a mummy leg. On the plus side, the wasp stings had stopped itching.

The Angel pursed her full, so attractive lips. "Yes, but—"

"But, nothing." Ray tried to sit up, but the Angel put a hand out on his chest.

"Billy, you have to rest and heal. You almost bled out. The doctors here aren't too familiar with ace metabolism. They had your medical records e-mailed—well, not all of them." She shook her head. "They fill seven complete CDs. They say your healing factor is slowing down. Your body can still repair itself, but not like it used to. You were very lucky this time."

For one moment his temper surged and he felt like shoving her aside and leaping up out of the bed. But he paused. Though they'd never actually tested it, in the best of times her strength was equal to his own. Maybe, as much as he hated to admit it, even greater. And this was not the best of times. He was weak. He felt tired.

Ray stared into space. "You're not telling me something I haven't realized. It's all catching up to me. I don't know how much I have left."

"Oh, Billy," Angel said, "you've got plenty—you're like a force of nature. Unstoppable. Fearless—"

"No. I can feel it in my bones." Ray took a deep breath. This was hard. "And you were the only fear I couldn't beat."

Her eyes went wide. "Me?"

"I was afraid of needing you," he said. "I'd never known anything like you. You became part of me so fast. But these past few months I've faced an even greater fear. A fear of never being with you again. Never sleeping, never waking, never eating, drinking, screwing, laughing, sharing the everyday stuff with you. Jesus Christ, Angel, *someone's* got to tell me what to do about Hillary Rodham. *Someone's* got to help me get through the crazy shit I call my life. God knows, you don't deserve to be stuck with the job, but only you can do it. I can't make myself whole anymore. Only you can."

" 'You're in my blood like holy wine,' " she said, leaning over and kissing him. The touch of her lips on his was like coming home again. He could feel his heart beat, the blood pound through his veins.

"This marriage thing—"

The Angel shook her head. "I know—"

"No," Ray interrupted. "Listen to me. Is my wallet around here somewhere or did someone steal it?"

"They put your personal effects in the bed stand," she said, leaning over and opening it. She took the wallet out and handed it to Ray. He looked through it, quickly counting the money and credit cards, then found a folded slip of paper, creased and dust-stained after the parking lot fight. He held it out to her.

"What's this?" she asked, taking it from him and unfolding it. Her eyes grew wide as she scanned it. "A marriage license!"

"I took it out a couple of months ago. I've been carrying it around. I just couldn't find a way—"

The Angel practically fell on him. Her hand went behind his head and she pulled his face to hers, and Ray nearly shouted with the sudden pain in his neck. They kissed again, this time with the fierceness he remembered so well. After a long moment, they broke apart, and Ray said, "I take it that's a yes."

"Yes," said the Angel.

"Good," Ray said, smiling freely for the first time in a long time. *Son of a bitch,* he thought. *This might all work out.* He scooted over in the bed, careful of the tubes coming out of the bags pumping antibiotics into his arm. "Come on, babe, join me."

"Billy!" She looked around. It was a private room, but with an open door and a big window on the corridor and nurses' station beyond. "Not here!"

"Nah, not for *that,*" he said. "I just want to feel you next to me again."

Carefully, she climbed up. He put his unencumbered arm around her, feeling foolishly triumphant. He soon fell asleep. Some time later, his cell phone rang. He awoke instantly, feeling refreshed and alert, untroubled by dreams. The Angel, still at his side, reached out and took it off the bedside stand and handed it to him.

"Yeah," he said.

"It's Jamal," a voice said. "We've found them."

Ray looked out of the tacky gift shop across the street from the seedy motel called the Love Lodge, where Moon had tracked the Racist and his companion after they'd abandoned the stolen car in a lot six blocks away. Fortunately, Ray thought, even ace criminals needed to sleep. They thought they'd muddied their trail enough, but they hadn't counted on Moon's hypersensitive sense of smell. They hadn't counted on a lot of things, including Ray's fanatical sense of outrage. And now they were going to pay.

Stuntman sidled up to him in the darkened shop and whispered in his excitement, though there was no way they could hear him in the motel across the street even if it wasn't 3:00 A.M. and they weren't asleep.

"All set," he said, putting a certain amount of grim satisfaction into his whisper.

"The Marines in place?" Ray asked.

Norwood nodded. Ray had requisitioned a platoon of Marines, as well as half a ton of material, from the base and placed them around the back of the motel. No one was going to slip away from this party.

Ray nodded. "All right then. Let's go."

He looked almost normal in his fighting suit, except for the bandage covering most of his neck, and his right leg, abnormally thickened and stiffened by the brace and wrappings that made it possible for him to move slowly and gingerly. The tendons behind his knee, severed little more than twelve hours earlier by the Racist's blade, hadn't totally healed yet. But the doctors had listened to his orders and sewn them together. They were holding precariously. Getting old, he reflected, was a pain in the ass. He set his crutch aside. The Angel took his left arm, and they shuffled forward together. Stuntman stepped in front of him.

"I'm going to get a shot at that loser, right?" he asked.

Ray looked at him. "I won't be up to any fancy dancing for a couple of days. You'd better take a *good* shot at him. Moon and Angel will back you up."

"Yes, sir," Stuntman said happily, almost as if he meant it. He went out through the back of the shop to join Moon in the adjacent alley.

"You sure you want to do this, Billy?" the Angel asked.

"Hell, I'm not dead, yet," he said. "I want to see the look on that shit-head's face when we bust him. And I *really* want to see the look on his face when he tries to run."

The Angel shook her head. "All right."

As they went through the darkened shop Ray stopped before they reached the door, grabbing an object that was dangling from the ceiling. "Hey," Ray said. "Just what I need."

The Angel looked at him, frowning. "What in the world is it?"

"It's a piñata shaped like Tachyon's spaceship," Ray said, putting it on the counter. "I promised my secretary I'd bring her one. Remind me to pick it up later."

The Angel started to say something, thought better of it, and shook her head. They went out into the dark street together, carefully, shuffling silently, Ray's disability only part of the reason for their slow and careful movements. They sidled through the motel's parking lot and came up to the right door.

Ray turned and waved back toward the alley mouth and two black shapes stepped out into the street. The man-sized one was Stuntman. The beast-shaped one was Moon in her most terrifying form, the dire wolf. Her hunched back was almost as high as Norwood's head. Her fangs gleamed in the moonlight.

Ray turned to the Angel. "Take down the door for me, would you?"

"Certainly," she said with a smile, and smote it off its hinges with a single blow. Ray followed it into the room if not as gracefully as usual then with at least the usual fervor. He flicked on the overhead light as he came in shouting, the Angel following him in with her blazing sword clasped in her hands.

"Wakey, wakey, scumbags. Time to go home to the big house."

The Racist and Deadhead were even more unlovely sleeping than during waking hours. The Racist lay on one of the twin beds in the threadbare motel room in his dirty underwear briefs, his lean body covered by crude prison tattoos, his greasy hair exhibiting an extreme case of bed head. He woke first, a snarl on his lips and the look of a trapped weasel on his face. Deadhead slept on, snoring, drooling, and naked. His skin was fish-belly white, his body managed to look flabby and scrawny at the same time, as skin hung off his bones in sagging rolls. He didn't wake until the Angel prodded him with her sword tip, and then slowly, with a snort, a yawn, and a slow lifting of sleep-gummed eyelids. He looked at the Angel blankly, rubbed his crusted eyes, then suddenly came to his senses and screamed, "Don't kill me, don't kill me!"

Ray grinned at the Racist, whose eyes were darting around the room, seeking some manner of escape. "I hope you'll be as reasonable as your partner," Ray told him.

"Fuck you, pig," the Racist said. He rolled out of bed, his legs entangled in the dingy sheet for an instant. Ray could have fallen on him then, but he held himself back. As much as he wanted to pummel the Racist into unconsciousness, he'd promised him to Norwood. He watched the Racist spring to his feet.

*Maybe*, Ray thought to himself, *I am getting old. Or maybe, just a bit more mature.*

He watched the Racist turn, hurtle across the room, and fling himself through the window next to the door.

"That had to hurt," Ray said conversationally as the almost-naked Racist shattered the glass and landed face-first on the sidewalk beyond. He leapt to his feet and immediately fell right down again. Stuntman had already crossed the street and was approaching with a shuffling gate, a growling Moon at his heels, as the Racist struggled to his feet and they again shot out from under him as he tried to run, and he again fell on his ass.

Ray laughed out loud as the Angel and a frightened, yet perplexed Deadhead joined him at the window. It had been hard, Ray reflected, to commandeer nearly every single ball bearing in the base's machine shop, but the look on the Racist's face had been worth all the arguing with requisition clerks and filling out all their goddamn forms. Come to think of it, he'd like to see the look on Rodham's face when she saw the line on the expense account for the half a ton of ball bearings that the Marines had surreptitiously spread around the motel's parking lot while the Racist and Deadhead were sleeping in their cozy little beds.

Stuntman reached him as he was scrabbling to stand again. "Let me help you up," he said, grabbing the Racist's long, greasy hair and lifting.

The Racist howled like a dog and struck Norwood.

"Hit me again," Stuntman said, and slammed him hard in the face.

His blow pushed the Racist back to the ground, and Norwood fell on him, hammering away.

Ray peered out the window, watching, and after a moment said, "I think that's enough."

Norwood let the Racist have one more for good measure in his already bloody mouth and stood over him. "What have you got to say about 'mud-men' now?" he asked.

The Racist lay there and bled.

Ray looked at the Angel. "I guess we can call in the Marines and let them take possession of the prisoners."

The Angel nodded, got out her cell.

"Can I put my clothes on?" Deadhead asked.

"Please do," the Angel said, and made the call.

The escapees were taken into custody with a minimum of pratfalls and no real problems. The Racist was still unconscious when they put the cuffs on him and Deadhead offered no resistance.

"Watch your step," Norwood said, grinning, as a pair of Marines helped the Racist up into the back of the detention van. Looking like he was auditioning for the role of the drunken wife-beater on *Cops,* the Racist just scowled.

Ray put Moon and Stuntman in charge of the prisoners, and they went back to Holloman with the prisoners and Marine guards. After the excitement died down, Ray found himself alone with the Angel. He checked his watch. It was a little short of 4:00 A.M.

"Let's go grab some coffee and a bite to eat."

"Don't you want to call Washington?" the Angel asked.

Ray considered, then shook his head. "No. Let's let sleeping dogs lie. There's no sense in stirring them up when we don't have to."

"What do you want to do?"

Ray pursed his lips. "I'm sure we can find some way to pass the time until the stores open."

"Stores?"

"So we can go ring shopping. There's a wedding chapel where we can get married by a Tachyon impersonator—or," he said, switching gears at the expression on her face, "we can wait until after we run down Little Fat Boy and have a church ceremony anywhere you want. Except Washington."

"Why not Washington?" the Angel asked.

Ray shook his head. "I'm staying away from there as long as I can. Can you imagine all the frigging paperwork I'm going to have to fill out once Rodham knows I'm back?"

♣

# Double Helix

## MAKE NO TREATY WITH THEM AND SHOW THEM NO MERCY

### Melinda M. Snodgrass

**A SANDSTORM IS BLOWING** across Mecca and the wind keens and howls around the corners of the hotel. The building across the street is a phantom shape looming in the dust and the sky is a strange yellow.

I teleported Siraj away as the first helicopters were descending on the Baghdad airport. He is just standing in the center of the room, head bent. His hands are trembling ever so slightly. Memory seizes me.

Of Siraj standing with just this attitude in our rented house in Cambridge. Without Siraj's wealth I would have been living in rooms at my college. It was Siraj's money that had given rise to the situation. *"Your money doesn't give you class. At base you're just another dirty little camel trader."* The final verbal barrage from one of our housemates who we had all agreed had to go.

I know Siraj is my enemy, but I suddenly want to be nineteen again and comfort my friend. His head lifts and he rolls back his shoulders. A man preparing for the fight again. I tense, wondering what order he will give me. He's always been civilized about the struggle. Is that about to change? Who will he send me to kill?

"We intercepted some interesting communications between SCARE and Washington." The tone is almost conversational.

Because of the mild tone I almost miss the import of what I've just heard. He intercepted an encrypted message *and read it.* Siraj isn't a technophobe like the Nur or a man living in the past like Abdul, the Nur's son. He has been building a modern intelligence service and I missed it. Because I'm a holdover from that earlier era—an *Arabian Nights* fantasy, a useful killer and very little else.

Siraj is continuing. "The explosion in Texas for which we were blamed." I give him a look of questioning interest. "It was an ace. A child. A little boy. You will go to America, and find him. Help him."

"Where is he being held?" And I'm terrified that Siraj will actually know, and then how in the hell do I get out of that?

"He escaped custody and the Americans are hunting him to kill him. We will befriend him, and your power combined with his . . ." Siraj smiles, a mirthless grimace that never reaches his eyes. "The West will withdraw from the Caliphate."

I salaam. "I must return home and change into Western dress. I will find him."

I turn and start for the door only to hear him say—

"Onc of you will."

*London, we have . . .*

◆

"*. . . a problem,*" Flint whispers.

We are walking around the base of Nelson's statue in Trafalgar Square. A gusty wind off the Channel is tossing the pigeons back as they try to land on the admiral's bronze head. It holds the promise of fall, and Mecca seems very far away. I'm still in my Bahir form. The effort of changing just to change again seems monumental.

"*Obviously you cannot deliver the boy.*"

"So, do I find him before the Americans, kill him, and tell Siraj so sad, too bad?" I consider. "Or maybe I don't need to be involved at all. Allow Bahir to be spotted a few times in America so the word gets back to Siraj that I'm trying, but let the Americans kill their little problem."

"*Siraj has a point. With your power and the boy . . . well, it would be a potent combination.*"

"So, you want me to find him, but for us."

"*Yes.*"

"I'd like to go home first. Check—"

"*No.*"

♥

# The Tears of Nepthys

## THE SECOND TEAR: ALIYAH

### Kevin Andrew Murphy

JONATHAN HIVE SAT NEXT to her on the plane in his camelhair sport coat, green eyes intent on his laptop. Apart from some guy called the Llama, he'd been the only ace left at the UN. "So," he asked with a reporter's intensity, "why do you want to join the Committee?"

Ellen had already been around the same mulberry bush with Secretary-General Jayewardene. She gestured to her cameo. "You know my power. I've been freelance too long. And I'm sick of hiding." She glanced out the window at the rolling scallop of the Gulf Coast as the plane began its descent. "So John Fortune's still in Africa?"

Jonathan didn't answer, but had probably just nodded. He clattered at his keyboard as Ellen fixed her makeup and adjusted her suit. She wasn't certain what one wore to a hurricane, but Chanel was classic and would have to do. It paid to have Coco's sewing machine.

Of course, there wasn't a hurricane. Not yet. The air in New Orleans was warm and balmy. And sweating on the runway was a study in opposites. With the crisp linen suit and little beard, Holy Roller looked like Colonel Sanders after a ten years' supply of fried chicken. To his right, garbed in a billowing kaftan, stood willowy blond supermodel Michelle Pond.

Who did not seem pleased to see Hive. "Bugsy, you're wanted by the Feds."

Jonathan shouldered his laptop bag over his sport coat. "Do you think they'll have time to arrest a hundred thousand wasps in the middle of a natural disaster?"

"He has a point, my dear." Holy Roller then turned to Ellen with a be-atific smile. "Reverend Thaddeus Wintergreen, ma'am, at your service. And you'd be?"

"Ellen. Or Cameo. Or, well, someone else." Ellen was tired of explana-tions. It was time to let another person do the talking. She took off her jacket and handed it to Jonathan. As she began to unbutton her blouse, Reverend Wintergreen averted his eyes. The Amazing Bubbles merely stared, remarking drily, "That shirt *so* does not go with that skirt."

Aliyah laughed and embraced her. "Bubbles, I'm back!"

Michelle pushed Aliyah away. "Who are you?"

Aliyah turned a pirouette on the tarmac. "I'm Aliyah!"

Bubbles wasn't buying it. "Funny. You don't look a bit like her. Who are you, really? What sort of game are you playing?"

Holy Roller was no longer averting his eyes, now that the threat of overt nakedness had passed. "If this is a prank, it is a cruel one, Jonathan. Aliyah is with the Lord now."

"Maybe," said Jonathan, "but Cameo here is with the Committee. Jayewardene and I already played twenty questions with her in New York. She's an ace. She channels dead people from, uh . . . well, jewelry and stuff. Hats. She's Simoon. Sort of."

The Reverend Thaddeus Wintergreen seemed willing to believe in mir-acles. "Can this be true?" he said cautiously. "The Lord works many won-ders, but even so . . . Aliyah, is it really you, returned to us like some Lady Lazarus? How . . . how are you?"

Aliyah flicked one hand. "Oh, just great. I got to go sailboating with my mom. But it would have been a lot cooler if I, like, hadn't been possessing the body of a forty-year-old woman."

*Thirty-something,* Ellen corrected.

Michelle gave her a cold hard look, then turned back to Jonathan. "I'm sorry, no. This is creeping me out, and . . . oh, crap, here comes Mayor Connick . . ."

A stretch Hummer pulled up. Out stepped a handsome man about forty years old, with bright blue eyes, pouting lips, and a casually rumpled gray suit. "Mr. Tipton-Clarke." Harry Connick Jr. nodded to Jonathan. "Welcome to NOLA. I never saw ya—but nice work on the Pyote story. An' I guess this'd be the latest member of your Committee," he surmised in a rich N'awlins drawl, extending his hand to Aliyah. "An' jus' who do I—"

"That's Cameo," Bubbles cut in. "She channels the dead. She's Simoon right now."

Connick's smile vanished as Attractive Woman My Age was swiftly replaced by Creepy Possessed Lady. He released her hand like it was a dead fish, and not a very fresh one either. "Well then," he said, "how many of y'all're in there?"

"Uh, just me and Ellen," Aliyah replied.

" 'The trumpet shall sound and the dead shall rise again,' " quoted Reverend Wintergreen.

Mayor Connick looked unhappy. "I'm sorry. The police get calls all the time about some hoodoo mama raisin' zombies in the French Quarter. The last thing we need is some ace showing up who can actually do it." He glanced at her clothes. "I have to say, I never would have guessed. Ya gotta be the least likely voodoo queen I've ever seen."

"Well," Bubbles said, still frowning, "I did ask Jayewardene for reinforcements. If Harriet changes course . . ."

*The dead that walk and the wind that wails,* Ellen thought immediately.

"The dead that walk and the wind that wails?" Ali repeated, confused.

Everyone looked askance. *Osiris had a prophecy,* Ellen explained. *Zombies and hurricanes.* "Uh, my uncle had a vision," Aliyah paraphrased. "Hurricanes and, uh, dead people. My uncle's Osiris. He, like, rose from the dead. . . ."

"Just runs in the family now, doesn't it?" Mayor Connick remarked. "Doesn't he have a lounge act in Vegas?"

"At the Luxor."

"You know, the National Weather Service keeps sayin' that Harriet is headed for Houston. It's not that we don't appreciate the help, but if it gets out that I'm evacuatin' NOLA on the word of a Vegas lounge act?"

"Well," Bubbles said, "I'm certain the secretary-general has other sources."

"You and the Reverend be sure to mention that at the press conference. And when we get there, launch all the bubbles you can in the air, make a big show for the cameras. Remember, this here's NOLA. If we want people to pay attention, what we need is li'l lagniappe. Before you go onstage, I'll have a garbage truck ram you as many times as you want."

The Reverend Wintergreen gave her hand a gentle pat. "I can do it instead."

"What about me?" asked Aliyah. "I can help." She stepped back, laughing defiantly, and raised her arms. "You can't kill the wind!" Her fingers crumbled, blowing away into sand, the particles whipping around as the wind arose and she spun like a dervish as she drifted and shifted into the sandstorm of legend.

*Don't drop the shirt!* Ellen thought frantically. *The earrings! If we can't touch them, I can't channel you!* Perspective was odd and crazy, and it took Ellen a moment to realize that as a whirlwind, Simoon saw the world as a 360-degree circle, their eyes a band at the top of the cone. But Aliyah was an old hand at this, and Ellen became aware that all her things were whirling around in the funnel, a crazy *Wizard of Oz* swirl of haute couture and luggage, Jonathan's joining hers as he dissolved, a cloud of green wasps taking their place in the eye. Ellen dimly remembered this trick from the "Crazy Ace Antics" bonus feature of the *American Hero: Season I* DVD.

Simoon whirled over the city until Ellen perceived a portion of the lakeshore where a forest was popping up like time-lapse photography. They spun down, Jonathan Hive's wasps swarming from the zephyr's funnel, going to where a tall young black woman in blue overalls walked scattering acorns from Johnny Appleseed pouches at her hips. Farther on, a young Hispanic woman crouched, one hand on the ground, the other clutching her necklace as the muck and silt heaved themselves out of the water. The wasps buzzed around her then up, a living green marquee, one word swarming into the next: EARTH * WITCH * TIRED * GET * SAND.

Ellen observed silently as the whirlwind scoured sandbars and silt from the lake and then the river. As the day's work continued, Gardener and Earth Witch and Simoon raising the banks and embankments, Jonathan Hive's wasps scouting for likely resources and scattering Gardener's seeds. At last, light was fading and everyone was spent. Aliyah re-formed, swirling down into the skirt, spinning the funnel on into the shirt, and finally coalescing back into Ellen's usual form . . . with both earrings in her left ear, her cameo off to the same side, and her slip hanging out. She squelched a few feet to where her shoes had landed in the muck.

"Well, I think we've done some good work here today." Gardener yawned as she got up from the base of one of her huge oaks. "Let's hope it holds." She smiled at Aliyah. "Nice work, but we better get you some different clothes. Those aren't made for gardening."

Earth Witch looked troubled. "Your power . . . it's the same as a girl I knew."

"It is the same." Aliyah smiled hopefully. "I'm Ali. I'm back."

There was a long silence filled with uncomfortable glances.

"I'm not a rotted corpse!" Aliyah yelled. "I'm just in the body of some flat-chested old lady!" She then burst into tears.

Ellen let the dead girl have her cry. It had taken a lot out of her, Ellen realized, to control her wind that finely, to keep contact with the tokens that tied her to demi-life while at the same time moving mountains or at least tons and tons of sand. It probably didn't help that Ana and Jerusha were similarly exhausted from the use of their powers.

Jonathan put his arm around her shoulder, letting Aliyah sob into his jacket as they walked. By the time she'd cried Ellen dry, the smell of river mud and greenery had changed to sweat and alcohol. Jerusha and Ana had gone. Now college students in Loyola sweatshirts and other bon vivants walked by slurping daiquiris from yard-long plastic flutes.

Bourbon Street.

Jazz music floated out of clubs and revelers wandered by in masks, gorgeous with sequins and feathers, like old newsreel footage of Jokertown before the Wild Card Pride movement. Or maybe after—Aliyah noted that one of the Loyola students had cloven hooves. Nearby, a woman with a beehive of flamingo heads peddled cups of shrimp cocktail. And next door, under a green awning marked LAGNIAPPE: THE GENTLEMEN'S CLUB WITH SOMETHING EXTRA stood two men—one man—two men. Aliyah was having a hard time figuring it out, seeing two aging bodybuilders from the waist up, but from the waist down, one grotesquely wide joker with extra-wide black wingtips. Even more disconcerting were the twins' T-shirts, the one on the right reading JESUS SAVES! and the one on the left SHOW ME YOUR TITS!

"Good sir," cried the Jesus freak twin, waving a Bible at Jonathan Hive, "do not go into this vile pit of depravity, this veritable Sodom! These joker Jezebels have sin in their hearts, and it would imperil your nat soul to even gaze upon them!"

"Don't listen to Momus here," said the other twin, who affected a goatee. "Listen to Comus. Come right in! We've got chicks with extra tits! We've got chicks with dicks!"

*Oh, my God,* thought Ellen as Aliyah looked at Comus and Momus. *It's Rick and Mick.*

"Huh?" said Aliyah, catching the eyes of the twins.

The first paid no attention, but the second one pointed. "It is the Witch of Endor!"

Rick or Mick—the one with the goatee anyway—rolled his eyes. "Excuse my brother for being a pussy. He got beat up by a mute hooker and now he thinks he screwed a zombie."

"Oh," said Jonathan Hive drily. "Can we see that on YouTube?"

"Yea, the dead shall rise to chastise the wicked, for Hoodoo Mama is their mother and the pigeons are her eyes!" Mick or Rick waved his Bible dramatically at some rather moth-eaten pigeons watching him from a nearby awning. "She's older than grave dirt and comes riding a pale horse—*a fucking dead one*—but Jesus Christ Joker is my shepherd and I shall not want!"

"Pussy," added his brother.

Jonathan began shepherding Aliyah away. "Lilith needs us at the Children's Hospital by nightfall. She's taking all the kids away, but she can only do a few at a time."

The pigeons cocked their heads, one of them fluttering off, and Aliyah nodded, drained emotionally as well as physically. She let herself be led through an arch to the Place D'Armes, a small preserve of historic homes, and upstairs in one to her own private room. And with great relief, Ellen observed her take off the T-shirt and then, hesitantly, one earring, then the other.

Herself again, Ellen tuned the old Philco-style radio to soft jazz, then quickly and numbly took a shower, touching the fixtures as little as possible. Most were authentic eighteenth-century elegance, coming with a history. One Ellen was in no mood to relive.

Instead, she dried her hair, did it up in a crown braid, and donned a man's suit, cool white linen, summer weight and sixties style. A tie hid her cameo and choker, and an old fedora slipped neatly over the braid. *Hey, Nickie . . .*

"Hey, Elle." He took in the brick walls and spindly legged furniture. "Where are we?"

*New Orleans. There's a hurricane coming.* She paused. *I've joined the Committee.*

"The Committee?" He chuckled. "Out of the sleeve and straight to the big league."

*Who needs* American Hero? There was a knock at the door. *That's Jonathan. Get the earrings and shirt over there by the radio—we may need them.*

"New look for you," Jonathan remarked, surveying Nick's suit. "Ellen?"

"Nick, actually." Nick put out a hand, which after a moment Jonathan shook.

The cab ride to the hospital was unremarkable, as was the vending-machine coffee once they got there. Like all waiting rooms, the one at the New Orleans Children's Hospital had pretensions to cheerfulness, with old kids' issues of *Aces!* featuring a pre-teen Dragon Huntress on the cover. But the adults waiting silently were ashen, and even the children did not escape the pall. At the end of one row, a skinny Creole teen stared out the window, her face sullen beneath a backward Saints cap, a blaze of red-dyed hair sticking out through the gap. Her stick-thin arms were crossed, framing a chest even flatter than Ellen's and the all-too-appropriate logo for some jazz band named Lost Souls.

*Aren't we all,* thought Ellen as Nick read it.

"Same crap as at the UN," Jonathan remarked, surveying the vending machines. His phone rang. "Hey, Lilith." He listened, turning to Nick, green eyes wide. "Trouble."

*"Security to third-floor reception,"* a voice from the intercom clarified. *"We have a code white emergency. Repeat, code white."*

Nick followed Jonathan up the stairs and through the door and took in the scene: Lilith, her black cloak flowing, was struggling with a little boy not more than ten with red hair and freckles and his fingers around her throat. "—fucking kill you, you vampire whore!" His voice was cracking, grating with rage as he snarled, "Bloodsucking motherfucking cunt!"

Security stood in a circle, except the one guard lying on the floor. A few doctors and nurses and parents also stood stricken as Lilith and the boy struggled.

"Cocksucker!" The boy's elbow shot out like lightning, smashing another guard's nose.

Nick formed a will-o'-wisp, a tiny shocker, and tossed it across to ground into the neck of the enraged child. The boy spasmed but continued to strangle Lilith, so Nick sent another, and then a third, a larger one, enough to take down a grown man.

His grip slackened. Lilith twisted, lithe as a snake, flinging the child to her feet with a sickening crunch. "You're dead, you little bugger!"

The boy snatched the hem of her cloak, clutching the fabric, pulling like he was ripping down an old shower curtain and choking Lilith with the laces as he pulled himself up. Green wasps landed on his cheek, stinging ineffectually, but a knife appeared in her hand then, a magician's trick. Laces parted with a flash of steel, yards of black silk pooling to the floor. But the boy had his own trick and instead of tumbling down with the cloak, he grabbed Lilith's long mane of raven locks, clambering like a monkey and whipping one around her neck to garrote her. Lilith's knife was razor-sharp, but hair was strong, and like a cable, only cut strand by strand.

Nick sent the fourth will-o'-wisp, the largest yet, dangerous to the border of deadly. With a crackle and a pop, the child spasmed, then collapsed to the linoleum, a lock of raven hair clutched in a death grip, a handful of wasps beside him like scattered peridots. Jonathan yelped.

There was a brief silence, then a woman exclaimed, "He's dead!"

The boy lay stretched out atop Lilith's cloak as if it were a rumpled coverlet—or a funeral pall. "It was only a shocker," said Nick. "He should be awake in a while."

"No," said the woman, "he's *really* dead."

Nick felt a horrible lurch in the pit of his stomach. He turned back to the boy. The child's ashen pallor was not the shade of unconsciousness, but of death. He caught his breath, praying the woman was wrong . . . then saw a twitch from the boy's eyelids, a jerk of facial muscles, and he breathed a great sigh of relief.

The child opened his eyes and began to sit up.

"He died three hours ago!"

A knife appeared in the dead boy's chest, and then a second one, blood blossoming around them to soak his hospital pajamas. A third blade hissed through the air, catching him in the shoulder as he stood up. *"That's what I was trying to tell you!"* snarled Lilith. *"The little bugger's dead!"*

The child removed a blade with one small hand. "So are you, you vampire whore!"

Nick sent a fifth will-o'-wisp toward the boy. The ward stank with burnt hair and ozone as the corpse fell to the ground again, twitching spasmodically.

The elevator doors opened then and more people came in. The child's corpse began to twitch back to animation, and everyone took a step back . . . everyone except the people who'd just come from the elevator. Nick realized with dull horror that the boy wasn't the only zombie present. Lilith had stepped back into the gray-faced parents from the waiting room. They caught her with merciless hands, gazing at her with glassy eyes. The dead boy pointed with the bloody dagger. "Make the bitch bleed! Make the fucking whore—"

The dead boy gagged as a thousand wasps filled his pie hole, more covering his face, blinding him with sheer numbers if not their stings. Nick turned to the other zombies as they began to beat Lilith, tearing her hair and clubbing her with their clenched fists. He hurled a giant orb of foxfire at the crowd on the left, blasting them back against the elevators. Jonathan interposed himself, pulling Lilith away, presenting himself as a target instead. The zombies accepted, tearing him wasp from wasp until all they held was a torn sport jacket. Jewel-tone wasps swarmed their faces, and Nick rushed forward to where Lilith lay like a bloody rag doll, pulling her away from the zombies as patients and staff clogged the stairwell.

*Nick*, Ellen thought quickly. *Blast out the back window.*

"What, you can fly now?" Nick hissed, dragging Lilith away from the walking dead.

*No, but Aliyah can.* Nick glanced to the back of the ward: no patients, but an oxygen tank. A single shocker and the blast took out the window, blowing the hat from Nick's head.

Ellen retrieved it, pulling off the jacket and pulling on the shirt and earrings. *Aliyah, whirlwind, now!* The thought was imperative and the dead girl didn't even question. *Get Lilith! Get Bugsy! Get Nick's hat!* The sandstorm blew, shards of glass mixed with its stinging particles, but the clothing came up, the wasps as well. The most difficult task was lifting Lilith, but she was slender and the wind was strong.

They blew out the window and into the air.

The New Orleans nightscape glittered, the Mississippi a glistening ribbon. Aliyah roared aloft, Jonathan's wasps trailing behind like a chain of stars. The brightest beacon was the lights of the Quarter, and in that, shining brilliantly, a fountain of fire. Aliyah headed for that.

Midcourse, Lilith simply vanished. *Teleported,* Ellen realized.

Aliyah re-formed on the patio next to the fire fountain, half-dressed, which was more than could be said for Jonathan. Diners gawked, but without missing a beat, Jonathan said to the nearest waiter, "Table for two, two of your souvenir T-shirts, and what's your special?"

The waiter didn't miss a beat, either. "That would be the Hurricane, sir."

"How appropriate," Jonathan remarked as Aliyah looked to a sign lettered in green and white: PAT O'BRIEN'S—HOME OF THE HURRICANE. Next to that was the outline of a jauntily tilted cocktail glass in the shape of a hurricane lantern. "Two of those while you're at it."

"Very good," said the waiter, gesturing to a free table. Apparently in a city used to drunken hordes of Mardi Gras revelers, partially clothed aces didn't raise many eyebrows.

They donned what clothes they had, Jonathan adding the T-shirt when it came along with their menus and two brilliant red cocktails in the distinctive glassware.

"I'm only sixteen," Aliyah said, looking at hers, then paused.

*Go for it, Ali,* thought Ellen. *I could stand a drink myself.*

Aliyah took a sip. It tasted like high-octane Hawaiian Punch. "What happened?"

"Zombies," Jonathan said. "We'll let Lilith explain it to Bubbles. And actually, that's not a half-bad idea . . ." He ordered some Zombies to go with the Hurricanes, paired with jambalaya and crawfish étouffée. By the end of the evening, they were both pretty giddy.

Aliyah squinted at Jonathan's forehead and watched as a lump traveled down, moving under the skin, then down the bridge of his nose. The next moment a luminescent green wasp stuck its head out his right nostril. "Ew!" She giggled, pointing. "You've got a wasp booger!"

Jonathan snorted, his whole nose dissolving into wasps that swirled around before settling back into a nose sans wasps. "Uh, sorry. It happens sometimes when I get drunk."

Aliyah giggled. "It's actually kind of cute once you get used to it."

"So are you." Jonathan bought himself time by taking another drink. "Uh, well, Ellen's pretty easy on the eyes, but I thought you were cute—though completely underage—when I first met you . . . before you, uh, died." He looked uncomfortable, and not just because a trio of drunken wasps were trying to figure out how to turn themselves back into his left eyebrow.

"How did I die?" Aliyah clutched her Hurricane. "I mean, how did the Djinn kill me? No one's wanted to tell me. No one's even wanted to talk to me much except you. . . ."

"Uh . . . well . . . the Djinn had all sorts of powers. He'd turned himself into a giant and nothing could touch him, at least until you turned into a whirlwind and sand-blasted his hands."

"And . . . ?"

"Um, he reached out kind of like this." Jonathan grabbed a leftover alligator fritter, "And, uh . . ." The appetizer came apart in his hands and the broken pieces fell to the tablecloth.

Aliyah gaped at the crumbles of wasted meat and began to tear up. "That's horrible!"

Jonathan moved his chair and put his arms around her. "It's okay. You're back."

"For how long?" She sobbed. "I never even got to have a real boyfriend!"

Ellen felt like an awful voyeur, but knew it was best to hold her tongue. Jonathan Hive seemed to be a gentleman anyway, seeing to it that the bill was paid and giving Aliyah a shoulder to cry on as he escorted her back to her hotel room. "Um, we're here. Got your key?"

Aliyah opened her eyes, wiping at them. "Uh, yeah . . ." She opened the door, then looked at Jonathan, blinking, his sweet face and brilliant green eyes, and reached a snap decision.

She stood on tiptoe, Ellen tall enough it didn't take much to bridge the gap, and Jonathan's lips parted almost immediately. Tongue met tongue. He tasted like nectar.

Drunk on alcohol and sorrow, Aliyah finally came up for air. "You're a good kisser."

He grinned his sweet grin. "Wasps know what to do with their tongues."

Aliyah grabbed his T-shirt and pulled him inside the room. After a second clinch, she admitted, "They do." She bit her lip. "I, uh, I've never been with a guy, but I . . ."

"Well, you're not exactly underage anymore, but is Ellen okay with it?"

*Just ask if he has protection.*

"Uh, yeah. She just wants to know if you've got a condom."

Jonathan's grin was still there. "That's one thing I was able to get at the UN gift shop." He took her for a third clinch, running his hands down her back, stroking her sore muscles.

It had been a long while since Ellen had been touched like that. And Jonathan *was* an excellent kisser. For Aliyah, it was all completely new. When she pushed back for just a slight breath, she asked, "Do you want to take my clothes off or let me do it the ace way?"

"Maybe a little of both."

Light jazz still crooned seductively from the radio. "Take off my jacket then."

He did, his fingers deft and supple despite the drunkenness, the dexterity of someone who worked with his hands. Next Nick's dress shirt, the buttons sliding free in sequence. Jonathan softly brushed his knuckles down the T-shirt underneath, between her breasts and over her heart.

Aliyah sighed, the soft sigh of a desert breeze, and allowed her form to blur slightly. The slacks pooled about her feet, followed by the dress shirt as it slid through the sand of her shoulders. With a soft susurrus, she re-formed, naked but for the baby-doll shirt and earrings.

Jonathan Hive's grin got wider. "Two can play at that game."

His figure blurred as well, but where Aliyah became dull brown sand, Jonathan exploded into brilliant green, bright as his eyes as thousands upon thousands of neon wasps flew across the room to swarm atop the coverlet, a half minute later forming into Jonathan, naked but complete, his head propped on one hand, the other hand . . . well, maybe not quite complete.

A cloud of drunken wasps swirled lazily through the air, doing some intricate aerial ballet as they brought him the condom from his wallet. They reattached to his wrist, becoming his right hand with the condom between his fingers. "Care to do the honors, milady?"

Aliyah giggled. "I don't know how."

"I'll show you."

Jonathan was drunk and hungry and desperate. Ellen knew that it was probably his first time in a while. A guy who turned into bugs probably got as much action as a woman who channeled the dead. But what he lacked in experience, he made up in enthusiasm, and Aliyah had enough enthusiasm for two. *Or even three when you came down to it.*

Maybe even four. As Aliyah closed her eyes and felt her growing wetness, Ellen imagined that Jonathan's hands were Nick's, Nick whom she'd never touched, never would touch. Nick who'd died before she was born . . .

She felt him sliding inside her, in and out, as Aliyah embraced him with her legs, held his arms with her arms, the old iron bedstead creaking with the rhythm and pounding the bricks of the wall, the rhythm of the jazz from the antique radio. "More," Aliyah moaned. "Touch me."

Jonathan slid out, making Aliyah moan harder, craving him, wanting him, but next he kissed her belly, tracing the way down with his tongue. Aliyah clutched his hair as he teased her, his tongue flicking in and out, and then he traced his way back to her navel, then reared up, his penis entering again as he reached one hand under her shirt and squeezed her left breast. "Oh, Jonathan." Aliyah put her arms over her head, allowing him to pull the shirt free.

The connection faded slightly as the shirt was pulled away, but Aliyah just pushed it aside, pausing to take out the earring where it had caught. The connection faded further but she was still there, heady but lucid. Jonathan reached for the last earring, not understanding, but Aliyah instead guided his hands to her breasts as she clenched him, letting him ride her in and out. Then, when she closed her eyes and began to quake with ecstasy, there was a tiny tug on her left lobe and *la petite mort* suddenly became *la grande mort*.

Ellen was back in her body as Jonathan still rode her, quaking himself as his eyes burned in the dark like green embers.

"Not bad for a guy who turns into bugs," he said afterward, falling into bed beside her. "How was it for you, Ali?" He placed his hand and the final earring between her breasts.

Ellen smiled. "Aliyah liked it just fine, but it's just Ellen now. I stopped channeling her when you took this off." She held up the fateful earring, the Eye of Horus twinkling in the dimness.

Jonathan's face fell. "So I swapped partners mid-orgasm?"

Ellen nodded.

"Uh," Jonathan stalled, "I should probably be going." A cloud of wasps literally buzzed across the room and next thing Jonathan was getting on his pants.

"You don't have to go. I was there the whole time you were with Aliyah."

"I've really gotta."

He almost ran from the room. Ellen heard the jangling of keys as he let himself into the room across the hall. Tears welled up in her eyes on their own. She'd been spending all day on someone else's tears, but in the end, there were still a few left for herself. "Oh, Nick . . ."

She didn't know how she could be unfaithful to a man she'd never touched, but it still felt like a betrayal, to a memory at least. The memory of a man she loved. Ellen clutched the pillow, listening to the soft music in the darkness.

Ellen awoke the next morning to the sight of a used condom, a couple of asphyxiated wasps trapped in the tip. It was not a lovely memento. She turned back over, fresh tears stinging her eyes, but sleep wasn't returning. Forcing herself, she got up, turned off the radio, and showered.

Ellen didn't want to touch the clothes from the day before, not Aliyah's, not Nick's. She opened her suitcase. The final outfit was a twenties flapper gown, midcalf spangled black silk with jet beads, with a matching cap with black ostrich plume and a steel mesh purse fringed with ermine tails. It was beautiful for a night on the town, but utterly impractical for a hurricane.

To hell with it, she was wearing it anyway. Everyone already thought she was nuts.

At the last moment, she paused and set the plumed cap aside. She reached down and retrieved Nick's fedora from where it had been crumpled into the pocket of his jacket.

Nick looked at himself in the dressing-table mirror, touching his fingers to the skin below his eye. "You've been crying, Elle. What's the matter?"

*Aliyah* . . . Ellen thought, but she couldn't lie to him, not Nick. The whole flood of memories came across in a tsunami.

"It's okay," Nick said. Her heart was now his and it calmed slightly, but only slightly. "I'll take care of it." He stood up, steeling his fingers on the dresser top, then surveyed the room, the wreckage of the night before. Reverently, he retrieved Aliyah's earrings and shirt, placing them neatly in the ermine-fringed mail purse, then less reverently, he picked up the condom by its edge and stalked across the hall.

After three sharp raps, Jonathan opened the door, looking disheveled and even more hungover than Nick felt. "You left something."

Jonathan sheepishly took the condom, and looked even more sheepish as the trapped wasps roused themselves, crawling out the bottom and buzzing up the leg of Jonathan's boxers. "Uh, thanks, uh . . . Ellen?" Jonathan's green eyes flicked to the dress, then the hat.

"Nick." He pushed the fedora out of his eyes. "We need to talk. Man to man."

"Man to man?"

"I'm being nice about it. I could say 'man to bug.' " Nick pushed his way into the room, standing on tiptoes to look Jonathan in the eye. "A real man doesn't treat a lady that way. Do you have any idea how upset Ellen is?"

*Nick, please, you don't have to make a big deal—*

"Yes, I do," snapped Nick. "A real man never treats a lady that way, and Elle is a lady. Do you know what I'd give to be able to touch her, hold her, just once? And you . . ." He fixated on Jonathan's small paunch. "God, man, don't you ever work out?"

Jonathan sucked in his gut and a cloud of fat wasps liposuctioned their way out of his navel and buzzed menacingly about his midsection. "Back off."

"You're forgetting who you're dealing with, aren't you?" Nick raised his hand and formed a ball of pure lightning floating on his fingertip. "My ace name was Will-o'-Wisp." As punctuation, he let his entire body limn itself in St. Elmo's fire.

Jonathan's eyes went wide and his fat wasps were even more horrified, funneling down his navel and hiding themselves as his love handles.

"Do we have a problem?" asked a voice from the hall.

Nick turned and Ellen saw Bubbles, slightly plumper but still recognizably supermodel Michelle Pond. "No, miss." Nick let his will-o'-wisp ground itself into his fingertip, blanking the rest of the charge as well. "I was just telling Jonathan here how a gentleman treats a lady."

Michelle looked to Jonathan, who still stood there, holding the condom.

Nick turned his back to him, searching her features. "You'd be Michelle?"

"That or Bubbles." She gave him a quick up and down. "Whoever you are, we don't have time for this. Harriet has just changed course. She's headed right for New Orleans."

♣

# Double Helix

## YE BRUTISH AMONG THE PEOPLE, WHEN WILL YE BE WISE

### Melinda M. Snodgrass

**MORNING IN NIGERIA.** I only have time for a few impressions. The way the edges of the leaves seem to gleam golden in the rising sun, the sweat that's already itching in my beard, the rich smell of wood smoke and coffee, and the rank odor of urine and the throat-clogging reek of shit.

The Radical has his back to me, shoulders hunched as he grips his dick, sighing with relief at the first pee of the morning. I can hear the piss pattering on the leaves in the bottom of the latrine trench. I want to rip his head off with 750 rounds per minute, but he's not alone in this morning ritual. A soldier standing next to him spots me. I don't have time for the careful aim. Instead I bring the Heckler and Koch G36 up to my shoulder, aim for the largest target—his back—and depress the trigger.

The stream of .223 rounds vomit from the barrel. I stitch my way up his back hoping to hit the kidneys, spleen, lungs, and spine. The shirt flies into blood-spattered rags, and the smell of gunpowder trumps even sewage. The force of the bullets throws Weathers into the trench. I change targets, and fire a short burst into the soldier. I risk a quick glance into the trench. Rivulets of blood trickle around the turds and stain the wet ground. The Radical's face has gone slack and smooth, the lids fallen over the eyes, forever hiding that mad glitter.

A sudden memory of Weathers's face gentled by love intrudes. Soldiers are converging on the latrine trench. I jump into the Between hearing in my mind a woman/child's cry.

*"Dadeeee."*

Flint is waiting in his office. I'm still wreathed with the warm scent of gunpowder. On the desk a silver carafe exhales steam like a soft breath. It carries the smell of fresh-brewed coffee. My chief holds out a plate of ginger scones.

*"All tidied up?"* he asks in the low whisper.

"Yes." I take a bite of scone, and feel crumbs drop. I brush them out of my beard, and decide to transform. I hate facial hair, it always makes me feel dirty when I'm sporting it.

It doesn't hurt, precisely, but it feels like the skin wants to tear before it suddenly softens, stretches, and shifts. I'm back to myself with the fatigues hanging a bit on a body that is slimmer than Bahir's.

"Why is it, sir, that our proxies always fight worse than the tin pot dictator's fanatics?"

I manage to maintain my bored drawl, but it's an effort. Why couldn't the politicians and the Helix let me kill Weathers back when I'd first offered? Instead they wait until the PPA's tanks and army have rolled across the border and Britain is scrambling to mobilize the army and Royal Marines to assist the Nigerian forces, and I get interrupted when I'm taking care of Dad.

Mum has a conference in Wells, and had asked me to look out for him. We'd had a very bad night last night. He had been in a great deal of pain and the hours between the morphine injections had dragged like centuries. In the midst of this I'd had to transform into Lilith and jaunt off to Nigeria to scout for a place to effect the assassination. Thank God Nigeria and Britain are in the same fucking time zone.

I help myself to a cup of coffee, and wash down a couple of lid poppers. Flint notices. *"Do you need more of those?"*

"I wouldn't say no. Got to fuel three people, don't you know."

*"When did you do it?"*

"This morning. I'd considered killing Weathers in his tent last night, but he was fucking someone, probably Snowblind, and I would have had to kill her, too. If I were spotted the Committee might wonder why Lilith was killing another member of the Committee. And since I always assume that what can go wrong will go wrong in these situations I opted to wait."

*"Must have made for an uncomfortable night."*

I nod, but it wasn't for the reason he thought. I hadn't waited out the night in Nigeria. I'd hopped back to Cambridge and sat with Dad until sunrise, then teleported back to Nigeria, killed the Radical, teleported to London to report, and now . . . I check my watch . . . I should get back to Cambridge in time to prepare his breakfast.

*"And to answer your question."*

I try to remember what the fuck *was* the question.

"Our fellows aren't fanatics, and we do try to maintain a modicum of civilized behavior." I can't help it, I glance down at the blood flecks that pepper my Kevlar vest. *"Oh, not you. You're our agent of last resort, the place where morality gives way to necessity."* That hangs between us, then Flint adds, *"You need to be debriefed."*

"No, sir, I need to go home. I left my dad alone."

*"Oh, yes, that's right. Dying, isn't he?"*

"Yes." The word emerges from between gritted teeth. Of course, why should I expect sympathy? I kill for my country. He must think that death holds no power for me.

*Dadeee.*

I put a hand to my head as if that will somehow silence that voice.

It's frighteningly quiet when I arrive in the hallway outside Dad's bedroom. I don't hear the thin whimpering moans that had tormented me all night. I rush into the room. He's managed to get himself propped up against the elaborately carved wood headboard. There's a luminous, almost translucent quality to his skin, and for an instant I have the illusion that I can see the vibrant colors of the starburst-pattern quilt through his hands. He has the Bible resting on his lap. It's open to a color plate. A picture of Abraham brandishing a knife while the child Isaac lays passively atop the stone altar. A brilliant stream of golden light pours through an opening in the clouds, pinning Abraham like a bug.

The smile of welcome loosens the knot in my chest, tension leaches out of my muscles, and my legs start trembling. I drop into the chair beside the bed. "You're all right," I say inanely.

"Well, I'm still dying, but the pain isn't so bad this morning." He glances out the window where a breeze is bending the overtall grass, and shaking the fall-splashed leaves on the big oak. "Or perhaps I can just bear it better when I can look out and see the world. Look, the leaves are starting to turn."

"Would you like me to carry you outside?"

"That would be lovely."

He whimpers when I pick him up. I feel my guts curdling with frustration, anger, and guilt, and then it hits me. Dad doesn't have to suffer between morphine injections. I can go anywhere in the world. I speak Arabic and a smattering of Pushtu. I can get heroin in Afghanistan.

I get him settled on a chaise lounge, and drop into the grass beside him. The blades prick through the fabric of my slacks. I pick up a fallen leaf and study the tracery of dark veins through the rampant colors. When I look up my father is gazing down at me fondly, but with a faint crease of worry between his graying brows.

I cough to clear the obstruction in my throat. "What?"

"I'm worried about you."

"Don't be. And why would you be worried?"

He smiles ruefully. "Well, we've been quite the best of friends, and I just hope you have other friends. I'm afraid you're a little too much of a loner. You take after your mum that way."

I'm startled at that. "Really? I don't think I'm much like her at all."

"Oh, no, you're very like her. Same drive, same intellect, same ability to have a very private but rich interior life."

As a child you aren't often offered an opportunity like this. "Did you love Mum?"

"Yes. And guess what, I still love her."

"But she seems . . . you're very . . . I mean, you're dying and she's not here." It just bursts out. Writhing at how inarticulate and juvenile that sounded, I try to cover my discomfort by plucking blades of grass. They leave green stains on the tips of my fingers.

"Couples carve out their own spaces and accommodations. I send her into the world, and she comes back with tales and wonders."

"And what did you get?"

The brush of his hand across my hair is like a sigh. "You."

♥

# Political Science 301

## Walton Simons & Ian Tregillis

HIS BUTT WAS SORE from getting bounced around in the back of the truck, but at least they were getting far away from BICC. Zane, the last of Niobe's babies, was keeping them camouflaged, but the kids apparently didn't live more than a few days and Zane might not be around much longer. The truck was stacked full of packages, and it was stuffy and cramped inside. In spite of the gas shortage, some things still absolutely, positively needed to get there overnight.

Drake felt the truck turn and slow, then stop entirely.

"If he opens up, do we stay or go?" Drake asked.

Niobe took a moment, then softly replied, "We get out."

He heard footfalls on gravel moving around the side of the car to the back, then the door opened. The driver stood on the right side and lit up a cigarette. Niobe gave Drake a gentle nudge. He sidled quickly and quietly past the man and into the driveway of what turned out to be a county courthouse. They moved far enough away from the truck to be out of earshot and checked their surroundings. It had the look of a small town, with few buildings taller than two stories, even in what appeared to be downtown. Drake spotted a water tower and squinted to make out the print on its metallic tank.

"I know this place," he whispered. "We're in Pecos."

"Well, that's something," Niobe said. "Now we just need to figure out where we're going."

There were few people on the streets, and even fewer cars on the road.

A number of the locals had obviously decided bicycles were a good way to get around, as a half dozen were in plain view.

Drake eyed a nearby bike and tugged at Niobe's shirt. "Come with me and have Zane keep us covered."

The trio headed over to the bicycle and Drake snatched a backpack from its wire rack. Niobe gave him a disapproving look, but when Drake fished out a plastic water bottle, her expression changed to a smile.

"You have some first," she insisted.

Drake took several deep gulps. In spite of being lukewarm, it was the best water he'd ever tasted. He handed the bottle to Niobe and checked out the rest of the contents of the backpack. The big find was a knife, which might come in handy. The other stuff inside was a bust, and included a shirt, sweatpants, and a copy of *Aces!* magazine.

Niobe suddenly looked at Zane, panic on her face.

"Not now," Niobe said, looking around frantically. "Please."

A champagne-colored Ford Taurus was pulling out of the parking lot of a hardware store across the road. Niobe pointed to it and dragged Drake toward the car at a near run. She held her remaining child to her chest.

An instant later the Taurus disappeared, but not its driver. He swiveled his head, then grasped frantically for the unseen door latch. Finding it, he leapt out of the car and sprawled onto the parking lot. The car popped back into view and Niobe jumped in behind the wheel of the slowly moving car, Zane still clutched to her. Drake didn't need to be told what to do. He ran around to the passenger side and got in. Niobe set Zane on the seat between them and backed out. The man pointed with an open mouth at his car.

"Go right," Drake said. "Head east on I-20."

They weren't far from Pyote, from home. Drake didn't believe it was blown up. The people at BICC were all liars, so why would they have told him the truth about Pyote?

Niobe looked down at Zane, tears starting in her eyes. He puddled out on the seat as Niobe was reaching for him.

"I'm sorry," Drake said, knowing how sad losing her kids made Niobe. "We'd never have gotten away without him."

"No," Niobe said, and then she was quiet.

Drake didn't know what else to say so he kept his mouth shut. An idea occurred to him and he started taking the backpack apart. First, he pulled out the laces. They were still in pretty good shape, not brittle or frayed.

One of the laces was slightly longer than the other, which was ideal for his purpose.

He cut a rectangular piece of leather from the shoulder strap and carefully bored a hole in either end with the point of his knife, then trimmed the sides so that the remaining piece of leather resembled an elongated octagon. After working the laces through the eyeholes in the leather, he tied them off and created a loop at the end of the longer lace, just big enough for his finger.

"A sling," Niobe said when he showed her the finished product. "You ever used one before?"

Drake shrugged. "Made one as a kid, I mean a really young kid, but I didn't use it much. I'm going to practice getting good at this thing. You'd be surprised how far and fast you can toss a stone."

Without Zane, they'd have to be much more careful about the people from BICC who were after them, for sure. More careful about everything.

Clouds hid the moon and stars, making it hard to see anything, but Drake knew where he was going. They'd hidden their stolen car behind a small rise. By now the cops were looking for it and it was getting low on gas anyway. Drake placed his feet carefully as they scaled the hill. It would be easy for one of them to stick a foot in a hole and twist an ankle, or worse. A broken bone and it was over. They'd be captured for sure. He wasn't sure what they'd do to Niobe, but it wouldn't be good. Drake they would probably kill. He remembered the tone Justice had used when they put Drake in the high-security wing. Like he was going to death row.

"Almost there," Niobe said, balancing herself with a hand on the dried and dusty ground.

Drake dug in with his feet and hands, using the last of his strength to make it to the top of the hill. Then he collapsed into a sitting position, head down, panting for breath.

"Drake, look."

He raised his head and looked at the horizon. The sky was glowing red and orange, like the aurora borealis but in the wrong color. Drake knew what it meant. It meant it was true. He *was* a murderer. He'd killed his own family and everyone else in town.

Niobe put a hand on his shoulder.

"Leave me alone, okay?" He shrugged her hand off his shoulder. "Don't . . . don't touch me." He collapsed to his knees, staring at the fire on the horizon where his home and family had been. Maybe it would go away if he just kept looking at it.

The glow continued to flicker across the night sky.

Maybe Justice and the rest were right. Maybe he did deserve to die. Drake closed his eyes. He beat the ground with his fists, sending dirt and sand flying. He'd never believed in hell, but now he'd made one. His family was there, and his friends, pretty much everything he'd ever known. Drake stood and started walking toward the distant glow. It was where he belonged, in hell with everyone else.

He felt a hand on his shoulder, pulling him back. "Drake, I'm sorry, but we need to get going if we're going to find shelter before dawn. We can't go that way."

Drake did not have the strength to fight her. It didn't matter. Nothing mattered. Wordless, he turned away from the blazing ruin that had been Pyote, and didn't look back.

Drake stumbled. Niobe caught his arm, steadied him. "Easy, kiddo," she said. "I got ya." She gave his arm a little squeeze before letting go.

He shuffled off like a sleepwalker. His body was going through the motions, but his mind was elsewhere.

She wished she still had her children. Drake needed Cameron, her piebald little healer, whose touch erased pain in its myriad forms. Or Gabriella, with her electric blue hair and infectious laughter. Or even Wynn, who sealed away one memory with every paper crane she folded. But they were gone, reduced to stains and memories before Niobe met Drake.

Niobe and Drake followed the contour of the hill until they found themselves standing at the edge of what appeared to be an arroyo. It stretched into the darkness to both left and right. She hoped it was shallow, so that they could cross it directly. She was too tired for detours.

Niobe pulled Drake a few steps back from the edge. "Here. Let me climb down first."

She crawled backward on her hands and knees. Gravel scraped her palms and dirt packed itself beneath her fingernails. She moved until her ankles dangled over the edge. First her ankles, then her shins, then her knees. She was perched with her waist on the edge of the arroyo when her feet sank into soft sand.

"We're in luck. It's shallow."

Drake needed her help to climb down. His legs were too short and he was moving like a marionette with tangled strings. Random, purposeless.

The poor kid was slipping deeper into his own head. Probably reliving memories of Pyote. She wondered if he'd had a large family. Drake's file at BICC had been scarce on biographical details.

"Wait," she said, when he trudged off again. "Let's take a break." The sand shifted as she sat down, making a depression where she could rest her tail. The sand was damp beneath the surface. It made the seat of her sweatpants clammy, but this was still the most comfortable she'd been since leaving BICC. "Oof. This feels nice. I could lie down right here."

Drake plopped down unceremoniously, as though a capricious puppeteer had cut his strings altogether. He mumbled something.

"What's that, Drake?"

"Might flood," he said.

"We'll get going in a minute. Just need a breather."

Niobe knew he was right. He'd warned her about flash flooding in the desert. It didn't take much for a rainstorm to spawn a deadly gullywasher. But she had larger concerns at the moment. She scooted closer to Drake. Sand trickled into her sweatpants.

"How you doing, kiddo?"

His shrug was so minute as to be almost invisible. She nodded in companionable silence.

A gritty breeze ruffled his hair. It dusted them with ash, traced new patterns of moonlight and sand along the soft bed of the arroyo. She hoped Drake didn't notice how the wind from Pyote smelled like soot.

She couldn't see his face; a cloud bank had swallowed the moon. Maybe it was time to get out of the arroyo.

"You know, Drake, there was a time when I hated my power and I hated myself for having it. It just hurt so damn much. But I eventually realized that if I didn't have my power, I'd miss out on lots of happiness, too."

He pulled away from her. "I'm not *happy* about what I . . . about what happened." His shoulders shook freely now.

"No, no, of course not. I'm not saying that. All I'm saying is that sometimes it takes a while to understand the full extent of these things. I used to think that my power was useless and cruel. But it isn't. We wouldn't have made it this far without my children. You see?"

"Nothing . . . good . . ." Drake struggled to force the words out between sobs. He fell against Niobe, pushed his face into her shoulder. ". . . killed them . . ."

He stopped holding everything in. *Finally.*

She held him while he cried. The moon set. He cried. The clouds thickened. He cried.

It didn't rain.

Drake was tired from their cross-country journey, but the thought of the BICC and cops on their trail kept him going. He'd done some practicing with his sling when they stopped to rest, but hadn't come close to hitting what he was aiming at. He was determined to get better at it, though.

They were near Wink, but the blazing remains of Pyote from the previous night were still etched in Drake's mind. Niobe decided they should move only after dark. Without Zane, a chopper could sneak up on them too easily, given how little cover there was. Tonight they weren't going any farther, though. Niobe had twisted her ankle earlier and it was still pretty swollen. She'd picked an area of scrub not far from a farmhouse for them to hide out in. It was a moonless night and she'd already crashed out. Her heavy, even breathing annoyed Drake, since he dreaded going to sleep. The dreams didn't come all the time, but they seemed more real now because he knew they were true.

Drake couldn't do much about most of the things that were making him miserable, but he had a plan for getting some food. A hope, anyways, if he was lucky; he was due in that department. The nearby farmhouse was a two-story job, which meant the bedrooms were almost certainly upstairs. There hadn't been a single bark to indicate the presence of a dog, since a pooch would have killed his plan altogether.

Moving as quietly as possible, Drake headed toward the house. There was a chain-link fence around the yard and he walked around it, looking for an alarm sign. Nothing. He struggled over the fence and plopped down on the other side, then crouched and hurried toward a shingled wall. Drake gathered himself for a moment and took deep breaths. The reality of breaking into a house was a little scarier than he'd thought it would be. He walked slowly to the back door, noting that there was no food bowl there. No dog for sure. Drake grasped the cold, metal handle on the screen door and it turned with a click. He crept up the steps and let the door close behind him.

Once inside, he took time to let his eyes adjust to the darkness. There was a single doorway leading into the house proper. He spotted a refrigerator directly on the right. Excited as he was, Drake waited a long time before opening the fridge door.

A rush of cold air from inside the refrigerator ran over Drake, but he hardly noticed. He grabbed a carton of milk and set it on the floor. This was the closest thing to happy he'd been in a long time. He closed the door and took a gulp of milk.

The beam from the flashlight caught him flush in the eyes. "Hold it right there, Mr. Thief." If the shotgun hadn't told Drake the man meant business, his voice sure enough did.

Drake raised his arms over his head. "Don't shoot, mister. I was just hungry." His heart was thumping in his chest.

The man turned on the kitchen light. He was old and had more hair in his bushy beard than on his head. He set the flashlight down on the kitchen counter. "Well, son, you can get food at a restaurant or a supermarket. My house isn't either one." He kept the gun leveled at Drake.

"I didn't mean anything. Just let me go and you'll never see me again." Drake pointed at the food he'd left on the floor. "Want me to put it away for you?"

The old man shook his head. "You go sit over there." He nodded toward the breakfast table.

Drake did as he was told.

"I'll get the county sheriff out here. He'll give you something to eat. And plenty more besides." The old man moved to the doorway Drake had come in through and picked up the phone from a handset mounted on the wall.

"Please." Drake started to feel . . . wrong. He tried to control his fear, push it deep down into his gut. It was going to happen again and there was nothing he could do about it.

"Put down the phone, or I'll blow your head off." Drake recognized Niobe's voice. His panic went away. "Get down on your knees and set the gun down behind you," she said.

Drake saw that Niobe had only a piece of pipe in her hand, pressed against the back of the old man's head. If the man turned around it was game over. But he didn't. He knelt and set the shotgun down.

"Find something to blindfold and tie him up with," Niobe said, then mouthed "no names." Drake understood.

Minutes later the man was bound and his eyes covered with a bandana.

"I'm cooperating," the old guy said shakily. "No need to do anything stupid."

They carried him into the next room, out of easy earshot.

It was a bedroom. Niobe took care not to brush the man with her tail, and to keep it hidden behind her back in case he could peek under the bandana, while she and Drake half lifted, half pushed him onto the bed. Mostly they pushed; Drake was too short and too weak, and her bad ankle wouldn't let her take most of the weight.

Drake panted quite a bit from the exertion. The kid needed to eat some vegetables.

The exertion worsened the throbbing in her ankle. She whispered in Drake's ear. "Check the bathroom. Try to find some painkillers. Aspirin, ibuprofen, whatever," she said. "But leave any prescription bottles alone."

He went. Niobe stayed behind, keeping an eye on their prisoner. Thanks to Drake the Feds would have a new lead on their location as soon as this man freed himself.

They needed help. She considered propositioning the man. It would obliterate their attempts at anonymity, but with luck her children could more than make up for that.

And then she realized she was thinking like Pendergast. Children as tools, means to an end. *Never. Never.*

Then again, Drake didn't have a chance if she didn't have another clutch soon.

She argued with herself, hating herself from both sides, until she noticed the computer on the desk in the corner. A beige box and a small monitor, with little brown smudges on the mouse and keyboard from years of use.

"Do you have an Internet connection here?"

The man on the bed was silent for several moments. He realized she was talking to him. "What?"

"Does your computer have Internet?"

"Now why the hell would I want that?"

Niobe slumped against the wall. For a moment, the briefest of moments, it had felt like they actually had hope. With an Internet connection, she could have sent a message to Michelle, could have begged her for help.

She roused herself, fearing what it would do to Drake if he witnessed her despair. She went through the closet. This, more than anything else, made her feel like a true burglar. But until Niobe had another clutch, they needed better disguises.

The man on the bed heard her rummaging through his things. "Take anything," he said. "Just don't kill me."

Niobe said, "We won't hurt you. I promise." She rummaged through the closet. "We're not here for your money or valuables, either."

She found a skirt that fit. It was sized for a full-figured woman, which was perfect for hiding Niobe's tail. She wondered where the man's wife was. Then she saw the jewelery atop the dresser, one gold band and one diamond ring, next to a wedding photo of a smiling couple. The groom was a younger version of the man trussed up on the bed; the bride was a zaftig brunette. One corner of the photo was draped with a black velvet band.

"I'm truly sorry for your loss," said Niobe.

"Gather up whatever food you want to take and put it in a garbage bag, then wipe down everything else you touched with this." Niobe gave him a handkerchief. "Hurry."

Drake quickly grabbed bread, cold cuts, cheese, some bananas, and a few other items like matches and the flashlight. After putting his loot into the bag, he dutifully wiped down the fridge door and chair for prints.

Niobe gave him a stern look and jerked her head toward the back door.

"What in the world did you do that for?" she asked, once they were safely outside. She was limping noticeably.

Drake shrugged. "I was hungry. I just want to try and feel normal again. Food helps. At least, it used to."

"I understand. Let's get as far from this place as we can before morning. Those knots are tight, but he'll get out of them eventually."

"Found these. They might help." Drake jingled a set of car keys.

"Good boy," she said, extending an open palm. He reluctantly dropped the keys into her hand.

They headed over to the garage and swung the creaky doors open. Inside was a beat-up blue Suburban. Niobe unlocked the driver's side door and let Drake in. She inserted the ignition key and turned it. The engine made a feeble effort at turning over, then died.

"Out of gas," she said.

The air went out of Drake. "This is Texas. How can people here be out of gas? There're oil rigs everywhere."

"Looks like we're still on foot," Niobe said, easing out from behind the wheel. "Wipe anything in the car you touched and let's get out of here."

Drake used his shirttail to do as she asked. "Are you okay to walk?"

"I'll be fine." She started off again, slowly, Drake at her heels.

He felt like there was a bottomless, black pit ahead of them somewhere in the distance, waiting to swallow him up. When the time came, Drake wasn't sure he wouldn't just walk right in.

Drake's skin was bright red from panhandling all morning. Niobe stayed hidden—the Feds had their descriptions plastered everywhere—so her sunburn was milder. She watched him from the shadows of an alleyway, where she sat on a trash can, trying to ignore the pain in her ankle.

The plastic shopping bag jingled when he set it at her feet. They'd fished it out of a trash can in front of the Walgreens around the corner. Now it was heavy with coins.

"Got a few quarters in here," he said.

Niobe fished through the bag. Mostly pennies. And a few paper clips. And lint. And gum wrappers. But here and there, sunlight glinted on dimes, nickels, and quarters. She counted out a couple of dollars.

"Good job." Niobe handed him the coins. He looked to be on the verge of heat stroke, the poor kid. "Why don't you go into the store and get an ice cream sandwich and some water. It's air-conditioned in there."

"Want me to get you anything?"

"Nah. I'm good," she lied. "Enjoy the ice cream but don't wander off, okay?"

"Yeah. I know."

She waited for him to disappear around the corner before taking up the bag and walking to the far end of the alley, where the shadows smelled like urine and worse things. The coins were heavy. The handholds in the plastic dug into her fingers.

The bag jingled again when she set it down in front of the crude cardboard shelter under the fire escape. It was basically just a refrigerator box, but the bundle of rags inside was a man.

"Hey," she said. "I'm back."

The man sat up. His face was streaked with grime. He picked at his hair. "You again. What'd you bring me?"

Niobe nudged the bag with her toe. "There's a little more than four dollars in here. That's ten dollars, counting the six I gave you yesterday." *Which meant sticking around here for an extra day,* she thought. *A day better spent on the move.*

When he didn't say anything, she continued. "That was our agreement, remember? Ten dollars."

The homeless man hunched over the bag and picked through it rapidly with two fingers, like an inexpert typist. "Lotsa pennies. Can't do much with pennies."

"Please," she whispered. *We won't last much longer without this.* Every second wasted in negotiation made her nervous. Drake would come back soon and she didn't want him to know about this. He'd feel guilty about it.

The man's gaze flitted between the bag full of change and Niobe's face. She tried to angle her body to keep the worst of her acne in the shadows.

The man grunted. "'Kay." He motioned Niobe to lie down in his nest.

"I—I can't do it that way." She playfully waggled the tip of her tail at him. The look in his eyes made her worry that he'd back out, and she regretted the vain attempt at bonhomie. But he shrugged, and relented.

After that, they worked out the mechanics quickly enough. He breathed with his mouth open, grunting in short little bursts. It smelled like he had a rotten or abscessed tooth. Niobe prayed it was his only health problem, and that if he was an addict, he wasn't using needles.

She jumped to her feet as soon as she felt the first egg forming. Her erstwhile partner rolled over, cleaned himself on his bedding, and didn't stir after that.

Trash cans rattled as she doubled over in pain. Her ovipositor widened and deposited the first egg under the fire escape. She already had the names picked out. Avender, Aubrey, and Abernathy, for boys; Agatha, Akina, and Allie for girls.

Another egg followed the first. Only two children this time around: a smaller than average clutch. *Maybe they'll be twins,* Niobe mused.

She felt the first tickle of consciousness, a tentative hello at the world, as the eggs hatched.

*Momma?* thought Avender.

*Ave, my darling! Give me a kiss.*

*Momma,* he thought, *I don't feel very well.*

Niobe's heart felt like it had been punctured with an icicle.

*No. No, no, no no no no no. Not now.*

Avender popped out of his egg. The boy was slender and beautiful, covered in fine golden hair, though missing one hand. He took a step toward his mother. "Mom," he said. "I lo—" It trailed off into a gurgle. He toppled over, clutched his stomach, then melted.

His sister Agatha also drew the Black Queen.

Niobe was still crying beside the puddles when Drake returned.

West Texas was the platonic ideal of hot, arid desolation. No people, no cars, just scrubland and dirt. It felt downright post-apocalyptic. Which, given what Niobe had seen of Pyote, wasn't so far from the truth.

They'd been walking since before midnight. A band of pink on the eastern horizon limned the gray sky; sunrise in the offing. The nascent day felt bright as noon to Niobe's dark-adapted eyes. When she stumbled over a snag of sagebrush or a dry streambed, it was from exhaustion.

They walked through a field, parallel to the highway but roughly fifty yards away, so that they wouldn't be seen. Not that it mattered—they hadn't seen a car all night.

Water sloshed in the near-empty bottle when she went to take a swig. Dawn twisted through the thin plastic, forming a little hourglass-shaped spot of light on Niobe's blouse. Two swigs left, at most.

She called ahead to where Drake trudged through the field. "Here. Finish off the water."

He didn't stop, didn't slow down.

"Hey, Drake. I'm talking to you."

The only sound from Drake was the scraping of his tennis shoes on hard-packed soil as he stepped around a creosote bush.

Niobe raised her voice. "You could have the courtesy to pretend to listen. I'm trying to help you, in case you haven't noticed."

Drake was becoming increasingly sullen. He'd withdrawn into himself again. They hadn't spoken about it, but clearly the Black Queen clutch had demolished his hopes.

Hers, too. She'd keep Drake alive as long as she could, though without help that wouldn't be long at all. In the meantime a little cooperation would have been nice. Maybe even a "thanks" now and then.

The bitterness receded as quickly as it had washed over her, leaving in its wake a profound shame. She hoped it was exhaustion making her feel this way. Resentful. Irritable. Or maybe she wasn't as maternal as she liked to think.

She picked up her pace, drew even with Drake after a few strides. "Drink this," she said, holding the bottle under his nose.

"Yeah. Okay." She studied him while he unscrewed the cap and drained the bottle. His sunburn didn't appear to be getting any worse. They'd swiped a tube of aloe vera lotion and some SPF 45 sunscreen from the farmhouse.

Something twinkled on the horizon. Then it disappeared. Then a flash and another twinkle. It came from where the highway receded into the distance.

"Car coming," she said.

Drake shrugged. He tossed the empty bottle aside. He knew better than that—they might be able to refill their bottles, if they got lucky. He was giving up; the decision manifested in countless little gestures, actions, evasions.

She examined the glint on the horizon. For all she knew, it was a cop or state trooper. But this death march was killing them just as surely as SCARE would. Sleeping in ditches all day, walking all night . . . It had to stop.

The car was closer now, a rapidly growing blob of red and silver visible through the haze. It was still the only car in either direction.

"Stay here," she said. "Keep yourself hidden."

Niobe took a deep breath, then half jogged across the field to the middle of the two-lane highway. Her ankle screamed in pain, but she ignored it as best she could. She stopped, facing the oncoming car.

Drake hunched down behind a bush. He called, "What are you doing?"

"We need a ride." The white-noise hiss of tires on asphalt reached her ears. Niobe swallowed, trying to keep the anxiety out of her voice. "Stay hidden, Drake."

She could see it more clearly now. A rounded, burgundy-colored thing bearing down on her. No lights on top, though with Niobe's luck it would probably turn out to be an unmarked cop car. Or SCARE.

Niobe raised her arms, palms out, toward the approaching vehicle. The car's shape became apparent in the rapidly closing distance. She recognized it from television commercials she'd seen back at BICC. A gas/electric hybrid. *That makes sense, I guess.* The question was whether or not the driver could see *her.*

The car didn't slow down. She waved her arms.

Closer. Louder. Niobe clenched her eyes shut when she could hear the whine of the engine.

The road noise lessened, the engine relaxed. Niobe cracked one eye open. The car was rolling to a halt.

Sunlight glare on the wide windshield prevented Niobe from seeing inside the car. She waved, tossing out thanks as she trotted over to the driver's side.

The window slid down with the whirr of an electric motor. Niobe got a strong whiff of clove cigarettes.

"Thank you so much for stopping," said Niobe.

"By Crom's beard! You scared the daylights out of me."

Niobe had no idea who "Crom" was supposed to be. But that wasn't the odd thing about the woman behind the wheel. Not compared to the fur-lined chain-mail bikini, the crimson-colored cape, and the axe sitting on the passenger seat. The bikini did not complement the woman's figure.

"I . . . uh . . ." Was that a *sword* on the backseat? Niobe wondered if heat stroke had scrambled her brain.

"What brings you out here, noble wanderer?"

"Huh?"

"Nah, never mind. Need a ride?"

"Yes. Badly. Please."

"It's traditional to just stick out your thumb when you're hitching."

"We've been out here for hours. There aren't any cars to hitch rides from."

The woman raised her eyebrows. "We?"

*Damn.* "Yes. Me and my friend." Niobe waved at Drake, motioning him to join her. "We ran out of gas money back in Wick," she improvised.

"You've been on foot since Wick?"

Niobe nodded. That much was mostly true, anyway.

The driver stuck her head out the window. She gave Niobe the once-over, then the same for Drake.

"You guys have been on foot too long," she said.

"Tell me about it," said Niobe. "Please, may we ride with you? Just for a while?"

Niobe had never imagined that the *clunk* of electric door locks could sound so sweet. She felt like crying. "Thank you. Thank you," she repeated.

Drake hurried over. Niobe opened the back door for him. He wrinkled his nose at the cigarette odor, but it didn't stop him from scrambling inside.

"Next stop, Barbarian Days," said the driver as Drake buckled his seat belt.

Niobe and Drake exchanged a silent look. *Barbarian Days?* He shrugged.

It sounded like some kind of festival. Well, that explained the outfit. Niobe held the axe in her lap when she buckled in. It was plastic.

The driver raised her window. She clicked the air-conditioning up a notch. The car was surprisingly silent when they pulled away, causing Niobe a moment's disorientation when the landscape outside the car started to slide past them. She had never ridden in a hybrid.

"You getting enough air back there, kiddo?" Niobe turned, looked over the seat. Drake's eyes were closed.

She slumped down in her seat, tempted to drift off under the caress of chilled air. It felt like heaven. The upholstery stank like a cheap bar, but at least her feet could rest.

"I'm Mandy," said the driver.

Niobe blurted out the first name that sprang to mind. "Yvette," she said. She motioned toward the backseat with a nod of her head. "That's Xander, in back."

"So," she continued. "Barbarian Days."

The driver smirked. "Never been, I take it."

"No."

"Lots of people there. Maybe not so many nowadays, with the oil crisis." She paused to light a cigarette.

"It hasn't stopped you," said Niobe.

"Most of the time I work behind a desk, processing medical billing for an insurance company. Three days out of the year I can strap on a cape and become Red Sonya."

Niobe nodded, unsure of what to say next. The driver dragged on her cigarette, then tapped ashes into a tray affixed to the center console. It hung over a charging cradle holding a cell phone.

Mandy saw her gazing at the phone. "You can use it, if you're wondering."

"I . . . Thanks. Again. It would be a huge help."

Niobe pulled the phone from the cradle, careful not to knock down the ashtray. She thumbed through the menus, thinking. Who could help her? Did she even know any telephone numbers?

No. But she did know a few e-mail addresses.

"Mandy? Where exactly is Barbarian Days?"

"Cross Plains. Birthplace of the late great Robert E. Howard."

*Michelle—Help, please. I'm in danger. Please come. I'm in Cross Plains, TX.— Niobe.*

Niobe wasn't accustomed to using such a tiny keypad. Thumbing out the e-mail to Bubbles took a long time. But after she finished, she thanked Mandy again, closed her eyes, and slept.

♥

# The Tears of Nepthys

## THE THIRD TEAR: NICK

### Kevin Andrew Murphy

**THE CAFÉ DU MONDE** prided itself on beignets, chicory coffee, and never closing, even for hurricanes. Ellen didn't know if the last was such a wise idea, but since Committee aces were like cops and got the two former items free, she wasn't exactly going to complain, either. The wind wailed outside the iron shutters, and Ellen shivered. Her beaded flapper gown was not exactly suited to the weather, but then again she had a psychic allergy to off-the-rack.

Jonathan had no such problem, and had somewhere acquired a new sport coat. Ellen was about to comment on it when Michelle blew in, her latest Endora-style kaftan flapping around her currently svelte figure. "Zombies," Michelle said succinctly. "They're at it again." She glanced to their table. "Grab your coffee. I'll explain on the way."

The explanation did not help much. All Ellen gathered was that A) Reverend Wintergreen had been holding a prayer vigil at the Superdome; B) buses were in the parking lot to evacuate people without transportation; and C) zombies had shown up, wreaking havoc.

Michelle found a spot at the edge of the parking lot. There were indeed a huge number of buses and an even more enormous crowd of people waiting for them, soaking in the rain. But havoc was a bit of an overstatement. "This is your fault," stated Mayor Connick, storming up to them, rain dripping off the brim of his umbrella. He was not looking at Michelle or Jonathan.

Ellen looked up at him. "How do you figure that and what is 'this,' exactly?"

"You . . . the dead . . ." He gestured wildly to the buses. "Look . . ."

Ellen took his umbrella and went around to the nearest one, glancing for a moment at the crowd, black and white and, well, joker—Ellen wasn't sure what race or even sex the individual with the shrimp chiton had started out as—but they were all looking with horror at the open door. Ellen glanced in. In the driver's seat sat a nattily dressed young black man, a gold grill in his mouth and a bullet hole in his forehead. He was beckoning with one hand and gesturing to the back of the bus with the other, clearly miming *Come in . . . come in . . . always room for one more.*

There was a bit more commotion at the next bus. "The Power of Christ compels thee!" roared Reverend Wintergreen, waving a large silver cross. "Get thee behind me, Satan!"

Ellen refrained from pointing out that if he wanted anyone on the bus to get behind him, he'd have to stop blocking the door. Instead, she just looked over his shoulder, seeing another zombie bus driver, but instead of welcoming gestures, this one was flipping him off.

"Same thing as at the hospital," Ellen said, "though these seem a bit friendlier."

"Safe bet it's this 'Hoodoo Mama' we've heard about," said Jonathan, coming to join them along with Jerusha, Ana, Michelle, and the mayor, "but fuck if I know what her game is."

"Ain't no game, you fuckers," said a voice, harsh but still clear over the rain, "it's fuckin' dead serious." An ancient black woman moved herself forward from the crowd, her wheelchair sluicing through the puddles. "You ain't got no call to take these poor fuckers, these old fuckers, these fuckin' jokers, away from the only homes they know, take them off to fuckin' Jesus knows where, have them sit around in the fuckin' rain while you play preacherman and hero so they catch their fuckin' death of cold like poor ol' Miss Partridge here."

"Who's Miss Partridge?" asked Michelle.

"I'm Miss Partridge"—the old woman glared through rain-specked bifocals—"and you fuckin' killed me, you fuckin' lily-white lard-ass bitch!" Her frail arms pushed on the arms of her wheelchair and she stood up, straightening her crooked back with a crack of snapping bones. "Go ahead, blow me up, you fucker!" She stalked forward as Michelle stepped back, a bubble forming between her fingers, pretty as a snow globe. "I seen you on TV, I fuckin' know what you can do." She gestured to the crowd, waving to several news cameras. "Go ahead and show all these nice people the sort of bitch who'd kill a little old lady with a fuckin' bubble!"

"Hoodoo Mama, I presume," Jonathan said, looking at her.

"Who the fuck wants to know?" she snapped, glaring at him, her milky eyes magnified to near the size of her face.

Ellen presumed as well. She handed the umbrella back to Mayor Connick and in three paces was at the wheelchair. She turned and sat down, placed her hands on the armrests, feet on the footrests, and closed her eyes.

Miss Partridge opened them.

She looked around, taking in the crowd. "Lan' sakes, it's a miracle," she breathed. "I ain't seen this clear in years."

*Not quite a miracle,* Ellen apologized. *The wild card. I brought you back—you're in my body—but someone else is using yours.*

Miss Partridge's shock was also kindled with anger and recognition. She wheeled her chair around to face where Michelle's team and the mayor stood in a confrontation with her former body. "Joey Hebert!" she called sharply. "What on earth do you think you're doing?"

"Jesus fuckin' H. Christ!" The old zombie woman turned, looking down at the woman in the wheelchair. "How the fuck do you know my name?"

"Don't you be speakin' blasphemy with my poor dead lips, Josephine Hebert," Miss Partridge snapped. "I know your hoodoo tricks. I knew you even before, back when you an' Shaquilla Jones was smokin' joints and drinkin' Mickeys under my porch an' you begged me not to tell your mama." She wheeled her chair right up to the zombie's legs. "An' I didn't, so don't you be sassin' me now. You ain't got no call to be abusin' my corpse after all I done for you."

"Fuck you," the old zombie spat, "you ain't Miss Partridge. You're some rich-ass white chick."

Miss Partridge raised one hand and looked at it in wonder. "Why so I is. But you sure ain't me neither, Joey Hebert, even if you be talkin' with my old lips." She put her hands on the wheels of her chair decisively. "An' I may be a white girl now, but I kin still tan your backside once I fine where you is." She wheeled, scanning the crowd, and stopped as she came to a scrawny girl-child, not quite a woman, with a ring in her navel, a red streak in her hair, and her eyes unfocused and glassy as any zombie's. "There you be. . . ."

She began to wheel forward but suddenly the connection was broken. Ellen felt claws around her throat, strong as a harpy's, tearing her out of the chair, throttling her from behind, and then there was a deafening explosion. Something spattered the back of Ellen's head and she fell to the ground beside the wheelchair, landing hard on her hands and knees, rainwater and blood splashing as the crowd screamed, nat and joker alike running in horror, trampling the press.

Ellen rolled, then Jonathan was helping her up, pulling her away from the headless corpse of the old woman as it staggered about in the rain, waving her gnarled hands, blood spurting from the stump of her neck. A bubble floated through the air and blew off her right arm.

There was a momentary echoing silence. Then, behind them, came the roar of the bus.

Jonathan shoved Ellen out of the way but was not so fast himself, the bumper throwing him to the ground, the wheels coming over his legs as the jauntily smiling zombie driver flashed Ellen a gilded grin. But rather than an explosion of red, the tires sprayed green, thousands and thousands of wasps flying out from under the undercarriage, swirling around her. Then came a horrible rumbling and a quaking of the earth and the bus moved another seven yards before its front end was swallowed up by a huge crevasse in the asphalt.

The second bus wheeled toward the panicked crowd, Reverend Wintergreen waddling after it, waving his cross. "The Power of Christ compels thee!" He fell on his belly in the rain, a sad and tragic figure until the next moment, when his legs pulled into his body, his arms as well, and then a huge fleshy sphere wrapped in white linen rolled over where his head had been, gathering momentum until it struck the bus square in the side, tipping it over.

Vines began to erupt from the crevasse, pale green with purple blossoms, but ginormous, a cross-pollination of *Jack and the Beanstalk* and *Little Shop of Horrors,* overgrowing the whole fleet, stopping the last bus in its tracks, and sealing the zombies inside.

"Kudzu!" Mayor Connick cried aghast. "I told her to plant anything but kudzu!"

Ellen heard a soft moan behind her then and turned as Jonathan crawled out from under the first bus—or more horribly, half of him did. Like a bisected wasp, his upper torso struggled forward until Ellen hoisted him up, cradling him in his sport coat. "Are you okay?"

"No, but—" He paused, wincing. "Well, no butt. It got my butt and my upper legs. Help me, I—" He winced again.

Ellen carried him over to Miss Partridge's wheelchair, the wasps swarming over him, forming a green lap blanket as the rain continued to fall.

"I've never really done this before," Jonathan admitted shakily.

"You've lost your legs," Ellen stated, horrified.

"No, just my pants." Jonathan winced and the green wasps seethed. "Most of my legs are here, just not all the bits that connect them." He gasped and squeezed her hand. "I can re-form pieces but . . ." Ellen just held his hand as he clenched his eyes shut tight and moaned in pain, and she watched as his paunch melted away along with most of the fat on his body, tiny lumps moving under his skin, moving purposefully down to what there was left of his lower half.

"Is everyone all right?" Bubbles asked, squelching over with someone's umbrella. She'd ballooned up fatter than the Reverend and then some, evidently having stopped another bus.

Jonathan opened his brilliant eyes and stared at her. "Apart from losing my legs, just peachy," he said at last. "You?"

She stood there, her kaftan now a skintight muumuu. "You lost your—"

"I think I can get them back. How's everyone else?"

"Ana's overdone it. Again." From the sound of it, this was a regular occurrence. "The Reverend's helping her. And the mayor's blown a fuse but Jerusha can deal with him. The zombies don't seem to be a problem right now anyway. They're just slumped over the steering wheels like someone cut their strings. Or maybe they're playing dead." She paused, then looked at Ellen worriedly. "That old woman I blew up . . . Hoodoo Mama's work?"

"Who else? I saw her at the hospital," Ellen said. "Nick did, too. And Miss Partridge knew her from way back. Young girl, Creole-looking, red streak in her hair. Looks like a boy."

Jonathan looked confused. "She was at the hospital?"

"You were paying attention to the vending machines." Ellen glanced to the crowd, but Joey Hebert had vanished in the throng. "Do you have anything to sketch with?"

"You're an artist, too?" Bubbles opened an exquisite Hermès bag with one fat hand and fumbled out a stack of glossy photographs and a Sharpie.

"Not really, but my mother was." Ellen took them, photos backside up, as Bubbles came over next to her, giving her shelter with her umbrella. She raised her hand to her cameo, touching her fingers to the smooth wet stone.

There was a blink and a familiar presence, and Ellen thought her explanation all in a rush: *Mom, please, it's an emergency—I need a sketch.*

"Well, nice to see you, too, dear," Mrs. Allworth remarked, glancing to Bubbles, then looking at the end of the upended giant-kudzu-covered bus. "Where are we?"

*New Orleans, but I swear, it's an emergency. We need a sketch of this girl.* Ellen remembered her, the girl Nick had seen in the waiting room, the glassy-eyed teen in the crowd, the child Miss Partridge had known and in some part loved, a dozen images.

"She'd be prettier if she didn't frown like that." Mrs. Allworth uncapped the pen. "Is this all we have to work with?"

*Yes, Mom. But please. I've been practicing, but I'm only good with fashions, not faces.*

"Of course, dear," said her mother. "Anything for you." With sure, swift strokes, she began to sketch a montage of Hoodoo Mama, aka Josephine "Joey" Hebert, one pose after another, angry, wary, sullen, none of them happy. "So," Mrs. Allworth asked conversationally, "are you seeing anyone?" Ellen couldn't shield a flash image of Jonathan, and Mrs. Allworth glanced over and raised an eyebrow. "Well," she sniffed at last, "at least this one's not dead, but honestly, young man, work on your posture." She then lowered the edge of her sketch and noticed the wheelchair and the lack of legs. "Oh, I'm so sorry, I—" Then she noticed the lap blanket of poison-green wasps.

She turned away. "I'm not even going to ask." With one finger, she lifted the choker from her throat, Ellen's throat, breaking contact between skin and brooch, severing the channel.

"Uh," said Jonathan as Ellen handed him the sketch, "nice to have met your mom?"

Ellen attempted a grin.

Jonathan looked at the images and his wasps did as well, turning as one to examine each face. A few crawled over them, then began to shake their rear ends, doing a waspish macarena. Then the whole cloud, the lower half of Jonathan Hive, took off, dodging raindrops. "Fly!" Jonathan called. "Fly, my pretties!" He turned to Ellen as she folded up the sketch sheet and slipped it in her purse. "I've always wanted to say that."

"I think you just said it to CNN," Bubbles pointed out, indicating the lurking news crews.

The Reverend came over next, his suit split down the sides and ground with mud down the front and presumably the back, but otherwise no worse for the wear. "Oh, my poor boy," the Reverend said, falling to one knee and grasping Jonathan's left hand. "May I pray for you?"

"Got any prayers for people who lose their asses?"

"Samuel 6:5 and 6:17," the Reverend said brightly. "God's right ahead of you there." He bowed his head, clutching his cross and his Bible in the other hand. "O Lord, please bless this poor sinner and fill him with Your Holy Spirit. Let him be filled and made whole. May—"

"Oh, my God," said Jonathan, getting religion rather abruptly, staring at the dark sky transfixed, eyes so wide they were almost glowing. "Oh, my God. Brace yourself. It's coming."

Reverend Wintergreen bowed his head. "Are you seeing God's Kingdom, my boy?"

"Worse," breathed Jonathan. "Harriet."

A swarm of wasps fell from the sky, clutching to Jonathan for dear life, and three seconds later, the wind followed, a raw blast of screaming fury. Ellen clung to the handles of Miss Partridge's wheelchair, Jonathan only anchored by the Reverend holding his hand, and the next moment, the hand ripped free, crumbling away at the wrist into green motes, the rest of Jonathan eroding away as well until nothing was left but an empty wheelchair that was wrenched from her grip. Ellen was flung back, finding herself caught by the even greater mass of the Amazing Bubbles—Michelle, her rock in the storm, almost literally—and after an interminable interval that was probably just minutes, the first wave passed, Harriet lulling to a driving rainstorm.

"Jonathan . . .," Ellen breathed, looking at the shamble of humanity. He was gone.

"Bugsy's been scattered before. He has to save himself." Bubbles held her. "Ellen, you're my ace in the hole. I need you to track Hoodoo Mama. How are your detective skills?"

Ellen clutched the ermine-tailed purse still slung across her chest. "Professional."

"Good. What I needed to hear. Meet me at the hotel at nightfall."

Of course, it was not Ellen who was the detective, but Nick. She walked far enough back to the Quarter to find a bar where she could seek shelter, then took out his hat along with the sketch. *Hey Nickie,* Ellen thought. *We've got a problem.* She briefly filled in the details.

"Good detective work," Nick complimented her. "You and your mom are hired."

*Nick, I'm serious. What do we do now?*

"No great mystery, Elle. Just legwork. Ask around." And so began what felt like a demented pub crawl, going from one shuttered business to another, pounding on doors until they found someone to let them inside and look at sketches. Josephine Hebert was known mostly by face. A few folk knew the name "Joey" and that she was sometimes seen around Congo Square.

*Doubt she'll be hanging out,* Ellen thought, *but she has to get her corpses somewhere.*

"Good thinking." They struggled to the nearest funeral home, where they found that Josephine Hebert had instituted a "Don't ask, don't tell, don't get strangled by the zombies that walk out the back" policy. She was also in the habit of sending them home when they got a bit ripe, but the traumatized mortician neither knew nor wanted to know where she lived.

Nick went back out into the storm, clutching his hat. Halfway down Royale, Harriet hit again. A shutter tore off a building nearby and Nick dove to safety, in the process letting go.

Ellen watched his hat go flying down the street. "Nick!" she screamed, louder than the wind, rushing after it. But as fast as she ran, a hurricane was faster and the old fedora blew up Royale until it caught on a wrought-iron balcony, plastered against the metalwork a story up.

Ellen raced. The ironwork was twisted with roses and vines, painted black, cutting into her hands, but panic numbed the pain. She was almost to the balcony when Harriet lulled and Nick's precious hat fell to the street. Ellen jumped down, stumbling, lunging for it. For Nick.

The wind rose up again, stealing him. Twice, she almost caught the circle of felt. Twice more, Harriet taunted her. Then the hat fetched up against the legs of a child. At least, the stature and the *American Hero* BRICKBAT children's jumper said child. Above that was a rubbery ebony-skinned cross between a golliwog, a cyclops, and a sea anemone.

The joker child picked up Nick's hat in his-her-its tentacles and held it.

"My hat!" Ellen called, rushing forward. "Give it to me!"

The child's eye went wide above its fanged mouth and it ran, Ellen chasing, her own mouth open in a wordless scream. Only when the water overtook her did she realize that it had not been her the child had been running from, but the levee breach behind them.

She tumbled end over end, swallowing mouthfuls of the muddy Mississippi, then came up, gasping and sputtering. But a lifetime on sailboats and yachts made for a strong swimmer, and a midcalf silk dress was not the least practical garment when swimming for your life.

Nick's hat bobbed a ways away, floating like a paper boat. The other direction, the child surfaced, squalling, thrashing its tentacles. Ellen knew drowning terror when she saw it. Despite having drawn a joker designed for water, it had never learned to swim.

She prayed for Nick to forgive her, but knew he wouldn't if she made any other choice. Wouldn't make any other choice himself. She swam for the drowning child.

Its tentacles whipped around her, almost drowning her in the process, but she ducked down and it released her. She surfaced and caught it from behind, letting it wrap its tentacles around one arm. It was hard going, but at last she got to solid footing. "You okay, honey?"

The joker child clung to her wordlessly, but seemed unhurt. Ellen glanced back to the flooded street. Blocks away, a speck may have been Nick's hat. The wind blew. It was gone.

Her shoes were also gone, lost somewhere in the floodwaters. But she didn't need shoes to hot-wire a car. At this point, she didn't even need to channel Great-Aunt Lila.

The joker child seemed enthralled by this and Ellen was glad it found larceny so entertaining. She didn't know what she felt. Joy at having saved another human life. Fear that she would never find Nick again. Anger that she had been forced to choose. Maybe grief.

Reverend Wintergreen was onstage at the Superdome, leading prayers. Ellen wasn't the only one who had lost someone, but she knew him. "Oh, yea," he said, looking down at what Ellen had brought him, "suffer the little children. . . . What's your name, my child?"

The joker child gurgled wordlessly into the microphone.

"It's PJ!" came a chorus. Actually, a duet—Ellen turned as Rick and Mick forced their way through the crowd of joker refugees near the front.

The joker child wrapped its tentacles around both their necks. "You find PJ's mama?" asked the one with the goatee.

"No," Ellen said. She didn't know whether PJ was Rick and Mick's son or niece or maybe just some child they knew. "Uh . . . PJ was alone." Ellen paused. It was a long shot, but maybe not that long. Mick and Rick had known everyone on the seedy side in Jokertown, and New Orleans couldn't be that different. "I'm looking for someone, too." She took out the sketch.

It was waterlogged but intact. The twins studied it. "Oh, yeah, that's Joey," said the one with the goatee. "Foulest fucking mouth in the Quarter. She lives in a red shotgun over on Treme. By the old St. Louis cemetery. Can't miss it. Hoodoo marks chalked all over the front."

"She's Hoodoo Mama, right?"

Rick and Mick both laughed. "Joey?" said the first. "Nah, she's just a street punk."

"Hoodoo Mama's this old Creole witch, blind as a bat and older than grave dirt. Calls up hellhounds to serve her, and the dead are her eyes, even the pigeons."

Ellen nodded. As she left, a young black woman reached into a suitcase and handed her a pair of pink sneakers, which Ellen wore back into the storm to make her way to the hotel.

Nick was gone. Nick, the brave one. He'd been with her so many years, and now a piece of her heart had been ripped out, blown away by the hurricane. But when she stepped into the main foyer of their house at the Place D'Armes, she heard a voice. Not Nick's, but . . .

"Jonathan!" Ellen cried, throwing her arms around him. "Oh, thank God. I—I lost Nick . . ." She hugged Jonathan, not knowing what else to do, and grief finally came in great wracking sobs.

"Sorry." Jonathan sat with her on the couch, held her. "Um, he was a brave . . . uh . . . hat."

"My, uh, condolences," Michelle said, "I only just met him. . . ."

Ellen scrubbed the tears fiercely from her eyes. "I know where Josephine Hebert lives." She took a breath. "She does dead animals as well as dead people. There were some pigeons the other day that I think were her spies."

"The creepy ones on Bourbon Street?" Jonathan asked.

Ellen nodded. "She's got a bunch of zombies, too. Checks them out like library books."

"Well, I'm pretty much invulnerable," Bubbles said.

"Nice to be you," Jonathan said. "What if she suffocates you with zombie pigeons? She's just a kid, anyway. You already blew up an old lady on CNN. Want to do a punk kid for an encore?"

"No," Ellen said, taking a deep breath and trying hard not to think of Nick. "Personally, I'd like to wring her scrawny little neck. But Miss Partridge didn't think she was all bad, and all we need is for her to stop pulling this shit." She exhaled. "And the easiest way to do that is to get her on our side. We need to talk."

Jonathan and Aliyah hid behind Bubbles as she knocked on the door of a chalk-marked red shotgun on Treme opposite the cemetery.

There was no answer. Bubbles knocked harder. A minute later the door was opened by a very tall cadaverous bodybuilder who loomed over Bubbles menacingly.

"Look, Morticia," Jonathan said to Aliyah, "she has her own Lurch."

"Fuck off," the zombie croaked.

Bubbles only held up a beautifully scintillating bubble. "Listen," she said, "we'd like to speak with Joey Hebert or Hoodoo Mama or whatever she wants to call herself, and we can do this the nice way or the not-so-nice way."

"You fuckers got balls," the zombie finally croaked, "but I ain't playin'. You fuckers steal little kids."

"Lilith was taking them to other hospitals," Bubbles explained. "There was a hurricane coming."

"Harriet." The zombie stared. "The weather fucker kept sayin' she was goin' to Houston, but I guess you cocksuckers knew what you were talkin' about after all." He opened the door farther, stepping back.

It was an invitation of sorts, and as they walked in past more and more zombies, Aliyah paused, stricken. The third zombie was a girl, barely seventeen. She could have been Aliyah's sister except for the cuts on her wrists. The *American Hero* T-shirt she was wearing showed the Jackalope from the current season instead of Simoon. Aliyah put out her hand, almost touching the girl's face, then stopped, looking her own death in the face for the first time.

Her hand began to shake, her fingernails drifting into sand.

*Take off the earring,* Ellen thought. *Now. I can handle this.*

Aliyah didn't have to be told twice. Even oblivion was preferable to the awful truth. And as she slipped the earring out with one hand, the sand snapped back into place on the other.

Ellen stood eye to eye with the dead girl. She was acutely aware that while Bubbles was invulnerable and explosive and Jonathan could turn into countless stinging insects, all she could do if the zombie decided to strangle her was scream and flail at it with her purse while trying to put on an earring—and even once she had the earring on, there were no guarantees that Aliyah would be any help. She missed Nick even more and for all the wrong reasons.

She sniffed then. Inside the apartment was the peculiar odor of lemongrass, and Ellen realized it was coming from the zombies. "That's Van Van oil and Chinese wash," a girl's voice said to her unanswered question. "Us hoodoo women use it for rootwork."

Ellen turned her head, looking away from the honor guard of zombies, across the room to where the young woman lounged in a purple wingback, flanked by two large, menacing, undead pit bulls and lit for mood or just lack of power by a dozen large votive candles marked with vodoun veve patterns. It was a pose calculated to intimidate and was doing the job admirably.

"It's your crutch for making the zombies," Jonathan surmised.

"Fuck no," said Hoodoo Mama, "I just use it to keep the fuckers from stinkin' up the place. Axe doesn't last long enough. Sometimes fuckin' old school works best." She gestured to the matching purple couch facing her chair, its back in convenient throttling range of the zombie honor guard. "Have a seat. Let me get you some refreshment. You fuckers like beer-can chicken?"

"It's pretty good," Bubbles allowed, sitting in the middle of the couch. Jonathan sat down to the right of her and Ellen perched on the opposite arm.

Hoodoo Mama smiled proudly. "Nobody makes it like I fuckin' make it."

There was a thumping and banging then, from the kitchenette to the right of the couch, and the closest zombie, a woman in a KISS THE CHEF apron, went and opened the door of the refrigerator. A quartet of headless plucked chickens gamboled out of the bottom drawer trailing butcher paper, clambered up to the nearest counter by means of a stepladder, and proceeded to sodomize each other with beer cans provided by the zombie.

She offered the remaining cans from the six-pack to Jonathan and Bubbles, who passed, watching the chickens in horrid fascination. Ellen, however, accepted, smiling, and popped her can as the zombie served the last to Hoodoo Mama. It was a test, and when the girl raised her beer, Ellen did the same and drank. It was cold, refreshing, and what she needed.

"You think I can get a job at Brennan's?"

Ellen shrugged and took another sip of beer, keeping the earring carefully palmed in the opposite hand. Bubbles and Jonathan continued to stare as the sodomized chickens proceeded to breakdance in a roasting pan coated with seasoning salt.

"You're a fuckin' cold bitch, you know that?"

Ellen chose to take it as a compliment. "I've been dealing with the dead for a while."

"So who the fuck are you? I seen these fuckers on TV." Hoodoo Mama jerked her beer can toward Bubbles and Jonathan. "I ain't seen you before."

Ellen gestured to her throat with the hand with the earring. "You can call me Cameo."

The girl squinted at her. "You're that fucker from the hospital!" The zombies all took a step forward. The zombie pit bulls bared their fangs.

Ellen came to her feet as well, armed with nothing more menacing than a can of weak beer and the earring of a hysterical teenage ace who'd probably be even less help. "So are you."

"So what? You're gonna electrocute me now?"

"I could," Ellen lied, "but my power's more than that. I channel the dead, and I channel their powers. You've already met my friend Nick." A beer can was not a will-o'-wisp, but if she held it in her fingertips, it felt the same, and Hoodoo Mama could see the pose. "He's the shocker." She gritted her teeth, forcing herself not to betray any emotion or any hint that she would probably never be able to call Nick again. "But don't worry, you got your licks in."

"Heh," Hoodoo Mama snorted, leaning back in her chair. "Guess I did." She gestured to the zombies and they stepped back to their former positions, all except for the chef, who proceeded to put the chickens in the oven and adjust the dials.

"You ran over my ass, too," Jonathan mentioned lamely.

The girl ignored him, still looking at Ellen. She took a sip of beer. "So," she said after a while, "this morning, that really fuckin' was Miss Partridge?" Ellen nodded. "Fuck," the girl swore. "I really liked that ol' lady. She was one of the few fuckers who ever gave a damn about me." She rubbed at the corner of her eye and then slammed her beer, seeming to reach a decision. "So what do you fuckers want?"

Ellen glanced to Bubbles, who was sort of official spokeswoman, even if Ellen had been doing most of the talking. "Well," Bubbles said slowly, "what we'd like is for you to stop screwing us up. We're trying to save people's lives here."

"What about that fuckin' vampire bitch, Lilith?" The girl glared. "She's been stealin' little kids. I ain't read much of the Bible, but I fuckin' *know* about Lilith the Child Stealer."

There was a glance between the Committee members, and Jonathan was the first to answer: "She just thought the name sounded sexier than Teleporting Eurotrash Girl."

Josephine Hebert handed her empty can to the chef zombie. "Okay, I'll fuckin' give you that."

"You know," Bubbles said, "there are two more storms. We could use your help."

Jonathan opened, "The UN does have some money . . ."

"Fuck that," Hoodoo Mama snorted dismissively. "You know how many fuckers die wearin' wedding bands and fuckin' diamond engagement rings? I've got a whole fuckin' box full of bling." She gestured to the mantelpiece. Amid the candles was a makeshift altar, with feathers and shells and the photograph of a woman who would have been attractive if not for the ravages of hard living. And beside the photograph sat an old wooden jewelry box.

Ellen stifled a ghoulish itch to open that box and see who lived inside it.

Bubbles sighed. "All we really need is a truce."

Hoodoo Mama shrugged. "Okay, fine, you've got it." She glanced to the three of them. "Anything else you fuckers want?"

There was a long uncomfortable silence with glances between Michelle and Jonathan, and between Ellen and the watchful eyes of all the zombies before she finally settled on Hoodoo Mama's. "Can you really see through the eyes of the dead? Even animals?"

Josephine Hebert grinned proudly. "Fuck, yeah."

Hope is a thing with wings. In this case, a dead pigeon. A whole loft of them. "I lost something when the levee broke," Ellen told her. "A hat. An old gray fedora."

"You fuckin' want me to look for a hat?"

"Yes." Ellen bit her lower lip. "It . . . it belonged to my friend Nick."

Hoodoo Mama gave her a sly look. "You can't work your mojo without a personal object, can you?"

"No," Ellen admitted. "I know you don't want money, but if there's anything else, anyone you'd want to talk to . . ." She glanced to the photo on the mantel, the candlelight flickering over the tired woman's face.

Josephine Hebert looked as well. "You're a fuckin' dangerous bitch," she said at last, "but fine, I'll keep my eyes out. But not because you'll let me talk to my mama. I'll do it because I saw what you did for PJ. You ain't as cold a fuckin' bitch as you let on."

Ellen broke eye contact with the dead woman's photograph to look at her daughter. "Thank you."

Hoodoo Mama nodded, then looked at all of them. "So are you gonna get the fuck out now, or you still wanna stay for dinner?"

There was a second awkward silence, broken a moment later by a digitized version of "Tiny Bubbles." Michelle looked to the zombies, then fumbled open her Hermès bag and got out her cell phone. Ellen glanced over and was able to read the text message just received: *Michelle—Help, please. I'm in danger. Please come. I'm in Cross Plains, TX.—Niobe.*

Bubbles quickly stowed the phone back in her bag but was visibly disturbed. "Would you be terribly offended if I took a rain check on the dinner? A friend of mine needs help."

Hoodoo Mama flicked a hand. "Fine by me. Y'all should come for Thanksgivin'. I do self-bastin' turkey."

Back at the Place D'Armes Ellen let herself into her room. She didn't like old rooms. They came with too much history, and this one was no exception. Whatever the reason, and today there was a particularly excellent one, the maid had not been in. Slowly, reverently, Ellen put her purse on the dresser, took out Aliyah's T-shirt, and hung it up to dry. Then she picked up Nick's jacket and sat down on the bed, clutching the fabric with both hands.

The tears came again, but there were no memories, none strong enough for her to call him back. It was an empty shell, without even a trace of the ghost of the man she'd made it for.

There was a soft knock on the door. "Who is it?" Ellen choked out.

"Uh, Jonathan. Can I come in?" She didn't answer, and he took that for a yes. "Are you okay?"

"Do I look like I'm okay?"

"Not really, but you seemed kind of glad to see me earlier, and, well, I was thinking about what Nick said to me before . . ." He sat down on the bed beside her. "About how a man should treat a lady. I haven't treated you very well."

"It happens. When you were sleeping with Aliyah, I was thinking about Nick."

"Ouch." Jonathan sighed.

Ellen looked at him. "Were you honest when you said I was easy on the eyes?"

Jonathan grinned, his eyes twinkling poison green. "I think we both know the answer." He reached out and touched her hair, which was in a state after the levee breach and the hurricane. "But I think we could both stand a shower."

Ellen looked mournfully at Nick's jacket. Then she set it aside. Nick was dead, had always been dead as long as she'd lived. To everyone but her at least and at last.

Jonathan was alive, and he wanted her. And if some bit of Nick's wisdom, his gentlemanliness, his simple gallantry, had passed to Jonathan, then good. And even if not . . .

He tasted like nectar to her, to Ellen, with no other soul in between. He reached up, pulling her dress and her slip both down by the shoulders, working the zipper and letting the whole fall into a beaded pool around her feet. She did the same with his pants, his bony thinness making this simple, and a half minute later they were both stumbling into the shower, laughing as they worked the taps and got the right temperature, soaping and exploring the shape of each other's bodies. Starting fresh, starting clean, with no other impressions.

The suds ran smooth down her body and he stroked her breasts, touching her nipples, bringing them full and alert until his talented tongue tasted each in turn, then traced his way down, and then up. Then he entered her, and embraced her, and they kissed, no ace powers except the honey of his taste and her hands on his back, feeling the impressions of the women who had touched him before. There weren't very many.

They tumbled out into towels, Ellen letting him take the hotel robe. "Fresh linen," she said. "It's . . . a bit of a fetish of mine. . . ."

Jonathan grinned. "Easily done."

He ducked out into the hall and a minute later came back with an armload of fresh sheets, stripping the bed and making it for her. She lay down atop the bed, naked, and they set to the second round of their love-making. Halfway through, Ellen reached out to the bedside table and retrieved the earring, the simple bit of silver and Swarovski crystal. She handed it to Jonathan. "Be a gentleman and do the honors."

"But I was wanting to be with you."

"And last time you were wanting to be with her." She placed a finger on his lips, stilling them. "This way, you can be with us both. Care for a three-some?"

He grinned. "I contain multitudes. Sex with me is never that few." He then leaned down and kissed her, then the next moment, slipped the earring into her ear. "Wake up, Sleeping Beauty. Your Prince Bugsy awaits."

"Jonathan?" asked Aliyah. "What happened?"

*Everything's fine*, thought Ellen. *Hoodoo Mama's not going to bother us.*

Aliyah took stock of her body, Ellen's body. "We've been having sex."

"Just picking up where we left off." Jonathan's eyes twinkled. "You okay with that?"

"Oh, yeah." She reached out and grabbed him.

◆

# Political Science 401

Walton Simons & Ian Tregillis

**MANDY PARKED THE CAR** near what looked like the center of Cross Plains. She adjusted her gear, which was probably a good idea, and they all got out.

He'd gone maybe two steps when his nose caught the scent on the wind. Corn dogs! There was no other smell like it on the face of the earth. Maybe Bubbles was near the corn dogs, maybe not, but that's where Drake was going.

The street he was walking down would have been the main road in Pyote, but even Cross Plains was a lot bigger than Pyote. He imagined what it would be like to chow down on a corn dog, cotton candy, and a huge Coke. Miserable as he was, food had always done the trick for him. He'd been starving lately, and had even been nibbling on bits of his own sunburned skin when he knew Niobe wasn't looking.

Drake stepped out into an open area and stopped dead in his tracks. It was like he'd gone from Texas to WoW in an instant. There were people, grown-ups, walking around with swords and helmets and shields. Some were wearing furry pants and others even smaller furry pants. There was one man wearing a scary-looking preacher costume. He had a sword and an old flintlock-style pistol. Then Drake saw a woman. She was wearing a chain-mail bikini. Even the she-elves in games wore more than this woman. Mandy fit right in with these folks.

There were plenty of normal people, normally dressed anyway, but they didn't get Drake's attention. There were also a Ferris wheel, some bumper cars, and one of those rides with the spinning cups. Right now, food was all he wanted. He had enough money to get what he needed. If Bubbles was going to take them away, he wouldn't need to beg anymore.

The first normally dressed person Drake came to, he asked, "Is this Cross Plains?"

"Yes, it is."

Drake's depression lifted a bit. The soreness in his skin and feet melted away. They'd finally made it.

A black man in a long, dark robe walked slowly by, nodding to the crowd and tossing plastic snakes to them, while loudly saying, "Doom, doom, doom." He had a deep voice that was scary in spite of the fact that he wore eye makeup.

Drake got in line at the concession stand, scanning the crowd for anyone who looked like Bubbles. He'd seen her on the first season of *American Hero,* and was confident he could spot her easily enough. She was big, not just big like Drake, but really big. The line moved quickly and soon Drake was at the front. A man wearing a red BARBARIAN DAYS apron and a horned plastic helmet gave him a quick smile. "What can I do for you, by Crom?"

"I just need a corn dog and a Coke."

"Small, medium, or barbarian-sized on the drink?"

"Small is okay, thanks." Drake wanted the big drink, but he also wanted to finish up quickly and get back to Niobe.

The vendor pushed the drink and paper-wrapped feast to the edge of the wooden counter. "Six-fifty."

Drake fished out the money and turned to walk away, but bumped into a large man. He was unsteady on his feet and his T-shirt smelled like beer.

"Sorry." Drake quickly sidestepped him.

The man pulled a plastic sword and waved it around. "Kill your enemies. Drive them before you. Hear the lamentations of the women."

"Okay," Drake said, through a mouthful of corn dog. "I'm on it."

Niobe had hated the smell of corn dogs for almost as long as she could remember. Ever since the time in fourth grade when she came down with the flu and sicked up chunks of hot dog and cornmeal under the jungle gym during recess.

Barbarian Days smelled like corn dogs, gamey turkey legs, cheap beer, sweat, and the occasional whiff of manure from an upwind feedlot. And it was hotter than hell.

"Where is she?" asked Drake.

"She'll get here. She has to," said Niobe. They'd been searching the crowds all afternoon. So far they'd found no sign of Michelle, or anybody else from the Committee.

Niobe wondered what Barbarian Days were like when a tank of gas didn't cost a small mortgage and people were more inclined to travel to the middle of nowhere. There were gaps in the midway where absent rides and games of chance should have been. She hitched up her skirt again. It hid her tail as long as she kept it curled around her waist. Her tail ached; it was like having a bad kink in her neck after sleeping funny.

Drake stopped next to an overflowing trash bin buzzing with wasps. "Are you sure," he said, retying his shoelaces, "she got the message?" He paused, watching her. "Niobe?"

She was staring at the trash bin, and the wasps. Niobe stepped closer to the bin, where the smell was stronger. "Thank God! Are we ever glad to see you."

"Who are you talking to?" Drake asked.

"Did Michelle send you? Or the Committee?"

Drake looked back and forth between the wasps and Niobe. He looked skeptical.

"Hello? Bugsy?"

The wasps did nothing to indicate that they were anything other than wasps. *Damn.*

Niobe sighed. "Well, it was worth a try. Let's get something cool and escape the sun for a while," she said. The sno-cone booth might give them some plain ice if they asked nicely; they couldn't afford to spend their last dollars on junk food. She could have sworn they had more cash. Drake's appetite at work again.

The sno-cone booth was situated next to a stand selling deep-fried candy bars. They stood in line behind a five-foot-tall Conan and a six-foot Valeria. Cute couple. Niobe eavesdropped on their conversation.

"But the Jackalope is dead weight," said Valeria. "I'll bet the Diamonds will drop him next. They have to."

Conan shook his head. "Jack hasn't had a fair shake yet. He can deliver.

Unlike Spin Doctor. All he does is change his hairstyle every week and hope people like it. That's just freakin' sad."

Zane would have enjoyed the conversation. He'd followed the new season of *American Hero* as closely as living on the lam would allow, right up until he died.

The breath caught in Niobe's chest as she thought about it. She shivered, tucked the sorrow away where she could embrace it later, and thought about what to do next.

Drake touched her elbow. "Hey. Look." He pointed toward a row of picnic tables under a green plastic sun shade. Through the crowd Niobe glimpsed a very large woman taking up most of one bench, her back to them. She appeared to be wearing a cape. Not Michelle's usual attire, but it made sense if she wanted to try to blend in.

Niobe took Drake's arm and pulled him through the crowd, calling, "Michelle!" Michelle didn't hear them.

Somebody jostled her. Drake's arm slipped out of her fingers. Niobe turned to face a tall woman in a skintight leather bodysuit. It wouldn't have been out of place among the other costumes, except that it covered a body much shapelier than was the norm here. Niobe wondered if the woman was a prostitute.

"Hey!" Niobe said. "Please watch where you're going."

The hooker tipped her head at Niobe. She flicked a waist-long black braid over her shoulder. "My apologies," she said, and melded back into the crowd.

They made their way to the picnic tables. In addition to a cape, the overweight woman also wore plastic armor and a toy sword. She wasn't Michelle.

"Crap," said Drake. "Face it. She's not coming."

They made another round of the festival, then another. At times they glimpsed other obese women—many of the festival goers weren't exactly small—in line for rides, or the tour of the Robert E. Howard house, but no Michelle. Drake and Niobe also cruised the midway, where the highest concentration of people lingered.

The sun was low on the horizon when Drake went to go use one of the Porta-Potties. Niobe waited for him. Here, near the toilets and Dumpsters, Barbarian Days smelled overwhelmingly of outhouses and rancid grease.

The crowd was getting louder. Rowdier. Some of these people had been swilling beer all afternoon. Meaning they probably suffered from impaired judgment.

Which gave Niobe a sad, desperate idea.

Drake returned, wiping his hands on his pants. She asked him, "Can you wait here? I want to try something."

Drake wrinkled his nose, as he had done in Mandy's car. "It stinks here."

"Fine. How about you wait for me over by the Tilt-A-Whirl?" She pointed at the ride, farther down the midway. "I shouldn't be gone long."

"Why? Where are you going?"

"To get help. I hope."

Finding a willing partner was easier than Niobe had expected. There was no shortage of men half blitzed out of their minds who'd spent the day staring at bikini-clad women. Additionally, it was getting dark out, so by keeping to the shadows she could ensure they didn't see her face easily. It didn't reflect very well on the patrons of Barbarian Days, but Niobe stood in no position to judge.

She met a man calling himself Solomon. He led her behind the Dumpsters, to stand against the tall retaining fence that separated garbage from the rest of the festival.

It wasn't love, but it was a private degradation.

"Is there anything I can do to help you along?"

"Shh," he slurred. "Tryin' to concentrate."

"This never happen' before. I swear."

"Uh-huh."

"Really."

♥

"Jesus Chris'," he said. "Thass a tail."

"Technically, it's an ovipositor."

"Ugh. That ain't helping."

"Just forget it," she said. "This isn't working."

"Wait. Wait, this is better."

In the end, Solomon gave her two boys and a girl: Benedict, Baxter, and Belit. Niobe named her new daughter after one of Conan's many girl-friends, in homage to Barbarian Days.

Benedict, scarecrow-thin with cobalt blue skin and white hair, was a one-man waste-disposal unit. He devoured half a dozen empty bottles while waiting for his siblings to hatch. An ability influenced by his birthplace.

Lithe but muscular Belit had the agility of an Olympic acrobat. Gold-medal material, without a doubt.

The lights on the midway went crazy when Niobe took the youngsters to meet Drake.

"Hope you like it, Mom!" said Baxter.

When they didn't find Drake in front of the Tilt-A-Whirl, Niobe pan-icked. *They caught him, and it's my fault. I shouldn't have left him alone.*

Belit somersaulted straight up one of the tall light poles. She scanned the crowd. *He's over there, Mom.* She pointed. *Buying cotton candy.*

Niobe sighed. "That figures," she muttered.

"Niobe!" A familiar voice came out of the crowd.

She spun around, looking for the owner of the voice. A woman darted through the throng toward Niobe. She waved.

"Michelle!" Relief coursed through Niobe so strongly that it threat-ened to wash away the last of her strength and leave her collapsed on the midway. "You found us."

Michelle winked. "Eventually. Sorry we couldn't get here sooner." She indicated her companion, whom Niobe had disregarded until Michelle in-troduced her: a stunning woman with long black hair and eyes like silver orbs.

"This is Lilith," said Michelle. "She gave me a ride."

"Thank you," Niobe said.

Lilith looked her up and down, studying her. Niobe shied away from an intense quicksilver gaze. The woman radiated sexiness in waves. Niobe felt like an insignificant bug next to her. "A pleasure to finally meet you," said Lilith. She even had a husky voice.

Michelle frowned. Niobe hugged her. "You found us," she repeated. Tears of joy tickled her face. "Thank you for coming. We wouldn't have lasted on our own much longer."

Drake returned, munching on a stick of cotton candy. In the corner of Niobe's eye, Lilith tensed, took a tiny step backward, then stopped herself.

When Drake saw Niobe talking to Michelle, his shoulders slumped in relief. Niobe grinned at him.

"It was worse than you realized," said Michelle. She took Niobe's arm, squeezing it. "But you're safe now."

"Worse? How could it have been worse?"

"Your friend isn't who you think he is."

"Oh, crap," said Drake.

Niobe, Michelle, and Lilith looked at him in unison. He was looking past them, up the street.

Niobe said, "Drake? What's wrong?"

He pointed. The crowd on the midway had thinned out. Probably, Niobe realized, because of all the cops at the edge of the throng. They cleared a path for the leather-clad woman they'd bumped into earlier in the afternoon. Her long braid swung back and forth like a pendulum as she strode toward them. Whoever she was, she wasn't a hooker. Assassins and kinky call girls had similar fashion sense.

"Wait," said Michelle, staring at Drake. She looked very pale, and not as pretty as she had a moment ago. "*That's* the friend you've been protecting? A kid?"

"Who'd you think I was with?"

"The most dangerous fugitive in America," said a man's voice. The words didn't frighten Niobe nearly as much as the cocksure tone of their delivery did. "Public enemy number one."

A man in a well-cut business suit swaggered through the crowd. He elbowed his way between two policemen to join the leather-clad woman.

Niobe turned back to Michelle. "What have you done?"

Michelle shook her head, looking dazed. "I—I didn't know."

It was all for nothing. Everything Niobe had done to protect Drake, everything she'd endured, everything—everyone—she'd sacrificed: meaningless. All flushed away thanks to the Amazing Bubbles. Amazing was right.

Niobe grabbed Michelle's arm. "What have you done?" Her face felt hot. So did the new tears trickling down her face. Whether they were tears of sorrow or rage, she couldn't say. "I *trusted* you! They're going to kill him!"

"They said . . ." Michelle turned to face the swaggering hick and his companion. "You didn't tell me he was just a kid! What else didn't you tell me?"

Niobe grabbed Drake's hand. "Run!"

They headed away from the man in the suit, toward where the crowd hadn't thinned out. Behind them, Michelle's voice rose above the hubbub: "I do *not* appreciate being *USED*!"

They hadn't run more than a few yards, Niobe pulling at Drake for him to keep up, when a paunchy, middle-aged woman stepped out of the crowd. She wore a silvery cape and a black bodysuit that covered every inch of her body except her face. The cape might have been natural at Barbarian Days, and she might have been just another festival goer, if not for the huge German shepherd at her side.

Niobe turned in a slow circle. Behind them, the Hound of the Baskervilles and the woman in the silvery cape. Before them, the swaggering man and his companion. And all along the edges of the crowd, half a dozen cops. They were surrounded and outnumbered.

For the first time in as long as he could remember, Drake had been happy. Now, looking at the people who were there to take them in, he felt almost sick. They'd walked halfway to hell across Texas, and for what? So the person Niobe had counted on to help them could turn them in.

The crowd was backing off, far enough to be safe from whatever was going to happen but close enough to see.

The big man in the suit spoke. "My name is Billy Ray. I'm a federal agent. Stand away from the kid, lady. If you cooperate, things will go better for you. Resist and we'll just drag your sorry ass away kicking and screaming." He smiled. Ass-kicking obviously was what this guy did.

Niobe put an arm around Drake. "Go away. He's just a little boy."

"Yes, go away." Bubbles walked up next to Drake and Niobe. Her large shadow enveloped them both.

Billy Ray made a fist. Drake turned his head to look behind them. The woman in the shiny cape and her dog stopped. "What do you think you're doing, Balloon Girl? It's four to one." Billy Ray pointed to his friends. "Not to mention the fact that we represent the government of the United States. Your government, in case your memory needs refreshing."

Bubbles looked around slowly. "If my government can't get by without harming children, maybe we need a new one."

Drake knew about Bubbles from TV and the Web. He started punching her with sharp jabs. Maybe it would help build up her energy a little, although she was really big already. It hurt his hands, though.

"You're making a life decision here, a mistake you won't be able to walk away from. The Committee means squat to me. If you cross us you will go down and it's going to hurt." Billy Ray grinned. It was the nastiest excuse for a smile Drake had ever seen.

Bubbles laughed. It wasn't a girly one like Drake expected, but more of a *you-are-so-dead* laugh, cold and brittle. He hadn't ever thought of Bubbles as scary, but he sure was glad she was on their side. For the moment, at least. "Really?" Bubbles said.

She turned sideways, holding one palm out toward Billy Ray and the curvy woman decked out in black leather, the other at Moon and her buddy. A torrent of small bubbles poured from her fingertips, like she'd dropped a hundred bags of golden marbles that moved in pools toward the government agents. It was a conservative move, just to keep them at a distance.

Billy Ray whispered something to the leather-clad woman next to him and patted her on the butt. A burning sword materialized in her hand and wings of flame sprouted from her back. She rose gracefully into the air, holding her flaming sword in a striking position, and flew toward them.

That was when every light in Cross Plains went out. All at once. An instant later they came on again. Some of the rides jerked to a sudden halt, while others began to speed up. The Tilt-A-Whirl was tilting and whirling madly, out of control, and shrieks were coming from the Ferris wheel. The lights went out again, on again. Shouts and screams echoed through Barbarian Days. Drake gave a quick backward glance and saw the giant dog waiting patiently on the edge of bubble carpet. The caped woman had vanished in the sudden chaos.

Bubbles tossed a couple of medium-sized missiles at the flame-winged woman, keeping her from closing in. Drake heard a gunshot from behind. It picked one of Niobe's kids off her shoulder, the dark blue one.

Niobe spun, slipped, and fell. Her momentum rolled her to the edge and two cops sprang from the crowd and grabbed her by the arms. One of the remaining kids, the really muscular one, started bouncing around like a rubber ball, pounding on the cops. The larger of the two policemen grabbed Niobe and twisted her arms behind her back.

Drake lost it. He was tired of being chased all over the Southwest and tired of getting pushed around. Crouching low, Drake launched himself across the bubbles, gliding on his belly to where the cops had Niobe.

The lights were going off and on, on and off. The rides had all gone crazy. People were running everywhere, knocking into each other. Bubbles hit the flying woman in the legs with a bubble, spinning her awkwardly in the air. Two more bubbles quickly followed; the first knocked the burning sword from her hand and the second caught her in the solar plexus, sending her to the ground. Down in flames.

The cops were too busy with Niobe to notice Drake, so he jumped the smaller of the pair and bit his ear. Hard. There was a crunching noise and a scream. A bit of flesh came off in his mouth. Drake felt a pair of hands rip him from the man's back and toss him to the ground. He got up as fast as his fat body allowed, spitting dust and blood. The shorter cop had a hand to his mangled ear, but his partner had drawn his pistol and pointed it at Drake's face.

"Go ahead," Drake said. "Try it and see what happens. The bullet will melt before it even gets to me."

A tiny spark of doubt crept into the cop's eyes, but he kept his gun leveled. "Get down on the ground, face-first."

Drake shook his head. "You've got three seconds to set down your guns. Otherwise, this town is going to end up just like Pyote." The memory made Drake sick inside, but he wasn't going to let it show. "They did tell you about me, right? Two seconds." His heart was jackhammering, but he wasn't afraid. "One second. Say good-bye."

The officers put their guns on the ground and exchanged frightened glances. Drake picked up one of the pistols and pointed it. He turned to Niobe. "Cuff them."

She looked at Drake like he'd transformed from a fat kid into a lion, but after fumbling for the cuffs, managed to get them snapped around the cops' wrists. "It's going to be okay," she said as the second of her kids joined them. He could tell from the expression on her face that Niobe was talking telepathically to her kids. It made him feel left out, but right now it was necessary.

Drake turned around to see how Bubbles was doing, just in time to see her turn to Billy Ray. "Next," she said.

Ray bellowed and launched himself at her, landing inside the bubble ring. He punched her several times, blows designed to kill or cripple. Bubbles swelled a bit and laughed. Snarling, Billy Ray dropped to his knees and grabbed a handful of dirt, flipping it into Bubbles's face in a single, swift motion. "*Now,*" he yelled.

Bubbles wasn't entirely blinded and reacted faster than someone as big as her should have been able. She grabbed Billy Ray and rocked backward, pulling him on top of her. A large bubble formed between her and Billy Ray and she sent it, and him, rocketing into the air. Billy Ray exited the fight in a trail of expletives, some of which Drake had never heard before, as he was catapulted into the bumper cars. Runaway cars started banging into him, keeping him off balance. *Niobe's other kid,* Drake realized.

Then he saw someone out of the corner of his vision. The woman in the shiny cape moved purposefully through the now-thinning globular carpet toward Bubbles, and clamped her hands on her shoulders. Drake could tell it was hurting Bubbles, but he couldn't imagine how.

It didn't matter what he thought, though. It was happening and he had to do something about it. He still had the gun. His dad had taught him how to fire one, but if he used it he might kill someone. One thing Drake knew for sure, he never wanted to kill anyone again, in spite of what he'd said to the cops.

He remembered his sling. With all the practicing he'd done, anything within twenty-five yards was a hittable target. That put the caped woman right at the edge of his range.

Drake pulled out the sling and tightened the loop over his pudgy, sweating finger, then fished out a stone and placed it in the pouch. He whirled it in several rapidly accelerating circles, then let go. Drake didn't see where the stone went, but clearly he'd missed his target. Maybe by a lot. Bubbles was on one knee now and the caped woman still hadn't let go. Drake focused his breathing like his aunt Tammy, a yoga teacher in Austin, had taught him and visualized his rock taking the caped woman in the head. He wound up again and let fly.

There was a sound like a walnut being cracked open a couple of rooms away. The caped woman collapsed. Bubbles staggered back to her feet.

Drake pumped a fat fist, but his celebration lasted no more than an instant. The giant dog had its teeth in his cuff and was dragging him away. He punched at the dog's face, but his blow barely caught the snout. "Help!" he yelled. Niobe's acrobat kiddo leapt to his rescue and bounded around the dog, whaling on it with her tiny fists. The dog snapped at the kid, catching a leg. The dog snapped again. For a fraction of a second the kid was free; then the dog's teeth crashed down on her small chest with a crunch.

Drake looked into the dog's cold eyes, wanting to gouge them out with his bare hands, but the dog continued pulling him along the ground, keeping him off balance.

There was a flash of metal. The dog howled and let him go. Niobe was holding a long sword in her hands, cocked at her shoulder for another blow. The dog bared its teeth. Somewhere nearby, a car engine revved. The dog was turning its head when the truck slammed into it, sending the canine howling into a small knot of people.

Niobe helped haul Drake up off the ground. "You okay?"

He nodded.

"This is Baxter," she said, lifting her last kid onto her shoulder. "He can, well . . . he's good with anything electrical." She got into the truck on the driver's side and set Baxter onto the seat. "Let's get out of here."

"Right behind you," Drake said. He piled through the open cab door into the seat.

Drake glanced back and saw the caped woman moving. He felt relief. Billy Ray ran up and helped her to her feet. They were shouting at each other when the woman with the coal-black hair and ball-bearing eyes wrapped them in her big black cape. All three of them disappeared.

"Buckle up," Niobe said. Her tail was taking up a lot of space on the seat. He wriggled his fingers under it and found the seat belt.

Drake frowned. "What about Bubbles? We'd be goners if not for her."

*Of course, she dropped a dime on us in the first place.*

Niobe glanced down at Drake's seat belt, which he'd dutifully buckled, then looked at the rearview mirror. "I've got a plan for that. Hang on."

She put the car into reverse and backed up into Bubbles. There was a heavy jolt that Drake felt in every part of his body, even though he'd braced himself. He stuck his head out the open window and looked back. Bubbles had gotten bigger. Niobe kept her foot on the gas, spinning the tires in the dirt without moving Bubbles an inch. She continued to swell in size. "Cool," Drake said, popping his head back inside. "Smart move."

"Time to hit the road." She changed gears into drive and off they went. "Nobody will be following us, Baxter's seen to that." Baxter looked up and smiled. Sure enough, when Drake looked back, the road was empty. Every other car in Cross Plains seemed to have a dead engine.

Drake looked out the side window and watched the town roll by, which didn't take long. He'd never seen much of the world outside Pyote. If things were different, and people weren't chasing him and trying to kill him, this might be fun. But it wasn't. "How much gas do we have?"

Niobe squinted to check the gauge. "About half a tank."

Drake checked the glove compartment. In addition to the owner's manual, maps, and receipts, there was a candy bar and a nearly full bottle of Jack Daniel's. He pulled both out to show Niobe. "Want to split the candy bar?"

"Fine, but put the booze back in the glove compartment."

They were munching happily on their respective halves when he heard a heavy thump above their heads and a burning piece of metal cut through the roof of the truck. Leather-clad fingers curled under the torn metal and ripped away the roof on Drake's side. "You can't escape, sinners."

Drake could feel the heat from her sword and fiery wings stealing away his breath. "The bottle, Drake," Niobe screamed. "Hit her with the bottle."

At first, what she said didn't register, but then he snapped to it. He snatched the Jack Daniel's from the glove compartment, turned his body to face the woman above him, and cocked his arm. He threw it at her hard and straight and she reacted instinctively, fending off the bottle with a sweep of her sword.

The glass shattered on impact and its contents sprayed outward, immediately igniting and enveloping their pursuer like a fiery hand. The leather-clad woman lost her balance, bouncing off the bed of the truck and into the road behind them. "Jesus," said Drake. "I forgot about her." The wind from the hole in the cab roof whipped his dirty hair about his face. "This blows." He looked down at Baxter, who appeared to be thinking the same thing.

Niobe was silent for the next quarter mile or so. "Drake, would you really have blown up back there?"

He gave her a look like she was from Mars. "Of course not. I mean, my power is awful and I wish I didn't have it. I don't ever want to blow up again. But since I'm stuck with it I might as well use it for scaring people. Sorry if I scared you, too. You're the only friend I've got."

"You did good, Drake. Particularly when you went Mike Tyson on that policeman."

"Yeah, we're a good team." He patted Baxter's head.

Drake leaned his head to one side and closed his eyes. It had been a long time since he listened to the sound of tires on asphalt. The rhythmic noise reminded him of life before the accident, and provided him just enough comfort to let his mind slip into sleep. Finally dreaming about the future, and not the past.

♥

# Double Helix

## I WILL REDEEM THEM FROM DEATH

### Melinda M. Snodgrass

"**KIDS COME OUT OF** eggs. I really shouldn't be telling you this. Carnifex will kill me when he gets back, but Jesus, she lays *eggs*," Stuntman is saying, and his disgust is evident in the way he almost chews the words as if looking to spit them out.

SCARE has brought in an RV to serve as a command center. Outside, the fallen Ferris wheel has lost its little cars like nuts spilling from a branch. A harsh wind is blowing, carrying dust through the door to coat the floor in grit. It carries the faint scent of corn dogs and cotton candy. The wind seems to be pursuing me across continents and time zones.

"Where is the director?" I ask blandly.

A fearsome hailstorm begins beating on the metal roof with a sound like giants banging pots together. I have to lean in to hear him. I'm back to being Noel. It feels odd and I realize I have been morphing between Lilith and Bahir for days with scarcely a stop in to visit me.

"In Paris. The attorney general is arranging for a plane to get him and Lady Black back. That creepy Committee chick teleported them to the Louvre and dropped them inside." I'm a touch offended at the appellation of creepy. That's not how men usually react to Lilith. "Since it was after hours, every alarm in the world went off and they got arrested."

I hide my pleasure at the memory. My last words as I dropped them and teleported away were, "Art is broadening, Mr. Ray. Take the opportunity to improve yourself."

Stuntman shakes his head. "And the arrests aren't going to stop there. Warrants have been issued for Bubbles and Lilith. God, I'd love it if I could catch Fat Chick before Ray gets back."

"This Genetrix . . .," I nudge.

"She's gotta fuck somebody to lay a clutch, so we've been trying to trace her that way."

"While I admit sex in times of stress can be a lovely release, why would she want to . . ." I make a gesture toward my trousers.

"She can't have the clutches without sex, and the freaks are helping them. They're like little mini-aces." His hand indicates something about two feet tall. I have to feign ignorance, but I had seen the power at work last night. "And the powers are always different. That's how she got out of BICC."

I wish him luck on the search, and tell him we'll pool information. I then step outside and proceed to backstab him. The street is awash with runoff from the abrupt thunderstorm. The air smells of ozone and dust and desert plants trying to grasp at the rare and valuable moisture. The smell of carny has finally faded.

I use my BlackBerry to log on to the VICAPP network that lists criminal activity across the fifty United States. The network tells an interesting story of two ATMs that have been mysteriously emptied of money. I'm finding it hard to read, my eyes seem filled with grit. I pop another Black Beauty and continue. The security camera on the first robbery shows only the top of a head. As if the robber is on his knees. Or a dwarf. Or perhaps . . . a mini-ace.

In the same vicinity as the ATMs there has been a rash of stolen cars, abandoned after they run out of gas, and a carjacking. One of the perps had been caught. A midget. He's in custody in Center, Texas.

I locate the place on Google Earth, unbutton my collar and loosen my tie, and unhook my belt, transform into Bahir, and make the jump Between. It's a relief to feel the flesh pull and shift and return to Noel. The binding in my crotch was becoming rather uncomfortable.

Center is another dismal Texas town that looks as if it has been dropped like a turd by a passing bird. It's easy to locate the jail. I walk in. The officer behind the desk is young, with a too-prominent Adam's apple, a shock of straw-colored hair. He tries to hurriedly hide the girlie magazine he was perusing beneath the desk. "Help you, sir?"

"Do you have an impound here? My car was jacked near Cross Plains."

"We may have the guy." He opens the gate and invites me back.

Jails the world over have the same smell. Stale booze, sweat, shit, piss, and blood. We walk down the hall while I check for security cameras. There is one, but the indicator light is dark. There are a surprising number of cells for such a small burg. I hear labored breathing as we approach the last one.

A tiny figure is seated on the thin mattress of the cot. He leans back against the wall, a hand pressed to his chest. He is whispering softly to himself. A prayer? A string of curses? I can't make out the words. A shock of carrot-colored hair falls across his sweat-beaded forehead.

I shake my head. "No, not the guy." The cop looks disappointed, but I don't want to spend time filling out paperwork for a crime that never happened.

The street is lined with low-end businesses. I slip behind the 7-Eleven and transform back into Bahir. I make the jump directly into the cell.

The little man opens his eyes and looks up at me. They are pain-filled but brightly intelligent, with a wry light in their cinnamon depths.

"Well, this is something you don't see every day," he rasps.

I press a finger to my lips, lift him in my arms, and take us out of there.

It's all mental, but I feel too tired to travel very far. I spent a relatively pleasant evening in the Old Town of Albuquerque, New Mexico, a few years back. There was a nearly deserted parking garage directly across the street. I jump us to the top floor. It's deserted. Americans really do hate to walk. I allow my features to shift back to me.

"Thanks for the rescue," the little man says, "but why?"

"I'm looking for Niobe," I say as I lay him down on the cold concrete floor.

"That's nice."

"You're the one who caused all the chaos at Cross Plains."

"Yep." The word resonates with pride and something else . . . love is the only way I can describe it.

"Got her some traveling money and a car, did you?" I kneel at his side.

"Might be."

I keep a flask of brandy on me at all times. Along with cigarettes, a gun, and a knife, it means I'm prepared for almost anything. I hold it to his blue-tinged lips and he sips hungrily.

"I don't suppose you'd tell me where to find her?"

"Nope."

Again there is a wealth of information in a single word. There is determination and, unfortunately for me, not a hint of bravado. Clearly the
homunculus is dying. Hurting it will only hasten its death, and probably
won't garner any results.

My knees are aching so I sit down and now the rough concrete is digging at my seat bones. Usually I'm not this aware of physical discomfort. I
must really be tired. Trying to keep my tone very conversational I say, "You
know I won't be the only person who will figure out how to find you."

"You seem brighter than they are," he says.

"Granted, but they do have the resources of the American government."

"And Mom has us."

My reaction surprises me. Instead of finding it unbelievably creepy I
find it sadly touching. "Your mom?"

There's a faraway look in the strange eyes as if he's hearing a distant
voice. "Yes. She loves us . . . love you, too." For an instant I think he's
talking to me, and there's a sudden tightness in my throat. I shake my
head hard. "I did my best," he whispers softly toward the stained concrete
overhead. His eyes close briefly and the pain-wracked features soften.

A pager starts to buzz. Breath-stopping panic constricts my chest and
sets my gut to aching. I start pulling them out. I can't remember where I
put them. I assign pockets for each pager. Why can't I remember? *Which
one is it? Oh, Christ, not that one, please. Not yet. Not yet.*

It's not the med-alert pager. It's the Committee pager. I'm holding one
in each hand. The urge to throw John Fortune against the wall is strong.
Instead I mute the page and thrust it back into a pocket. I start to put
away the med-alert when a small hand closes on my wrist.

"Who's sick?" The tone is gentle.

I answer. "My dad." *Why did I answer?*

"I've had one. Mom's had one," the little man adds quickly. It snaps
into place. There are more than two people in this garage. *She's* here, too.
"So she would know when we were dying. 'Course she knew anyway. We're
part of her."

"You always die?" A mute nod. "How many?"

"One hundred and seventy-nine. I remember all their names."

"He has a name?"

"Of course I do. I'm her son, I'm Baxter. You don't forget your children."
I'm suddenly back in my parents' yard.

*"And what did you get?"*

*"You."*

The sob erupts from my chest, tears across my throat, and echoes in the garage. The little man lays a hand on my arm. I wave him off with one hand, cover my eyes with the other. "I'm all right. Just tired."

I pull away my hand and stare into his eyes. Can she see me? Or does she only know what he's telling her? I try to look through him to the woman. "I'll bring him to you."

"What?"

"I can bring him to you. So you can see him before he dies. I just need to know where you are."

"Don't do it, Mom. It's a trick. He'll hurt Drake."

"No!" Urgency makes my voice rough. "Don't let him die without seeing you." It hurts to swallow. I don't know this man who's suddenly living inside my skin. *Bloody hell, I'm melting down. Dad, are you listening?*

The homunculus grips my hand. "She says to bring me to her," he whispers, and he tells me where they are.

It's like carrying a corn husk or a nautilus shell when the inhabitant has vacated. I can't pinpoint a hotel room so we arrive in the parking lot. The asphalt is cracking and there's only one car. The Rube Goldberg contraption on the hood and the faint smell of rancid grease and french fries indicate that it's been rejiggered to burn cooking oil. The motel is two stories with exterior entry. Just a concrete strip. The sign declares it to be the Sleep Inn. Underneath it used to read AMERICAN OWNED, but someone has tried to paint over it. As I hurry past the front office I smell the pungent aroma of vindaloo.

I'm taking the stairs two at a time. Is he still breathing? I can't feel his heart over mine, which is wildly beating. They have the corner room at the far end from the office. A pudgy young teenager is holding open the door. I recognize him from the photo Ray displayed. I rush into the room. It's dingy, the spreads are threadbare, but it's meticulously clean.

She's waiting. The photo from BICC doesn't capture her. In the photo she's ugly. In person, her life and soul are in her gray-green eyes. She spares me not a glance. She gathers Baxter into her arms, and settles onto the end of one bed holding him in her lap. It's hard for her to arrange the fat, bristly tail, but I scarcely notice that. It's a pietà.

"It's okay, kiddo. Momma's here." She has a warm, low voice with a husky little catch in it, and that overlay of East Coast money. The little ace reaches up and tangles his hand in the chocolate-colored hair that falls over her shoulder. "Drake," Niobe says. "Would you go get me a Coke? I think there's still a few cans in that machine."

The nuclear ace goes.

"Is that wise?" I ask.

She shrugs. "You either brought people or you didn't. And I don't want him to see this. He knows too much about death." She leans forward and gently kisses Baxter on the forehead. The small chest is barely rising and falling.

She's softly humming. I don't recognize the tune. I stand there feeling gauche and decidedly de trop, but I can neither move nor look away. *So, this is death when you care.*

I try to remember all the deaths I've dealt. I can't.

I try to remember if I cared. I didn't.

I try to picture holding Dad when he passes. I can't.

I'm afraid.

The death is so subtle that I miss it. Only Niobe's soft sobs tell me it's happened. She closes Baxter's eyes, quickly kisses each cheek, and hurriedly lays him down on the bed. The small body melts, leaving only a smear on the worn bedspread. She looks up at me. Her eyes are filled with tears, but she seems at peace.

"Thank you."

I squat down in front of her. "How do you bear it? I don't think I can."

She pushes her hair behind her ears. She is frowning, thoughtful. "You'll do it for him. Because you love him, and he wouldn't leave you alone if you were dying."

And that says it all. We sit together in silence. Then she asks, "Who are you?"

"I'm Noel Matthews. I can get you out of here. They're going to kill him." I jerk my thumb toward the absent Drake. "And if you try to stop them they're going to kill you, too. There's nothing you can do."

"I can *not* leave him. That's what I can do."

"He's a living bomb. They're right, he's too dangerous to be allowed to live." I can feel my frustration rising.

"A lot of people are dangerous, and when they kill they mean to. Drake is a little boy. He doesn't . . . didn't want to hurt anybody. We have to give him that chance."

"Why do you care so much?" I ask.

The sensitive, overly soft mouth tightens with determination. "Because this is one death *I can* stop."

The door opens. "I had to get an orange pop. There wasn't any more Coke," Drake announces. His eyes slide across the stained bedspread and slide away. He goes to Niobe and gives her a rough and awkward hug. "I'm sorry," he says gruffly. She hugs him tight.

I can't believe I'm hearing myself saying, "All right, I'll take you both, but I've got to make a little change first. . . ."

♣

# Won't Get Fooled Again

Victor Milán

**A FIGURE APPEARED IN** midair beside the open-topped Land Rover Wolf. It floated eight feet off the crappy road and easily paced the vehicle's twenty-two miles an hour. Which was fast enough on this surface to make John Fortune's brain feel Shake 'n Baked. "Jesus!" Simone Duplaix yelped. Their Croat peacekeeper escorts jumped and pointed and yelled. The car swerved.

"Tell them to take it easy," John said over his shoulder to Zvetovar, the shave-headed corporal with ears that stuck out like hairy amphora handles beneath his blue UN beret. "It's just the Lama."

"It creeps me out when you do that," Snowblind said from the backseat beside the corporal. She wore a black T-shirt with the words BITCH GODDESS written on it in gold glitter. John wondered if that was really appropriate for an official UN fact-finding mission.

"I merely manifest myself in astral form," the Lama said. He smiled in a way he probably thought was benign. John thought of it as a shit-eating grin.

<*You should assert your authority over this one,*> Isra-who-was-Sekhmet said. <*Teach him to fear you.*>

*Oh*, great *idea*, John thought back. *How?*

The Lama was a devout coward. Right now his physical form squatted in a tent miles away from potential trouble in the middle of an armored column from the Simba Brigades, the PPA's regular army, guarded by Brazilian peacekeepers.

"I have discerned a Nigerian roadblock awaiting you around this curve in the road," the floating figure said.

"Good job," John said grudgingly. "Thanks."

"Let us see that asshole Llama do that," the Lama said. "He lacks the Buddha nature."

Snowblind said, "You're a monk. You can't be supposed to talk like that."

"You are not the boss of me."

She flipped him off. He gave her a sardonic *namaste* and vanished.

*How the hell did I ever let DB talk me into changing teams?* John Fortune wondered. *I should be in Arabia, with Kate.* "Tell your guys to look sharp," he told Zvetovar. "We got Nigerians up ahead past these palm trees."

Zvetovar grinned and bobbed his head. To say he understood English might be stretching things. More accurately, he occasionally responded to what John said, and even more occasionally said something John could make out. He did pass *something* along to his men. Probably orders.

"I don't like this," Simone said, shaking her head. The streaks were magenta today. The stud in her left nostril looked like a gold Egyptian scarab. It made John Fortune's own nose twitch to look at.

The day was hot and bright. They always were, here in the Oil Rivers region of the Nigerian coast. Unless they were hot and rainy. "We're the UN," John said. "The Committee. We're legit. What could go wrong?"

"Everything," she said. "There's *war.* I wish the Radical had not been killed. We could use his backup."

"Yeah," John said. "Well." They could have used some of the Committee's heavy hitters, too. Lohengrin, Earth Witch, Bubbles. Not that any of them could have matched Tom Weathers for sheer power.

He hadn't much cared for the guy. But getting backshot into a trench full of piss was a hell of a way to go. And Simone was right. It *would* be comforting to know the world's most powerful ace had their backs. Instead of what John did have: a redneck who turned into a big toad. A flying Apache with an attitude. An even surlier astral dude. A French-Canadian princess who could make people temporarily blind.

<*You do not need him,*> the voice said in his head. <*We are powerful. You must learn to use your power more.*>

*Don't start,* he thought back. "Nothing's going to happen," he said aloud. He drummed his fingers on the outside of the door, ignoring the way it scorched the tips. *We are not here to fight,* he reminded himself. *This is just a fact-finding mission.*

The Wolf rolled around the bend. A Fox armored recon car blocked the road. *It's menagerie-of-war day in the Oil Delta,* Fortune thought. The armored car was narrow and precariously tall, like a normal sedan with big tires and a turret stacked on top. Its long-barreled cannon pointed straight at John's nose. It was only 30mm but looked as if they could drive right up it.

A pair of utility trucks angled into the ditch to either side. Troopers in Nigerian battle dress slouched around. They didn't point their long FN-FAL rifles at the newcomers. Maybe they thought the autocannon was enough.

A tall man in a maroon beret held up his hand. "Halt," he commanded. That was one good thing about the Nigerians: English was their official language. Their accents got a bit dense sometimes, but John could talk to them.

Snowblind had to translate with their PPA allies. She could be a bit of a diva, but wasn't a bad type. And her ace might actually come in handy if things got crosswise.

"What is your business?" the Nigerian demanded.

<The fool! Can he not read?>

Isra had a point. UN PEACEKEEPERS was painted on both sides of their car in four-inch white letters. "We're the United Nations fact-finding commission," John said. He kept his voice level despite Sekhmet's influence stirring in his blood like angry bees. "We're legally entitled to go wherever we need to."

The officer looked doubtful. He wore no rank badges: like most modern armies the Nigerians had figured out that officers' insignia served as wizard sniper aim-points in the field. The Browning Hi-Power in a holster on his web gear in lieu of a broomstick-long assault rifle marked him as head guy even to John Fortune, who wasn't exactly Gary Brecher the War Nerd. It struck him as kind of a wash.

The officer turned to shout in some tribal dialect to the guy in the helmet and goggles peering at them from the Fox's cupola. John wasn't sure that was a good sign. Nigeria usually mashed up its innumerable ethnic groups among its military units, he knew from the briefing dossiers

Jayewardene had loaded onto them. Tribal strife had wracked the country since independence.

The Nigerians fought hard and mean to suppress Oil Delta ethnic groups, primarily Ijaw and Ogoni. The UN recognized their right to do so. The issue that had John Fortune and his fellow Committee members driving around through the swamps enjoying bugs and heat and having guns pointed at them was whether the horrorfest the Chinese had shot—currently the world's hottest viral video, even though YouTube yanked uploads as quickly as they could for graphic violence—was aberration or policy.

The guy in the space helmet spoke into a chin mike. "What're they doing?" Simone asked.

"Probably bumping us upstairs," John said. "Must have a radio in the armored car."

Simone sighed. She flipped open her phone and began texting somebody.

To either side of the road rose dunes of white sand, overgrown with brush and tall grass, all wispy and pale green. It didn't look healthy. Maybe petroleum seeping from the ubiquitous oil pipelines poisoned it.

John was just feeling grateful they weren't near a bayou right now, so that the meanest bugs had farther to fly and consequently had less energy to torment them, when a plump figure pushed through the grass on the hillock to his left.

<It is the get of a dog!> Isra said. <Slay him!>

Butcher Dagon grinned at them and gave them the reverse V-sign that was the Brit equivalent of the bird.

<It is a trap!>

Fear blasted through John's veins. His grip, always tenuous, snapped. He just kept presence of mind to yank open the door and spill himself onto the broken-shell road. Then the beast broke free. Sekhmet seized the ascendant.

The Nigerians opened panic fire at the sight of a giant golden lioness appearing in the road. Sekhmet the Destroyer saw the Croatian corporal stare at her in gap-mouthed shock before a bullet pierced his head and he slumped. The copper-haired girl yelped and dropped from sight.

The Fox's turret gun erupted in thunder and fire. Like the troopers on the road the gunner fired high. The muzzle blast still blew the Wolf's windscreen in. The safety glass obediently sugared. The force of the blast shotgunned the particles into the face of the driver, who hadn't been quick enough to hit the floorboards.

The Destroyer's ears rang from the horrific noise. It stoked her primal fury.

A flash. Sekhmet's head swam. Her vision turned all formless white, as if she drowned in a Nile of milk. She understood: the strange-looking girl had used her power, blinding all in the vicinity. Even a Living God was not proof against that, it seemed.

But Sekhmet did not need to see. She had the senses of a beast, as well as the brain of a man.

And the wrath of a god.

Though her sensitive ears rang from the unnatural loudness of *guns* she smelled the soldiers' sweat, laced with adrenaline bright as silver. Smelled the hot metal of the great iron beast, the petroleum farts of its diesel exhaust, the strange chemical reeks emitted by its weapon.

She breathed flame. The horrific shrieking that answered it was sweet as the music of *ugab* flute and lyre, accompanied by the crackle of fire and the smells of burning cloth and hair and man-flesh.

She bunched muscles, leapt. Her mind and body knew where her target lay. She struck the squat metal monster's turret and clung like a locust. Her claws dug deep into metal that the men inside thought armor to protect them. She roared in amusement as much as triumph.

She heard screaming, smelled man-breath that carried traces of tobacco and a breakfast of gruel, bread, and pulses. She lashed out with a forepaw. The strike of a mortal lioness could break the neck of a wildebeest. Sekhmet the Destroyer was much stronger than that.

She felt the impact of the plastic helmet on her pads. Felt more than heard the skin and tendons and tissue and bone give way as her fury tore the gunner's head from his neck and spun it toward the ditch.

Hot blood sprayed her face and shoulders. She yanked the headless corpse from the hatch and flung it aside. Then she drew a deep breath, thrust her muzzle into the opening that reeked of sweat and metal and chemicals, and filled the car with fire.

The screams of those trapped within exalted her.

With a bound she reached the crest of the dune from which the foe had shown her—her, Sekhmet!—disrespect. She roared again in triumph and challenge.

But the blindness still fogged her eyes like cataracts. The stinks of burning and the knife-edged clamor of ammunition bursting in the burning vehicle blanketed nose and ears. Yet she knew.

Her enemy had escaped.

She raised her head and roared. In nature lionesses did not roar. But she was Sekhmet the Destroyer. She roared.

*We shall meet again, dog-spawn,* her roaring said. *And when we do, I shall taste your blood.*

◆

"*Hei-lian!*"

Walking through a well-lit corridor on the palace's ground floor, Sun Hei-lian stopped and turned. Sprout broke from her female handlers and ran to her. She wore shorts and a short-sleeved shirt. Tears streamed down her cheeks. Her blond hair streamed behind her. Hei-lian had a moment to wonder why she was being taken for her usual exercise in the garden. With her father's fall, why would the Nshombos indulge this unnatural creature?

The creature hit her in a hug so desperate it was almost a tackle. It took all Hei-lian's *taijiquan*-honed balance to keep from being bowled over.

Sprout clung to her like a handful of flung muck and wept, drenching Hei-lian's blouse. "My daddy! They killed my daddy!"

For a moment Hei-lian stood rigid. Her stomach heaved with revulsion at the contact, at the disgraceful display she'd been made a part of. Many times her life depended on fast thinking followed by faster action. Now she had no idea what to do.

*I should push her away and go about my business,* she thought.

Instead her arms went around the young woman and tentatively returned the hug.

Vision blurred. She felt wet heat on her cheeks. *I'm crying!*

Holding awkwardly on to Sprout, Hei-lian shook her head. *It's pent-up emotion—fear of what loss of Weathers might do to our hard-won position in the PPA. That's all.*

"Oh, Hei-lian," Sprout moaned.

*He means nothing to me,* Hei-lian thought.

Mechanically she stroked the long golden hair. It struck her that for all the many things she knew how to do, she had no idea how to comfort someone. "There," she said. "There, there."

*Nothing.*

Even in the glaring morning sun the tracers from the BO-105 attack helicopter's strap-on mini-gun made red streaks in the sky. Brave Hawk wove deftly between them, great falcon's wings spread wide.

"He can't keep that up long," Simone said. She had gotten minor scorches and punctures from the autocannon blast and flying glass. Our Lady of Pain had healed her without putting herself out of action for more than an hour. *How* she did that still made John cringe, and left Simone inclined to guilt up over it.

"Isn't there something you can do?" he asked. "Blind the chopper dudes?"

"Not without a chance of blinding Tom. So close to the ground he might crash."

Sitting in a fresh Land Rover, with fresh Croat escorts, John Fortune felt frustration crawl like ants throughout his body—felt the scarab stir beneath the skin of his forehead. Since Butcher Dagon turned a routine highway stop to carnage, the UN mission had been functionally at war, fighting alongside the Simba Brigades.

John couldn't say that bothered him. The Nigerians and their Brit pals were playing the monster here. The kind of things they were doing were the things the Committee had been formed to stop. But with the Mideast occupation unraveling in sabotage and suicide bombings, he was seriously worried if the Committee would be *enough*.

<You must not hold back. Strike. Strike!> Sekhmet said.

*There's nothing we can* do, he thought. Kate could have brought the chopper down with one well-thrown stone. Michelle could have taken it out with a bubble. But Kate was in Arabia, and Bubbles in New Orleans. *This was just supposed to be a fact-finding mission, damn it.* He squeezed his eyes shut so hard brief tears came.

Two attack choppers had jumped the small convoy out of a clear blue sky. The flat coastal swampland of green canals and white sand offered nowhere to hide. Diedrich sprang fearlessly into the air. He'd actually managed to wrench a landing skid off one gunship and whack it a few times, causing black smoke to pour from its engine housing and the bird to turn north and run for home.

But then its partner had gotten stuck on the ace's tail.

John's eyes opened to see a half-dozen 57mm rockets ripple from the launcher beneath the chopper's right stub wing. They were unguided ground-attack missiles. The gunner clearly hoped their blasts would swat their pesky prey from the air.

Brave Hawk flew into a red fireball rising from the sand. Snowblind moaned. John felt his nut sac contract.

The ace emerged. Smoke streamed from his wings. Dazed, he flew straight and level. Not a hundred feet behind him the chopper jock steadied for a can't-miss shot right up his ass.

Something long and pale streaked up out of the weeds and hit the helicopter's sandy-camouflaged belly. It stuck. The gunship's nose dipped toward the marshy ground. Its Allison turboshaft engines whined. It gained ten feet of altitude. Twenty.

From the grass appeared a toad the size of a Volkswagen Beetle. The tip of its tongue was glued to the helicopter.

The aircraft wobbled. It dipped, bouncing the toad off the ground. Simone cried out. Engines straining, the helicopter rose and fell twice, slamming the giant toad into the ground each time. The toad vanished behind a dune. It stayed down. Somehow it had caught a grip on the planet.

The helicopter pivoted straight into the ground. It blew up with a series of white flashes, engulfed by an orange fireball when exploding munitions lit off its fuel.

John piled out of the car with the UN flag fluttering from one antenna and the red-and-white checkerboard of Croatia from the other, and raced into the weeds. As he reached the dune crest the grass parted and a tall, rawboned man appeared. He walked as if more disoriented than usual. "Buford," John said, "what the *hell* do you call that?" Improbably, he liked the redneck. It was hard not to.

Toad Man smiled that big goofy smile of his. "Leadin' with my chin, Mr. Fortune," he said. "Kinda my specialty."

"Jesus."

Brave Hawk touched down. His wings vanished. He didn't look to have any more holes in him than he started out with, it relieved John to note.

"You know what they say," Diedrich called out. "If a frog had wings, it wouldn't bump its ass a-hoppin'."

"Toad," Buford corrected reflexively.

Diedrich flashed a rare grin. "Thanks for the hand, there," he said. "Tongue. Whatever. For a white-eyes, you ain't half bad."

"That's what I like to think," Buford said.

Fragrance dense as fog and the buzzing of myriad bees enveloped them as they walked in the rose garden of Mobutu's old palace, surrounded by high white stone walls that kept the Kongoville traffic noise at bay.

*Not that there's much, with the fuel shortages,* thought Hei-lian.

"The Arabian occupation has disrupted Mideast oil shipments, Your Excellency," she said in her flawless French.

"As the imperialists should have known in advance it would," President-for-Life Dr. Kitengi Nshombo said. He walked at Hei-lian's side. He was a head shorter than she.

"These circumstances increase the value of the Niger Delta oil fields."

Nshombo nodded his big head, which shone like hand-rubbed teak in the sun. "As the People's Republic's appetite for oil increases daily, Colonel."

He knew what she was. He seemed to prefer to treat with her over the regular diplomatic delegation when possible. It made them crazy.

"Don't worry. The oppressed people of Africa, whom I unite under one purpose, one flag, shall not forget those who aid us in our hour of need."

"That isn't what worries me, Excellency," she said. "With Tom Weathers gone"—to her surprise and annoyance, the name caught briefly in her throat—"the war of liberation has slowed."

"We feel the loss of Mokèlé-mbèmbé most keenly," Nshombo said.

He could have fooled Hei-lian. The president was renowned for never showing visible emotion. But his utter nonresponse to the loss of his revolutionary comrade, the man whose crazy genius and unmatched powers had put him in this palace, struck even her as cold.

"Now that the UN has joined us," he said, "I think they and my Simba Brigades, along with help from our LAND brothers, should suffice. Don't you?"

She wondered. She didn't care to say so aloud. Her job required selfless courage, not folly. She searched for words to frame her true concern. The PRC had backed Weathers's guerrilla-style strategy for liberating the Oil Rivers. With him . . . gone, the campaign had shifted to conventional warfare. And the Simba Brigades were largely trained and subsidized by India: China's bitter geopolitical foe and, more specifically, rival for Nigerian oil.

Shrill, excited barking broke out ahead. They walked from among the high rose-jeweled hedges, across white gravel that crunched beneath their shoes, toward a wire-mesh fence. A white-clad attendant opened the gates to admit the president and his companion.

A horde of mop-headed white Dandie Dinmont terriers yapped ecstatically as they jumped up Nshombo's trouser legs. The president chuckled and clucked to them in the dialect of his and his sister's tribe, which apparently had about a dozen living speakers. They didn't include Hei-lian.

"I know what your interests are, Colonel Sun," Nshombo said. "You look after them ably. And you have served me well. As Tom did." He knelt and let the tiny dogs lick his face. He actually smiled, in a manner that reminded her, remarkably, of Sprout in better times. "But I know that in all the world, only Alicia and these dear little creatures truly care for *me*. Remember that well, Colonel."

"Thanks," Tom Diedrich said. "I feel better already." Which, John Fortune thought, was total macho bullshit. Not even Our Lady of Pain's super-accelerated healing could take perceptible effect that fast.

"You still look like twenty miles of bad road," Buford said helpfully.

"We all serve the Revolution as best we can," the young woman said. Her English was just shy of too thickly accented for John Fortune to follow. She smiled through bloody gashes and the glaring red burn that now covered half her face.

She was already moving slowly when she'd entered the cheery, brightly lit room in the presidential palace. John couldn't imagine what weight of hurt she carried from wounds she had taken to herself. He didn't want to try.

Simone Duplaix sat in a chair beside the bed, almost hidden by bursts of roses, red and pink and yellow, Alicia Nshombo had sent from her brother's garden.

"You sound just like Tom Weathers," she said. Out of consideration for her fellow Committee members she spoke English, too.

"Do I? He . . . left his mark on me. On all of us."

"Yet he was a warrior," the Lama said. He sat in a chair like a normal person, sipping bottled orange Fanta through a straw. "You are a healer. Is it not strange you are being disciple of one such?"

"What I saw in the Delta made me accept that the Revolution won't be won by good intentions."

Which, John knew, was another of the Radical's damned bumper-sticker homilies. He'd seen it on enough Prius bumpers. *I guess she spent enough time with Weathers in the few days before he got whacked,* he thought. *That Chinese TV chick didn't look too thrilled about it, either.* Ah, well. He wasn't here to sort out the PPA's domestic affairs.

*<You should court this girl,>* Isra told him. *<Even though she is black. She is strong, and has good hips. She could bear you strong sons.>*

*Please,* he thought. *I'm in love with Kate. And this girl has got a self-mutilation thing going that makes the most razor-happy emo girl look a wimp. Plus I get enough from you without putting up with hearing revolutionary slogans twenty-four/seven.*

Dolores Michel bent to stroke an uninjured part of Diedrich's forehead with gentle fingertips. "You will be well soon, well-named Brave Hawk."

"Thanks, ma'am," he said.

She left. "Well," John said, "she seems to be taking the Radical's demise pretty calmly."

"Don't be a dick, John," Simone said. "She's trying to hold in so much pain, she can't give in to sorrow."

"Poor gal's carrying the world on her shoulders, that's sure," Buford said.

"When the lion lies down with the lamb," said the Lama, "who knows what issue may come forth?"

"Wait," Simone said. "Back up. What?"

He smiled.

John Fortune never saw what toasted the lead tank.

He rode in the backseat of a fresh Land Rover with six fresh Croats. Buford Calhoun and Simone followed in a second Wolf. In front and behind rolled a PPA mechanized company, Brit-provided Ferret armored cars and beefy, tracked BMP-2s from Russia, hauling infantry. A quartet of Indian-made Vijayanta main battle tanks flanked front, rear, and sides. The Western aces called them Va-jay-jays.

With all that serious steel and firepower surrounding them, and the Lama scouting ahead in invisible astral form, John felt fairly safe, even deep in enemy territory. Until the Va-jay-jay two hundred yards up the road went up.

The Land Rover's doors flew open. Blue-helmeted Croats blew out of them like shell splinters. *Screw* that, John thought. *This may be an open car, but some cover's better than none—*

A blast bellowed from the stricken Va-jay-jay. It lifted the heavy turret six inches and dropped it skewed to one side. Blue-white flames gushed up from the hull.

It occurred to John that that was what modern weaponry made of a massively armored, forty-four-ton *tank*. He wasn't even sure the Wolf's body was real metal.

He dove into the weeds to his left.

He found most of his crew huddling in a ditch with four inches of stagnant salt water in the bottom. "That fucking Lama!" he shouted, jumping in with them. "Why didn't he warn us?"

The radio quacked. No more cell reception. Their buddies in the Liberation Army of the Nile Delta had helpfully blown up all the repeating towers. What he had was an overweight Croat kid squashed beneath a humongous radio pack, red-faced and puffing asthmatically, looking ready to puke from heat stroke and terror.

John snatched the microphone. "Fortune here, over." They always said that in the movies.

"*Brave Hawk,*" the radio crackled. "*Nigerians are in our base, killing our dudes. Dagon's beast form's ripping Brazilians to pieces.*"

"What about the Lama?"

"*Hiked up his skirts and ran off like a rabbit.*"

John dropped the mike without even saying "out." Instead he said, "Oh, fuck *me*."

His half-dozen Croat escorts huddled in the ditch like frightened mice. They all stared at him with pathetically open optimism. They—his *body-guards*—plainly expected him, the great American ace and son of aces, to rescue *them*.

On the dune-line to the right across the road, Nigerian armored vehicles appeared. Zippy little Scorpion tanks with 76mm guns and much bigger Warrior personnel carriers whose long 30mm autocannon quested side to side like monster bug antennae. A Scorpion promptly exploded in a billow of red fire and black smoke.

John's blue helmets might be a bunch of lovable losers, completely out of their depth here. The Simbas were hard-asses who'd carved a chunk bigger than Argentina from Africa's bleeding heart. And their mostly Sikh officers were as warm and fuzzy as the daggers they all carried.

A line of explosions stitched the road. Their abandoned Wolf blew up in their faces. "Shit!" John yelled. His Croats all jumped up and raced off over the dunes behind them. He followed.

*<You must not run!>*

"Shut *up*," he shouted.

Facedown in a clump of rough grass he struggled to get a grip on what was happening. War's like that, he was finding out: if you're *in* it, you miss about 99 percent of what goes on.

He smelled gasoline burning. And something else. *I think I may be over barbecue for a while,* he thought. To his right a vehicle went up with a roar. His heart jumped into his throat. It was Simone and Buford's Land Rover. "Oh, shit, oh, Jesus, no."

He felt . . . total helplessness. He was the man in charge. He was an *ace* again. Or the next best thing, at least. His friends had just gotten fried and he *couldn't do a fucking thing.*

*<Then let me,>* Isra urged.

*What? Like you can bring them back? You're not that kind of god.*

He heard a colossal plop. As if . . . as if a one-ton toad had jumped over a dune to land on packed white sand beside him. *Exactly* like that.

The toad stared at him with those huge eyes. Moss green. Like Buford's, but bulbous and the size of cantaloupes. But still with that unmistakable goofy good nature.

The mouth opened. And opened. And out upon the sand plopped a whole *Québécoise* ace.

Simone's eyes weren't much smaller than Toad Man's. Her hair stuck out as if her head had played octagon for a death-match between a weed whacker and a quart jar of mousse. She looked like a kitten fished out of a washing machine. Only more *viscous.*

She opened her mouth. She closed her mouth. Sounds came from her nose, along with bubbles of toad mouth slime. She squeezed her eyes tight shut. *"Eww,"* she said.

There was a *pop!* and Buford stood beside them in all his Florida cracker glory.

"Thanks," John rasped. His throat felt as if he'd gargled battery acid.

"Wasn't nothing," Buford said. "My uncle Rayford always said to help a lady when I could."

From his right John heard a noise like a sheet ripping, times a hundred. He looked around in time to see a machine-gun burst tear into one of his Croats. The guy's body bucked. He rolled on his back and stared up at a sky whose painful blue was stained with gray smoke.

A quarter mile behind them more Nigerian AFVs rolled out of the scrub. Fire flashed from their guns. "Okay," John said. "This officially sucks. White 'em out, Simone!"

Snowblind shook her head. Her face had gone pale as her namesake. "Can't. Too far!"

John sucked in a deep breath and almost choked on fumes and stench. He had mostly been ignoring Sekhmet's increasingly furious yammer in his brain and blood. It hadn't been hard: he had things on his *mind.* But now was the time to hear her. Now was the time to give her what she clamored for.

He let go and exploded in a flash and boom like a shell going off.

Gun flames reached for the huge golden lioness like hungry tongues as she raced toward the line of machines. Lion laughter rippled through her body as she effortlessly eluded their foolish fire. Did they think so easily to stay the wrath of a Living God?

She struck the lead Scorpion tank like a lightning bolt. She leapt to the turret. Her jaws crunched its metal as her rear claws raked the tank's hull, the way she'd gut a Cape buffalo. The vehicle's armor was aluminum treated to steel hardness. It yielded like butter to her fangs and talons.

She expected that once she was among the flocks the other vehicles wouldn't dare fire for fear of hitting their own. She reckoned without the power of panic. With a clang and a bang a main-gun round from a neighboring tank struck the Scorpion she was savaging.

She sent a burst of flame toward the other tank. It was too far to do damage but would confuse and terrify the gunners. She pounced as the machine she had eviscerated exploded.

When she breathed fire the tank's commander ducked down his turret, slamming the hatch above him. She hooked claws into the hatch and tore it away. Then she blew fire within.

The hideous screams of commander and gunner were drowned as 76mm shells racked inside the turret cooked off. The Destroyer had already turned and leapt onto her next victim. Joyously she rampaged among the Nigerians, tearing and burning. She was vaguely aware of PPA armored vehicles shooting at their enemies with seeming disregard for whether they hit her or not. She paid them no heed.

She was crouched on a Warrior's front deck, worrying its long gun in her jaws like a bone when something smashed into her right side. Hurtling weight drove her off the personnel carrier. She landed hard on her back with the weight crushing down on her. Teeth plunged into her shoulder.

Squalling outrage, she kicked with her rear legs. Her new opponent bellowed in pain as she threw it away from her.

She rolled to her feet. Her right shoulder bled. It meant nothing. It *was* nothing, next to the punishment she would inflict in return.

Eight meters away her enemy faced her. A huge, hairy beast whose muscle-mountainous body narrowed to a pointed snout. A naked pink tail lashed behind it. It reminded the lion-goddess of nothing so much as a gigantic rat.

She drew breath and sent it forth in flame.

The rat wasn't expecting that. Yellow fire briefly obscured it. It rolled away, shrieking. Unfortunately distance had attenuated the blast. Sekhmet had done no more than singe the beast. It jumped back on its four legs with a score of smoke-tentacles waving from muzzle and shoulders.

The Destroyer was already flying at it. The rat-monster reared back to grapple her with what more closely resembled arms than an animal's forelimbs. She struck.

Over and over the two monsters rolled, snarling, clawing, and snapping. Their blood dyed the sand pink. To the Destroyer's fury the rat-thing's bristles and thick hide resisted her talons and fangs better than Nigerian armor plate had. She felt chisel-like teeth and claws dig deep into her own golden-glowing skin.

But she was Sekhmet the Destroyer. A Living God was *not* to be defeated by an outsized rodent. With the strength of righteous rage she snapped her jaws. Her opponent squealed. By the luck of the Gods of the Nile she had bitten its neck.

But she had muscle, neither windpipe nor spine. It gave her leverage. From her back she threw the rat from her with a spasm of mighty neck and shoulder muscles.

It landed three meters away. Huge rents showed red-raw on its body. Its fur was dark-matted with their mingled blood. Yet it instantly began to roll upright to counterattack.

The Destroyer stretched her head back and enveloped it with fire.

Screaming like a ship's whistle, the rat-creature reared up. Its fur burned with blue flames and a stinking smoke that filled her nose like burrs and clawed her throat and lungs.

She came up rampant. With a swipe of her forepaw she knocked the huge beast through the air. It struck, rolled over and over in the sand, extinguishing the flames. It landed in a bush and lay still.

Its outline writhed. Blown sand and steam swirled up to hide it momentarily from her sight. Then it cleared.

A man lay in the bush on his back. His fat, nude, blue-white body was gashed and torn and washed with gore. His limbs stirred feebly.

Dismissing him instantly from her mind, the Destroyer turned away. Grievously wounded she might be, but she had better prey than a mere *man*.

But instead of the armored cars and little tanks among which she had rampaged as if they were baby gazelles, she faced a crescent of full-sized tanks. Their cannons were trained upon her.

Even if she had all her strength she could not prevail against such monstrous power. And she felt her strength draining through a hundred wounds. Within, John was silent, stunned. <We are only half of what we were meant to be, Isra thought sadly. He was meant to be Ra, with all the powers of the sun, and me but his handmaiden.>

She was Sekhmet the Destroyer; but she was also a protector. She felt duty to her comrades, puny though they were. She turned and loped back to where they huddled against the white flank of a dune. She could at least shield them with her body as she fell. She turned back to snarl at the tanks where they squatted like vast impervious turtles. Her grip began to slip. Exhaustion and injury—and despair—had sapped even the will of a goddess.

She raised her muzzle and roared defiant denial: *No!*

It did no good. She whirled down and down, away from being.

In an ecstasy of fearful frustration Sun Hei-lian paced the palace terrace, hugging herself tightly beneath her breasts.

Since Tom's murder Nshombo had refused to let her and her team leave the capital. Hong monitored radio traffic from the front in real time. Even when it was encrypted his specialized Guoanbu equipment and training easily cracked it.

The war went badly. That morning Simba armor had thrust triumphantly along the Niger Delta coast toward Lagos. Abuja, well inland, was the national capital. But capturing the huge seaport would seal the conquest— strike that: *liberation*—of the country. Or at least its coastal oil fields.

Then Nigeria mounted a massive counterattack. Taken by surprise, the PPA spearhead was cut off. Now half-coherent reports claimed a terrible monster was ravaging the Simbas. A giant golden lioness—appropriately enough, she supposed, given "Simba" meant "lion"—had miraculously appeared to fight it.

John Fortune and Butcher Dagon were going at it in their alternate forms. But Nigerian traffic revealed an armored battalion closing in to deliver the killing blow. Not even the Destroyer could deal with that.

Hei-lian shook her head. The other Committee aces were useless in an armored battle. Toad Man, the Lama, Snowblind, Brave Hawk . . . *the Committee sent us its B team, not the powerful aces who broke the Caliphate's army at Aswan last year.* Whether John Fortune had simply misjudged, or had regarded Africa as unimportant, his parsimony was about to lose it all. *If only Tom still lived.*

"Hei-lian?"

She stopped and spun and glared. Sprout had emerged from the French doors of the palace onto the terrace. She wore jeans and a T-shirt. She clutched a slim picture book to her chest. "I'm sad," she said. She held out the book. "Will you read to me?"

*No!* Hei-lian's mind raged. *Get away from me, you unnatural thing!*

*Why do they suffer you to wander the palace still, without your father to protect you?*

Her eyes welled. "Yes," she heard herself say, as from the depths of a pit of sadness. She took the book. *Charlie and the Mouse Ace,* the cover read. "Let's sit here in the shade."

They sat on white-enameled metal chairs beneath an awning. Heilian's fingers trembled as she opened the brightly colored cover.

"'Charlie was a little boy with a big secret,'" she read. "'He had a friend who was a mouse. And more than that—'"

"So when I was little," Buford was saying when John Fortune opened his eyes, "Uncle Rayford, he had him these naughty magazines."

John raised his head from the sand. "Oh, shit," he said with a groan. His head dropped back. His neck felt like boiled pasta. "Am I naked?"

"I don't think it matters much now, John," said Simone. She knelt beside him. "Just try to rest."

"Did I see like half a dozen tanks pointing their guns at us?"

"Eight tanks, yes," Snowblind said. "Nigerian ones. Look just like Vijayantas."

"Anyways," said Buford, who sat beside them with his legs drawn up, "I never saw no bad pictures nor wanted to. But Uncle Rayford, he showed me the funnies. I liked them."

"How badly am I hurt, Simone?" John asked.

She flicked a glance along his body. Then she turned her head. "Don't worry about it."

"Now, he showed me this one I still remember. It had like this big hero guy with a big old mace, and a couple little scrawny guys with a pitchfork and a club."

"Why aren't they killing us?" John asked.

"I think they wait to see if we have any more surprises. Then again, they may just be toying with us."

"All around them, see, there was thousands and thousands of these knights on horses. And they all had spears pointed at them three fellas."

John's sense of detachment from reality was beginning to fade. Which *really* sucked. Even Isra's voice was stilled. Exhaustion had overcome her.

For the first time since that dramatic evening in his mother's L.A. home, he was alone. *I should be with Kate,* he thought, picturing her face, her smile. *I never had a chance to say good-bye.* "Snowblind," he croaked. "You couldn't, like—"

He had his eyes closed but somehow felt her headshake. "What's the military term for lots and lots of vehicles?"

He sighed. "A shitload."

"There's a shitload of Nigerians, John. They are all around us."

"So anyway," Buford said, "this fella with the big chest and big old shoulders, he's saying to his pals, 'Don't worry, boys. They can't stop men who want to be free!'"

He laughed and laughed. "Kill me now," John said.

"Be careful what you ask for," Simone said. "Their gun barrels are ze-roing in on us."

John wondered if their deaths would make the evening news. Back home, the second season of *American Hero* was the most watched show in America. The fighting in Nigeria made page six in the *Times,* maybe. The only news crew on the scene was the one from China. *It's just Africa,* he thought bitterly. *No one cares.* "Help me," he said. Simone lifted his head and scooted a knee under it to support it. Which he needed; it weighed at least a ton. No question the gunners in the tanks were tuning up their aim. "I guess the douche bags're just gonna smoke us—"

Down from the sky speared a shaft of white light. It transfixed the middle MBT like a pin through a bug. It was so bright it cast shadows on the dunes.

The tank erupted in blue-white fire.

Another sunbeam stabbed down, another.

Another.

Each left a pyre blazing on the sand.

Big diesel engines growled. The Nigerian armor began to mill. Main guns probed the air, seeking targets.

A man landed on a tank's front glacis. A white man with shaggy golden hair. A man who laughed. He grabbed the main gun, heaved. The whole multiton turret came right up out of the well. Grunting, he threw it end over end through the air. It smashed down on top of another tank, dented in its turret. Yellow fire enveloped both as their ammo stowage went up.

From twenty meters away another tank fired at him. It couldn't miss. Yet somehow he still stood, laughing.

"Shell went right through him," Buford said. "Pretty fine trick, you ask me."

The man stretched out his hand. Red flame lanced from the palm. It shot down the gun barrel and gushed out of the breech, which the loader had opened to receive a fresh shell.

The shell blew up. So did all the others.

Just like fucking *that,* one tank remained. It churned away as fast as its treads would carry it, throwing up a great bow wave of sand. The infantry and lesser vehicles had already fled. Simba armored vehicles fired after them, over the heads of the three Committee aces. They didn't try to pursue.

"You have *got* to be shitting me," John Fortune said. "Tell me I'm hallucinating." Maybe they would live to see another day after all. *Kate,* he thought.

Somehow his companions heard his feeble croak above all the explosions. "It's the Radical," Snowblind said. "*Ce n'est pas possible.* But it is him."

Tom Weathers vanished. Reappeared at once, ten feet from John and a yard in the air. He landed a little unsteadily, walked forward a couple steps.

"Whew," he said. "Takes it right out of you. But I'll get my second wind in a minute. Then we'll get it *on.*"

Somehow John remembered his duty. "Leave it, Weathers," he said. "It's good to have you back. But you're part of a team, now. Just chill with us. We'll sort things out."

Smiling, Weathers shook his head. "That's a big no-can-do, Mr. Establishment Man. It's time to deal out some *revolutionary justice.*"

He vanished.

"How does he *do* that?" John asked the air.

A Simba infantry squad came down the dune. Their tall, turbaned Sikh officer shouted for medics. Dark hands propped John to a sitting position and held a canteen to his torn lips. Simone got up and went to stand next to Buford.

Away across the dunes, white light flashed against the sky like distant lightning. A black smoke stalk sprang up in response. A moment later, a rumble reached John's ears. Another flare lit the sky. "I got me a bad feelin' about this," Buford says. "Never seen a feller look so crazy."

Snowblind crossed her arms and leaned against him. "What he said," she said.

Tom burned through energy like a drunk playboy's bankroll in a Monte Carlo casino. But all he had to do was land and breathe for a few minutes. Then he was good to go again.

It was as if killing these running-dog colonial lackeys *recharged* him.

He leapt into the sky, seeking more lives to take. A mile ahead he saw a sizable village. As he approached, climbing for a clearer look, he saw fleeing Nigerian armor had locked the narrow streets up tight.

He smiled like the Angel of Death. And swept downward like a scythe.

Noisily Simone barfed over the side of the Land Rover.

Around them smoldered the ruins of a murdered town. The stench was as thick as the flies. The flies were thick as monsoon rain.

"There must be hundreds dead here," John Fortune said. He wasn't feeling so good himself.

The Lama floated by the car. "One thousand," he said.

A reserve Simba column had routed the Nigerians raiding the base camp where the Lama's body had sat in lotus while his spirit did its astral scout thing. Without Butcher Dagon to back them they didn't put up much fight. Another Wolf and some intact Brazilian peacekeepers had been found. They drove the Lama up with Brave Hawk flying top cover to pick up their comrades.

The team followed Tom Weathers's wake of massacre. To his crowning horror.

Simone had quit puking. Now she sobbed. "How could he *do* this?"

"His power," John Fortune said. He shook his head. "It's like nothing I've ever seen. Like nothing I could've *imagined.*"

"I didn't mean that," the young woman said. "I meant, how could he do so horrible a thing? It's worse than what happened in that village. A hundred times worse."

John could only shake his head some more. He had no words. In the seat behind him Buford muttered under his breath. John could only make out the words "terrible bad."

"Why the long faces, children?"

They all looked up. The taunting voice came from ahead and above.

Tom Weathers hung thirty feet in the air. He descended slowly to stand before them with hands on jeans-clad hips.

Anger boiled up inside John. "What the *hell* did you think you were doing here?" he shouted.

"I told you. Dealing out revolutionary justice."

"But these poor villagers," Simone said. "You killed them. You killed *civilians.*"

He shrugged. "They were collaborators anyway. They had it coming."

John almost released Sekhmet again. But he was held together by duct tape as it was. And more than for himself, he feared that if he let the Destroyer out now, she'd prove no more discriminating than Tom Weathers had. "You're a war criminal, Weathers," he said. "That's the only way to say it."

"What? When colonialists bomb or shell neighborhoods full of indigenous people you call it 'collateral damage.' What makes this worse?"

"Just because others do it doesn't make it right," Simone said.

"I cannot *believe* what a bunch of posers you are!" Weathers yelled. "Bourgeois phonies. You come here saying, 'Long live the Revolution,' all that dorm-room shit. But when it comes down to hitting the barricades, man, when it all gets *real,* you can't fucking take it."

"This wasn't revolution," Simone told her fallen idol. There was no heat in her voice. No life at all. Verbal flatline. "It was murder."

Weathers sneered. "You can't make an omelet without breaking eggs."

Buford gripped John's arm. "It's all over here, Mr. Fortune," he said. "This is a bad place. Let's go home."

"Yeah," John said. "It is over. We're not part of this."

"Yeah!" Tom flared at them with wild hateful laughter. "Your work here is done, right? And I did it for you. Now you want to run on home. Run, then.

"You're all fucking fascists. Just like the rest of them."

♠

Standing amid the devastation he had created, the Radical watched them drive away. His chest pumped like bellows. His stomach was a surging chaos of nausea. He had spent himself unimaginably. Soon his body would pay the price.

He gave it no thought. What he thought was, *There, Meadows, you simpering hippie fuck.* That's *what I think of your peace-and-love horseshit.*

"This is all for you, man," he said aloud. "All for you.

"*I hope you fucking like it.*"

"Why are we here?" Chen asked. He clutched his heavy camera to his chest like a teddy bear.

"No idea."

Hei-lian glanced around the helipad next to the palace. A crowd had gathered. Wide-eyed, Sprout stuck close to her. She had panicked when Leopard Men came to escort them brusquely here.

So had Hei-lian, almost.

"Look," Hong said. "It's Nshombo. And his sister."

"Are they going to shoot us?" Chen asked in Mandarin.

"I don't think they'd have had you bring your gear," Hei-lian said. "Since they did, you'd best start shooting. *Something's* going on."

"Hei-lian?" Sprout asked in a small voice.

Quick headshake. "No idea, honey," she said. "Just stay close."

She saw the young healer-ace, Dolores. She stood between Nshombo and Alicia, dressed in gleaming white. Her face shone as if with inner radiance.

Someone shouted. Pointed to the sky. Everyone looked up.

A hundred voices gasped. A pale-skinned, golden-haired man floated above their heads. He raised a fist.

"*Vive la Révolution!*" shouted Tom Weathers. "*Vive Dr. Kitengi Nshombo!*"

"Long live *Mokèlé-mbèmbé,*" roared a claque of Leopard Men.

To mad cheering, Tom descended from the sky. Palace guards in powder-blue uniforms held the mob at bay as he swapped handshakes with Nshombo and an embrace with his sister.

Sprout hit him at a run. He laughed and kissed away her tears.

He turned to give Hei-lian a big grin as she approached. She was too stunned to talk for the benefit of the microphone she'd clipped to her shirt collar moments before.

"Sorry to scare you like that," he said. "But we had to keep things secret. We wanted to spring a little *surprise* on the imperialists."

She flung arms around his neck and kissed him deeply. Then she stepped back.

"Why are you still alive?"

Dolores was suddenly by his side. Still holding Sprout in one arm he slipped the other around the Congolese girl.

"She healed me," he said. "She's the real heroine."

He turned and kissed her on the forehead as camera flashes flickered.

Hei-lian wondered why she felt so hollow.

◆

# Double Helix

## UNTIL THE DAYBREAK, AND THE SHADOWS FLEE AWAY

### Melinda M. Snodgrass

**SHADOWS ARE STRETCHING AND** dancing on the plaster walls of the old cottage as Niobe clears the battered table. The air is redolent with the smell of beef stew. After delivering them here I teleported to Kirkwall for supplies.

We're using oil lanterns for light, saving the generator to heat water for baths. Drake's face is rosy from the heat of the fire and a large meal. He is nodding, then suddenly jerking back awake. Niobe ruffles his hair.

"Go to bed, kiddo."

"Can I have some more pudding?"

She smiles indulgently. The soft golden light and the shadows hide the worst of her acne. Drake spoons more chocolate pudding into his bowl and shuffles out. A few moments later I hear the springs on the old bedstead creak.

"Why here?" she asks me as she starts to wash the dishes. I fill the chipped glass with more wine.

"Because there are seventy islands in the Orkneys and only seventeen of them are inhabited. If he loses control nothing but gulls and rabbits will die."

"He won't."

"I want to be damn sure of that."

"How did you know about this place?"

"My mother took a month one summer to look for Roman influence in the Orkneys. We crawled all over the islands, and found this abandoned farm."

The smile is back. It's very warm and genuine. "But no Romans."

"No Romans."

The hot water won't last long, so I stand in the chipped and stained claw-footed tub, hand resting against the wall, and let the water sluice through my hair and down my back. The tightness is back in my chest, as if I'm filled with tears fighting to escape. It's just because I'm so tired. That's all it is. I should head to London. Report. Wait for dawn and check on Siraj.

The water is starting to cool. I soap up and rinse. The handles squeak as I spin them to turn off the water. The rings on the cheap plastic shower curtain rattle like chattering teeth on the rail as I pull it back. Suddenly the door to the bathroom flies open and Niobe and Drake rush in. She has one hand between his shoulders. The other is pressed against his forehead. He has a pudgy hand clasped desperately over his mouth.

I'm naked, and acutely aware of my deformed genitalia. She looks at me and her eyes widen. Once again rage is coursing along every nerve. I lunge forward and grab the frayed towel.

They reach the toilet and Drake folds up like an origami figure. The smell of vomit tinged with stew and chocolate pudding fills the steam-filled room. I feel my own gut heaving in sympathy. I'm frantically trying to wrap the towel around my waist.

Niobe holds out an imperious hand. "Wet a washcloth with cold water," she orders. I don't act immediately. I'm getting the sheltering towel in place and tucked. "Would you get me a damn cloth!"

This time I obey. It's a tiny room, and my back is against the wall as I try to shuffle out. I watch as she wipes Drake's face, and murmurs to him soothingly. I remember just such nights, but it's my father's warm baritone I hear. Drake is crying. I don't think it's just because he's puked. I leave them.

I should be sleeping. Instead I'm standing at the edge of the ocean, smoking. The waves hiss and giggle on the rock and sand shore, and the sound of the rising and falling water is like the breathing of a great beast. I want to walk into it and let the waves close over my head.

I have that writhing feeling in the belly when you feel like you've said or done the wrong thing with someone you want to please. Why did the little bastard have to get sick right then? Why couldn't it have happened five minutes later. I should have put the towel right by the tub. Dried myself in the tub.

Carried on the night wind, the squeak of the sagging front door seems like a scream. I listen to her footsteps. *Oh, crap, she's joining me.*

"You didn't have to be embarrassed. I've seen a few penises." I don't answer and the silence yawns between us. "Is that what the wild card did to you?" she asks.

Anger shakes me. "No. That's what a genetic fluke did to me."

Nervous, she gathers her thick, bristly tail into her arms and cradles it. "Isn't it the same thing?" she asks.

"Somehow it seems more cruel." I cough to clear the harshness from my voice.

"At least your deformity is hidden." And she drops the tail as if horrified to find herself holding it.

"I'm not sure that helps all that much. I can't tell you the number of times my classmates jumped me and pulled down my pants and underwear for a firsthand look. Children are such little animals." I see her blanch at that. "I'm sorry. You obviously don't feel that way."

"Children are a blessing."

"That's what my father says."

"But not you."

I should just walk away from this uncomfortable conversation, but I find myself answering. "A little side effect of this cosmic joke is that I'm sterile," I lightly add. "The noble line of Matthews dies with me."

She doesn't realize I'm joking. "And your father blames you for that?"

"Oh, Christ, no, he doesn't give a damn about all that. He just would have liked to have grandkids." I take a long drag on the cigarette and release the smoke in a sharp exhalation.

The tips of her fingers are cool as she quickly touches my wrist. "But you feel guilty." And I realize it's true.

A flick of the fingers sends the butt soaring away over the water trailing red sparks.

"When did you find out? That you couldn't . . ." Her voice trails away.

"When I was twelve. My teenage years should have been fantastic—*stick with me, baby. All the fun and none of the risk.* But it didn't work out that way."

"Why?"

"Christ, woman, are you dense? You saw me. I'm grotesque."

She reaches back, feeling along the length of her tail. "Do you know how I ended up at BICC?"

I shake my head.

"I was twenty-two when I learned this isn't just a tail," she said. "As if things hadn't been bad enough already." She looks up at me, challenging me to engage. I decide to go along.

"And what, exactly, does that mean?"

"My parents never had any interest in raising a joker. I was, um, embarrassing to them. They distanced themselves from me as much as they could. They called me their niece, said they'd taken me in after my own parents died."

"Charming. They must live in a world where image is more important than anything else."

She seems startled at my words. She nods slowly. "I had no idea I was an ace until it just sorta happened." Her eyes have gone dark, and her expression is bleak. "I thought he liked me, but he just wanted sex. And it happened almost instantly."

"What?"

"The eggs. It hurt so badly, I thought I was dying. I thought God was punishing me. That this was what happened to wretched little whores."

"I hear a quote in that." I find I'm suddenly fascinated, and furious at whoever would have said such a thing to a frightened teenager.

"My father." The words are spoken so quietly that I have to lean in to hear her.

She draws in a deep, shaky breath and forges ahead: "But the eggs hatched, and suddenly, I had kids. They were so wonderful. They bounced and laughed and flew around the house. They infuriated my parents and terrorized the help, but I didn't care, because they were my children and I loved them so intensely. And they loved me, too." Her voice is fierce, passionate. "I was simply delirious with joy. Until they died." The three words seem to hang in the air. "When my children died, my heart was crushed. My joy extinguished. I took it badly. I hurt myself.",

Her tone is so dispassionate that I know she is holding back a storm of emotion. I don't know why I'm hearing this story, but I know I want to hear it all. I speak very softly as if I'm dealing with a frightened foal. "What did you do?"

"I tried to cut my tail off. I've never felt pain like that. It surged up my spine and erupted in my skull like magma. I passed out." She gets a crooked little smile. "It's funny. I've been in therapy for years and I just remembered this. As the floor was coming up to meet my face, I noticed the way my blood ran in little rivulets between the tiles, toward the bathtub. My last thought was how upset my parents would be when they learned their remodeled bathroom had an uneven floor."

I look down at the bumpy ridge where none of the bristly hair grew. "I presume they shipped you off shortly after that."

She nods. "And then they had the bathroom redone."

We stand in silence listening to the ocean's soft murmurs.

"Can Drake control himself?"

"Yes."

"Then let's go."

"Where?"

"I'm going to take you to meet a truly decent man."

"I think you're pretty decent."

"You'd be mistaken."

♣

# Dirge in a Major Key: Part II

S. L. Farrell

**THE CHINOOK WAS LOUD,** crowded, and uncomfortable. Underneath them, lit only by starlight, sandy, low hills crawled toward the horizon and more hills emerged to replace them, until finally the sun rose to color the world red and then yellow. Rusty was in the chopper with him, along with four dozen UN troops and their officers, Lieutenant Bedeau among them. They wore flak jackets and helmets and carried live ammunition in their weapons, but there had still been no real resistance—not at Kuwait International, not at any of the places that Michael had been to in the endless parade of days and nights.

Michael had lost count of time. All the places in the Ar-Rumaylah field in southern Iraq were starting to look the same, blurring in his memory. The employees of each facility had packed up and left, leaving papers and half-eaten snacks on their desks. In each place, the wind wailed mournfully as it blew dun-colored sand between the buildings. The army of the Caliphate was an eternal no-show.

The other teams—Kate with Lohengrin in the Al-Burqan field in Kuwait; Tinker on the Az-Zuluf platforms out in the Gulf—reported the same: no resistance. The wellheads, the pumping stations, the pipelines, the refineries: they'd all been abandoned. Michael, Rusty, and their blue helmets would stay a day or two or three until UN contractors and support troops were sent in from HQ at Kuwait International, and then they'd be on to the next place.

The ease of the operation was a relief to everyone, Michael no less than the others. He'd not been looking forward to another battle in some god-forsaken locale, especially when the enemy carried a special hatred for him.

He glanced out the window nearest him. The radio headset squawked with terse updates. DB kept tapping on the flak jacket that covered his chest, but the dull sound it returned gave him no comfort. Easy or not, the whole operation still felt wrong. Everything was *too* easy. Michael was sweating, and it wasn't the heat. He slipped one of his hands under his flak jacket and rubbed at the bruise on his chest, the fading remnant of the sniper attack at Kuwait International.

*They hate you for what you did in Egypt. . . . The people of the Caliphate, they don't like you very much. . . .*

"Wellheads, one minute." The warning came from his headset. Around him, soldiers checked gear and readied themselves: their group was French, as were the bulk of the UN ground forces, armed with stubby FAMAS G2 assault rifles. The Chinook tilted, then dipped with nauseating suddenness as the rotors wailed. Michael caught a glimpse of the towers of derricks, several buildings, and a trio of huge storage tanks for the crude oil, but then dust and sand rose in a dense, choking cloud, blocking sight of the landscape, and he felt the shudder as the wheels touched ground.

The rear door yawned; a squad of blue helmets jumped out, ducking their heads against the rotor wash and running across the sand with weapons ready. Alongside him, Rusty coughed in the gritty air. "Cripes," he muttered. More troops tumbled out. Michael checked the two M-16s he carried—still leaving his upper set of hands free—and lurched to his feet. "Let's go," he said to Rusty.

"Why don'cha stay behind me, fella?" Rusty suggested. "Just in case." Michael thought that an excellent idea.

They lumbered down the ramp and onto the sand at a jog.

Their Chinook had landed alongside the administration building for the facility—Lieutenant Bedeau was leading the first set of blue helmets, and had already kicked open the doors of the building and gone in. As with all the wellheads they'd taken, there didn't seem to be anyone around: no cars in the parking lots, no one near the storage tanks or near the oil derricks set in a mile-long arc just to the east, no one moving in the village five hundred or so yards away to the west near the main road. The pipeline-linked refinery a half mile to the south looked equally deserted. The Tigre choppers hovered overhead menacingly, loud in the sunlight, but their guns were silent.

*Maybe,* he thought, maybe Jayewardene and Fortune were going to get what they'd hoped. He rubbed the bruise under his Kevlar again and crouched behind Rusty, scanning the rooftops and half expecting to feel the kick of a slug against his jacket.

"We're secure here," he heard Bedeau say in his headset in French-accented English. *"Aucun problème."* The relief in the man's voice was palpable. Someone laughed nearby; he saw the closest soldiers let the tips of their weapons drop slightly.

These assignments were already becoming routine. They were beginning to *expect* it to be easy. That worried Michael more than anything.

"Nobody home again," Rusty said. In the midst of the pipes and derricks, he looked like a piece of old equipment that had decided to become ambulatory. "Good deal."

They swept the facility closely and made certain that the employees had indeed abandoned the place, that there were no soldiers of the Caliphate or snipers hidden about, and that the facility hadn't been either sabotaged or booby-trapped. Rusty had been given the task of using the metal detector on the grounds, with two demolition experts a careful dozen steps behind him, checking any hits he found. He grinned at Michael with the earphones stretching dangerously around his orange-red head. "I found lots of pieces of old pipe, and a whole buncha coins." He held out a large palm, and Michael saw several silver and bronze-colored coins there, adorned with Arabic lettering. "Souvenir, fella?"

Michael took one. He brushed the sand from it and stuck it in his pocket.

A few hours later, Michael, Lieutenant Bedeau, and a six-member squad of blue helmets trudged out to a small village along the narrow paved road passing the complex, while Rusty and the others continued to sweep for mines and booby traps. The village was a collection of small houses huddled together in the sand with a few stores and a petrol station. All the houses looked the same: prefab, cheap company housing. The veiled faces of women watched them from behind shuttered windows as they approached.

There were children—a dozen or more, their ages seeming to range from maybe seven to perhaps fourteen—playing soccer between the houses. Usually, no matter where he went, the strangeness of Michael's spidery figure would bring them running and chattering toward him, but these only stopped their game and stared as they approached before melting away into the bright shadows between the buildings. ". . . *Djinn* . . ." He heard the word in the midst of the stream of whispered Arabic, and it gave him a chill. He began to watch the windows of the houses carefully, half expecting the muzzle of a rifle to appear. The children vanished, the soccer ball abandoned on the sand. The village seemed preternaturally quiet; it made the small hairs stand up on Michael's arms. His lowest set of hands clutched the single M-16 he was holding tighter, his finger sliding close to the trigger.

*It's all kids, women, and old men here,* he reminded himself, but that gave him little comfort. Any of them could just as easily press a trigger.

Lieutenant Bedeau, in addition to English, also spoke Arabic. He called out a greeting, his voice sounding terribly small. For several seconds there was no response at all, and Bedeau shrugged at Michael. "We'll go building to building looking for weapons," Michael began, but then a door creaked on rusty hinges and an elderly man stepped out from one of the houses. His *thobe*—the standard white robelike garment of the region— swayed as he moved, revealing a stick-thin body underneath. They tensed, all of them: had the man made a wrong gesture, he would not have lived to take another breath. But the grizzled elder kept his hands carefully in sight as he spoke to Bedeau in a burst of rapid-fire, gap-toothed Arabic. Bedeau nodded; they exchanged a few brief sentences.

"This one's name is Dabir," the lieutenant said. "He says that all the men—the workers—are gone. His son was one of them. Big trucks from Baghdad came here three days ago and took them away. The wives, a few old men like him, the children; they were told more trucks would come for them, but none have. There's no one here right now but the elderly, the women, and the children." Dabir said something else, pointing at Michael. Bedeau grimaced and hesitated before translating. "He said that you and the other one are abominations in the face of Allah, that you must leave so the men can come back."

"Well, that's nice," Michael said. "Rusty will be happy to hear that. Tell our friend Dabir that we don't think the men will be coming back at all, that tomorrow or the next day more of our people will be coming to work here. Tell him that we'll talk to Prince Siraj and try to make sure that the trucks show up to pick them up to take them to wherever their men went."

As Michael spoke, he saw movement behind the old man; a boy, probably no more than ten or eleven. The child crept out to stand next to the old man, who put an arm protectively around him as he listened to Bedeau's translation, scowling. The boy said something in response—again, Michael thought he heard the word "Djinn" in the torrent—and Bedeau's face colored.

"This is Dabir's grandson Raaqim. He's . . . not exactly happy with the news," Bedeau told Michael. "The rest, it's not worth translating."

"Yeah, I kinda gathered that." Raaqim was staring at Michael, scowling like Dabir with his arms crossed defiantly in front of him. "Tell the old man we're sorry, but that is the way of things. It is the will of the Caliph and Prince Siraj."

Bedeau shrugged. He translated, and Dabir's scowl deepened. With a middle hand, Michael dug in his pocket for the old coin Rusty had given him. He crouched down in front of Raaqim, the muzzle of his weapon pointed down at the sand, and held out the coin. "Here," he said. "You can have this."

The boy stared; the old man watched without saying anything. "Go on," Michael said when the kid didn't move or respond. "It's yours."

Raaqim unfolded his arms. He stared at Michael, his gaze roaming up and down his long, muscular body, staring at the several arms, at the snarl of tattoos decorating his skin, at the sextuplet of tympanic rings covering his chest and abdomen. His eyes widened. He looked at the coin.

With a violent lurch of his head, he spat in Michael's face.

Michael recoiled, dropping the coin and standing abruptly. Raaqim flinched, stepping quickly backward; the old man snarled something in angry Arabic, his hands coming up as if to ward off a blow. The soldiers' weapons snapped up, all of them.

"Stand down!" Michael shouted. He wiped the spittle from his face with an upper hand; he forced himself to smile. He spread all his hands wide. "Shit. Everyone take it easy . . . Lieutenant, tell the old man I'm sorry. I didn't mean to offend anyone. I'm sorry the men were made to leave and I hope they're all together again soon, but we have the wellheads now and there are more people coming to take the oil. That's the way things are. We need to check their houses for weapons, but once we've done that, we won't trouble them again. We can give them food or water if they need it. There won't be any trouble for them as long as they let us do our job." He waited until Bedeau had finished translating, watching Dabir's leathery face, watching the doorways and windows around them.

He'd dropped the coin when Raaqim spit at him. He could see it glinting on the sand. He shouldered his weapon with a flourish of many arms, and nodded in the direction of the houses. "Let's get this done," he said. "And be fucking careful."

The connection over the satellites was static-ridden and erratic, and Michael had to strain to hear Kate's voice. "Everything's still going easy here," she said. "Clockwork. Last place, there were villagers wandering around and scavenging stuff from the facility, but they scattered when we landed. We had some shouting and cursing, but no real resistance." The line squealed; he could barely make out the last words.

"Yeah. Same here," DB told her, half yelling into the cell phone. Across the lobby of the Administration Building that had become their base, Rusty glanced over at him. "No problems. Makes me happy; I wasn't looking forward to another dustup with the Caliphate, especially not over oil."

"What we're doing is about people," Kate said. "That's what matters. Half the world is suffering because of the embargo. That's the reason we're here." Then, a laugh that made him grin. "That sounded like John, didn't it?"

"All you need is a scarab beetle in your forehead."

There was silence, and he worried for a moment that she'd taken offense. "Sorry," her faint voice responded at last. A squawk of static cut off most of what she said afterward. ". . . watch yourself, especially. And see you soon back home, okay?"

"Right," he told her. "Soon."

"How's Curveball and the others?" Rusty asked.

"It's good," Michael told him. "Everything's good."

The rest of the day was uneventful. Michael and Rusty toured the wellheads that their team had secured; all seemed well. The evening subsided into semi-boring routine as the workers arrived from Baghdad International: derrick workers whose job it was to get the oil flowing again. The feeds they received from the news channels were full of praise for the work of the teams. Fortune sent word through Barbara that the aces would be brought out within the week—there was more need of the Committee elsewhere with this operation going so smoothly.

The next day, Michael and Rusty, along with two blue helmets—Lieutenant Bedeau and Marlon, another French soldier—decided to sweep through the refinery area to the south of the Administration Building, where crews were scheduled to begin work. Tomorrow, Michael and the others would be heading somewhere else, landing in some other desert wellhead.

They walked along a large open area set in the middle of the cluttered refinery: weapons shouldered, their Kevlar vests unbuttoned against the day's broiling heat—Michael, against orders and his own nagging paranoia, was entirely bare-chested in the fierce sunlight. Marlon was snapping pictures with a digital camera; Bedeau was speaking into a satellite phone, reporting in to Colonel Saurrat's adjunct. "The refinery looks to be operable," Michael could hear Bedeau saying in French-accented English. "There's no—"

The voice cut off with a grunt. Michael glanced back. Bedeau had dropped the phone and was clutching his stomach with both hands, a look of surprise and shock on his face as blood poured through his fingers and bloomed on his uniform shirt. A strangled, wet cry came from his open mouth as his knees gave way and he crumpled. At the same moment, there was a familiar, chilling metallic chatter: small-arms fire. Something *pinged* from Rusty's body and whined away past Michael's left ear, leaving behind a burning line from his ear to his forehead. He could feel blood sliding hot down his cheek.

"Shit! Take cover!" Michael screamed. A four-foot-tall set of thick pipe sections was stacked a dozen feet away. Michael took two running steps and flung himself behind them. Marlon was trying to get his FAMAS up when a round took him in the biceps and spun him around; he managed to crawl behind the pipes with Michael, puffs of sand kicking up around him from bullets.

Rusty hadn't moved. He stood in the open, pointing to the north and a tangle of steel pipes laced between two buildings a hundred feet away.

"The fellas are over there," he said calmly. "I see six or seven of them."

"Great," Michael told him. "Now get the fuck down."

A trio of bullets struck Rusty's body and caromed away, leaving shiny scratches on his chest. He grunted. "I'm fine," Rusty said. "Let me try—"

A stream of orange fire and black smoke raced past well above them and slammed into the side of the main refinery building fifty feet behind. The concussion of the explosion was like a fist, the sound was deafening. Michael could feel the heat of the fire as debris rained down around them. A brick slammed into the sand a hand's breadth from Michael's right side, burying itself several inches deep. "RPG," Michael shouted to Rusty, wondering if any of them could hear anything over the lingering roar. He was trying to wrestle his own M-16 from his back. "*That's* why you have to get down, Rusty! Marlon? You okay?"

The man was cursing loudly in French, and blood stained the sleeve of his uniform. "Fuck," he said in English. "I think so, but the lieutenant, I think, is dead."

Rusty had stooped to grab Bedeau's body, then came lumbering behind the piping with the others. "How is he?" Michael asked, glancing at Bedeau's open-eyed stare and already knowing the answer. Rusty shook his head.

Michael felt his stomach turn over. He gulped acid.

They huddled behind the pipes. It was the only cover—they had been caught in a large swath of open ground, the nearest building the one now burning behind them: a good twenty running strides away and already a conflagration, vomiting black smoke and fire from the hole the RPG had punched in it. Rifle fire rang from the pipes like a Midwestern hailstorm. To their left and right there was nothing: just sandy ground for a hundred yards or more—a killing field if they tried to retreat.

Michael could hear more small-arms chatter to the north and to the east—separate firefights on the compound. Someone with a high, thin voice was shouting in Arabic near where Rusty had said their attackers were hidden. Through the din, Michael heard the dull k-*WHUMP* of another explosion somewhere in the distance, followed by the *thrup-thrup-thrup* of a chopper's rotors starting up. He hoped it was one of their people at the controls. *Christ, it wouldn't take many of them to get us all.*

Marlon was moaning as he ripped open his medical pack. Michael helped him apply the pressure bandage to his arm. "Can you still use

that?" Michael asked him, gesturing at the soldier's weapon. Marlon nodded grimly. "Good. Look, it sounds like the others are dealing with their
own problems right now. We can't just sit here and wait for someone to
rescue us—and if our friends have another RPG and send it our way, we're
dead. Rusty, you willing to take a few more hits? If we can see the muzzle
flashes, Marlon and I can return fire and hopefully take a few of them out,
and maybe then we can figure out a way to get the fuck out of here."

"Sure thing," Rusty said. He lumbered to his feet behind the pipes as
Marlon and Michael moved to either end of the pipes. Gunfire popped
and hissed; Michael could see the glint of fire from the muzzles—their attackers were settled in a snarled nest of piping and flow valves between
two buildings; judging by the flashes, there seemed to be five or so separate
people with guns. Twenty feet over their attackers, a heavy pipeline
bridged the structures. Michael heard the chatter of Marlon's gun and he
pressed the trigger on his own weapon, the recoil slamming into his upper
shoulders, his lower set of hands bracing himself on the pipes. The Arabic
shouting returned, more alarmed this time, but Michael doubted they'd
hit anyone. Michael saw a bloom of fire and smoke—"Rusty! Down!"—
and another RPG arrowed toward them. Rusty stood there gaping as the
round passed a bare few feet over his head before slamming into the burning building behind them with a new eruption of fire.

Rusty hit the ground belatedly with a grunt. He stared at Michael wide-
eyed, his steam-shovel mouth open. "Yeah," Michael said. "I know.
Cripes. We're lucky that bastard's a lousy shot, but we can't sit here waiting for him to get more practice."

Another bullet ricocheted from the pipes, the sound like a drumstick
on the bell of a cymbal. The heat from the fire behind them was searing;
Michael began to wonder what was going to kill them first.

"They be amateurs, these ones," Marlon spat in his broken English.
"Professionals would now spread to come from different angles; but
these—they stay all together." He made a quick sign of the cross. "This is
good, yes? If they are well trained, we would be already like poor Bedeau."

"Yeah, there's some comfort," Michael told him. The gunfire had
slowed to erratic single shots. Michael hoped that wasn't because they were
taking Marlon's advice. The wind was whipping the choking smoke away
from them, but flames were gushing from the ruined building and the heat
was nearly unbearable—Michael was almost afraid to touch the pipes in

front of him. The fire hissed loud and throatily and suddenly leapt thirty feet into the air as a gas line in the building ruptured. They all felt the fiery embrace of the inferno. "We really can't stay here. We gotta make our move. Rusty, you willing to take a chance on being a target again?"

The ace's shoulder lifted and fell. He didn't look thrilled at the prospect, but he didn't say no.

"Okay, then. Marlon, I want you to start firing from your side of the pipes—keep them down as much as you can. Rusty, I'm hoping they're even worse at hitting a moving target. Head toward them, but zigzag it—maybe about ten steps' worth, then go down just in case Mr. RPG is waiting. I'm hoping that they'll be a lot more interested in a fucking big steam shovel coming their way than me."

"What are you doing?"

"I'm going to give them a free performance that'll bring down the house. I hope."

Rusty's eyes widened. "Oh," he said, somewhere between question and statement.

"Yeah." He touched the wound on his forehead, looking at the blood that stained his fingertips. "Sorry, I don't have a better idea. Do either of you two?"

Rusty slowly shook his head. Marlon just stared and clutched his weapon. "Then wish us luck," Michael said.

Rusty, his knees creaking, got to his feet; Marlon, lying on the ground, began to rake the space between the buildings on full automatic as Rusty came around the pipes and started toward them, shouting and waving his massive arms.

Michael, on the other side of the improvised cover, stood up. He started drumming with all six hands, the multiple throats in his neck pulsing as he shaped and focused the sound as he surveyed the target area. At first it was merely noise (as Marlon continued to fire, as Rusty weaved and roared while bullets pinged from his body). Michael could hear the stacked pipes in front of him rattling in their racks with sympathetic vibrations, and he forced his throat openings to narrow, to toss the sound farther out and focus it—as he had when he killed the Righteous Djinn. He aimed the torrent of percussion between the two buildings, hitting himself harder and harder, his arms flailing. There was a new sound now: a metallic wail as the piping set between the buildings started to respond.

(Rusty took a few more steps, a lumbering, bearlike dance. Marlon's weapon went silent for a moment as he changed clips. Through the fury of Michael's drumming, there was a percussive cough, and a smoky lance arrowed in Rusty's direction, hitting the ground six feet to his left and erupting; Michael saw Rusty lifted and tossed.)

He drummed, grimacing at the effort of finding the right notes, the right timing, and the right frequency. The pipes shuddered and danced angrily in response. He could see figures there, pointing toward him, and muzzle flashes. Bullets whined past him and he forced himself not to respond. The huge pipe above their attackers groaned loudly enough to be audible over the racket and Michael concentrated on it, forcing all the sound toward it; he saw dust and bricks falling as it shook itself loose from the walls, shaking like a wet dog. Dark, thick fluid gushed out in a wide stream.

The man-high steel tube fell, much of the walls of the two structures going with it. He could hear screams as it slammed into the ground, taking out the nest of smaller piping underneath. A dust cloud rose; within, something sparked violently and then there was fire and more screams—high-pitched and desperate.

Michael stopped drumming. Marlon was staring. Rusty had pushed himself back up to a sitting position on the sand, shaking his head as if dazed. Michael snatched his weapon from the ground and ran toward the buildings.

He saw one of their attackers, on his back with his arms outstretched as if he had been trying to escape the fate he had seen falling on him, the bottom half of his body crushed under a section of brick wall. The thick tube of the RPG launcher lay near him.

"Oh, fuck," he breathed. He stopped. His weapon drooped in his lower hands. "Fuck."

He stared at the body—at the beardless, smooth face of a child, a face he recognized: Raaqim, the boy who had spat at him yesterday.

None of them were soldiers. None of them looked to be older than their midteens, while the youngest couldn't have been more than ten. The weapons they'd brandished were a strange collection of ancient single-shot rifles to modern automatic weapons, probably scavenged from a dozen different sources. The RPG launcher had been the most sophisticated and dangerous piece, but it had no more rounds left.

Twenty kids, all told, and not all of them boys. Their surprise attack had cost the lives of three UN soldiers, but twelve of the twenty kids were dead; of the survivors, all had serious injuries. The unit's medic had done what triage she could; the four worst they'd choppered out to Baghdad after frantic communications to Colonel Saurrat and Barbara Baden; the medic didn't seem to have much hope any of them were going to make it. They'd laid out the dead children in the lobby of the main building, covering the bodies with whatever sheets they could find, and they'd permitted the villagers to come in to identify the bodies and take them away for burial.

The wails and screams, the accusing glares, the accusations, were something that Michael knew he could never forget. Dabir, his ancient body shaking with rage, had screamed curses over the body of Raaqim. A woman in a black *abaya* and head scarf had charged at Michael after seeing her granddaughter's body. She'd reached him before anyone could stop her, beating at him with her fists as she screamed in Arabic, her fists making the tympanic rings boom and crash in a mockery of his playing. Michael endured the beating, his arms at his side like a stunned spider while two soldiers grabbed the woman's arms and pulled her away, still screaming and wailing, tearing at her clothes, gesturing with hoarse, sobbing cries.

He was weeping with her suddenly, the tears coming unbidden and unstoppable, hot and harsh, his throat clogged with emotion. Michael had left then, going outside into the heat and glaring sun. He slumped against the side of the Administration Building, his back on the rough stone wall, staring outward toward the oil derricks.

He touched his chest where the woman had struck him, so softly that he made no noise at all. His throat openings pulsed and yawned, silent. Under the bandage the medic had wrapped around his head, the scabbed track of the bullet throbbed and burned. Part of him wished it had killed him instead.

Afterward, he'd tried to call Kate and hadn't gotten her; he sent her a text message: FUBAR. That said it all.

"Hey." A shadow drifted over him. Michael glanced up.

"Hey, Rusty."

"Bad deal, huh?"

"Yeah. The fucking worst."

With creaks and groans, Rusty sat down next to Michael. "Kids. I don't want to fight kids."

"None of us should have had to." Michael glared outward. Against the sky, the derricks were ink lines drawn on a blue canvas, and he'd killed children for their sake. He imagined the blood flowing dark like oil. "This shouldn't have happened. It shouldn't have been *able* to happen."

Rusty said nothing more. He and Michael sat there for a long time, each lost in his own thoughts, until the sun slid away and abandoned them in the cool shadow of the building.

The old man Dabir stared with slitted, dark eyes at the nervous squad with Michael. He barked something in Arabic and spat on the sand between him and Michael. The squad's translator spoke to Michael without taking his eyes from the old man or his finger from the trigger of his FAMAS. "He says you are the afterbirth of a syphilitic camel and that you are not welcome here."

Michael might have laughed at that, before. Now it only made him feel ill. "Tell him . . . tell him that I want him to know that I had no choice. He needs to know that."

That earned a bark of dry, hollow laughter from Dabir. "Allah always gives us choices," the old man said through the translator. "What choice did Raaqim have? You come here, you take away his father's job, you ruin our family, you take the land that belongs to us and our people, you steal our oil. Why shouldn't my grandson defend what was his? Why shouldn't he fight to take back what you've stolen?" Dabir glared at Michael. "I am proud of my grandson. His was a good death. Are you proud, you abomination in the eyes of Allah?"

Michael clenched his jaw at the torrent of vitriol from the man. "You don't know," he told him. "You don't know the suffering the Caliphate has caused with its oil policies. You don't know—"

"Suffering?" Dabir interrupted as the translation was given to him. "Look around you, Abomination. Do you see people here with automobiles and televisions? Do you see mansions? Do you see stores full of things to buy? I have seen pictures of your West. I have seen the way you live. Suffering? You know *nothing* of suffering."

"People have lost jobs from the lack of oil," Michael persisted. "Some are going hungry as a result, or can't pay for care that they need, or have lost their houses. And some have even died." It was what Fortune might have said. The words tasted as dry and dead as sand.

"So you come to steal the job from my son, who has been taken away?" Dabir waved a hand toward the buildings of the wellhead and spat again. "You come to steal the food from our table? You come to kill my grandson?"

"Your grandson tried to kill me. I was only defending myself." It should have sounded angry; it sounded apologetic.

"Raaqim was defending the land that is his from you. You come here saying you want to ease the suffering of all people, but it is only *your* people you care about, and you bring the suffering and the pain and the death here instead. You want to leave it here when you go." The old man spat again. "You wonder why we hate you, Abomination? Because you do not see us. We will fight you with an army of children if we must. We will fight you with an army of old people, because there is only one way to make *any* of you see. Only one way."

The translator was still speaking the last few words when Dabir reached under his white *thobe*. Michael saw the gleam of metal, but before he could react, the others already had. Two of the FAMAS opened up, and the old man danced spasmodically backward to the barrage of sound, an ancient handgun flying from his grasp and splotches of arterial red spraying over the bone-colored clothing. Dabir thumped loudly to the floor of the house as the FAMAS went silent. Someone screamed inside the house and a figure hurled itself from the darkness of the interior toward Michael. He struck at it with all his hands, using his full strength with his adrenaline and fright; the figure slammed hard against the door frame of the house. He could hear the crack of bones and glimpse the deep lines and liver spots on her half-covered face even as he realized the ancient frailty of her body. She was unconscious by the time she slumped, half over the body of Dabir. "Pull them all out!" someone ordered behind him. "Anyone moves or resists, shoot."

"No!" Michael yelled. "No!" He grabbed at one of the soldiers who tried to move past him toward the house and shoved him away. "Damn it, back the fuck off!" He glared at them all, waving all six hands. "We're going back. You hear me? We're done here. We're done."

The old woman moaned on the floor. He could see other people inside the house, watching and too afraid to come forward. "I'm sorry," he told them. "I'm sorry . . ."

They didn't understand. They only stared at him with hatred diluted by fear. At him.

The Abomination.

♥

# Just Cause: Part III

Carrie Vaughn

**HOT, EXHAUSTED, SWEATING RIVERS** inside her Kevlar vest—this, she had decided, was a Kevlar situation—Kate looked out the helicopter window at the desert sliding past below her. In a few minutes, they'd reach the pumping station in Kuwait, twenty miles from the coast of the Persian Gulf.

This was their second stop of the day. At the first, they'd spent six hours keeping a crowd of sullen locals at bay while technicians started the wells pumping.

Not a single person on either side had been happy to be there. This wasn't like Ecuador, where the lives they saved stood right in front of them. Hard to see the lives they were saving here.

Her phone beeped—incoming text message.

One word: FUBAR. From Michael.

"What's wrong?" Lohengrin said. Somehow, even in the heat and sand, with everyone around him boiling, he managed to maintain his cool, almost arrogant demeanor.

She showed him the screen. The German ace raised an eyebrow.

"From DB? He wanted to come here," he said. "He shouldn't complain now."

This wasn't complaining. Complaining was bitching about the heat and the food, pouring sand out of your shoe and yelling at your teammates for nothing at all. This was different.

It wouldn't do any good to argue with Lohengrin. He'd just look down his nose at her with the sort of condescending pity people used on children with skinned knees.

The helicopter landed on a concrete pad outside the station in a whirlwind of grit. Like Simoon. Ana had called from New Orleans to tell her about the weird ace who showed up channeling the girl's ghost. Kate was happy enough to not be there dealing with that particular mess. She shook the thought of the fallen ace away. She and Lohengrin piled outside first. Despite his confidence, he wasn't taking any chances—he already wore his armor.

They were in a dusty valley, a bowl of sand ringed by rocky outcrops. Some grasses clung to the wasteland, tossing in a constant breeze. The station itself was an industrial complex covering acres. Dozens of wells were marked by steel trees thrusting up from the ground, attached to angled collections of pipes and valves. More pipes, a twisting maze of them, connected various stations of hunched machinery of arcane purpose. It was a sci-fi landscape from some depressing post-apocalyptic future. The air smelled thickly of oil, sulfur, and waste. Kate sneezed.

Sun glared off everything. Even with sunglasses, Kate's face felt like it had frozen in a squint.

A control building and a collection of prefab barracks lay off to one side. But nobody was here. No workers had gathered to block the gate in the chain-link fence surrounding the site. No crowd milled around the barracks. She should have been relieved. The whole place was quiet, still.

Throwing a pebble, she blew the padlock and chain securing the gate. Still nothing. Maybe the place had been abandoned. She waved back at the helicopter, and the team of technicians, with their bright blue UN vests and helmets, ran to meet them.

"Keep your eyes open," she said to Lohengrin.

"You think I would let down my guard?" He sounded offended.

*You're sleeping with Lilith, aren't you?* "Of course not," she said.

They followed the team to the main building. Their attention was out, looking for trouble. The helicopter's motor was still running, just in case. A trio of UN soldiers stood near it, also keeping watch.

"Curveball!" one of the techs called from the door. He was middle-aged, British, and had a weathered look to him. "It's locked. Care to do the honors?"

She kept looking at the barracks, waiting for someone to lob a grenade from there. "Yeah. Sure." She pulled a pebble from the pouch over her shoulder.

"I could cut the lock off," Lohengrin said.

"Yeah, but people like it when things go boom." She smiled. The techs chuckled. "Stand back, guys."

She almost didn't look at the door before making her pitch, but she lowered her arm at the same time Lohengrin said, "Wait a moment."

They both approached, their attention drawn by a thin line of discoloration at the top of the frame. Like a bad paint job, or a place where someone had tried to patch a crack. It looked almost like caulking.

"Bill?" she said to the British tech. "What's this look like to you?"

He joined them at the door and studied where she pointed. It only took a second for his expression to turn slack, his eyes growing wide.

"Bloody hell," he murmured. "I think it's plastique."

"Set to detonate when the door opens? A booby trap?"

"Probably."

They all backed away.

"What do we do?" Lohengrin said.

"We call it in," Curveball said. "Go back to HQ. This isn't worth blowing ourselves up over."

The technicians trotted back toward the helicopter without argument. She and Lohengrin brought up the rear as they'd initially led the way—watchfully, looking over their shoulders.

They heard the machine-gun fire before they saw the gunman.

Instinctively, Kate dropped as squibs of sand burst around her. Then a weight fell on her. Lohengrin, in full armor, including bucket helmet with decorative wings, playing human shield. She couldn't move to reach her pouch.

"Get up!" she hissed, elbowing him. He did, just enough for her to slip out, take shelter, and take stock.

The firing continued. Bullets pinged off Lohengrin's ghost steel.

There was only one of them. A basic-model automatic rifle. It was coming from the corner of the control building. She was actually getting experienced enough with this to discern that much from a noisy burst of gunfire.

Golf ball in hand this time, she cocked back and threw over Lohengrin's shoulder. Didn't have to aim, because she steered the projectile, sent it rocketing around the corner. She hoped that would silence the weapon.

It impacted with all the power of her surprise at the turn of events. People shooting at her brought this out. This *anger.* It translated well, and that side of the prefab building went up in a crack of thunder, a burst of dust and debris.

But he'd already run. Lohengrin pointed, and she caught a glimpse of someone peering out around the corner of the other side of the building.

Still just one of them. No army bearing down.

A second explosion blew out the front of the building. Fire ringed the door—the booby trap. Her detonation rattled the door and set the bomb off. Shit.

Billowing flames swallowed the building. She ducked, Lohengrin hunched over her, and debris pummeled them. Pieces of siding, of corrugated roofing, furniture even. Sheltered by Lohengrin's body, she felt the impacts against him.

She didn't see what struck his head, hard enough to whip it back, too fast, too hard. He slumped, boneless—and his armor vanished. She found herself holding a two-hundred-plus-pound unconscious German in her lap. The ghost steel couldn't protect against everything—like getting knocked out inside the helmet.

In a panic, Kate felt for a pulse, looked for injuries. She didn't see blood, no obvious marks. She shook his shoulders. "Lohengrin? Lohengrin! *Klaus!*"

They were in the open, totally exposed, and that guy was still out there with a gun. But the rain of fire didn't come. She threw another stone.

And at that moment the gunman emerged and revealed what he was doing. He'd set down his gun and was pulling the pin from a grenade. But he wasn't facing toward them. He'd turned to the tangle of pipelines, the wells, the pumps that held back the pressure of oil and natural gas.

He threw. The grenade sailed up.

She turned her missile toward the grenade. Didn't know if this would work. Was she good enough, fast enough, clever enough? Had to believe she was. Good enough to get this far, couldn't hesitate now.

She wondered what would happen the time she wasn't good enough. It would only take once.

Her missile, glowing red-hot, sailed in a straight line toward the grenade, which was falling toward the pipes.

Squinting, she could barely see her target. But she could see it in her mind, follow the arc. She reached toward her missile, her arm taut and trembling, guiding it faster, still faster. She let out a cry of rage.

It sped up, then slammed into the grenade from the side, carried it forward some twenty yards, and exploded. Both projectiles vaporized. Nothing else happened. Nothing broke, nothing ignited. These oil fields wouldn't burn.

The gunman—young, wearing plain trousers and a T-shirt—screamed in his own fit of rage and ran toward her, waving a handgun, a weapon of last resort. He fired at her again and again in an obvious suicide run. She picked up something—stone, a piece of plastic from the destroyed control room. Didn't matter, because it was solid in her hand, and her arm burned. She pitched.

The missile went through him, all the way, just like a bullet, complete with the spray of blood, a splatter raining from the front, a gory mess spilling from his back. He exploded from the inside and fell like a stone.

She stared, almost smiling with satisfaction.

Lohengrin tried sitting up, shaking his head, blinking until he managed to focus on her. "My lady! I am in your debt."

She pursed her lips.

Blue helmets ran toward them. The UN team, with machine guns. They were shouting.

"Curveball!" one of them called. French accent. She couldn't remember his name.

"Help me get him to the chopper!" she shouted, trying to lever Klaus to his feet. He tried to pull away.

Everything moved quickly. Two soldiers were suddenly there, taking Lohengrin's arms, pulling the big ace away from her. She scrambled after him. "He's hurt, we have to—"

"Curveball!" the French peacekeeper said again. He pulled her to the helicopter. In moments, they were airborne and getting the hell out. But the soldier wouldn't let go, and she started to get angry, especially when another soldier started tugging at her left arm. What the hell were they doing? Between the two of them, they pinned her to the seat.

"What—"

Lohengrin was the one who said, "Kate, your arm!"

She stared at him, blank-faced, confused. Then she looked at herself.

Her left arm was covered with blood. Her own blood. The soldier was swabbing at her with an alcohol wipe, searching for the wound. She hadn't even felt it. Why couldn't she feel it?

"Just grazed. You'll be fine," the medic said, poking at her biceps.

He did something—and every nerve lit with pain. She clenched her teeth and pressed her head back while he wrapped a bandage around the arm.

She thought, despairing—what if it had been her right arm?

A few long, terrifying moments of shock passed. After sunset, they arrived back at the tent city that served as their local base of operations. Kate ended up in the infirmary, on a lot of painkillers, sitting on a chair and looking away as a medic stitched the wound in her arm. Eight stitches. She'd have a scar to show for this.

Lilith, still managing to look suave and stylish in black fatigues, regarded her.

"Don't tell John about this," Kate said. She didn't want him to worry. But God, she wanted to see him. Wanted to fall into bed with him and sob about the close call. But he'd try to send her back to New York. "I'll call him later. I don't want him to get distracted because of me."

"You're loopy on drugs," she said. "You're not thinking clearly."

Kate gritted her teeth. "Lilith, I know we don't get along. But please don't tell him just to spite me."

Lilith stepped close and glared down at her. "After everything we've been through together, you don't think I'd go out of my way to spite you, do you?"

Of course she would. Spite was her bread and butter. "Bitch," Kate muttered.

She tsked. "Dear, don't aggravate yourself. And you really shouldn't call me names when you want me to do you a favor."

Kate closed her eyes and tried to settle herself. She didn't have anything on hand to throw.

"What are you going to tell John?" she said softly.

Lilith shrugged. "What I have to." She swirled her cape and vanished with a hiss of air.

"Funny. The guys all seem to get along with her just fine." DB pushed through the tent flap.

She wasn't sure she wanted to see him just now. At the same time, she was relieved to see a friendly face. He pulled a chair over with one hand, tapped a patter with another. After sitting, he just looked at her for a long moment. His face was a picture, a conflict of emotions. Shadows darkened his eyes. A multicolored bruise melded with the ink of tattoos on his rib cage. He hadn't slept since his own disaster. Hadn't smiled, either. Together, the two of them must have looked war-ravaged.

"Christ, Kate, when I heard you'd been hurt—"

"I'm fine—"

"Would you listen to me? After everything that's happened, all the shit that's come down, I don't know what I'd do if anything happened to you."

"Michael. I'm not sure I can handle that sort of thing from two sides."

"Is it so fucking wrong that I care?"

"No. Of course not. But—"

"But you've got John. I know."

Incredibly, she felt her lips turn in a smile. He stared at her. "What? What'd I do?"

"You didn't call him Captain Cruller. Or Beetle Boy."

For a moment it looked like he might spout obscenities. Then he ducked his gaze and chuckled. She reached for his nearest hand and squeezed. Friends in a tight spot. She didn't want to lose that. He wrapped three of his hands around hers. All she had to do was say the word, and he'd wrap his whole, immense body around her like that, smothering her with warmth and affection. She didn't say the word.

Sighing, he said, "This mission is completely fucked up."

She pressed her lips in a line. "I know."

That evening, Kate found a TV that picked up CNN and watched John's mission go to hell even worse than this one was. The footage of Sekhmet the Lion shrugging off gunfire and tearing the treads off tanks left her nauseous. That was John in there, she kept telling herself. The Committee hadn't stopped a genocide. They'd ignited a war. Reports of injured Committee members were sketchy—all anyone knew was that there were injuries. Calls to John weren't getting through.

When Ana called, Kate left the crowd gathered around the TV to get some privacy.

"How are you?" Ana asked, her voice scratching over the cell connection.

*I've been shot.* "I'm okay," Kate said instead.

"You're lying," Ana said, a little too flatly for it to be a joke.

"Well, so are you." Both women sighed, unable to explain how much they were really hurting. "Have you been watching the news at all?"

"Haven't had time," Ana said. "Not sure I want to. I take it things aren't going well."

"They could be worse. We haven't lost anyone yet." Then Kate wished she hadn't said it. It was such a close thing.

"Same here. We got through Harriet, but there's a second hurricane on the way. Category five this time."

When it rained, it poured. And that was a *really* bad joke.

"Are you getting any rest at all?" Kate said.

Ana sighed. "I'm doing okay."

"No, Ana, you're not. I'm ten thousand miles away and I can hear that you aren't."

"I swear, you're as bad as John with the overprotective thing," Ana said, as frustrated as Kate had ever heard her. Kate didn't know what to say to that. "I'm a big girl, Kate. You worry about your own skin, okay?"

Her own skin, with its gunshot wound and eight stitches.

"Okay," she said weakly.

"I have to get going," Ana said with new urgency. "Chopper's here to take me across the lake." It must have been midmorning in New Orleans. Ana was just getting started.

"Be careful."

"You, too. See you later." She clicked off.

Kate tried not to worry about what was happening on the other side of the world. Too much worry, in too many places. She returned to her room, sitting in the dark, on her cot, in sweatpants and sports bra, curling her left arm protectively to her body.

She didn't know what to do. What the fuck were they going to do?

A brief breeze, maybe a second of whooshing air, passed through the room, like a draft through an open tent flap.

Lilith swept back her arm, flourishing her cape. Beside her stood John.

Her first thought: she didn't want John to see her like this, hurt and defeated. Her second: Lilith told him. The bitch. But she forgot all that when John knelt by her cot and pulled her into his arms. He didn't look a whole lot better than she felt. His face was ashen, almost sickly, his eyes bloodshot. She could smell soot and gunpowder ground into this clothing.

"Are you okay?" they asked each other at the same time.

She hugged him as tight as she could with one arm. "I'm okay, John."

He pulled away to look at her, cupping her face in his hands, smoothing back her hair. "Kate. You were *shot.*"

"Grazed. Just a few stitches. Left arm, even. I can still throw."

"Kate—" His look darkened, and Kate braced. Here it came, he was going to try to yank her from the mission.

She tried to beat him to it. "John, we're done here. We're cooked. We need to pull out before something ridiculous happens."

"Lilith says this was an isolated incident. One guy. A disgruntled worker lashing out."

She almost laughed. "You can actually say that with a straight face? After what happened to Michael and Rusty? John, we've seen what's happening here. These people don't want us here. This is an invasion. Michael will tell you the same thing—"

"You're siding with him now?"

She huffed. "God, what is it with you two?"

"It should have been me here. I shouldn't have let him talk me into switching."

"John, would you listen to me? It wouldn't matter if you'd been here. It isn't about you or him or me or who's doing what. It's this place. The situation here is totally fucked up and Jayewardene's crazy if he thinks us being here is going to help anything. The UN needs trained diplomats on the ground here, not . . . not . . . a bunch of reality show rejects!"

John looked over his shoulder. Lohengrin was standing in the doorway.

"You lack faith," the German ace said. He'd recovered from his bout of unconsciousness with no ill effects. Hard-headed, that one. "We're symbols. Powerful symbols. Have faith."

This wasn't a game, she wanted to scream. This wasn't a divine calling. And there wasn't always going to be someone around to save your ass.

"Kate," John said, somber. "We're pulling out of Africa. The mission there's a bust. Tom Weathers—he's psychotic. Insane." He shook his head, as if still trying to understand. "There's nothing we can do there. Which makes it even more important that we do some good here."

Recalling the spray of blood from the man she'd killed, she almost laughed at him. *That* was doing good?

Lilith cleared her throat. "Let's leave these two to their little conversation, shall we?"

Predictably, Lohengrin seemed all too happy to leave with the British ace.

When they were gone, Kate touched John's face and kissed him. He looked surprised. His brow—his marred, gem-embedded brow—furrowed. "You're hurt."

And if that was going to stop him, he lacked serious imagination.

"Sit with me," she said, scooting back to give him room.

He did, shifting onto the cot. When he was settled, she curled up against him, pulling his arm around her shoulders, resting her head on his chest. Cocooned herself with him. He held her tightly, stroking her hair.

In spite of her plans, the painkillers and exhaustion conspired against her. Feeling safe for the first time in days, she slept.

◆

# Double Helix

## GO UP INTO GILEAD, AND TAKE BALM

### Melinda M. Snodgrass

**SHE'S READING TO MY** father—*Lucky Jim,* one of his favorite books for its vicious look at the British education system. Her voice is a low chuckle like the sound of water in a fast stream. Last night I slept in my own bed for ten straight hours. I had heard Dad moaning in the wee smalls, but when I'd gone to his room Niobe had been there before me, bathing his forehead with cool citrus water. They had both ordered me back to bed, and their air of command had been both charming and amusing. I allowed myself to be dictated to.

There's the yeasty smell of toasting bread from the kitchen. Drake has discovered the joys of Nutella. He emerges into the hall holding seven slices slathered with the chocolate/hazelnut concoction in one hand and a large glass of milk in the other. My mouth is suddenly watering. I snag one of the slices.

"Hey!"

I smile down into his round, outraged face. "It's nice to share."

The blush dots his face with red splotches. "They're not all for me. They're for Niobe and your dad." He shuffles a bit. "And me."

"If you can get my father to eat one of those slices I will bless you."

He scurries away and I follow at a more sedate pace. Mum is off at another conference in London. I know she's sought after, but it's starting to feel like she wants to miss the actual death, too. Maybe we are more alike than I realize. If she does come home I wonder what she'll make of the guests.

Drake is alternating bites of toast with slurping sips of milk when I enter the bedroom. It seems that the counterpane covering my father lies a little flatter each day. Niobe kneels Japanese style on a pillow on the floor. It keeps the tail out of her way. I give her shoulder a grateful squeeze as I move past. My dad lifts his hand. I take it and kiss his forehead.

"Thank you, you've brought me the most delightful nurse and assistant."

He smiles at Niobe and Drake, revealing crooked teeth, legacy of a lifetime of British dentistry. I wonder how he appears to her. Nothing remarkable, medium height, gray-brown hair, neither handsome nor ugly, a deeply lined face from a lifetime of invalidism, but, like Niobe, he has wonderful eyes. Niobe blushes. She looks rather adorable.

"The state nurse is coming," I say to Dad. "I thought I'd show Niobe and Drake about a little."

"Go, go," he urges, shoving at me with the back of his hand. It's stippled with dark bruises from the IV needles.

Out in the hall Drake makes a face. "Are you gonna, like, walk around?"

"Probably," I lie because I want to have Niobe to myself.

"Can I stay here and use the computer? I could play WoW."

"No! Use the Game Boy, but don't go online." Drake looks mulish as only a teenage boy can. Niobe hugs him and ruffles his hair.

"Come on, kiddo, I know it feels like we're safe, but we're not, not really."

I feel a stab of regret and resentment that I can't make her feel secure. But reason reasserts itself. In truth they're not safe.

I take her out the back door, across the swale of grass, and through the gate in the hedge. The Cam rolls slowly past, the color of caramel. We keep a punt pulled up onto the muddy bank. I squelch across to the punt. Leaves have gathered in the bottom, and I realize how long it's been since I've had it out on the water. I toss some of them out, and hold out my hand to Niobe.

She's hesitating, staring down at the mud. I realize there is a tear in the side of one of her tennis shoes, and it's the only pair of shoes she possesses. I need to buy them some changes of clothes. I pick her up and carry her across the mud. There's a sharp intake of breath as my arms go around her followed by a squeak as I swing her up. Her tail thrashes a bit against my leg as I carry her, the bristly hairs penetrate the fabric of my slacks.

"Is this okay?"

"Y-yes."

I deposit her in the punt and arrange pillows behind her back. A sharp push and the punt slides into the water. I jump in. Niobe squeaks again as the punt rocks a bit under my weight.

"Pardon me, not trying to be fresh," I say as I reach down next to her leg and pull free the long wooden pole, and step onto the platform at the end of the boat. I like to punt. There is something both relaxing and empowering as you time the push, let the pole slide through your hands, pull it up and thrust again.

She leans back, exposing the line of her neck. My eyes linger on the hollow at the base of her throat. She opens her eyes and smiles at me. "You're a fibber," she says.

"Guilty."

"Drake could have come."

"Yes, but I didn't want him to come."

She's blushing again. "Why?" Her color deepens even more. "Oh, I'm sorry, that sounds like I'm angling."

"I wanted to spend time with you."

Her face is almost scarlet, but those amazing eyes fill with delight.

"Really?"

"Truly."

We're only gone for an hour, but I'm straining toward the house, feeling like I can't quite draw in enough air to satisfy my lungs. I realize I'm outdistancing Niobe, the tail makes her clumsy, and I moderate the length and speed of my steps. I feel I owe her an explanation. "I feel guilty when I go away. When it's just for me, not work."

She catches me by gently touching my arm. "You have to take time for yourself or you can't be there for him. Not when he'll really need you there."

"But he may not know I'm there. Not when . . ." I clear my throat. "The time comes."

"He'll know." She lays a hand on her breast. "Souls yearn to each other when people care for each other."

I'm roused by the soft murmur of voices and running water. The glowing green numbers seem suspended in the darkness. Three A.M. Niobe is in Dad's room. She supports him in one arm while with her free hand she spreads another urine pad beneath him. Our eyes meet over his head. I take the shell of his body in my arms as Niobe straightens the sheet and plumps up the pillows.

The mattress dips on one side. I wake, startled, disoriented. My hand is reaching for the pistol suspended on the side of the bed. The heavy aroma of coffee reassures me. Niobe is seated on the edge of my bed, a tray in her hands. A right proper breakfast adorns the plate. The yolks of the eggs look almost orange against the white china, but all I really see is her smile.

The first one to go was the Committee's pager. Next Bahir's. I called my agent and had him cancel my upcoming performances. Another pager down. The last one to go is the pager from the Silver Helix. As I press and hold down the button and watch the lights dim to darkness I realize I'm not even feeling very guilty. It joins the other four in the desk drawer.

A gale off the North Sea moans around the house. It whistles down the chimney and captured sparks whirl away back up the flue. Startled, Niobe looks up from her book, *The Nine Tailors*—I approve of her taste. She is curled up in a nest of pillows that supports her and keeps her tail from making her too uncomfortable. Her hair falls across one side of her face, polished chestnut. I'm seated in my father's favorite chair, shoulder pressed into one of the wings, reading. The fabric is redolent with the smell of tobacco and his aftershave. But a new scent is in the room—lilies and jasmine. I had found the unopened bottle in the bathroom. I remembered when I had bought it for my mother at a boutique in Paris while on tour. That had been three years ago. Well, it's Niobe's now.

The wind shrieks, a sudden, sharp cry. I know why my ancestors created the legend of banshees and lost souls. I picture my father's soul spinning away into that maelstrom of clouds. I wonder if the souls of all the men I've killed are wandering tonight. The close and constant presence of death has made me fanciful. Niobe shivers, and rubs at her arms.

Setting aside my book—*Three Men in a Boat*—I hurry to her side, and rub her upper arms. The skin is pimpled with goose bumps. She's still in the T-shirt I found her in. I still haven't bought her . . . them, clothes. But shopping would take me away from the house.

"You poor darling, let me get you a sweater. It'll swim on you, my mother is . . . large." She is smiling up at me. There's nothing conscious or planned about it. I bend down and kiss her. Her lips are dry, and a little chapped. For an instant they part. She tastes like vanilla and honey. Then she draws back. I, too, rear back. "Sorry, sorry. I don't usually behave like an ass."

At the same time I'm sputtering the apology she is saying, "Wha . . . what are you doing? What do you want my kids for? Why do you want me to have a clutch? You're up to something!"

I'm completely at sea here. I wave my hands in front of her face. "Stop, stop, stop. It was just a kiss. If I wanted to seduce you I'd bloody well do it better than this."

She clambers awkwardly to her feet. "Bullshit! This whole thing has been a seduction. The punting, the tea and crumpets, everything!" Her voice is spiraling into a tight, high soprano, and the words come like the chattering of gulls. "Well, I've got news for you, I can't just whip up a clutch with the powers you want!"

"I say, hold on there! I'm sterile, remember."

"Not with me you wouldn't be. Not for my ace kids." Her face is a bright red. "Just the act of sex starts it."

Well, that stops me. "I could sire children?" My mind juxtaposes images of fathers at playgrounds with youngsters and the dying homunculus in the alley, but I can't quell the buzz of excitement. "I wouldn't be sterile with you." I thrust my hands deep into my pockets and feel the pressure of a half-formed erection.

"You really wanted to kiss me?" She sounds very young and very insecure.

I turn back to her. "Yes."

"But I'm ugly."

"And I'm grotesque." I force a smile. "I might get the kiss, but once my pants come off I get the kiss-off."

"It can't be more horrible than this." She gathers the fat, bristly tail into her arms and stares down at it. "I'm sorry I got so weird. I just haven't been kissed in a long, long time. He never kissed me at BICC. He just fucked me." I can barely hear her now. "He never stayed to see the kids. He never came to say good-bye to them when they . . . when they . . ." Her voice is thick with unshed tears.

I take her in my arms and this time she doesn't pull back.

They're absolutely delightful. Four. Three girls and a cocky imp of a boy. It amazed me how quickly it happened after we made love, and alarmed me how much pain Niobe endured. I held her as the eggs were deposited and we watched together as they hatched.

The black-haired, blue-eyed boy clambers up onto the bed and gives Niobe a hug. "Hi, Mom." She hugs him back fiercely.

Two of the girls join us on the bed. The joker is tiny and having trouble with the big four-poster. I pick her up and set her on the bed. She's charming. She's like those pewter and enameled figurines of fairies with shimmering translucent wings that flash in the sun like an opal, feathery antenna over her eyes, and pointed little ears that poke up through a profusion of lavender-colored hair.

Niobe is looking distressed. "I can't remember. I think I was up to 'D.'"

I remembered something from the reports from BICC, how they worked their way through the alphabet so they could keep the test subjects straight. My spine stiffens.

"No, these are our kids. We get to name them." She looks frightened, then delight brightens her face and shines in her eyes. She looks up at me shyly, her arms are full of children. "You should name your son."

I feel taller and broader and I realize I'm preening like a bantam cock. "Gabriel."

Niobe nods in agreement, but Gabriel pipes up. "You better not call me Gabe."

I give a bark of laughter. Niobe kisses the dark hair of two of the girls. "Delia and Bethany."

I pick up my delicate princess. "And Iolante." Her arms go around my neck. "Let's go show your grandfather," I say.

# Woulda

Caroline Spector

I REALLY NEED TO get a new job.

Oh, I could handle the crazy hours and never having a moment to myself. But zombies? Christ, no one ever said anything about zombies.

I looked up from where we were working on the levees and saw a row of the ugly buggers watching us.

Earth Witch, Gardener, and Cameo (channeling Simoon today) were working with a Corps of Engineers guy to shore up the levees. I was too far away to hear what he was saying, but Earth Witch nodded after a while, then knelt down and put her hands on the ground.

A trench opened up a few feet away from her. But it wasn't a deep one. It was low and wide and looked more like what you'd get from a bulldozer. Dirt flew from the edges as it sped toward the levee. A mass of earth was forming at the front of the trench. Enough dirt and they could do a decent patch on the weakened portion.

Cameo began to whirl. Even though the ground was still pretty wet, she managed a decent—if kinda slow and muddy—dirt devil. She spun toward the front of the trench and dropped a load of dirt on top.

Gardener pulled a pouch from her belt and ran to the edge of the water. Earth Witch and Cameo's efforts had paid off. There was a substantial mass of earth bolstering the weakened side of the levee. Gardener opened her hand and threw some of the seeds out. They began to grow as they flew through the air. By the time they hit the mud, they were ready to root.

Cypress, live oak, and magnolia trees soared into the air. Their roots grabbed at the earth like gnarled hands, intertwining and sinking into the mud. Gardener threw a few more handfuls of seeds, and reeds and water plants began to fill in where it was still bare. In minutes, what had been stripped away by Harriet was lush vegetation.

Earth Witch flopped down to the ground. Cameo dropped next to her. "God, how many more of these are we going to have to do?" Earth Witch asked. Sweat was pouring off her. I was supposed to be her friend, but right now I couldn't afford friends. Nothing I liked more than being head asshole.

My cell phone rang. I checked the caller ID and saw it was Bugsy. I slipped away because I didn't want Cameo (or Simoon or whoever of the smorgasbord that could potentially come through her) to know it was him. It rarely ended well when team members slept with each other—and Cameo/Simoon/Bugsy had added new twists to an old story. What a cluster fuck—as it were. Oh, and color me less than thrilled at having to deal with the not-quite-as-dearly-departed-as-I-thought via Cameo. I think the dead should stay dead. I'm wacky that way.

I walked to where it was a little quieter, and answered. "What's up?" I asked.

"We've been able to get help from Mayor Connick's office," he said. "We're coordinating our efforts with his. They even gave Holy Roller a block of time to broadcast evacuation instructions. They'll replay that speech every hour."

I let a bubble float up from my hand and hover above my palm. "Did you get the evacuation website up and running?"

I could almost hear him sigh. "Yes, of course I did," he said. "Honestly, you'd think I was a massive screw-off the way you treat me."

I let the bubble go and watched as it slowly rose into the air, drifting higher and higher.

"I don't think you're a screw-off, Bugsy," I said. I was leaning backward, to keep an eye on the bubble. "I think you're a massive smartass. Big difference. How's the preacher doing?"

"If you like long-winded speeches with loads of references to Jay-sus, then he's doing great."

Suddenly Bugsy started giggling.

"What's happening?" I asked. This was hardly the time for laughing.

"Sorry," he said. "I just found a YouTube video of Holy Roller with fart noises inserted into his praise Jesus stuff."

I rolled my eyes. We were trying to evacuate the city for a second time, and Bugsy was looking at fart videos.

"Send me a link," I said.

I was checking my e-mail on my phone when the TV crew finally arrived. I'd asked Ink if she could find anything out about Niobe and Drake. There was a message from her:

---

To: prettybiggirl@ggd.com

From: tatsforless@ggd.com

Honeypie,

SCARE did *not* get Niobe and Drake. Like you, Billy Ray is going nuts trying to find them. He's got agents looking for them all over Texas. It's like they've vanished into thin air.

But he wants your ass. (He can't have it because it's mine, mine, MINE! LOL!)

You are in a world of shit right now. SCARE and BICC are hugely pissed about what went down in Cross Plains.

There are warrants out for your arrest. Aiding and abetting, resisting arrest, assault and battery, and a bunch of stuff I'm pretty sure they made up.

Hugs and Kisses,

Ink

---

I scrolled through my messages but there was nothing from Niobe or Drake. Their silence was beginning to frighten me. I knew they were angry about what had happened in Cross Plains. God knows, I wanted to throttle everyone at SCARE. I'd screwed up things there royally. There's an ace talent to have: Fuck Up Girl. *When she's there, something's bound to go wrong.*

"Miss Pond!"

I turned off my phone and slipped it into my back pocket. One of the local TV anchors was mincing her way toward me. It was still pretty muddy. The sun had come out and the stench of sewage and dead fish rolled over us in waves. She looked out of place in her tidy pastel suit.

"Well, Miss Pond, you're looking amazing, I must say," she said.

Of course I did. I'd bubbled off almost all my weight for the media appearances I knew I'd have to do as team leader. Good thing Holy Roller was around. A few run-ins with him and I'd be back to bubble-icious.

I pulled myself up to my full height, which meant I towered over the anchor. "Are we ready to start shooting?" I asked.

"I, uh, thought we'd take a moment to set the shot," the anchor stammered.

I gave her my sternest Team Leader look. "You're joking, right? I'm trying to coordinate levee repairs, the evacuation of the city, and making sure people aren't coming back into town, and you're worrying about shot setups?"

She looked chastened. I was being a jerk, but I needed the TV people to get the message out and it couldn't be fluff bullshit. Harriet had been bad. She'd been a category four storm, but Isaiah was turning into a category five. And coming on top of Harriet, I didn't know what kind of disaster we'd be dealing with.

The people of New Orleans needed to know the Committee was here to help them—that we weren't trying to destroy their homes or drive them from the city.

"Uh, let's start rolling and we'll do pickups later," the cameraman said.

"Susan Wright here with the Amazing Bubbles, Michelle Pond," the anchor began. "She and other members of the Committee have been here in New Orleans since before hurricane Harriet hit. What is the Committee doing as hurricane Isaiah is bearing down on our already sodden city?"

*Sodden city? Ye gods,* I thought.

I started walking toward Earth Witch, Gardener, and Simoon. They scrambled to their feet and tried to dust themselves off. But I was glad they looked dirty. It showed they'd been working.

Zombies. God, I hate zombies.

I walked up the sagging wooden steps to Hoodoo Mama's dilapidated house. The smell alone could have dropped a horse. It was drizzling, though, and that dampened some of the odor. There were a couple of moldy pigeons eyeballing me. Zombie pigeons. Ew.

I was still checking e-mail as I went up the steps. But there were no messages from Niobe or Drake. And I couldn't stop thinking about the Nigeria job, either. I was worried about John, Brave Hawk, Toady, and Snowblind. I worried about Lama even though I wasn't that close to him.

The usual "doormen" were in place, but they didn't flinch as I approached. I guess Hoodoo Mama remembered me from our last meeting. There was no one else on the team available to try and get Hoodoo Mama and her people to evacuate for this storm. And I didn't know why Holy Roller thought zombie girl liked me. She called me "fucker" just like she did everyone else.

The door opened. A shambling corpse looked at me with dead eyes. "Come in, Miss Thang," it said. That was Hoodoo Mama talking.

"Thanks," I muttered. I didn't want to be rude, but I was pretty sure a chunk of this zombie's arm was about to drop off in the hallway.

I was led into the living room, where Hoodoo Mama was ensconced on her makeshift throne. The room was populated by a variety of zombified creatures. Most couldn't have been dead more than a few days. But they were all definitely less than fresh. The smell was *awesome*.

And they were all watching TV.

"What the fuck do you want?" Hoodoo Mama asked. She was a tiny thing, swimming in her oversized clothes. Her hair was dark brown with a bright red shock running through it. I knew models that would have killed for her creamy coffee-colored skin. But most of all, there was this feral quality to her that made her a little scary.

"I'm here to convince you to move your people out of New Orleans before Isaiah hits."

She gave a short, bitter laugh. "You fuckers want me to bail again? I'll tell you what I told you the last time—'Fuck no.'"

I sighed. This was going pretty much how I had expected. "Look," I said. "Harriet is going to seem like a cakewalk compared to what's going to happen with Isaiah."

"Yeah, you fuckers said something like that last time. We're still here."

I knew that besides the zombies, she had a bunch of nats living with her. I didn't think she had any wild carders, but there were con artists, grifters, prostitutes, and French Quarter street performers hanging here with her. How many we had no way of knowing.

I put my hands on my hips and gave her my very best Team Leader look.

"The reason you're all still here is because Earth Witch saved your hash and kept the levees from bursting. And the soil wasn't completely saturated the way it is now."

She shifted on her throne, looking a little less confident. "You been watching this *American Hero* shit?" she asked.

I stared at her for a moment, nonplussed.

"You know, that show you were on."

"I know what you're talking about," I said testily. "What the hell does that have to do . . ."

One of the zombies got up and moved the TV so I could see it, too. The all-too-familiar theme was playing, and I saw they'd gone a little more up-scale on the sets. Kandy Kane was tossing her "treats" out, and the other contestants were fighting one another to get them.

"She's a bitch," Hoodoo Mama said. "Why do they always have a bitch?"

The screen went to black, and then Holy Roller appeared. He started into his evacuation pitch, and I was pleased at how persuasive and caring he sounded.

"Damn, I don't wanna hear any more of that," Hoodoo Mama said. One of the zombies got up and turned the set off.

"Look," I said. "I understand that you think everyone like me is full of shit."

There was a wicked grin on her face at that. Her sharp white teeth shone. "Are you trying to convince me that you're 'street' by saying 'shit'? That's fucking hysterical." One of the zombie dogs growled at me.

I rubbed my eyes with the heels of my hands. I'd had virtually no sleep since Harriet hit, and here I was having to cajole this . . . this brat. "Look, I don't care what you think about me," I said. "You've got people here who are in danger. You know, *live* people. Why don't you ask them if they'll evacuate?"

She leaned forward. "I don't fucking tell my people what to do," she snarled. "I already fucking asked them if they wanted to leave, and the ones who did were gone yesterday."

I threw my hands up in exasperation. "Well, why didn't anyone tell us?"

She leaned back and smiled. "Guess they didn't feel like they could fucking trust you. And it's really not you fuckers' business, now. Is it?"

I wanted to smack her. She was so smug. So sure she knew everything and was in complete control. She was going to get someone killed. "Okay," I said. "I see that you're way ahead of us. But can't you imagine a situation where things could get dire here?"

She shrugged. "I s'ppose."

The wind picked up outside. We didn't have a lot of time to chitchat about it. "Do you have provisions and water for your people if they're stuck here for a week, maybe two?"

She glared at me and leaned forward in her chair. "I'm not fucking stupid. We have a larder. And anything we need, one of my children can fetch it for us."

"While I admit that your zombies are handy," I said, dropping my voice, "even they have limitations."

"Bitch, you have no idea what their limitations are." She snorted. "You fuckers have it easy. Show up at a place and take all the fucking glory."

*Oh, crap, not this tired song again.*

"I know it appears that way," I said. "But things often aren't what they seem."

I had to remind myself that her life had been really hard. She'd been on the street for years. Her mother was dead and there was no father. Shitty as my parents had been, at least they'd been there. Until they, you know, stole all my money and skipped the country.

My cell phone rang. It was Bugsy. "I gotta take this," I said.

Hoodoo Mama waved her hand in an imperious manner.

"This is Michelle," I said.

"Any luck?" he asked.

"Not so much."

"You should try to charm her."

I glanced at Hoodoo Mama and I noticed a piece of the wallpaper behind her was peeling off the wall.

"Uhm, that's really not going to happen," I said in my dubious voice.

"Then I hate to say this, but if you can't get her people out of there, you need to get out yourself. The outer edge of Isaiah has made landfall."

I looked at Hoodoo Mama and her zombies. And I thought about the people she still had here. And that she was too young to know what she was getting herself into.

"I'm going to stay here," I sighed. "Help out if I can."

"What the fuck?" Hoodoo Mama said, jumping from her chair. "I didn't invite you, bitch."

I wagged a finger at her. "Where's that famous Southern hospitality?"

"Are you insane?" Bugsy said. There was static on the line.

I turned and walked out of the living room.

"Look," I said. "She's practically a kid. There are people here who she's supposed to be taking care of. I can't just leave her here alone. This might be a way to show her we're more than just a PR stunt. Maybe make her trust us."

"Well, we're *all* practically kids, Michelle," Bugsy said.

I had a flash of fire and smelled the burning flesh again. I slumped against the wall. "I know," I replied.

There was a long silence. I thought maybe we'd lost our signal. "Be careful, Michelle," Bugsy said.

"You bet."

The line went dead. I hoped it was just Bugsy hanging up and not the cell tower going down.

I went back into the living room. Hoodoo Mama glared at me. "And what the fuck do you think you're doing? You fat dumb fucker."

I guess I could have been offended. But I *was* fat at the moment. Holy Roller had taken care of that. And there was no doubt that what I had just done was really dumb.

I went and flopped down on the ratty couch, dropping my emergency goodie bag on the floor. "I think I'm fucking staying here and fucking helping you, whether you fucking want me to or not."

The zombies leaned in toward me in a threatening manner. I stretched out as best I could and closed my eyes for a nap. I couldn't help but smile.

Zombies. I hated them, but they couldn't do a damn thing to me.

"Wake up."

I was on a cool beach. The lake spread out before me. But the water would be cold when I jumped in.

"Wake up, you fat bitch."

I opened one eye. Hoodoo Mama was crouched next to me. My back ached from sleeping on her ratty couch.

"Well, a happy good morning to you, too," I said.

"It ain't morning yet," she replied. She pushed her shock of bright red hair out of her eyes. "We've got a problem."

"We?" I sat up. We were alone in the living room. No zombies—yay.

"There are some people trapped in a building in the Warehouse District."

"I thought we got everyone out of there," I said. I stood up and stretched. Something popped in my back, but it felt good.

"Not everyone," she said. Her voice shook, and that got my attention. "Some of my people are still there."

"I thought *all* your people were *here*," I said. I couldn't help the exasperated tone. "Damn it, you should have told me that there were more out there."

She looked chagrined. *About time,* I thought.

"They didn't want to stay here," she said. "They don't like the zombies."

"Well, big points to them for showing good taste in companions, but the Russian judge is going to give them a major deduction for staying in New Orleans when there's—you know—a *hurricane* coming!" I ended up shouting that last bit. "How do you know they're in trouble?"

She shrugged. "Anything dead I can zombify. And there's lots of mice around."

I thought I might hurl. "Okay, no need to say more," I said.

"*Fuck* you, you don't know what it's like!" she yelled. She took a step toward me, raising her fist as if she were going to hit me. *Oooo, scared of that.* "You fucking rich bitch. They might only have the house they're in. Or the clothes on their back. And then someone tells them they have to pack up and get out because a hurricane might hit. Who can afford a fucking motel? And who's to say the landlord or the bank won't take your house away while you're gone?"

Her zombies had come into the room while she was ranting. They looked pissed. But I knew they weren't. It was her. She was possessing them, after all.

"Look, we don't have time for the niceties here," I said. "Let's just get your people out."

She glowered at me. God, I was sick of people who had a hate on for me while I was trying to help them.

I went to the front window and looked outside. It was pouring. Water covered the street and sidewalk.

"Do you have a boat?"

"Yeah, we got one," she replied.

"Can your zombies carry it?"

"Yeah," she said sullenly. "My zombies are *handy.*"

"Okay, get your boat and your zombies and meet me outside."

For a moment I thought she was going to argue with me, but then she just set her lips into a thin line and led the zombies toward the back of the house.

After I pulled on my slicker and grabbed my emergency bag, I went outside. Even standing on the wide veranda of Hoodoo Mama's house, I could feel the rain pelting me. It was coming down harder now, and I knew we didn't have a lot of time.

Hoodoo Mama appeared around the corner of the house. Behind her were two big zombies carrying a boat between them. There was a small outboard motor clamped on the stern and a pair of oars inside.

"Don't they get tired?" I yelled. The wind and rain were howling.

"They don't feel shit," Hoodoo Mama replied. "They're dead."

There wasn't a lot to be said after that.

Hoodoo Mama maneuvered the boat toward one brick building that was covered with graffiti. She steered us toward a fire escape at the rear of the building. The zombies dropped off the boat and dog-paddled to it. Hoodoo Mama tossed them the rope, and they pulled us to the fire escape and tied up the boat.

Hoodoo Mama led the way up to the second floor. She grabbed the doorknob, but the door was locked.

"Shit." She kicked the bottom of the door.

"I can blast it," I said. I really wanted to blast something.

"Can you just take out the lock?"

I hadn't bubbled since I'd gotten up to this weight, and I really wanted to do something big. On the other hand, the neighborhood was kinda crappy already, and after the water receded, there didn't need to be a big gaping hole in the side of the building.

"Yeah, just a sec," I said. I held my hands up and concentrated on the lock. Liquid fire surged through my veins. When it got hot enough, I let the bubble fly.

The lock exploded with a crunching sound, and Hoodoo Mama smiled at me. It was surprising to see such a sweet smile. Then it vanished. She turned away and opened the door.

Gray light filtered in through windows high up on the walls. There were offices ringing a wide balcony, with the center open to the warehouse floor below. We ran to the railing, looked down, and saw people clinging to rickety wooden shelves.

"Help us! Jesus, help us!" I saw arms waving here and there in the pale light.

"Why didn't they just come up here?" I whispered to Hoodoo Mama.

"Look over there," she said, pointing. The stairway had broken off halfway up.

"Then why didn't they go out the door down there?"

"They went down to check the barricade on the door when the water started coming in. The stairs collapsed when they went back up."

"And you know this because . . . ?"

"Remember? Zombie rats."

I sighed and bent over to rest my head on the railing. I could taste bile in the back of my throat. I wanted to be anywhere but here with the responsibility for these people.

A tremendous crashing sound came from outside. A shriek came from below.

"It's okay," I shouted, straightening up. "We're here to help you."

"I think the levee may have broken," Hoodoo Mama said. "That sound . . . there's one not far from here."

"Listen up," I yelled. "I'm going to make you some flotation devices. I want you to grab them and paddle over here. We'll pull you up. Okay?"

There was no answer.

Before I could say "Okay" again, Hoodoo Mama had stepped to the railing.

"You fuckers know who I am, right?" she said loudly. "Bubbles here has a good idea, and I want you to follow it."

"I can't swim," came a faint voice.

"All you need to do is grab hold of the bubble and paddle it over here," I said.

"What if I fall off?"

"I'll jump in and get you," I said. "Ready?"

I extended my hands as if I were holding a playground ball, and shimmering iridescence formed between my palms. I made it larger—about the size of a beach ball—and I made it nice and firm, so it wouldn't burst when they were holding on to it.

I glanced down to see where I needed the bubble to go, then sent it on its way. It flew across the warehouse and splashed into the water close to one of the men. The bubble skittered across the surface and he grabbed it.

I kept making bubbles. My pants loosened, and I stopped bubbling for a moment to cinch them tighter. In the pale light, I could see that a few people had actually bobbed over to us already.

"I've got a rope in here," I said, slinging my emergency bag at Hoodoo Mama.

She grabbed the bag, yanked the zipper open, and pulled out the rope. Her zombies came to the edge of the balcony and stood next to me. It was creepy as hell that they didn't breathe.

"Okay, here's the rope," I said to the bubble-floater closest to us. "What's your name?"

"Floyd," the man in the water said. His teeth were chattering a little and it made "Floyd" come out as "Ffffloyd."

"Floyd, I want you to grab the rope as high as you can. You'll have to let go of the bubble."

"I can't swim," he said.

"No problem," I replied. "I can. You get in trouble, I'll come for you."

"Are those zombies up there?" His voice quavered.

I sighed. "Yes, Floyd, they're zombies. But they're not going to do anything to you. You've got nothing to worry about."

But Floyd just clung to the bubble.

Hoodoo Mama flung herself against the railing. It groaned and swayed. *"Grab the rope, fucker!"* she yelled.

He did. The zombies hauled him up.

One down.

Leaning toward Hoodoo Mama, I whispered, "Got any idea how many are down there?"

She whispered back, "I dunno. Maybe twenty."

The zombies pulled more people from the water. After a while, the men we'd rescued started helping pull people up, too. Then the water began to rise. I didn't want to say anything, but it looked like Hoodoo Mama was right. The levee had broken.

I pulled Hoodoo Mama aside. "We can't get them all out of here," I said. "One small boat isn't going to cut it."

She grabbed my hand and led me toward one of the offices. "Look," she said, opening the door to one of the offices.

Inside there were cots folded up against one wall and cases of water stacked in a corner.

"They've been planning for this since Harriet," she said. "I helped them."

"This isn't enough for that many people."

"I know that," she said. She planted her fists on her skinny hips and gave me a look I was now all too familiar with. "Every office on this floor has cots, blankets, water, rations, first aid kits. We didn't know how many people would be staying. Luckily, fewer than we expected."

"What about a generator? Bathroom facilities?"

"We got stuff covered. Oh, *fuck!*" She ran out of the room to the railing.

Down below, a man was floundering in the water. I started to bubble up another floating ball, but I could see he was already panicking.

"Crap," I said. I kicked off my shoes and pulled off my baggy pants. I was not looking forward to jumping into that stinking mess. Outside, with the rain coming down, it was harder to tell just how bad the smell was. But in here, it was foul.

I grabbed the rail, hoisted myself over, and dropped into the water.

It was a shock when I hit. I'd expected it to be warm, but it was pretty damn cold. The guy who'd been floundering had sunk. I dove for him, but it was too dark to see anything. So I surfaced and yelled, "Get my flashlight out of my bag!"

A few seconds later, I saw Hoodoo Mama at the railing with the flashlight in her hand. She tossed it to me, but she was no Curveball. I had to lunge for it. It was my trusty, waterproof, small-but-bright flashlight. I'd had it since Egypt.

I switched it on, clamped it in my teeth, and dove under again. There was slightly more visibility now, but not loads. The next time down, I found him.

It was tricky getting him up. He was kicking and flailing. I hooked my arms under his arms. As we surfaced, he started sputtering and thrashing harder. So I held him tighter and said, "Dude, I'm trying to save you here. Don't make me sorry I did."

He settled down after that, and I got him under the railing.

I released one arm and bubbled with my free hand.

"Hold on to this," I said as I slid the bubble into his hands. "Lay back like you're in an easy chair. Yeah, that's perfect. I'm getting the rope and we'll get you out of here. Okay?"

He gasped, then squeezed the bubble for dear life. "Yeah, okay."

I swam to the rope, grabbed it, and swam back.

"What's your name?" I asked the man.

"Dave," he said.

"Okay, Dave," I said as I began to ease the bubble from his hands. I got one hand off and gave him the rope. He grabbed it and let go of the bubble with the other hand. The zombies pulled him up.

As they pulled him up, I noticed that the water had gotten much deeper. The railing was closer now.

He rose out of the water like a landed fish, water sluicing off him in a sheet.

The zombies had just gotten Dave hauled belly-first across the railing when it gave a rusty moan. He squirmed himself the rest of the way home, kicking off the railing. It tottered for a moment, and then it came down on top of me.

Of course, it didn't hurt, but it did shove me underwater. I sank, thinking I would be able to push myself away from the railing. But it was moving faster than I had expected. I couldn't get out from under it. And I couldn't see anything.

I banged into something and a whole pile of stuff fell over on me, pinning me facedown on the warehouse floor. One of my hands was palm-up, so I let some bubbles go, but I missed whatever was on top of me.

And then my stomach clenched with fear. I didn't know if anyone else could swim, but I wasn't optimistic. Who could get all this crap off my back anyway? I thought about bubbling downward and blasting through the floor, but odds were I'd hit either more water or just dirt.

My breath was running out. I tried to twist around, but I was stuck. *Don't panic,* I thought.

Too late.

Yellow blotches bloomed in my vision. The urge to breathe was too great. I gasped and water rushed into my mouth, down my throat, and burned in my lungs. The yellow blotches went red. And then there was the endless blackness of the water.

It was really a relief. I didn't have to think about the people who'd died because of me, or little girls who'd been raped, or Ink, or John Fortune, Niobe, or Drake, or anything anymore.

"Is she all right?"

I opened my eyes. Crap. Zombies. Then I rolled onto my side and started coughing and puking up water.

Someone wrapped a blanket around me.

"I thought you were fucking indestructible," said Hoodoo Mama, holding my hair back.

"I'm like the Wicked Witch of the West. Water can kill me," I croaked. My throat was sore and my sinuses burned. I pushed myself onto my hands and knees. "How did I get out?"

"I don't swim," Hoodoo Mama said. "But the zombies don't breathe. So I sent them in for you."

My throat and lungs were on fire, but in an "Oxygen Is Our Friend!" way. I never thought stale, fetid, sewage-tinged, flooded-warehouse air could smell so good.

"Did we get everyone out?"

"Yeah, every one of them." Hoodoo Mama smiled at me. That surprised me. "I've got Dave and Floyd setting up the cots in each office. C'mon, we've got one for you."

I stood up, but I was still a little unsteady. "What about everyone else? Is the water still rising? Are we safe here?"

"Jesus Christ, the water has stopped rising. This place is a dump, but has good enough bones to make it through this. That's why I chose it. Fuck all, stop worrying and come lie down."

"I smell terrible."

She rolled her eyes. "Tell me, Jesus, what did I do to deserve this fucker? I think we've got some wet wipes."

♥

"Bubbles."

I woke with a start. I was never going to get a full night's sleep again.

"Yeah, I'm here. Anything wrong?"

"No," Hoodoo Mama said softly. "I just wanted to talk."

I rolled over to face her and pushed my hair back. "Okay, what's up?"

She was sitting on the floor next to the cot, hugging her knees. "I guess, I, I just wanted to say that as fuckers go, you're not too bad."

"Mmm, high praise indeed."

"Now why the fuck would you go and say something like that? I was being sincere."

I pushed myself up onto my elbow. "I'm sorry. I've been dealing with some stuff lately. And my God, it smells like ass in here."

"*You* know what ass smells like? I find that mighty difficult to believe."

I stifled a laugh, but it really did smell awful.

"C'mon," she said as she stood up, grabbed the blanket off my bed, and went to the door.

I got up and followed her. We went toward the back of the building where we'd come in. She opened a door and led me into a stairwell. We went up to the third floor.

I'd thought there would be offices, but it was just a big unfinished area. There were windows around the perimeter of the room. Some were broken and let in the air. It wasn't a lot cooler than downstairs, but it didn't stink as much.

Hoodoo Mama went to the window closest to us and opened it. We were in the eye of the storm, and things were oddly quiet. We both leaned out of the window, sucking in the fresh air.

"There's a lot of bodies in that water," she said softly. That was part of her power, no doubt, knowing where the dead bodies were. It was a terrible power, I realized. Always knowing death.

"So, you were saying that you're going through shit," she said suddenly. "You want to tell me about it?"

I was surprised. I'd come to the conclusion that Hoodoo Mama had three modes: kill fuckers, annoy fuckers, ignore fuckers. And what could I say about my life? Killing people who are trying to kill *me* isn't as much fun as it's cracked up to be?

I shrugged. "You'll probably think it's stupid, but I got a friend of mine in big trouble with SCARE. They're this government agency that . . ."

"I know what SCARE is," she said coldly. She turned away from the window, then shook out the blanket and laid it on the floor. "Anyone got a wild card know who SCARE is."

We plunked down on the blanket together. I sat Indian style and toyed with a loose piece of weave.

"So, I get sent to do a mission to save this friend of mine. Only after all hell breaks loose do I find out that the guys who are asking me to do all this stuff have lied to me." It still made me mad thinking about it. Thinking how they lied to me and almost got Drake and Niobe killed.

"Lied to you about what?"

I could feel my hands shaking again. I shoved them under my butt. "They told me that there was this wicked powerful ace I had to 'contain.' Turns out that the ace was a kid. He was only thirteen," I said as I began to rock back and forth. "And so I accidentally betrayed my friend, Niobe, who was helping him escape these other assholes—who I now know want to kill him."

Her face went cold. "These SCARE guys want to kill some kid because he's powerful? Fuckers."

I nodded grimly. "Yeah, they are. At least the Committee was trying to get him away from them."

"So, the Committee protects kids?"

I nodded. "I'm still pissed as hell that they didn't tell me everything about him, but they were trying to keep him safe." I closed my eyes. "When we went to Egypt, I brought down these helicopters with soldiers in them." My voice broke. I bit my lip and took a deep breath to steady myself. I continued. "They caught fire and when they fell I could smell them. Like burnt pork. And they screamed." I opened my eyes and looked at Hoodoo Mama. "I can't tell you how it sounded when they screamed."

She shrugged. "From what I heard, sounded like those fuckers deserved it."

I hugged my knees to my chest.

"Maybe they did, maybe they didn't. If I had died, would I have deserved it?" I stared out the open window. The light was tinged a strange green color. And all those people I killed would never see any light again. "And there were other things. The Behatu rape camp. Jesus, you don't want to know what that was like."

"Did you kill the fuckers who did *that*?"

"Yeah, that doesn't bother me much. It was the women we found there that haunt me."

"I know what that's like," Hoodoo Mama said. It was so quiet I almost didn't hear it. And when I looked at her face I knew what had happened to her. I swallowed hard and then I leaned forward and whispered, "Did someone rape you?"

For a moment, her hard expression collapsed. The naked pain there was terrible to see. She didn't answer me, but she nodded.

"I'm so sorry." Then I took her hand in mine.

"That's how I got to be Hoodoo Mama," she said after a few moments. "My card turned then." She wiped her nose on the back of her shirt sleeve. "The fucker died screaming."

"Good," I said. I gave her hand a squeeze. Then she put her arms around me. So I put my arms around her.

We held each other for a while. I felt her stroke my hair. Then she slid a hand up my arm to my shoulder and started caressing my neck.

"I, uhm, Hoodoo Mama," I said.

"Call me Joey. That's my real name." Her lips were hovering over mine, and then she kissed me. And, heaven help me, I kissed her back.

It started tender, and then it became hard. She ground her lips into mine and jabbed her tongue into my mouth. She shoved me backward. And I was startled by how strong she was. But it wasn't as if she could hurt me.

"I shouldn't," I said. I felt like someone had just punched me in the gut. "I have a girlfriend."

"Fuck her. Fuck me instead. I'm here." It was filled with pain and desire.

She yanked my arms over my head and pinned them and then she mounted me, grinding her hips into mine. A shudder ran through my body. I was trembling and hot. She slid her hand into my panties.

I opened my eyes and saw her face. It was angry and excited and hurt all at once. And I knew that this was the only way she knew how to have sex. I started to move away from her, trying to think of some way to stop us from doing this thing I wanted to do so much it frightened me.

She grabbed my breast with her free hand and squeezed it hard. Then she yanked up my T-shirt. Her mouth came over my nipple. At first she just licked and sucked, but then she began to bite. It hurt and thrilled me.

And so I let myself be drawn into her rage and pain. She bit, slapped, and scratched me . . . but, of course, it didn't damage me. I tried not to come, but she kept biting and licking me. She punched and slapped me until I started shaking and couldn't stop myself.

And then when she came, she dug her hands into my flesh as if she would never let me go.

The wind and rain howled outside. The back door of the hurricane was passing over us now.

Pale light streamed in through the windows. I blinked, then rolled over and saw Hoodoo Mama watching me.

"Do you think the Committee would be interested in me?"

"Uhm, yeah," I said. I looked away, then rolled onto my side and sat up. I started looking for my clothes. My stomach hurt.

"Then I'd like to join. If you think they'd have me."

"Oh, well, that's great." I tried to keep my voice neutral. A stab of guilt surged through me, but I shoved it aside. Fortune and Jayewardene were always looking for powerful aces for the Committee. And Joey certainly would fit the bill. They'd be thrilled to have her. And that it was her idea would appeal to them even more.

I grabbed my phone and turned it on, hoping I would get some kind of signal. And there was one, but it was faint. I tried calling Bugsy, but he didn't answer.

I downloaded my e-mail. I still had no word from Drake or Niobe, but there was another e-mail from Ink.

My stomach hurt worse. I opened the message.

To: prettybiggirl@ggd.com

From: tatsforless@ggd.com

Sweetie,

Last thing I heard, Billy Ray is taking a team to NOLA to arrest you. If there is anything I can do, you let me know. I'll try to come to New Orleans as soon as they start letting people back in the city.

Be safe.

All my love,

Ink

I wasn't afraid of Billy Ray or his team. I'd cleaned Billy Ray's clock the last time we'd met. But here I was screwing someone else while Ink had risked her job to tell me they were coming. God, I sucked.

"So, soon as we're out of here," Hoodoo Mama said, "we're going to hook up with the other Committee members, right?"

I nodded. I didn't think I could speak. But I thought I might throw up. *Fuck Up Girl strikes again.*

# Dirge in a Major Key: Part III

S. L. Farrell

**JERUSALEM, THE OPEN CITY.** Jerusalem, owned by no one and everyone.

Jerusalem was loud and crowded, with a large population of those touched with the wild card, and even Michael could find anonymity, however momentary, in its warrens.

"Michael . . ." Kate's voice was burdened with sympathy and shared pain; her eyes searched his face. Her hand touched the bandage on the side of his face and fell away again. Kate's left arm was still bandaged, the edges of the wrapping visible under her T-shirt.

"How's the arm doing?" he asked.

She grimaced. "I wish you'd quit mentioning it. I wish everyone would quit mentioning it. Look, Michael. I don't know what to say. This has turned into such a mess. For everyone."

He gave her a six-shouldered shrug. "Not for everyone." A middle hand tapped a newspaper sitting on the table. "Says here that our mission was 'a tremendous success marred by a few unfortunate fatalities.' No mess at all. Like the kids I killed were some lousy, unnoticeable scratch on a piece of furniture."

The grimace on her face matched his, and he knew she was remembering her own experiences in the desert. "Have you talked to John or Jayewardene?"

"Yeah. I talked to Beet—" He stopped. "John," he said, and one corner of her mouth lifted at that. "For about thirty seconds, which was all the time he seemed to have for me. It was enough. I told John, or that fucking bug in his head, what I thought about what we did out there. Past that, I don't have nothin' else to say to either of 'em, and they don't seem inclined to talk to me, either. They're all wrapped in their success."

They were sitting at an outside table of a café on Emile Botta Street, near the King David Hotel in Jerusalem. The street was crowded with both tourists and locals, speaking in a dozen languages. Anonymity was indeed fleeting—Michael's recognizable form (or perhaps it was Kate's) was attracting stares from those passing the café. Occasionally someone would stop to snap a quick picture before they moved on. He could hear the comments, and some of them seemed to be tinged with disgust. Michael glanced up at the bright wink of a flash, unnecessary in the bright, mocking sunshine.

"They'll try to cover this up, Kate. Those kids I killed literally don't exist anymore. Never existed. We can't *allow* them to exist—they're just part of the price we've paid for our oil. Invisible. We can't permit the sight of their bloodied, dead faces to tarnish the image of the Committee or the UN. No, we're all too goddamn important for that. Getting that oil flowing is too important."

Her face had flushed under the blond hair. "The man . . . the man I killed was going to blow up the pipeline, and he didn't care if any of us died in the explosion. And your kids weren't entirely innocent, Michael. You know that. How many of the soldiers did they kill, after all? They would have killed you, too."

"I know," he told her. "That's what I told myself afterward. All I was doing was protecting myself. But they were fucking *kids*!" He nearly shouted the word, slamming his two lower hands down on the table. The wrought iron rang and bent, the glass top shattered, the coffee cups fell to the stones of the patio and shattered loudly. A waiter started angrily toward them, then stopped, evidently deciding that discretion was a better tactic than confrontation. "They were children who had decided that if the Caliphate wasn't going to protect their home, well, they'd do it themselves. A stupid goddamn decision, but you know what, Kate? I could see myself making the same choice when I was their age. Hell, when you're twelve you think you're immortal, and you believe the Good Guys are always gonna win, and that the Good Guys are always on your side. And it doesn't matter what Fortune or Jayewardene or Baden or any of them say: *I killed them. Me.*" He stabbed at himself with a sextet of forefingers. "I

gotta live with that. And for what? For what, Kate? Please tell me the fucking answer, because this really hurts and I haven't got anything for it."

He wanted to weep. He could feel the tears starting again, and he
growled and looked away because he couldn't trust himself to talk and not
break down.

She said nothing. Her lips were pressed tightly together and she had a
marble in her right hand, running her fingers over the glass ball as if she
were about to toss it. "You're bleeding," she said finally. He looked at his
bottom hands; the glass had cut the right one, and blood spattered his jeans
and bare stomach. He picked up a napkin from the wreckage at his feet
and tied it around the injured hand with his middle set. The pain somehow felt good. "What are you going to do, Michael?" she asked him.

"I don't know," he told her. "I really don't know."

Rusty had left Michael a message on his room phone.

"I don't know if John got the message to ya, fella. There's a press conference or something at the King David Hotel: Jayewardene, John, Prince
Siraj." Rusty's voice overdrove the phone speaker, crackling and static-
laden. "Somethin' about withdrawing the UN troops in exchange for oil.
They said I should be there; the fella that called said it's about the settle-
ment with the Caliphate. . . ."

♥

The King David Hotel, in the New City just outside the Old City walls, was
a palatial and imposing structure that had once served as a fortress, set
high enough to overlook the Old City, and catering to the rich who came
to visit the ruins of the open city of Jerusalem. By the time Michael reached
the lobby floor, he could see the crowd outside the main meeting room:
videographers jockeying for position, still cameras flashing like heat lightning, reporters thrusting microphones into the faces of anyone they could
find. He pushed through the crush, ignoring the cameras and microphones
that were suddenly aimed at him. "Hey, Drummer Boy . . ." "What do you
think . . ." "If you have a moment . . ." "I have one question . . ."

They pressed around him like hornets; he walked through them, not making eye contact and not caring who he pushed aside. Security guards in blue berets started toward the commotion, saw who was at the center of it, and stopped. One of them whispered into a lapel mike.

He pushed through the hall doors, closing off the shouting of the reporters left outside. There was no shortage of reporters inside, either; the room was packed, every seat taken and the walls lined with people with video and still cameras.

"I wish to thank everyone for coming." Secretary-General Jayewardene was already on the dais, smiling to the reporters arrayed before him, his soft, Indian-accented voice booming from the speakers. Barbara Baden was there with him, and John Fortune with Kate standing next to him, while Lohengrin, Rusty, and Tinker stood to one side. Lohengrin was armored up and glowing white for the cameras; Rusty seemed shabby and dull alongside the German's glory. Kate appeared to be uncomfortable as she watched, not standing as close to Fortune as she usually did, not touching him at all. Once, that would have been all Michael noticed. She saw Michael and her mouth opened slightly, as if she was about to say something.

To the other side of the secretary-general, Prince Siraj stood smiling, portly under his formal Arabian dress. There were men around him—bodyguards, Michael decided.

At the dais, Jayewardene nodded his balding head. "It's my pleasure to say that we have good news for everyone. We're all very proud of what John Fortune and his team have accomplished and the restraint they displayed, and the restraint shown by the Caliphate. I am prouder still of what we have come here to announce. This is a momentous day."

There was a stir at the head of the dais as the heavy curtains were pulled open. On the wall, a huge canvas sign had been hung. A COMMITMENT TO PEACE, the letters read, with the logo of the United Nations to one side and the banner of the Caliphate on the other.

Seeing it, a fury rose inside him. Michael flailed at his chest with his upper four hands, the raging of wild drums causing those nearest him to clap hands over ears and cower, which brought everyone's gaze around to him. His throat openings flared, open-mouthed, as cameras swung their glassy cyclops eyes toward him; flashes popped and flared. "Hey, I've got the fucking *real* news!" he shouted, his voice louder than the PA system as Jayewardene tried to bring attention back to the podium. Now the entire room was looking his way; now the microphones were pointed in his direction with eager faces behind them. Jayewardene was standing mute in his expensive suit behind the podium, Barbara Baden whispering to him. Prince Siraj glanced worriedly from Jayewardene to his own guards, who scowled angrily in Michael's direction. Fortune pointed toward Michael, shouting orders to the security people.

"You people want the truth?" Michael roared at the crowd. "Do you want to know what actually happened, and why they don't want me standing up there with them? They sent me out there, and I . . ." He took a deep, gasping, half-sobbing breath. "I ended up killing kids for your goddamn oil. I killed *children*. They won't show you the pictures, they won't talk about it. They've paid off people in black, liquid money to keep them quiet. They'll tell you there's no proof and no one will admit it ever happened, but I was there and . . ."

Michael stopped. His hands dropped to his side. Somewhere in the midst of his tirade, the faces that turned to him went quizzical. They'd stopped listening. They gaped at him, whispering to each other. Michael saw a face he recognized, a reporter and blogger for *Salon* who had interviewed Michael a half-dozen times in the past. "Carl," he said, "you know I'm not making this up. This is import—"

He stopped again. Carl's gray eyes were wide and astonished. The man shook his head. *"Adesque ad muilen freinet krium,"* he said.

"What the fuck . . ." Michael listened to the chaos around him—no one around him seemed to be speaking English. He could hear nothing but the babbling of nonsense syllables—no recognizable language at all. Up at the podium, Barbara Baden was smiling down at him. She lifted a hand to him as if in greeting.

Barbara Baden. The Translator, the ace who could make anyone understand anyone else. The realization hit him a breath before the cold fury: she could turn language into a babel just as easily.

He screamed, a wordless cry, and started down the aisle toward the podium. Security moved to stop him; he shoved aside a quartet of burly men, his six arms sending them careening backward into the crush of reporters. The crowd scattered wildly out of his way, and he leapt up onto the dais as Jayewardene and Baden were ushered quickly through a door at the back of the room, as Tinker quickly and discreetly followed them, as Prince Siraj's men clustered around him and fled the dais, as Rusty and

Kate watched uncertainly from their side of the stage, as Lohengrin's hand went to the hilt of his sword, as Fortune stepped directly in his path.

Michael shoved the man aside—hard, with a sense of deep pleasure. He reached with his top set of hands for the banner—to Michael, it now seemed to read E CIKWUGADF RO WIAKL—and ripped it from the wall, the canvas tearing and ripping. Behind him, he heard a sinister growl and a strange light flared, sending his spidery shadow moving on the wall.

"Oh, good," Michael said, turning to see the glowing form of the lioness of Sekhmet, her tail thrashing angrily. "You want to play, you fucking bug? Hey, I've been waiting for this chance."

The lioness spat fire and leapt at him and he went to meet her. They collided near midstage. Claws raked down Michael's arms, tearing deep into muscle and ripping into tattooed flesh as Michael shouted with the pain and the blood. The pain was catharsis; it gave him strength.

Michael grasped Sekhmet's paws with all six hands, letting the momentum of her charge take him backward, allowing himself to fall and roll as he used multiple arms and two legs to throw her past him. Sekhmet slammed into the podium, crushing it to splinters that sprayed the crowd as she tried to regain her feet. She gathered herself with a low, sinister growl; Michael began to drum madly, blood droplets flying from his arms, slamming waves of pure sound toward her, his throats tightening to shape it: as he had with the Righteous Djinn, as he had in the oil fields. The lioness roared and reared back with the sonic assault, a high and pained wail, then her haunches lowered as she readied herself to charge again.

Something slammed into the dais between them: a marble from Kate's hand. It exploded, tearing a massive hole that gouged a crater in the tile floor underneath. "Don't," he heard Kate say, and he wondered which one of them she was talking to.

The white-armored form of Lohengrin stepped in front of Sekhmet at the same time, his gleaming sword waving warningly. Michael looked at Kate, already with another marble in her hand. At the same moment, Rusty plowed into Michael from behind. "Cripes, fella," he heard Rusty say as the ace's huge, strong arms went around him, trying to stop as many arms as he could. "You gone crazy?"

Lohengrin, facing Sekhmet, had his hands up, though Sekhmet growled and paced furiously, her tail lashing. Her claws tore at the carpeted wood of the dais, but she didn't charge. Michael shrugged aside Rusty's bear hug, freeing himself. He stood, blood dripping down his arms and spattered across his body. Rusty was still holding one arm.

"Michael," he heard Kate say. He couldn't read her face. "I mean it. Don't."

He looked at Kate. And away. He'd understood her; he'd understood Rusty. He could read the letters on the shredded banner on the stage—which meant that Barbara was no longer using her power.

"I quit," he declared loudly, glaring at Sekhmet. "The Committee is a fucking travesty. We had something that was supposed to be wonderful and pure and moral, and you've turned it into exactly the kind of organization all those power-hungry tyrants and despots we're supposed to be fighting would create. I won't be part of it anymore. I won't fight for oil, I won't fight for money, and I won't fight for political power. I sure as hell won't kill more kids for any of those. I quit."

He put his back to the stage, to Kate, Rusty, Lohengrin, and Fortune.

Without another word, alone, he left the hall.

♠

# Double Helix

## I WILL TREAD THEM IN MINE ANGER, AND TRAMPLE THEM IN MY FURY

### Melinda M. Snodgrass

I FLIPPED THROUGH THE *Times* and finally checked my pagers. The headlines were all about the imminent collapse of the Nigerian forces. Not even the addition of Royal Marines had apparently helped. It felt strangely removed from me and my situation. Just as the six calls from Flint, twelve from Siraj, and seventeen from Fortune didn't seem to much matter.

My manager had only called once to tell me tearfully that I was killing him here. He was going broke. His children would starve. His wife would be forced to shop at Wal-Mart. I didn't call him back.

I also blew off Fortune. In his case the number of calls did not indicate urgency, merely hysteria.

Flint wanted to know if my father was all right. That rather touched me. But lest I think he was going soft when I called him back he told me to *do my damn job.* He wanted a report from Mecca *now.* What was the status on the search for the living bomb?

"I'll get on it, sir. Who do I talk to in Nigeria?"

*"Forget Nigeria. It's pretty self-evident what's going to happen there."* And he hung up.

After checking in on Dad, I changed clothes and made the transition to Bahir. Niobe came in as I was settling the black rope *Igal* over the *ghutra.* She stepped back and I realized she had only seen Lilith.

"Oh, sorry, this is the day avatar. Bahir at your service." I sweep her a bow. "Hell of a fellow, isn't he? Much more virile than that effete Englishman."

Now she's smiling and she comes into my arms. "I prefer the English-man."

"What about the elegant Euro-trash?"

"I am not that broad-minded." I laugh at her expression and she tugs hard on the edge of my mustache.

"Ouch."

"You won't be gone long?" she asks. Anxiety clouds her green eyes like emotional cataracts.

"No."

It speaks of such insecurity, but she often hugs herself tightly. She's doing it now. "I just get afraid when you're gone."

Since all I've done is go to the market once since we've been here I decide not to tell her I'm going to Mecca. "You'll be fine."

"You'll tell the kiddos good-bye?"

"Of course."

Gabriel, Delia, and Iolante are in the backyard. Gabriel is turning the flower beds into riots of blossoming flowers. The clashing perfumes are almost overwhelming. Iolante flits about half dancing, half flying. Delia is surrounded by rabbits, squirrels, dogs, a few mice, a mole, a pony, and God help me, a milk cow who lies in the grass contentedly chewing her cud.

"You have to put them back from wherever you summoned them," I say sternly as I kiss the top of her head.

"Finders keepers," she says.

"I will not be known as a horse thief and a cattle rustler," I say.

"Have fun," says Gabriel with an off-handed wave.

"Be careful," says my princess.

Bethany is in the kitchen with Drake. They are making tea. Whatever Bethany is creating out of the ingredients on the counter smells wonderful. I dip a finger into the batter and get my hand slapped.

"No, Daddy, not 'til it's cooked."

"You're in charge," I tell Drake and then I can put it off no longer. I picture Siraj's hotel room and make the jump.

He's behind the desk twining a pen between his fingers. Siraj is not a restless man and anxiety goes shivering down my spine. Perhaps it's because of the way he trapped me in my Noel form back in Cairo, but I allow my soft peripheral vision to take over and I catch a sense of movement behind a connecting door of the suite.

I'm teleporting even as a blinding flare of pain rips through my side. I need to concentrate before I jump. Think about where I'm going. Visualize the place. This time it's purely unconscious. I hit the ground amid the piping screams of children. I'm lying on my back half in and half out of the sandbox at the local playground in Cambridge. My father had taken me there to play when I was a kid.

My left hand is slick and sticky with blood as I press it hard at the point of my agony. I'm six blocks from home. But I can't go home like this. Niobe will freak. I roll over and manage to get to my knees. The swings on the tall steel swing set are swaying lightly in the breeze, the chains squeaking. I realize that blackness seems to be closing in from either side, narrowing my focus. I need a doctor. *Now!*

I concentrate and find myself collapsing among the chairs in the emergency room of Charing Cross Hospital. Their clattering is like the distant sound when a row of punting poles goes tumbling. There is again screaming. I can feel my body morphing and shifting and it hurts like hell where the bullet hit me. The screams start again at higher intensity, then rough hands grip my shoulders and legs, there's the sound of tearing as my shirt is torn open. They're trying to drag my hand away from the wound. There's enough of them so that eventually they succeed.

The first thing I see when I awaken is the puke-colored curtain that has been drawn around my bed. Beyond the cheesy fabric comes the beep and wheeze of medical equipment, the sounds of coughs and moans, and a querulous old voice calling, "nurse, nurse." My torso is swaddled in a tight bandage from just below my nipples to just above my navel. It hurts to sit up, but I manage and pull back the curtain. Through a window I can see a night sky. *Shit, Niobe is going to be so worried.*

The next thing I notice is the broad back of a copper. The rattle of the curtain rings has him turning around. *Of course. I arrived as an Arab man, and I was armed to the teeth.*

"There now, sir, you just settle back down."

I hold up a hand. "I'm Noel Matthews, ID number 232751. You need to call the office of the Silver Helix."

We have a pretty decent quality of cop in this country. They don't argue, they take the obvious step when presented with information—they check it out. After a call to his superior officer, and a call back from said officer, the cop is flapping his hand at me and saying, "You ought to take it easy, sir," as I am pulling the IV out of the vein in the back of my hand.

"I've got to get home."

Twenty minutes later they've brought me clothes, returned my pagers, cell phone, weapons, cash and wallet with Bahir's information, and the idiot doctor is still remonstrating with me.

There is a text message on my Noel cell phone. *Call me, Siraj.* My spine seems cold and not just because of the open back of the hospital gown. Flipping open the phone I call him.

"Siraj, dear fellow, haven't heard from you since I escaped your hospitality in Cairo." I fill my voice with that insufferable British drawl that makes almost everyone in the world hate us. Particularly if they've been crown colonies.

"Yes, and now I have a pretty good idea how you did that." His tone is equally conversational. "I also understand why Bahir was so quick to kill Abdul and switch allegiance to me."

"Pity it turned out so badly. How did you figure it out?" I'm actually curious.

"Bahir was a hick from Afghanistan, or Kazakhstan, Baluchistan, or some other fucking *stan*. But suddenly he begins to show a great deal of sophistication. And then there was the little trick with the cards. Not to mention your stunning failure to locate the boy. You're too dangerous to be allowed to live, Noel. I will try to have you killed."

"Well, thanks awfully for the warning."

"A gesture to our past friendship," he says.

"You won't target my family?"

"No," and I hear fourteen years of British public school and sportsmanship on the cricket pitch echoing in his voice.

"Good of you. I have to go now."

I hang up, force the doctor, the cop, and the orderly to go the hell away, and pull shut the curtain around my bed. I feel the bandage slip as my waist narrows as I make the transition to Lilith. I picture the front hall of the house and jump.

Cordite has a distinctive smell. I know it well. I've shot a lot of guns over the past seven years. *Someone has fired a gun in my parents' home.* I struggle into a shuffling run, cursing Siraj with every breath. *"Dad! Niobe!"*

I find them in the study. Dad is out of bed. His skin is gray and seems to be drooping off his bones. Dark circles are under his eyes, and there's a smear of blood on the back of his hand where he's pulled out his IV. I look down at the scabbed bubble of blood on my hand. He is standing next to the wing-backed chair, using it for support. Niobe is curled up in the chair. Dad's free hand is softly stroking her shoulder. On the threadbare oriental rug there is a wet smear. I've seen it before—on a threadbare spread in a hotel in Texas. I plunge out of the room and find the other three. One in the hall. One in Drake's bedroom. The other in the kitchen. My children. Dead.

I return to the study and Niobe looks up at me. I seem to be staring into an infinite darkness. Her face is rigid, and tear-stained. "They took Drake," she says. "A stone giant and a bunch of men with guns. The kids tried to stop them. Protect him." I hear or at least think I hear the accusation. *You weren't here. You didn't keep us safe. Why weren't you here?* "They killed them. I felt the bullets." She lays a hand on her chest. "It hurt so bad. I couldn't do anything." Her voice is shaking. It translates into her body. She's shuddering like a woman lost in a blizzard.

I kneel next to her, my arms outstretched, hanging in the air an inch or so from her body as if held back by an unseen barrier. She falls against me and Lilith's long black hair hides us. Rage engulfs me. Rage at all the masks. I will be myself and they will fucking *fear* me. Niobe gasps a little as she feels my body morph against hers. But then I'm back and she rests her head on my shoulder with the air of a bird settling into its nest. "They've taken everything from me," she says, so quietly that it's more like puffs of air against my cheek.

"I'll get him back for you. I swear I will if it's the last thing I do."

Her arms close convulsively around me, and she whispers something that I can't hear.

"What, honey, I didn't—"

Dad suddenly pitches forward. I jump up, feel the stitches in my side give way and the tickle of blood running down my side, but I manage to catch him before he hits the ground. Niobe is at my side, brushing the tears off her cheeks.

"We need to get him back in bed," she says.

A clawlike hand seizes my forearm. "They put him in the back of a big truck." My father's voice is like stone on a file. "It was bloody strange. It started driving. Very fast. Then it was gone."

Niobe reads something in my expression. "What? Does that mean something?"

"Yes, darling, it means I know how to find Drake."

The pub is empty at 3:00 A.M. The truck is parked out front, the streetlights glittering in the raindrops dappling the hood and roof. The silly little bell tinkles madly as I push through the door. Beneath the long leather coat I'm wearing tight leather pants and a laced vest that pushes up my breasts. Bruckner only knows Noel.

He knows I'm an ace. He knows I'm a killer. He doesn't know my power. That leaves Lilith free to do her job—get me close.

The fat bartender looks up from his washing. A glass hangs in his hand slowly dripping soap suds off the rim. The Highwayman is at his table by the window, but instead of watching his truck, Bruckner's watching me. His face is slack with lust. I saunter over to him. His eyes follow every undulation of my hips and sway of my hair. I'm reminded of a fakir in India I once saw dancing with his mesmerized snake. I lean down and whisper in Bruckner's ear, "I hear you're a man who can give me a ride."

"Which kind you want, love?" The last word turns into a whistle of pain as I reach into his crotch and close my fist around his balls.

"The kind that takes me to the boy."

The bartender yanks up a rifle from behind the bar. The silenced Glock coughs once and the bullet takes him between the eyes.

"You crazy bloody bitch!" Bruckner gasps.

"Try bastard," I say and let my body slide and twist back to myself.

"Jesus!"

"Not to sound like the hero in one of those dreadful American action movies, but you will be seeing him if you don't answer my question." I grind the muzzle of the gun into his temple, and tighten my grip on his nads.

"You know I can't do that, lad." Pain has him panting between the words, but now that he knows it's me he seems more relaxed. "Captain'd skin me alive."

"Actually he wouldn't. But *I* would. Where's the boy? Where did you take him?"

He shakes his head. I release his balls, and pull handcuffs out of my coat pocket. Once he's secure I get down to business.

For all his bravado and bluster it actually doesn't take that long. The wood floor is sticky beneath the soles of my high-heeled boots. Bruckner's blubbering. The wet sounds become words forced between split and swollen lips, "Nigeria. Took him to Nigeria. Dumped him out in front of the PP army. Captain's orders. Not my fault. Just doing my duty." He sees something in my face and screams out, "Don't hurt me anymore! Christ Jesus, no more!"

I put away my knife and draw my pistol. Then I look, really look, at the scene around me. The dead man. The nearly naked old man on the floor in front of me with pieces of skin missing. Blood staining the wood floor. I think about Niobe. How she would see this scene. How she would see *me*. How she would look at me.

I return the gun to its holster. "Congratulations. You get to retire. Tell Flint to expect my resignation later."

"He'll never let you live. Not after this."

"Yes, I think he will. I'll be much more talkative after death. It would look so very bad for the Silver Helix and the government. Ta." And I lock the door behind me as I leave.

I look like an S&M drag queen sashaying down the street. I need to change and make preparations. If Drake can't control his power I'm going to need protection. As for finding him . . . well, if he's blown, that won't be a problem.

◆

# A Hard Rain Is A'Going to Fall

## Victor Milán

"DOLORES, *CHÉRIE!* THERE YOU are."

Already elevated, Dolores's heartbeat seemed to stumble in her chest at the voice behind her. Having one's name called by Alicia Nshombo was always cause for concern. Even when she had just hung a medal around one's neck in front of the global media and the adoring populace of Kongoville.

She turned. The corridors of Mobutu's erstwhile palace were bright and airy, belying the compound's fortresslike construction. High windows let late-morning sunlight pour in to raise a glow from whitewashed walls. Native flowers burst from vases in niches like static explosions of color. Floral-patterned carpets ran along a floor of royal blue glazed tiles.

Dolores was lost. She had been on her way to an assignation with Tom Weathers after escaping the great public fete.

Alicia moved toward her at a purposeful waddle. Continuing the motif she wore the same dress printed with Congolese blooms that she had at the ceremony at which she had made Dolores and Tom Heroes of the People's Paradise, in the proudest moment of Dolores's young life.

The large woman was alone. Clearly she felt no need of bodyguards. Rumor said she was herself an ace, with the power to transform into a leopard. Whatever the truth, no one who feared death, or pain, would dare attempt to harm the president's sister here in the palace.

Alicia hugged Dolores around the waist with a big arm. Dolores felt sweat soak through the white jumpsuit she wore to her skin. The smell of violets almost overwhelmed her.

"Your state has need of you, my Angel of Mercy," Alicia said. Though not whispering she spoke at a low volume for her: she had a bellow like a bull hippo at need. "There is a man you must heal for us. You must tell no one. Do you understand?"

Dolores nodded. The president and his sister—and Tom, dear Tom!—had brought order to the anarchy of Central Africa. With order came the need for discipline. The heart of discipline was obedience.

Alicia led her up broad stairs, to a room on the second story. Dolores smelled harsh cigar smoke before they even entered the room.

It looked like a study. Shelves of books, their dark covers age-cracked, lined the walls. The floor was hardwood with a Persian rug laid on it. A fan circled lazily beneath the high ceiling.

A man sat smoking in a leather chair. Dolores gasped. Half the hair on his round head and his beard had been burned away; it amazed her he wasn't literally smoldering. What of his plump pallid face wasn't black or glaring red was gouged bloody. He wore loose blue hospital-style trousers. Bandages wrapped his lumpy upper body. His blood had soaked them through and was actually beginning to run.

Blood-crust concealed one eye. The other glared madly at her.

Dolores swayed. He must have been in terrible pain. It amazed her he was able to remain conscious, let alone sit in a chair and puff a cigar.

Alicia clucked and shook her head. "You shouldn't smoke," she said in English. "It is bad for you."

The man barked a laugh, then groaned. "I'll take my bloody chances," he rasped in what Dolores thought was an English accent.

Alicia frowned and shook her head. She looked to Dolores. Dolores pressed her mouth to a line and nodded.

She knew what she had to do. All she had to do was steel herself to do it.

As she approached she could feel heat beating from his body as if still radiating from his burns. *He must be burning up with fever,* she thought. That, at least, would not affect her. Any tissue damage infection might have done would transfer to her; the pathogens themselves would not.

There was something repellent about him. Yet he suffered. It went beyond orders, now, even from Alicia. God had given her this gift, this curse. She could not withhold it. She was the Angel of Mercy; she was Our Lady of Pain.

She drew in a deep breath and stepped forward.

As always it hit her hard. As always it was bad. She ground her teeth against a scream.

"Ahh, Christ," he said. "That's good. That's good, girl."

His head lolled on his thick neck. He grinned up at her. "At least you won't need to grow your bloody arms back this time, eh?"

Cold shot through the fire that enveloped her. She stepped back. Instantly it was as if a furnace door had been shut. Dolores's cheeks felt sunburned; she felt blood run from gashes in her face and body. The torment dulled to an ache; no longer was his pain being loaded directly into her nervous system.

Recognition came like a slap. "I saw you!" she exclaimed in French.

"Speak English, bitch," he rasped. "Why did you stop?"

"You were there! I saw you."

Wild-eyed she looked at Alicia. "Why do you stop, child?" the woman asked.

"He's the enemy! He was there with those men in the Ijaw village where—where they chopped the boy's arms off!"

The injured man barked a laugh. "Too bloody right I was. People's Paradise wanted Niger Delta oil, didn't they? Needed an excuse to go to war with the whole world at their backs, didn't they? So it's play both sides, now, Butch Dagon, innit? For dirty work, I'm your man. Bloody Nigerians thought I was theirs, but it was your dirt I was doing all along. So get back here, girl, and finish what you started. I earned it, right enough!"

Through a curtain of hot tears Dolores looked to Alicia. Knew she would deny the man's words, damn his lies.

Instead, Alicia smiled encouragingly and made urgent hand motions for Dolores to continue.

Dolores turned and walked out. "Wait!" she heard Dagon bellow. "Get bloody back here!"

She went left down the hall, back in the direction Alicia had led her. Hot tears fogged her eyes and streamed down her cheeks.

"Don't fucking walk away from me!" Dagon shouted. "That bloody lion buggered me right up. You're a healer. Heal me."

She refused to look back. Guilt tore her, and the sense of duty. *I cannot bear to heal such a creature,* she thought.

"Heal me, damn you to hell! *Bitch!*"

Behind her she heard a sound unlike anything she had heard before. Half rustle, half gurgle. A breeze blew past her down the hallway.

She spun.

A monster crouched there. A great mound of fur-covered muscle. Half its fur was burned away; great red and char-black wounds had broken open and begun to seep. Its eyes were bloodshot.

A pointed maw opened. Jagged yellow teeth filled it. The monster vented a squealing snarl and charged.

Dolores stood frozen. As the horror gathered itself to leap upon her the hallway lit with dazzling white radiance. Heat hit her left side.

The sunbeam impaled the leaping monster. It blew apart into chunks and splatter. She screamed as hot clots hit her in the face.

A strong arm caught her from behind. She stiffened. Then knowing the touch she turned, melted against her lover's strong chest.

"Oh, Tom," she said. "It's terrible. We have to tell the world. It was all a lie! That monster was working w-with Alicia all the time!"

Even with the arms of the world's most potent ace wrapped around her it took all her courage to say that. She accused the president's own sister of terrible crimes. Knowing Alicia was capable of terrible acts of justice.

Tom grunted softly. "Too bad you heard all that," he said, stroking the short hair at the back of her head.

"This cannot be allowed. The truth must be told. I—I'll find the Chinese reporter. She'll get the story out!"

"I'm sorry you feel that way," Tom said. "Really, really sorry."

"Oh, Tom, why did it have to turn out so? I thought we stood for truth and justice. For revolution! Now I learn it was all oil and power."

His strong hand cupped her head from behind. She raised her face to his and smiled. "You won't change your mind?"

"I wish that I could," she said. "I wish I could unhear what was said. But the world must know."

His fingers tightened on the back of her skull. They twisted her head viciously clockwise. Dolores actually heard the pop of her cervical vertebrae breaking. A red spark shot through her brain.

Then she wasn't anymore.

♥

"Oh, sweet Lord," Alicia Nshombo said from the doorway. "The poor dear! Did it have to be so?"

Gently Tom lowered the dead girl to the floor. "I told you, babe," he told her softly. "You can't make an omelet without breaking eggs." He straightened, brushing absently at some wet furry clumps of Dagon she'd left on his blue chambray shirt. "She was going to blow it all," he told Alicia. "She wasn't objectively Marxist yet, you see."

Alicia's ample face clouded. "But she was heroine of the hour! Kitengi just gave her a medal in front of God and everyone. She's still *wearing* it, for sweet Mary's sake. What am I to tell the media?"

He grinned. "The truth," he said. "She died a martyr. Raised the alarm when that notorious tool of the British Empire, Butcher Dagon, infiltrated the palace to assassinate Doc Prez." He shook his head. "Poor kid. She was the Butcher's last victim."

"Uh-oh," said Hong.

They sat in the gloom of one of the suite of rooms they'd been assigned in the palace. Sun Hei-lian sat beside a junior tech named Li, helping edit video of today's medal ceremony. She hit pause, freezing a quartet of Chengdu Jian-7 fighters her government had provided the PPA in mid-flyover, and swiveled her chair.

She frowned. "Why are you showing me stock footage of a mushroom cloud, Hong?"

"It's . . . not stock footage."

The image on the wide-screen television was grainy, shot from ground level. A round head of smoke and dust rolled up a blue sky, a shape unmistakable and chilling. In the foreground white dunes and wisps of pale grass framed the terrible image.

The setting looked familiar. Feeling as if her blood had been replaced with liquid nitrogen, Hei-lian said, "Where?"

"From the Nigerian coast, near Brass. France 24 TV's sending it real-time."

Li turned beside her. "Wait, Brass? Isn't that—?"

Hong nodded. "Ground zero's the head of the invading PPA army."

♣

*"Still getting no readings,"* Tom's voice said. His voice crackled over the radio. A storm had gathered over the blast site with unnatural speed. Lightning laced the clouds and raked the ground.

"That is not possible," said Professor Évariste Tiwari, from Kongoville's Liberation University. An internationally known physicist who had worked with UN antinuclear proliferation teams out of Los Alamos, he was a small, stooped Congolese with a big bald head and a round belly pooching out the front of his rumpled black Western-style suit. "Even if it was an airburst, it *must* have left a plume of fissile material not converted to energy by the reaction."

*"No joy, Doc. Geiger counter barely registers a peep."*

A dozen people crammed the room where the Committee aces had been debriefed. The smell of nervous sweat almost overpowered the smell of Alicia Nshombo's violet soap. The wide-screen monitors mostly showed various satellite news feeds endlessly replaying the France 24 video, which had started right after the detonation's distinctive flash drew the cameraman's attention. A couple, muted, showed live debate from an emergency session of the UN Security Council, where Russia and China furiously demanded sanctions if not worse be imposed on both Nigeria and its sponsor, the British Empire, for crimes against humanity. It was sheer formality: the Empire held a veto.

Glancing that way occasionally Hei-lian gathered that the U.S. ambassador sat and said nothing to defend Great Britain. Which might mean his own government was none too pleased with its old ally for letting loose the nuclear demon.

Mostly she, like the others—her crew, President Dr. Nshombo, Alicia, Professor Tiwari—focused on the monitor showing the feed from the video camera strapped to Tom's chest. What it showed horrified even Hei-lian, accustomed as she was to the endless iteration of sorrow and atrocity that comprised modern Central African history.

In this land frost never touched, the green grass had gone winter gray. Skeletal trees smoldered beside the bent and burnt-out wrecks of a Simba Brigade armored column. The chassis of some Russian-made tank cradled upside-down in the branches of a stout tree. It had shed its massive turret somewhere as the blast flipped it through the air like a tiddlywink.

*"I see something moving down there,"* Tom said. *"I'm going down for a look."*

"Be careful," Nshombo said. It was a measure of the strain he was under that he consented to sit in a chair. His hands grasped the arms so hard Hei-lian half expected he'd leave grooves in the hard wood. Standing beside him, Alicia reached down to pat one hand reassuringly. "Your instruments might be malfunctioning. There might be fallout anyway."

*"No sweat,"* Tom came back. *"A little radiation doesn't scare me."*

Hei-lian kept her face impassive at the implied slap at the People's Republic. After some quick satellite consultation between Hei-lian and her superiors Tom had used his gift of hyperflight to bounce to orbit and then down to Beijing, where he picked up hastily gathered radiation-detection and air-sampling gear. He now wore it on a makeshift harness along with the video camera and a *Guoanbu* satellite-link radio.

Hei-lian caught Hong's eye. He monitored the telemetry from Tom's sensors. He gave her a scarcely perceptible headshake. *No malfunction.* He might have a weak stomach, but he was shaping up well under stress.

The camera's eye angled down. The scorched earth swept up. Tom leveled his flight off at perhaps thirty meters' altitude.

Six figures shuffled toward him along the road. They had a mottled reddish color.

*"Closing in,"* Tom reported.

*"Mon Dieu,"* Alicia said, choking.

For a moment Hei-lian's brain resisted making sense of what her eyes saw. Then she could no longer hide from it. Their clothes had been burned or blasted away. Their skin was gone. Their eyes were shiny tracks glazed down flayed cheeks. One cradled coils of his own intestines in stubbed arms. A purple greasy tail trailed in the white dust behind him.

"Use the wastebasket, Hong," Hei-lian said through teeth clenched so hard they squeaked. The tech caught it up just in time. The room filled with the acid reek of vomit.

Hei-lian barely noticed.

*"Going back up,"* Tom said. If the horrific and pathetic sight affected him his voice gave no sign. Hei-lian wondered what went through his mind.

*"I can see a crater ahead of me now,"* he said. *"Not very big. Maybe fifty–sixty yards across."*

"This cannot be!" the professor exclaimed. "A crater would mean the fireball came in contact with the surface. Vaporized soil and rock would be sucked up and mingled with unconsumed radionuclides. It would produce substantial fallout."

He took off his glasses and polished them furiously with a handkerchief. "Substantial."

But the instruments continued to show radiation levels scarcely more than background. Something strange was going on here. Hei-lian felt relief at having a mystery to distract her from the images that kept shambling through her mind.

*"I'm coming up to the crater,"* Tom said, in effect narrating the action they saw on the screen. *"Wait—there's something down there in the middle of it.*

*"It's—a kid. A naked kid. In the middle of the fucking crater."*

Tom Weathers touched down. The heat from the lumpy green glass walls baked his skin and forced him to squint his eyes to prevent their drying out. His Geiger counter chattered; the voices from Kongoville assured him he could endure it for a few minutes without permanent harm.

The boy lay sobbing in the midst of a patch of unaffected sand.

"Hey," he called. "Hey, kid." The boy was white—fish-pale all over, in fact, and jiggling chubby. Maybe he spoke English.

The kid had his head on his arms. He kept crying.

"Listen," Tom said. "It's okay. I'm gonna get you taken care of."

"Go 'way!" the boy shouted with a wave of his arm. *English. Cool.*

Tom squatted down at the edge of the patch of sand. "You want me to just leave you here to the mosquitoes? Not a good plan, man."

"I—killed them. I kill everybody. I shouldn't be around people. I didn't want to do it. I want to die!"

"Hey, buddy," Tom said. "Just take a deep breath and tell me what happened."

The boy sat up. His pale belly spilled sadly over plump thighs. "I didn't *mean* to. I never mean to. But the Highwayman shoved me out of the truck and drove off and then he was gone and these tanks were coming down the road. They started *shooting* at me. I got scared, and—" He drew in a big shuddering breath and waved his hand around. *"This."*

"You did this?"

He nodded. "It always happens when I get scared."

"Let me get this straight," Tom said. "You cause nuclear explosions?"

"Yes! Haven't you been listening? When I get real scared I fucking blow up. Are you some kind of 'tard?" The spasm of anger passed and his eyes gushed tears again. "I wish I was dead. I'm too dangerous to be around!"

The voices in Tom's head were going ape-shit now. He ignored them. The warm feeling—like the aftermath of a good fuck; that three-way with Hei-lian and Lilith, say—spreading up through his belly from his loins told him what he was dealing with, and what he had, at any cost, to do.

"What's your name?"

"Drake." He sniffled and dabbed tears from his eyes. "Who are you?"

"Pleased to meet you, Drake. I'm Tom Weathers. Locally I got hung with some unpronounceable handle. I used to go by *the Radical*."

"The revolutionary guy on the posters."

"That's me. You can call me Tom. Unless you can say *Mokèlé-mbèmbé*. Even if you can, call me Tom."

The fat boy fell over and curled right back into fetal position. "What the fuck?" Tom burst out before he could stop himself.

*"You're gonna kill me!"*

"Say what?" Tom was no slave to Western linear thought. Still, he thought that was a pretty funny worry for somebody who'd been announcing his desire to die so loudly thirty seconds ago. "Why the f— Why would I kill you, Drake? I wanna *help* you."

"But you're with the People's Paradise."

"Yeah."

"Before they dumped me, the kidnappers were talking about, about the PPA. I think I just blew up your army."

"We'll get more," Tom said. He imagined steam coming from Doc Prez's ears at that. But the Indians would give them more tanks. Shit, if he could only bring this kid around, nobody would deny the PPA anything. *Ever.*

"But there's only one you," he said. "Right?"

The boy nodded.

"The People's Paradise of Africa is a place where people can breathe free and never have to fear oppression again. Hell, I make sure of it."

A blue eye peeked at him. "Oppression?"

"Shit, yeah. *You've* been oppressed. Wouldn't you say? I mean, you tell me you got kidnapped, roughed up, dumped out on the road. And shot at by tanks. Sounds like oppression to *me*."

"And if I go with you—"

"You're safe. Nobody picking on you anymore." Although it struck him you'd have to be an exceptional dumbass even for a jock to pick on somebody who could vaporize you and everything within seventy-five feet of him, toss fifty-ton tanks into trees a mile down the road. "You'd be appreciated. Hell, you'd be a *hero*. We'll give you a parade."

"A parade? *Really?*"

Tom nodded, solemnly. *Fuck, Kitengi'd probably give you his sister's virtue. And a nerd like you might even go for—*

He straightened. "Okay, Drake. Let me help you up. Then I'll bounce us back to Kongoville, get you cleaned up, get some decent food in you." Not that the last looked too urgent, but the kid was probably hungry. All the time.

Drake looked past him and his eyes went wide.

Tom had been caught by surprise once. That was one time too many. He stepped quickly left and wheeled.

A man stood in the crater, as muscular as himself. And even more golden: not just his hair but his skin. Even his eyes. He held a scimitar.

Tom's eyes narrowed. "A teleport, huh. So you're the sneaky sack of shit that shot me in the back. What, no Kalashnikov this time?"

"Figured it out, did you?" The newcomer had a fruity Brit accent.

"Just now."

"You're not so dim as you look. A gun didn't work so well last time. Beheading's pretty final, though. If needs must."

"Needs must?"

"I didn't come for you," the golden man said. "I came for the boy."

"Ah, well then—" As if surrendering, Tom raised his hands.

Fire flashed from both palms. But the man was gone.

Tom threw himself into a forward roll. He heard the scimitar swish behind him.

"Your powers aren't much use against a teleport," the man said. He lunged for Tom, sword upraised—

Tom stood twenty feet away. It was as close as he could manage, doing a hyperflight bounce to near Earth orbit and back. Better than he expected, actually. He smelled the soles of his tennis shoes melting on the hot glass.

"Kinda hard to kill someone who can move at light speed, too," he said.

The golden man glared. Then he smiled. "Ahh. But if one doesn't know when and from where—"

He vanished.

"—the blow will strike—"

The words came from close behind. Tom looked down his nose to watch the scimitar tip slash beneath his chin. He turned.

His opponent stared at him with eyes like gilded saucers. "The blade," he said. "It passed right through your neck!"

"I'm just full of surprises."

He hit the man in the center of his broad muscle-bulging chest. The bastard was fast; he almost managed to turn away in time to slip the tank-armor-buckling punch. But not all the way. Tom's fist grazed him and spun him through the air to slam into the slanted green crater wall.

Tom heard a sizzle, smelled burned hair. The golden man squalled like a cat and vanished.

A moment later he was right in Tom's face and the sword came whistling down between Tom's eyes. It passed harmlessly down his body.

"Can't . . . hit me when you're insubstantial," the man grunted, whipping the sword around in a figure-eight through the center of Tom's torso. "I'll wager you can't . . . shoot fire, either. . . ."

Tom hung in space. The sun's heat scorched him; he felt the vacuum trying to suck the breath from his chest and tugging at the tender membranes and capillaries of his eyeballs.

Then he floated twenty feet above the golden man. He flung out a hand and sent down a sunbeam that filled the crater with brilliance.

It spattered gobbets of glowing-molten sand in all directions. Drake yelped and threw a hand up in front of his face.

Tom landed. He felt his legs buckle under him. He had to put a hand down to keep from planting his face in the little patch of sand.

He shook his head. "Whoa. Takes it *out* of you."

"Over there!" Drake shouted, pointing off and up toward the crater rim. *Glad to know he's picked a side,* Tom thought.

He wheeled quickly around and sent a fire blast toward the golden figure that stood against the bruised and roiling sky. It didn't much surprise him when it vanished. *Hope he didn't notice that last shot was a bit feeble,* he thought. *I haven't really recovered from letting it all hang out when I trashed the Nigerian Army.*

He was already spinning in place, cocking his right arm. His straight right caught the teleport square on the bridge of his aristocratic golden nose as he materialized behind Tom, sent him staggering back three steps. Smoke curled from beneath his slippers as he blundered into the hot glass.

He doubled over, emitting a thin keening wail. He put hand to face, looked at it. Looking up at Tom in shocked outrage he said, "You broke it! Bloody hell."

"That's just the beginning of a world of hurt," Tom said. He was *righteously pissed.* Stutter-stepping forward he side-kicked him. Not hard enough to break anything, or much. Just enough to *launch* him.

As the golden man reached the apex of his flight Tom raised a hand. But his sun-hot beam flashed through air and up into the dense clouds. They boiled away from its fury.

"Shit," he said. He stood tensed, casting from side to side, awaiting the next attack.

After a minute he decided the glowing Limey had had enough. Too bad.

"Next time, motherfucker," Tom said. "Next time."

Elation hit him, like a jolt of all the drugs he so rigorously denied himself. *We won!* he thought. *We won it* all. *We've joined the nuclear club, baby. Nobody can fuck with us now.*

"Okay, buddy. Let's get you out of here." He went to Drake, pulled him up by the arm. The boy felt like a pillowcase full of wet cement. Dead weight. But Tom could clean and jerk a Vijayanta. Important thing was, the boy didn't seem inclined to fight him.

The teenager slumped against him. Putting an arm around his fat bare back wasn't Tom's favorite thing to do. Compared to what else he'd done today, it wasn't so bad. "Ever wanted to see Earth from outer space, kid?"

"Naked?"

"Don't worry. You won't feel a thing."

They landed in the middle of a parking lot outside the palace. A pair of guards in crisp sky blue uniforms came trotting up.

They looked wild-eyed. Tom recognized them, so they must know *him.*

His sudden appearance out of thin air couldn't have rattled them that badly.

Drake sniffled. "Why are there sirens going off?"

Tom opened his mouth to explain an alert had been called after the armored column got nuked. Except why were they *still* going off?

Terrible certainty struck him like a blast wave. He thrust the plump, naked boy at the two guards. "Here. Take him to the president pronto. Don't let anything stop you!"

He turned and ran for his rooms.

The wailing of Congolese caretakers confirmed his sickest fears when he was halfway down the corridor.

He blew in through the open door. Sun Hei-lian sat amid a gaggle of hysterical local women, stiffly upright and apparently emotionless. The shiny tear-track down either exquisite cheek gave that the lie.

The women stopped their lamentations to stare at Tom in horror. Presumably a good part of their distress arose from their fears of what he'd do to them.

"A golden guy—"

Hei-lian nodded. "He took her," she said. "I ran up here as soon as the fight started. I realized, a teleport—no one was safe. Anywhere."

He nodded briskly. "Smart. What happened?"

"When I got here he was just chasing off the caretakers. He grabbed Sprout and held a sword to her throat. He said that the Committee would be in touch, with instructions where and when to bring the boy if you want your daughter back."

"The Committee," Tom said. "Those cocksuckers."

He noticed something on a table: a black handgun, a compact 9mm CZ-100. His eyes followed several frightened gazes and one as unnaturally calm as his own to a wall, where a divot had been knocked from faintly pinkish stucco. He frowned.

"You *shot* at him? When he was holding my daughter?"

She lifted her chin. "You know what I am, Tom. I'm counterterror-trained. Sprout was in no danger. I would have hit him"—she reached up to touch between her eyes—"here."

"You missed."

"I did not miss. He teleported."

"Yeah." He sighed and rubbed his hands together. "Bastard does that."

"What will you do?"

"Give 'em the kid."

She blinked and jerked back as if slapped. "What will Nshombo say?"

"Better be *yes*." Tom said. "I'll take them the kid. I'll get my little girl back.

"And then I'll kill every single motherfucking one of them."

# Double Helix

## THEY HAVE SOWN THE WIND, AND THEY SHALL REAP THE WHIRLWIND

### Melinda M. Snodgrass

**SPROUT WAS COMPLETELY AGREEABLE** when I said I'd come to take her to her daddy. But now we are standing in Jackson Square and no daddy is in evidence. Her head is jerking from side to side like a hummingbird guarding its stash as she scans the crowds of emergency workers.

The sky looks like boiling soap scum and the hot wind, heavy with moisture, shakes blossoms off the azaleas. There is the roar of diesel engines as earth-moving equipment scoops up and deposits sandbags. I can see Ana standing on the top of the river walk frowning out across the river. I spot Bubbles walking swiftly beside a man in a suit. Something about him screams "politician." She's making good time because she's surprisingly slim, a testament to how much energy she's been expending.

Since she has met Drake and dealt with Drake it seems prudent to explain the situation to her. But I am currently Bahir and she knows Bahir from the battles in Egypt last year. She's just as likely to flatten me with a bubble as listen to me. Which means—

"What the fuck!?"

A warbling tenor wail breaks across my musings. It's Bugsy and he's spotted me.

"Holy shit! Bubbles! Ana!"

The covey of aces are pounding across the flagstones and cobblestones with murder in their eyes. I allow the muscles and tissue to soften and flow. The ace stampede stutters, slows, and comes to a confused and milling halt.

"What the fuck?" Bugsy says again.

"Good you should ask," I say, and thrust Sprout toward them. "*This* is Tom Weathers's daughter. Weathers and the People's Paradise have the nuclear ace." They are goggling at me. "You know. Drake. Little Fat Boy, so to speak." It's a terrible pun. They don't seem to get that, either.

"You're that magician," Ana says. "The one who kicked our butts on *American Hero.*"

"I'm an agent for Her Majesty's government." *At least until Bruckner reports to Flint,* I think. "I operate in the Middle East. Recently I've been working in Africa."

"But you tried to *kill* me," Bugsy whines.

"Well, not really. If I had wanted you dead, you'd be dead. You were making a dreadful hash of things, and I had hoped to make you reconsider your involvement. Therefore it had to look good."

"Hey! We saved those people—"

"Not now!" I let it snap with command and they subside. "Weathers is a dangerous psychopath and President Nshombo and his sister are equally murderous. They now have a living nuclear bomb." I overenunciate the final three words. "I've left a message for Weathers that I have Sprout and he'll get her back when I get Drake."

Hearing her name the woman suddenly says, "Where's my daddy? Is he coming soon?"

Bubbles can't help herself. She puts an arm around the older woman's shoulders. "He'll be here soon. Would you like something to eat? Are you hungry?" And I realize that Bubbles really is kind.

"Actually we stopped in Iceland and I bought her breakfast while I waited for the sun to rise here," I say.

"Why us?" Ana asks in her blunt way. "Why bring her here?"

"Because Weathers will try to kill me rather than make the exchange. I need your powers. Individually none of you can stand against Weathers, but together . . ."

"Yeah, well, I say you can just go fuck yourself," Bugsy says. "Why should we risk our lives?"

"Because Weathers won't make a distinction between me and thee." I give him a smile. "And my message strongly suggested that the Committee was behind this."

"You fucker," Bugsy says miserably.

"You should broaden your repertoire of invective," I say. "How do I get a cup of coffee?"

The day is dragging by. I sit on one of the benches in Jackson Square drinking the strong, chicory-flavored coffee and setting myself abuzz eating sugar-drenched beignets. Around my feet is a halo of crushed butts. I ran out of the Turkish cigarettes hours ago, and have been making do with Lucky Strikes. Ana, Gardener, and more disturbingly, an army of the dead are still working to raise the levees. Bugsy and I are keeping watch for Weathers. I've warned Bugsy that Weathers will do something surprising and to consider every possible avenue for an arrival, no matter how remote.

My phone rings. "Hi, babe," I say as I answer. I know it's Niobe. We've been calling each other every hour.

"Oh, Noel." Her voice is husky with tears. "It's your dad."

It feels like a fist has closed hard around my guts. "Is he—" I can't say the word.

"No, but he's unconscious. I think it won't be long now."

I feel like a butterfly on a collector's pin. I want to be with her. I want to see him. I need to be here for Drake. All I can manage to say is, "I don't know what to do," and there's a five-year-old's wail in the words.

"He said to tell you to 'live forward.' Then he was quiet for a long time, and then he murmured something. I think he was still talking to you. He said 'for love is strong as death.' Do you know what he means?"

The agony in my belly is gone. My throat is tight and my chest tight, but I'm oddly calm. "Yes. Yes, I think I do."

"Are you coming home?"

"No. I need to be here for Drake."

"Then I'll be here for your father." Her voice is very soft.

"I'll see you soon," I say and hang up the phone. "Good-bye, Dad. Godspeed. I love you," I whisper. But the words are whipped away by the rising wind.

## Shoulda

Caroline Spector

"YOU'VE BEEN A BAD, bad dolly," Sprout said. "Now you have to go to bed."

I walked into the room where Hoodoo Mama was watching Sprout play. Their heads were together, and it was hard for me to reconcile the hard-ass zombie chick with this gentle girl who was so tender with Sprout.

"My dolly has been very bad," Sprout said, looking up at me.

"Oh, what did dolly do?" I asked.

"She walked funny. See."

Sprout put the dolly on the floor. It got up on all fours and staggered around the room.

"What the fu—heck is that?"

"Uhm," Hoodoo Mama said.

I strode over to the dolly and picked it up.

"Oh, hell no," I said. "Joey, you can't let her play with zombie cats." I opened the door and dropped the cat in the hall.

"I want my dolly!"

"How about we go out shopping and find you a new dolly?" Hoodoo Mama said.

Sprout frowned. "But I want mine."

"Tell you what, I bet Michelle will make you some bubbles."

They turned back toward me with expectant looks. I gave Hoodoo Mama a glare, but I couldn't be mad at Sprout. She was sweet beyond all measure.

"Okay, Sprout," I said. "What kind of bubbles do you want? Soapy? Rubbery?"

"Balls!"

"Rubbery it is."

I made an assortment of bouncy, soft, moderately tough bubbles. Sprout giggled and began to chase them around the room. Ever since Noel had dumped her in our lap, we'd been trying to think of ways to keep her happy. And not scared.

Once Hoodoo Mama had realized that Sprout was a child mentally, she was pissed as hell at Noel. "Fucker just dragged that poor little girl into the middle of all this shit about to go down," she hissed at me.

"She's in her thirties," I said.

"That don't mean dick." Her hands curled into fists and her breathing was harsh. "You can tell by looking at her that she's special."

"Well, her father is at the center of all this mess," I replied. "If you're going to be pissed at anyone, be pissed at him. He snatched Drake and set all of this in motion."

Hoodoo Mama's eyes narrowed. "Don't think I don't know that. That fucker will be sorry he messed with any of this."

Her rage was so pure and clean. I envied it. But I was also trying to avoid spending too much time with her. We hadn't talked about what had happened in the warehouse the night of the hurricane. Just thinking about it made me feel queasy. And excited. And confused.

I didn't know who I was anymore. I didn't make love to other girls. I mean, girls other than my girlfriend. But Hoodoo Mama had needed me then. And I had wanted to help her, but then things got carried away. And . . . and I was making excuses.

I left Hoodoo Mama with Sprout and walked across the hall to Bugsy's suite. Since the rest of the Committee had shown up, we'd taken over the entire top floor of the Royal Sonesta. I could hear the arguing through the door, but I knocked anyway.

". . . you bastard . . . Weathers . . ."

The door flew open. Bugsy had a pissed look on his face. Behind him it looked like an *American Hero* reunion. Except there were no cameras and no one was smiling. But the furniture was better. Nice Louis XVI–style couches and chairs. All done up in tasteful blues.

Drummer Boy was missing, though. I was still trying to decide if that was a good thing. He'd been an asshole during the show, but afterward, in

Egypt, he wasn't as bad. And Curveball, Lohengrin, Rustbelt, Toad Man, and Brave Hawk were here in addition to my own team.

"Bad time?" I whispered.

Bugsy's body began to look fuzzy. He was going all insect-y on me. "It's not great," he replied.

Fortune was glaring at Noel. Curveball, Rusty, and Lohengrin were leaning against the far wall of the room. They all had their arms crossed and they looked pissed.

"I don't see what the big deal is about Weathers," said Gardener, leaning forward in her chair. "Between us, we can take him."

Noel rolled his eyes. "Honestly, John, where do you get these girls? TV? Weathers is terrifyingly powerful and completely mad—and he's been around longer than most of you have been alive."

Toad Man's tongue snapped out and popped loudly behind Noel's head. His tongue rolled back into his mouth and he morphed out of toad form. "You should really watch who you're being snotty to," he said. "Far as I know, you're a double-crossing, cross-dressing liar who shouldn't even be here."

I didn't say anything. Right now, Noel wasn't exactly on my Favorite People list. He'd been playing, well, *everyone* off each other. And Drake was in the soup because of him, no matter what excuse he gave.

Oh, and if my eavesdropping was accurate, he was also screwing Niobe. If he broke her heart, I would kick his sorry ass from here back to whatever warm-beer-drinking blood-pudding-eating dental-hygiene-impaired London borough he came from.

"Fortune," he said in his most supercilious voice, "you should be able to rein your people in by now. Regardless of their opinion of me, we have Sprout now and a way to retrieve Drake. So that should make me—what's that American expression? Your new best friend."

A groan ran around the room. Noel was about as popular with the rest of the Committee as he was with me.

"Everyone calm down," Fortune said. He was looking tired. Then he stopped and got all daydreamy-looking and I wondered what Sekhmet was saying to him. Then he said, "Noel's right. If it hadn't been for him, we'd have no leverage with Weathers at all."

"Oh, c'mon!" yelled Bugsy, jumping up from his chair. "Noel tried to cut my head off! I don't care how 'helpful' he's been. He's a menace."

I walked over to the side table where a coffee service had been set up.

As I poured a cup and started loading it with sugar, I heard Curveball say, "Look, I know everyone's unhappy with Noel, but he really isn't the problem right now. We've got to figure out how to handle the Sprout/Drake exchange."

I glanced over my shoulder. Fortune was giving her a wan smile, but she didn't smile back.

"What I want to know is how we're going to make the swap," said Earth Witch. "I mean, if Weathers is as powerful as you say, he's going to be a bitch to handle."

Fortune rubbed his eyes, then took a pull off his coffee. "The swap team is going to be me and Michelle. Weathers wants me, so if I'm part of the swap he'll be thinking he's going to have a shot at me. And Michelle is there for two reasons. First, she knows Drake. And second, she can take almost limitless damage. Probably anything Weathers can dish out."

"You got any opinions about this, Bubbles?" asked Rustbelt in his flat Midwestern voice.

By now, I was sitting on one of the chairs next to the door. I was almost back down to my thinnest and had wanted to stay there until the PR part of the mission was over. Though it made me a little less able to kick ass right out the door, it was nice not to worry about the furniture when I sat down.

"If I'm the best choice for the job, then of course I'm fine with it," I said. I could feel my hands tremble, so I put my coffee cup down. "But we'll need a backup plan in case things go wrong. And do we hand Sprout over even if things start to go bad?"

"Of course we're going to have backup, Michelle," Fortune said. "Everyone else will be stationed around Jackson Square to keep things chilled out. Weathers is extremely dangerous, but he can't take all of us. And I don't think he'll do anything that'll put Sprout at risk."

Brave Hawk whispered something to Lohengrin, who nodded. I wondered what that was all about.

"Okay," Fortune said as he unrolled a map of Jackson Square onto the large coffee table. "Here's where I'm going to position each of you."

"Are we going to meet Daddy?"

"Yep," I said. "You remember what we said, right?"

Sprout smiled at me and tugged on my ponytail. "Yes, Daddy needs to talk to John Fortune before we can go home. I need to stay with you until Daddy and John Fortune are done talking."

I brushed back the fine tendrils of hair that had escaped her braid. She looked up at me with guileless blue eyes.

At that moment, I hated everyone who had put her and Drake into this position. Her father, Noel, and the rest of the assholes who thought that Drake was a pawn for their megalomaniacal dreams. And I really hated myself for helping them.

She took my hand, and we went back into the living room where Fortune and the others were waiting.

John Fortune, Sprout, and I were standing in the middle of Jackson Square. We'd done a pretty amazing job of getting some of the Quarter back on its feet. Though the lamps on the gate were shattered, the square was looking remarkably good. Gardener had replaced the trees and other plants that had been destroyed. And the statue of Andrew Jackson was unchanged. We stood at its base.

My clothes felt tight. Before coming for the meeting, I'd had one of Hoodoo Mama's zombies pound on me a bit. I still wasn't big, exactly, but I wanted *some* firepower, just in case.

We were in a good tactical position. On all four sides we had a clear sightline. Odds were that no one was going to sneak up on us here.

"Where's Daddy?" Sprout asked.

"He'll be here soon, honey," I replied. "Why don't you stay with John Fortune for a moment and I'll see if he's coming."

I walked around the statue, checking our position. Cameo and Earth Witch were sitting on benches near the entrance to the park. Hoodoo Mama had helped clear the usual street people from the square, so we didn't have to worry about civilians getting caught in the middle should anything bad go down. I knew Hoodoo Mama was still somewhere nearby, but she was really good at hiding.

Bugsy was in swarm form. He kept making swooping passes around the square. And it was hard to hide Toad Man—Volkswagen-sized toads, kinda hard to explain. From the other side of the park, I could see Lohengrin's armor shining in the sun.

I went back to Fortune and Sprout.

"Did you see anything?" Fortune asked.

I shook my head. "Not yet. I can't believe he's delaying this."

Fortune shrugged and kept looking around. "My mother says he was bad news back in the day. He's clever and more than a little nuts."

Sweat began beading on my forehead and upper lip. It was muggy as hell, but I was also feeling nervous. I'd gone up against Golden Boy and gotten my ass handed to me. This Weathers guy was known to be unpredictable, and there was no telling what we might get. Those old aces were scary.

There was the whooping sound of a helicopter. I looked up. We'd talked to the local flight authorities, and they'd agreed to suspend all traffic over the Quarter for the afternoon.

A black helicopter appeared over St. Louis Cathedral, heading right toward us.

"What the hell?" Fortune said. "That can't be Weathers."

Then, over the sound of the blades, we heard, "This is William Ray, head of the Special Committee for Ace Resources and Endeavors. We have warrants from the United Sates government for the arrest of all Committee members. Surrender peacefully or we will use deadly force."

Then the side door of the helicopter opened and I saw one ace fly out, swooping around the square. Ropes dropped and more SCARE agents slid down, landing about fifteen feet from us. I recognized Lady Black, Moon, and the Midnight Angel from Cross Plains. I figured the rest were aces, too. No one else could handle us. The helicopter flew off.

Billy Ray emerged from the midst of the aces wearing his usual pristine jumpsuit. He strode up to us followed by the Midnight Angel. I knew they were married now. Ink had said so in one of her e-mails.

Sprout gave a frightened cry and ran behind me. I understood why. Billy Ray's face was a mass of scars. Thick pink tissue crisscrossed the suntanned planes of his face. His eyes were cold. But I wasn't worried. He was strong, but brute force didn't frighten me in the least. And I had the psychological advantage. I'd taken him once already.

I saw the rest of the SCARE agents fanning out across the park. Crap. This was not good. These SCARE jerks could hose our trade with Weathers.

"John Fortune, Michelle Pond," Billy Ray said. "I am placing you under arrest."

Sprout had wrapped her arms around me and buried her face in my back.

"Are you insane?" Fortune asked. "Billy Ray, you have no jurisdiction over us. We're part of the UN. And there was a no-fly order for this section."

"I'm an agent of the United States government," Billy Ray said, coming closer to Fortune. He leaned in until his spittle was hitting Fortune's face. "You're on U.S. soil. You're U.S. citizens. Do I really need to draw you a map here?"

John's forehead began to glow. Sekhmet was getting pissed.

"Look around, Billy Ray," I said, trying to keep my voice from shaking with anger. This asshat had almost gotten Drake and Niobe killed. Not to mention that his Lady Black bitch had put a mad hurt on me. "You've got about a dozen aces. Not only do we have as many, but we've got a little extra somethin' somethin'." I pointed and Billy Ray turned around and saw what we'd been holding back for Weathers.

An army of zombies had suddenly surrounded Jackson Square. A lot of them had been floaters, which gave them a really horrible appearance. They stood there, silent, impervious, devoid of humanity.

I looked around, checking on our people. Earth Witch was flexing her hands, glancing around, looking for lines of sight. Cameo began to spin slowly, building up layers of dust. I saw a swarm of insects hovering near one of the SCARE aces, so I knew Bugsy was good to go.

Lohengrin was doing a propeller-fast pattern with his sword. The sunlight was glinting off his brilliant armor. Something small and lethally fast pinged into the dirt between me and Fortune and Billy Ray and the Midnight Angel. Curveball was making her presence known.

Noel was somewhere close by and I was hoping that Billy Ray would get the idea that this was a fight he didn't want. Weathers was due at any moment, and the last thing we needed was a full-on brawl in progress when he showed up.

Fortune began to glow even brighter. Crap. I did *not* want Sekhmet appearing right now.

"Daddy!" Sprout cried. She let go of my waist and ran in front of me, flinging her arms into the air and dancing around with her head tilted back.

We all looked up. Coming down out of the sky at an incredible rate was a bright yellow streak. Then the streak landed, and a bare-chested man dressed in low-slung, faded bell-bottom jeans appeared. He had sun-streaked hair that fell halfway down his back and a peace medallion around his neck. He was holding Drake tucked under one muscular arm.

Fortune grabbed Sprout and pushed her toward me. I folded her into my arms in a hug.

"I want Daddy," she said, pouting at me.

"I know, sweetie, but remember what we talked about."

It was getting hard to look at Fortune now. An aura surrounded him, bright gold.

"Let the boy go, Weathers," Fortune said.

"Oh, The Man wants me to let the boy go," Weathers said in a nasty voice. He flexed his biceps, squeezing Drake. But Drake didn't start crying. I wanted to bubble the hell out of Weathers.

"The Man's got to control all the power in the world," Weathers said. It was freaky how persuasive he suddenly sounded to me. "Can't let anyone else use any power."

"Let the boy go," Fortune said again. "Sprout wants her daddy."

Weathers glanced at me and Sprout. His face softened and you could see that he loved her. He dropped Drake, who landed hard on his hands and knees.

"Drake," I said in as calm a voice as I could. "Come to me."

"Let Sprout go," Weathers said.

"Not until Drake is over here." I stared right into Weathers's face. I knew he had a lot of power, but I also knew I wasn't going to let him intimidate me.

Drake scrambled to his feet and ran to me. As soon as he touched my hand, I let Sprout go.

She ran to Weathers and they embraced. Their golden heads bent together. Family reunion.

After Weathers checked Sprout and saw she was okay, he looked back at the rest of us. The expression on his face was pure, mad hatred.

"Don't try anything," Fortune said. "There are dozens of aces here. You can't take us all down."

I glanced around. The SCARE aces had obviously decided that Weathers was a bigger threat than we were. They had turned their attention from us to him and were slowly circling.

"To hell with you and the Committee, Fortune," Weathers said. "And those nimrods from SCARE. What I want now is Bahir. I frown on people who kidnap my child."

Fortune laughed. "You're not getting Bahir," he said. "You've got Sprout. We've got Drake. End of conversation."

A cruel smile formed on Weathers's face. Bad as his angry face was, this one was worse. There was a horrible feeling in my gut. Worse than when those helicopters had gone down in Egypt and all those people had died.

Weathers gave a yank at the medallion around his neck. The leather cord broke, leaving a thin line of blood on his neck. He began to swing the medallion around. It reminded me of Lohengrin patterning his sword. It spun faster and faster, glinting in the sun.

My hands started shaking. Drake had hold of one of them, and he squeezed it.

"You were always a clever boy, Fortune," Weathers said. The medallion whirred. "I could have used you in The Movement. But you had to go and work for the government." He moved backward, taking Sprout with him. "Oh, wait, you work for *all* the governments. That makes you the worst traitor of all."

He kissed Sprout on the forehead and opened his free arm wide. "Hop up, baby." Sprout wrapped her arms and legs around him as if she really were a four-year-old. And he began to slowly rise into the air.

"I can't kill you all," he said, looking around the park. "But *he* can."

The medallion flew from his hand and hit Drake in the chest. Drake stood there, frozen for a moment. Then he staggered back, pushing me into the statue of Andrew Jackson, and we both fell against the statue. Weathers shot into the sky and disappeared.

"Drake!" I cried. "Oh, my God, Drake!"

I slid out from behind him, then looked down and saw that the medallion was buried in his chest. Drake reached a shaking hand up and touched the blood, then pulled the medallion out of his chest. He held it up in front of his face as if he couldn't decide what it was. His eyes began to glow.

A cold knife went into my heart.

I looked up and saw Cameo, Hoodoo Mama, and Earth Witch running toward us.

"Stop!" I shouted. As if that would save them.

"God help us," I heard a velvety voice say. I looked up and saw the Midnight Angel hovering above us.

"Get out of here! Get everyone out!"

"Michelle!" screamed Cameo.

"Go! Everyone go! *Now!*"

I turned to Fortune. But at that moment, he started screaming. His golden glow had intensified. Squinting, I saw his hand go up to his face.

"No," he said as his body twitched and spasmed. "No . . . NO . . . NO!"

His head jerked around like a hooked fish. The scarab that was always outlined against his forehead was moving . . . getting bigger . . . expanding . . . until his flesh burst apart. Fortune shrieked, and blood covered his face and ran down his chest.

Sekhmet.

The golden radiance abandoned Fortune, and he collapsed to the ground. Sekhmet scurried toward Drake, and I was too shocked to stop her from crawling up his leg and then into the hole in his chest.

Sekhmet and Fortune had struggled for control between them for as long as I knew. But maybe she could control Drake. Maybe she could stop him.

Drake began to kick, and his back bowed. He began to babble in a language I'd never heard before. But the light wasn't just coming out of his eyes anymore. It filled his mouth, beamed out from his ears. The hole in Drake's chest began to sizzle and smell like frying bacon as the white-hot light poured from his wound.

"NO! NO!" he yelled in a strange voice. "By the light of all the Gods, I cannot stop him!"

"Drake," I said, shaking him. "Drake, Sekhmet, look at me!"

He looked at me and I was afraid.

"Let it go," I said. "But let it come to *me*."

I guess there's always a moment when we have to make a choice. And sometimes, there's just no choice to be made. You do what you can, and you hope it's enough.

I pulled Drake into my arms and held him as tight as I could. I hoped that Ink would find someone who would love her better. And I hoped that Niobe would be happy, even if it was with Noel. I hoped like hell that the whole damn city wouldn't be ruined.

I hoped that I would be enough.

He exploded.

I felt my body instantly expand to its maximum size. The power raged into me like molten lead. It burned and sang and made me want to bubble forever. The concrete cracked under us as I became heavier and heavier.

The power went on and on, building inside me, but I couldn't let it escape.

I dropped to my knees with Drake collapsing in my arms. And still the power came into me. It was like being bathed in a never-ending fire. I couldn't have stopped it even if I'd wanted to. And I didn't want to.

This was what it felt like to touch God.

I opened my eyes to the sky, and I looked directly into the sun overhead.

And it didn't blind me.

◆

# Just Cause: Part IV

Carrie Vaughn

## LIMBO

**KATE SAT CURLED UP** in a chair by John's hospital bed. She'd come here to explain to him in person. She hadn't known he would be in the hospital. The timing of all this was shitty.

He'd have a scar, the doctors said. They'd stitched the wound as well as they could, but Sekhmet had done a lot of damage when she tore out of his head. He was lucky he hadn't bled to death.

Sekhmet had done a lot of damage to him, period.

His forehead was bandaged, so she couldn't see the wound. Probably for the best. John seemed to be sleeping soundly for the first time in . . . For the first time since she'd started sleeping with him. His expression was slack rather than tense with unconscious anxiety.

She thought she might try to find some soda or coffee or something. Straightening, she winced—her arm was still sore. She'd stopped taking the pain pills. They made her fuzzy. She wanted to stay sharp, for just a little while longer.

Then she could collapse into a sobbing puddle of tears, when no one was looking.

As she stood, John opened his eyes.

"Hey," she said, moving to his side.

He gave a tired smile. He might not be able to do much more than that for now. Maybe they ought to enjoy this time, this moment in limbo, before they had to make any decisions.

"You're here." He even managed to sound surprised. "I thought you were pissed off at me."

"I am," she said. "I was. We can talk about that later."

He shook his head, annoyed, and tried to sit up. Winced, slumped back, and picked at the IV line, which had become tangled with his hand. She helped straighten it.

"This changes everything. It's all different now," he said.

"What are you talking about?"

His weak smile turned bitter. "I'm right back where I started. No powers. Nothing. I'll be resigning from the Committee. Then . . . I don't know."

If ever there was a moment she wanted to throw something at him, this was it. "Is that what this is about? You feeling sorry for yourself because you don't have a beetle woman living in your head anymore?"

He frowned. "She wasn't that bad."

"Not that bad? She—"

"She left me," he said. "She chose me, and then she left me, and it's like I'm . . . I'm *empty*. I feel empty."

Kate felt the expression of horror on her face, and she couldn't erase it. John actually sounded sad that he had his own life back.

And for the first time Kate realized that with their telepathic and emotional link, he'd been closer to Isra than he'd ever be to her.

Kate closed her eyes and took a breath. Probably shouldn't be yelling in a hospital room. But she wanted to.

"John. It's so nice to be talking to just *you* for a change."

"Even if I'm just a nat."

"I liked you before Sekhmet ever came along. It has nothing to do with anybody's powers."

"You liked Drummer Boy, too."

"Wait a minute. Do you think I only hooked up with you because you suddenly got powers? It couldn't possibly be because you were the nicest guy on the set? Because I had such a good time just hanging out with you?" Not to mention John hadn't fucked almost every other girl on the set like DB had. Those days on *American Hero* seemed like such a long time ago now. "You were the only one who saw *me*, not Curveball the ace or the hot chick."

He still wouldn't look at her. "You said you were coming here to talk to me."

He had to know what she wanted to talk to him about. Couldn't put it off any longer.

"I can't do this anymore. It's changed from when we started. I feel like someone else's tool. And I don't like it. So I'm going to take some time off."

"Leaving. With DB," he said. Like a dog worrying a bone.

"Just leaving," she said.

He smirked. Like he didn't believe her. With sudden clarity, she realized the Committee wasn't the only thing she couldn't stay with anymore. She had thought—hoped—she could leave one and not the other. But maybe that was wishful thinking.

She didn't want to have to say this to him. Not like this. But pity was a trap she didn't want to fall into. Feeling sorry for him would make them both unhappy. More unhappy, rather.

"You don't trust me, do you?" And he didn't say anything. She wanted him to deny it. To grip her hand, however weakly, and reassure her. Plead with her. But he didn't say anything. "You're always going to be worried that I'm going to leave you for him. Or the next flashy ace that comes along."

"DB was right. Maybe I was trying to keep you two apart. Because I was right, too. That if you two were together, you'd end up with him—"

Enough of this. Enough of being batted back and forth between them like a tennis ball. They all needed a time-out.

"I don't think you even see me anymore," she said. "I think I'm just . . . just this *thing* to you. Some kind of validation."

"Kate—"

"So I'm going to take some time off."

"Wait a minute—"

"I'm sorry, John." She kissed him. Lingered. Met his gaze for a moment, and didn't like the misery she saw there. But staying wouldn't change it. They'd hash this argument out again, and again—and sooner or later, she'd walk out just the same.

She left the room. Her steps came faster as she traveled down the hallway, looking for the front door. When she reached it, she left the hospital at a run and kept going.

♥

# Double Helix

## MY HEART WAKETH

### Melinda M. Snodgrass

**THE WIND IS MERELY** swirling now, the rain pattering on the leaves of the bushes and bouncing on the cobblestones. Drake's eyes are half closed and he's nodding. A golden glow surrounds his body, extending for about a foot. Fortune never looked this peaceful when Sekhmet lived inside him. I wonder what she's saying to the boy. Drake's a frighteningly powerful ace now. Ra the way Ra was meant to be. He's going to have to be trained and taught until he's of an age to actually use these powers. I hope Sekhmet guides him well.

Across the square Hoodoo Mama, assisted by the dead, works with Ana to construct a tent to cover Bubbles. The flagstones have cracked and sunk into the wet Louisiana soil because of the weight of her body. I find the mound of flesh disturbing and disgusting, and yet I owe my life to that quaking mass. I can't tell if she's trying to move or it's just the skin reacting to the strike of the raindrops.

Billy Ray is standing with his hands clenched at his sides, jaw working. The Midnight Angel is at his side. She looks quite amazing in her rain-drenched leathers. We're all sopping wet from the hurricane. Ray is staring daggers at Bubbles while the Angel whispers frantically in his ear. I saunter over just as Ray gives an emphatic shake of the head and starts walking toward Bubbles.

Lohengrin has been standing near the women working around Bubbles with his sword drawn. He moves to intercept Ray. I fall into step with the head of SCARE.

"Little hard to arrest that," I offer. "I'm not sure there's a crane that could lift her."

"I should arrest you all. Every goddamn one of you." His misshapen face turns toward me. "Oh, not you of course." Bitterness laces the words. "You'll wave your British passport and your diplomatic immunity and go waltzing out of here. But I know you're involved in all this somehow. I just can't prove it."

"You will not touch Bubbles," Lohengrin says. His voice is a Germanic rumble. "She saved all our lives. Yours, too. You should be grateful. She is a great heroine."

It's absolutely true, and I still want to belt him. He's such a naive, sanctimonious prig.

Ray's chest puffs out. Lohengrin makes himself even taller. The smell of bravado and testosterone fills the air. I step in before there's a macho-off.

"If you're smart you won't arrest any of them. The press has been showing round-the-clock pictures of the Committee saving a historic American city. You'll look bad. And it won't be general knowledge, but we all know that a million people could have died today." I nod toward Bubbles. "Lohengrin is always a little too operatic, and this is totally a cliché, but she did save the day at great cost to herself."

"You should report to the AG. Let her make the call," says the Angel with a fine sense of when to pass the buck upstairs.

Ray nods and they walk away together. His arm goes around the Angel's waist. I suddenly miss Niobe horribly. I need to get home and tell her about Drake. That he's safe.

Bugsy joins Lohengrin and me. He's wearing pants, his shirt is unbuttoned, and he's carrying his shoes. "Hey, we did it."

"Yes. We won . . . this time."

"This time. That implies there'll be a *next* time."

"Bet on it. Weathers is a man who holds a grudge."

Bugsy looks alarmed "Who do I talk to about this? John's in the hospital. We've got nobody in charge."

"You better figure out who that person should be," I say.

Looking like a dejected basset hound, Bugsy starts buttoning his shirt. "Are you going to stay and help us?" Lohengrin asks.

It's an interesting question. I've spent a year trying to blunt their effectiveness, but what ultimately blew them apart wasn't my petty manipulations, but fundamental questions of fairness and governance.

I have quite comprehensively burned the bridge to the Silver Helix. Siraj wants to kill me. Weathers wants to kill me. I'm going to need the Committee to handle Weathers. Which means I have to patch them back together, and expand their abilities. I glance over at the tent which now covers Bubbles's inert body. Hoodoo Mama kneels at Bubbles's head, gently stroking her hair.

"Yes, yes, I believe I shall."

"*Wunderbar,* we should start talking to the others right now."

"Actually, I've got someplace better to be. I'm going home."

I make the transition to Lilith. Lohengrin looks like he's swallowed all the mud, detritus, and insects in Jackson Square. It would probably have been kinder to make the change in private, but why cut the puppy's tail, or dick, off by inches?

"Oh, dude, you've been sleeping with her. Except she's not a her. She's a him. Actually she's two hims. That's kind of gay," Bugsy says.

Lohengrin's face is suffused with blood. He looks like he's about to cry. "You betrayed me."

"Welcome to romance," I say, and make the jump Between.

"'. . . come away—'" There's a knock on the door. Niobe breaks off reading and rears up out of the crook of my arm. Alarm tightens the soft line of her jaw. The single reading lamp next to the chair forms a pool of light on the worn carpet. My shadow flits across the wall dancing to the rhythm of the crackling flames. I draw the Glock and let it rest against my leg.

It's Flint. The rain is hissing on the pavement and running in rivulets down the crags of his stone face.

"*I need you back.*"

I shake my head.

"*What happened to you?*"

"It's interesting how the death of one good man can put everything in perspective," I say.

His disgust is evident as he says, "*So this is about losing Daddy.*"

"No, actually, it's about not wanting to be part of an organization that would make a twelve-year-old into a mass murderer."

"*It was the cleanest solution.*"

"Not for Drake."

*"What do you want?"*

"To be left in peace. Oh, and your resignation." The fire in his eyes seems to burn brighter. "I have every action I've ever taken on behalf of the Silver Helix and Britain detailed. It will be released to the papers and to a particular blogger if anything happens to me or mine."

*"All right."* My surprise at the capitulation must have shown. *"You can try to deny what you are, but nothing has changed. At heart you are still a killer, Noel."*

Oddly the attempt to play head games doesn't faze me. I chuckle and begin to close the door. "Good night, Captain. Stay dry."

I return to Niobe and snuggle in close against her. "Now, where were we?"

She picks up the book and resumes reading. " 'For lo, the winter is past, and the rain is over and gone.' "

♣

# THE
# WRITERS AND CREATORS
# OF THE WILD CARD
# CONSORTIUM

| | |
|---|---|
| George R. R. Martin | Lohengrin, Hoodoo Mama, Holy Roller |
| Melinda M. Snodgrass | Double Helix, Lilith, Bahir |
| John Jos. Miller | Carnifex, the Midnight Angel, Simoon |
| Victor Milán | The Radical, Our Lady of Pain |
| Stephen Leigh | Puppetman, the Nur al-Allah, the Oddity |
| S. L. Farrell | Drummer Boy, Gardener |
| Walton (Bud) Simons | Little Fat Boy, Demise, Mr. Nobody |
| Caroline Spector | The Amazing Bubbles, Ink, Tiffani |
| Ian Tregillis | Genetrix, Rustbelt, Sharky |
| Carrie Vaughn | Curveball, Earth Witch, Tinker |
| Lewis Shiner | Fortunato, the Astronomer, Veronica |
| Walter Jon Williams | The Racist, Moon, Justice |
| Roger Zelazny | The Sleeper |
| Leanne C. Harper | Bagabond, the Hero Twins |
| Edward Bryant | Sewerjack, Wyungare |
| Chris Claremont | Molly Bolt, the Jumpers, Cody Havero |
| Michael Cassutt | Stuntman, Cash Mitchell |
| Kevin Andrew Murphy | Cameo, Will-o'-Wisp |
| Pat Cadigan | Water Lily |
| Gail Gerstner Miller | John Fortune, the Living Gods, Peregrine |
| William F. Wu | Lazy Dragon, Chop-Chop, Jade Blossom |
| Laura J. Mixon | The Candle, Lamia, Clara van Rennsaeler |
| Sage Walker | Diver, Zoe Harris |
| Arthur Byron Cover | Quasiman, Leo Barnett |
| Steve Perrin | Brave Hawk, Digger Downs, Mistral |
| Royce Wideman | Toad Man, the Lama, Crypt Kicker |
| Bob Wayne | The Card Sharks |
| Howard Waldrop | Jetboy |
| Daniel Abraham | Jonathan Hive, Spasm, Father Henry Obst |
| Parris McBride | Elephant Girl |
| Christopher Rowe | Hardhat |